# Home
## C O U N T R Y
### AN ELROY BODE READER

# Books by Elroy Bode

*Commonplace Mysteries*

*This Favored Place*

*To Be Alive*

*Home and Other Moments*

*Alone: In the World: Looking*

*Sketchbook II*

*Texas Sketchbook*

# Home
# COUNTRY
## AN ELROY BODE READER

by Elroy Bode

Foreword by Bryan Woolley

Texas Western Press
The University of Texas at El Paso
1997

© 1997
Texas Western Press
The University of Texas at El Paso
El Paso, Texas 79968-0633

First Edition
Library of Congress Catalog No. 96-061727
ISBN 0-87404-244-5

∞ All Texas Western Press books are printed on acid-free paper, meeting the
guidelines for permanence and durability of the Committee on Production
Guidelines for Book Longevity of the Council on Library Resources.

Some sections of this book were originally published in *The Texas Observer*, *Nova*,
and the *El Paso Herald-Post*. "Deborah's Shoes" originally appeared in the *Dallas
Times Herald*, 1984. These works are reprinted with permission.

For Phoebe

# Contents

# Foreword

One time in the early 1970s I returned to my hometown of Fort Davis, Texas, to visit my mother and my grandmother. I had lived far from the state for a number of years and was becoming reacquainted with the West Texas land, air, and sky, letting them renew me as they always had before I moved away.

One lazy afternoon I walked down to the courthouse square to browse in the town's only bookstore, as pleasant an occupation as I can imagine for the heat of a day. There I happened upon a slim volume called *Elroy Bode's Texas Sketchbook: A Sheaf of Prose Poems*, which had been published by Texas Western Press in 1967. What attracted me to the book was the volume itself, which was a typical Texas Western Press book of that period: sturdy, simple, and beautiful, designed by the great Carl Hertzog, with drawings by the incomparable José Cisneros. These names I knew; of Bode I had never heard.

I bought the book, took it home, and sat down with it on the front porch swing. I opened it and read this beginning sentence: "In March, when the mornings begin to lose their chill and the elm trees begin to bud, the downtown plaza in El Paso ceases to be the bleak, wind-swept bus stop of wintertime and once again resumes its rightful character as the heart of the city."

I knew this place! As a student at Texas Western College and a kid cub reporter at the *El Paso Times* back in the 1950s, I had passed through San Jacinto Plaza almost every day and had absorbed its various colors, sounds, and moods. And in a sketch only two pages long, Bode was able to make real in my memory a place that I hadn't seen in almost twenty years.

I became a Bode fan on the spot. That copy of his *Sketchbook* is still a treasured part of my library, as are copies of his subsequent six books. Their author and I eventually would exchange letters, then meet and quickly become friends.  I treasure his friendship as I do his books.

Like "Spring in the Plaza," the piece that drew me to him, nearly all of Bode's writings are short.  Indeed, many of the pieces he calls "sketches," which are the main body of his work, are only a few paragraphs long.  But, like Thoreau, Bode can pack a world of wisdom into a single line, often creating a sort of prose haiku in which a single image can open up a whole universe.  A cedar limb or an orange peel lying on a dirty Juárez sidewalk becomes his Grecian urn, embodying all the truth and beauty there is.

In his preface to this book, Bode says the only adventure he has ever had is "the attempt to know the depths of myself and my surroundings."  Those surroundings have been mostly the Kerrville and hill country ranch of his childhood and the El Paso–Juárez borderlands where he has lived, taught, and written most of his adult life, with a few side trips elsewhere.  And the self he is trying to know is a feeling, observing, reading, writing man in the midst of that vast Texas landscape, his home country, truly *experiencing* the loves, the deaths, the work, the pleasures, the ordinary days that slip so poorly noticed by nearly everybody.

In the volume which you hold in your hand is collected the best work that Elroy Bode has produced over the past forty years.  Drawn together as it is here, it becomes the spiritual autobiography of an extraordinary man.  It's with great pleasure that I commend it to you.

Bryan Woolley
Dallas

# Preface

My home in Kerrville was across the street from a vacant lot and one block from the school grounds. It had oak trees, side yards, back lots, a garden, a chicken house, various sheds and pens for a few sheep, and, once, a cow.

My father ran a feed store; my mother was there in the rooms of the house, in the yards – a constant, sustaining presence.

I was there forever, it seemed, in that familiar, important place.

The pieces in the "Home" section of this book attempt to capture some of those small-town satisfactions and stabilities I had in the 1930s and '40s – experiences that vibrated within me for years thereafter like tuning forks.

My grandparents' ranch was about twenty miles out of town, near Harper, and it, like my home among the Kerrville oaks, anchored my life as I was growing up. I never grew tired of going there and I think it provided me with the concept of perfection – of an accessible and aesthetically satisfying private world.

I remember the afternoon in my mid-twenties when I was sitting in my car beside a cotton field near Corpus Christi and first began to think of my grandparents as people to write about. It suddenly was clear to me that if I didn't tell about them, nobody would. Nobody else who knew enough would care enough to preserve their ranch in words, and thus their fifty-plus years of ranch life – their legacy, their heritage – would be lost. Sitting there, staring into the coastal haze, I accepted the responsibility, in a sense, of trying to keep the ranch "alive." The section, "The Ranch," records, in part, the fulfilling of that responsibility.

When I left the familiar structures of home at seventeen and went off to college it was as if I had walked flat-footed and casually whistling into a brick wall called life. I spent the next twenty years or so trying to recover from the impact.

I was stunned by the knowledge that I was alive on the earth and didn't know what to do about it; it was as though I had been reborn, wide-eyed and vulnerable, into a world of gigantic, hidden meanings. Others seemed to know, almost serenely, what they ought to be doing; I did not. I was haunted by memories and almost paralyzed by the awesome shapes of reality. What was the purpose of my life, I wanted to know – the purpose of anything, for that matter?

As I walked through the days, as the years passed, I kept trying to find satisfying answers to the questions that plagued me. I wanted values I could believe in, and I thought if I looked hard enough, long enough, I would find them. I was on a quest – a private, intense search for truth, for God, for myself – and I was determined to discover, or perhaps create, some kind of order out of the chaos around me.

The "Journals" section near the end of the anthology represents part of that single-minded attempt to make sense of the world. The journals are also a record of my concern with the written word – the power, the lure, the mystery of writing. For as I looked and reflected and waited I wanted to do the impossible: to lift life out of itself and make it live a second time on my pages. The desperate urge to explore life gradually became, therefore, a desperate urge to tell about it. As I typed and retyped my conversations with myself I guess I secretly hoped that the scenes, thoughts, observations, sketches I was writing down might some day form the mosaic of that Absolute I was so doggedly seeking. Of course this was not the case. Yet such a journal did serve to record the only adventure I have ever had: the attempt to know the depths of myself and my surroundings.

Perhaps it would be appropriate here to explain the origin of what I have called "sketches" – especially since they have formed the bulk of my writing effort for the last forty years.

After college I ignored my instincts and my deepest interests and tried to write what people were supposed to write: "stories." Routinely I sent them off to national magazines – *Harper's, The Atlantic, The*

*Saturday Evening Post*, even *The New Yorker* – and routinely I got them back. Usually there was only the rejection slip attached; sometimes a handwritten note of encouragement was added at the bottom.

Then one day I did it. I was a second lieutenant in the air force, stationed in San Antonio, and I had come back from the base post office to my desk in the Information Services office. I dropped my just-returned – and rejected – story into the wastebasket, sat at the desk, looked out the window for a while, and made a decision: I would never again write anything the way I thought I was "supposed to." I would never write in order to make money, and I would only write about those things that I cared about. If I never got published – fine. I would write strictly for me about those moments of intensity that would not let me alone – that seemed to be the very stuff of my life.

Of course, since I had just about lost every ounce of my self-confidence, I wasn't sure how to proceed. I was back at Ground Zero in my writing life and didn't think I knew enough about anything to fill up a whole page. But maybe if I just wrote directly and honestly – no frills, no fancy stuff – about a few scenes and people and places and times of day that I cared about – on just half a page – it would be enough.

That afternoon I went to my quarters, got some typing paper, cut the sheets in half, and began to think about what "moments" I wanted to put on each of those half-sheets.

In the weeks that followed I didn't have a name for what I was doing so, for lack of a better term, I simply called them "sketches." I wrote one after another until I had thirty or forty (and on some of them I would cheat: I would get to the end of the half-page and find that, amazingly enough, I *did* have something to say – something that seemed to flow, to have a beginning, middle, and end – so I would turn the sheet over and continue on the back).

It was a special and rather memorable time – those first days in my middle-twenties when I was finally working at something I believed in. Those sketches were *mine*. They were shaped out of a need to make sense of things that haunted me, perplexed me, pleased me. They were the first tentative tracings of my own personal territory, and I was finally beginning to see a bit more clearly through the confusing mists of youth. I had begun the process of turning the world into words.

After my brief tour in the air force I taught in public schools here and there in Texas – Kingsville, Garland, Bandera, and El Paso. When I would return to Kerrville during the summer or at Christmas I would look out hungrily at hill country pastures, at the rocks and grasses and slopes of ground, at the country lanes and fences, the agarita and mesquite and yucca on distant ridges. I would look and I would be struck by their *goodness* – how else can I say it? If there is a morality in life, then the land has had it for me. A tree was as good as any human. A cedar limb held truth and beauty.

Harper, Mountain Home, Bandera, Comfort, Junction, Medina, Fredericksburg – their names became part of me, of my consciousness, my flesh. Like cattle guards and low-water crossings, like goats in a field, like cypresses along the Guadalupe, they marked my territory. "The Hill Country" section presents some of that territory which has always been my emotional lodestone.

But as important as Central Texas has been to me, I made a fortuitous and decisive move in 1958 when I came west. As I drove up Alameda Street and into El Paso I had the curious feeling of being immediately at home in this desert place among the mountains. I was ready for new boundaries, new vistas, and the spare symmetry of western horizons and sky gave them to me. And somehow – inexplicably, gloriously, constantly – El Paso was the *present tense*. Each day was new and shining and comfortable; I was alive under the sun and glad of it. "On the Border: El Paso/Juárez" features some of the special concerns and satisfactions I have encountered here.

Although the pieces in the "Commentary" section are, I believe, self-explanatory, I would like to stress one point in connection with

"Requiem for a WASP School," the piece about Austin High School in El Paso. Since 1957 I have basically earned my living by teaching in Texas public schools. In the late 1960s I started teaching at Austin High, and except for a four-year teaching stint back in Central Texas, I have been there ever since. It has been another unforgettable home of a kind for me, and I was fortunate to find it. I have felt committed to it the way one is committed to a family or a cause and I plan to remain there until I run out of erasers or breath.

"Anais" – the story in the middle of the anthology – is a fictional piece based upon a woman I met in Bandera after my divorce. She was ambling down the middle of the sidewalk behind two magisterial grey-hounds – one coal-black, the other copper-gold – that she held casually on a leash. She wore blue-jean cut-offs, a kind of skimpy blue-jean halter, and high heels. Her skin was a death-bed white; her hair was cropped short and dyed jet black. She wore large dark sunglasses. She turned slightly every now and then and gave big smeared-red-lipstick smiles to the faces of cafe patrons and insurance office employees who were staring at her through their windows.

Wherever "Anais" went, she made sure that she made an impression.

The last section, "Witness," is part of a work-in-progress and contains material which has not previously appeared in book form. Since in my mind there is no fixed chronology – past and present remain in a continual flux – the pieces range back and forth from Kerrville to El Paso, from childhood to my first marriage, my two children, my divorce. They also deal with the single constant in my life, the land: hills, rivers, deserts, mountains: the land that has allowed me to endure and to thrive.

# I

# HOME

# Moments

As a boy I walked near the river that went beside our town. The day was still, full of the large quietness of the early hours of afternoon.

I was there with the smell of the trees and the closeness of the ground; and below me, down the bluff, the river was in the sun at two o'clock.

I was there in that place, on a mild October afternoon: where cypresses stood on the banks of the river and oaks grew along the country road and patches of caliche ground shone like powdered light – intimate, timeless.

I was alone in the two o'clock silence of the world – the silence of berries hanging, of weeds growing, of deer moving through the cedar trees on the surrounding hills.

It wore a groove in me as deep as memory goes: four-thirty in the afternoon on a warm, spring day. It was the heart of my childhood life.

Four-thirty, and shadows beginning to spread out along the east side of the house and under the trees; four-thirty, and school kids coming down the street, their shoes crunching gravel, their voices lifting and fading as they passed our house and walked on toward the creek; four-thirty, and "Front Page Farrell" on all the radios in the block – the sound of it almost seeming to blend into the white caliche dust that hung above the unpaved streets and then settled on the ligustrum bushes along our fence; four-thirty, and the privacy of self starting to blend into the stronger privacy of later afternoon and night.

The chicken yard at dusk had come to this still, familiar moment.

The cow lot was there to the south; the garage was there to the east; the house was to the north, unseen.

Rusted baling wire hung in neat twists around the cedar fence posts. Water sat in pans. Weeds grew strongly among rocks and chicken droppings, and odd bits of tin and boards were scattered next to the cowshed. Clabber lay sour in crocks.

It was seven-fifteen in the summertime.

In the vacant lot to the west, under many large oaks, the air was heavy with tree-privateness. Late afternoon silence streamed into the chicken yard through the sagging wire fence.

Earthworms lay hidden in the moist ground beneath scattered boards. Pigeons were smooth and clean-feathered in their coop.

Nothing moved. Everything was.

I sat, looking on.


My mother, father, and I would rake leaves in the west side yard and burn them in the long twilight.

I would carry a tubful of brown oak leaves to the pile and dump them on the flames, and as I turned away I would see the bullbats dip into the yard and then angle away quickly above the low roof of the chicken house.

I would stand there, smelling the leaves burning and looking at the clean dark earth where the leaves had been raked away and listening to the sound of the mourning doves in the vacant lot across the street, and the moment would be so good and deep and so very much ours – our family's – that it was as if time had stopped and we were fixed there forever: the eternal familiar three of us, working next to the fireplace chimney and the white side of the house, our bodies perpetually blurred in the slowly fading light.


Mother, ironing in the bedroom under the yellow ceiling bulb. Nine o'clock on a Wednesday night. In summer. I had just finished listening to "Mr. District Attorney" and now it was time for Kay Kyser and his "College of Musical Knowledge." Daddy was still outside in the back lots, doing up the chores. It had just turned full dark.

The iron made rhythmic clumping sounds as Mother kept turning it on end and setting it down on the board. She shifted each shirt around, dampened it, continued to iron again. She was sitting on a high black stool – an old-fashioned barber's stool with an adjustable seat. She said it eased her back as she ironed.

The windows were open to the summer night, and from the vacant lot below our sudan patch voices of boys still outside playing drifted toward us. There was a slight breeze but it did not cool the hot, close bedroom.

Mother did not talk, and she did not seem to pay any attention to the radio. She ironed slowly, meditatively – as if with each stroke she ironed in another of her thoughts – while I listened to Harry Babbitt, Ish Kabibble, and the Kay-dettes.

# Childhood Days

As I played in the endless childhood days among the oak trees around home I came to love many things: a gray-faced terrier, so painfully shy that she came up sideways, apologetically, to be petted; acorns, with their beautiful bullet sleekness; a red-striped mackinaw smelling of chalk dust from school and arm loads of wood carried indoors for the fireplace; a backyard tree house where I sat by myself and watched the summer mornings drift by.

It was there, in the tree house next to the garage, in the midst of boards and oak limbs and many green leaves, that books were better to read and the ground better to look at: it was there that I learned special knowledges about the day. I learned how reliable ten o'clock in the morning was – how it came around, dutifully, at the very moment that the sun was edging across the top layer of shingles on the garage and the postman's arm was beginning to reach out of his car into our mailbox on the corner. I learned how ice glistened on the smooth bed of the ice truck, and how, without warning, acorns would fall onto the garage roof and roll noisily for a while and then lie dramatically still –

as if joining in the death of something huge and important and unknowable.

I learned the noise that a back screen door makes as it opens against the wooden side of a house, and the way emptied dishwater hits the ground. And I could not help but learn this too: that boys shouting in a neighbor's yard and cars racing along on a gravel street and dogs barking at delivery trucks and birds gathering continuously in trees were the sounds that structured a child's world – that gave it its sense of innocence and glory and stability and peace.

# The Radio

On winter nights we gathered before the fireplace with the lights off and listened to the radio. A lot of the time it was full of static, but no one jumped up to twist a knob or shake it. We indulged it as we would a sick relative who belched and wheezed at the supper table.

It was an old Crosley with a deep tone and it gave us the voices of the '30s and '40s: Walter Winchell, who swept toward us with crackling authority; Gabriel Heatter, who mourned over the news as if it were a dying or disappointing friend; Helen Hayes, who mourned also but with a little poetic spirit – who sounded as if she were trapped at the far end of a long tunnel, raising thin defiant hands to damp walls. And there was always Al Pierce and Fred Allen and Lanny Ross and Lum and Abner.

There were the Joe Louis fights too. On those rare nights Daddy would get the chores done early and his cigar lit and he would sit in the darkness beside me, our chairs drawn a little closer to the radio than usual, the whole world shrunk for a while to the size of the yellow Crosley mouth. The announcer would talk in his terse, sing-song way and then the bell would sound through all the excitement and Tony Galento or Max Baer or Billy Conn would try to last out the fifteen rounds, and couldn't, and after a while we would hear again

through the final clanging: "Tha winnah...and...still...heavyweight...
champ-yon...of...the world...." And it was like the sun going down each
day beyond the oak trees and Roosevelt being president: Joe Louis had
won again. Daddy would clear his throat from the cigar juice and turn
off the radio and say, "Well, son, the old Brown Bomber, *he did it again.*"

I had favorite programs that came on at bedtime – "Blondie," "Red
Skelton," "I Love a Mystery" – but I rarely got to stay up for them,
despite my begging. Instead, I went off into the cold wintertime bedroom and got deep under the quilts, trying to keep rigid and stoic
against the cold sheets and also trying to ignore Mother and Daddy as
they went about their routines in the rest of the house. But before long
I would edge gingerly over to the living room wall and press my ear
against the cold wallpaper. Just on the other side, the old Crosley was
roaring dimly on. It was there, with my shoulder raised uncomfortably
and my head cricked to one side, that I would fall asleep – usually
while suave and tolerant Sherlock Holmes was allaying some new fear
of bumbling Dr. Watson.

# Home from Work

When I was young Daddy belonged to a lot of different things:
to cigar smoke and horseshoe pitching and family reunions in pecan
groves; to funny papers read aloud in a droning, sing-song voice on
Sunday morning and Hurlbut's *Story of the Bible* with the pictures of the
burning bush and Jacob wrestling with an angel; to his feed store
beside the railroad tracks and to his small Stetson hat and khakis that
smelled of body odor and mashes; to alfalfa hay and the sun warming
the big splintery boards of the loading platform; to deliveries in the
old pickup truck made after closing time....

But most of all he belonged to that first rattle of loose truck fenders as he came around the corner by the vacant lot in the late afternoon: the sound always made me drop whatever I was doing and run

to the back gate and drag it open and stand beside it, waiting, as Daddy rumbled and clattered down the dusty street toward home. The truck always came slow and black and sure: the motor would be running in a high extra whine and the fenders would be jangling at each familiar bump and dip in the gravel street and the sideboards would be squeaking against the metal sides and to me it was all a sweet music. I would see Daddy's hand raised in a wave from within the cab and then he would make his last little tight swing to the opposite side of the street before turning in quickly through the gate and coming to rest beneath the clothesline in our backyard.

Daddy would usually have some kind of feed in the back of the truck. As he carried it toward the cow shed all the chickens in the sudan patch below the garden would begin running toward him in their frantic, armless way, barely stopping long enough to squeeze under the wire fences and gates. And for the rest of the afternoon, like a Pied Piper of the Back Lots, Daddy would do up the chores: he carried his pungent mashes and grains and clumps of pulled Johnson grass to the many pens and coops while dogs and chickens and pigeons – and I – followed peaceably in his wake.

# Summer Evening

Day is long in quitting, the summer twilight long and mild like a deep soft hole in time itself that has opened now just before dark.

The air seems to have thickened and blurred, and trees balloon darkly behind themselves into spreading shades. Chickens going to roost within the trees look like scraps of white paper pasted against the leaves. In the garden where I work, the ground grows thick and solid – an immensely sober and familiar thing resisting the time of mysterious change.

And all of a sudden, when I am not expecting it, night falls. I am looking past the wire fence of the garden into a patch of horehound and weeds below – just for a moment letting my mind blend with the twilight, letting it reach out and touch the vagueness of the air – when suddenly two katydids begin to sing and I look back to the fence and it is gone, dissolved. Night has descended on the earth, bringing with it its own sounds: cars hum and rattle and speed on neighboring streets, doors of houses slam more noticeably, katydids increase their singing.

I walk across the soft, loose, yielding dirt of the garden to the gate, putting my arm through and by instinct finding the latch. As the gate swings open a cow lows with a long distant eloquence somewhere to the south. I stand a moment listening, my face pointed in the darkness toward the lowing as if my eyes could still see. I stand there, suspended somewhere between listening and thinking, until I finally shut the gate and walk up the slope of the rocky yard toward the house, where the yellow light of the kitchen window shines like a beacon through the trees.

# Family Reunions

The four of us – my mother, father, brother, and I – walked out of the noontime glare of the field, where the cars were parked, into the shadows of the pecan grove.

They were there, already, the other family groups: the few surviving old men, the many small children, the young married couples, the aloof and distrustful-looking adolescents, and men and women in their fifties and sixties who were the backbone and flesh itself of such yearly reunions.

My father did not get beyond the first long wooden table before he was met by the waiting hands of gray-haired cousins. Three or four men in small white Stetsons and boots – from Junction, Fredericksburg, Llano – reached out sun-browned, calloused hands and my father took each in turn, shook it, called the man by name, then did not stop

to talk but continued on down the line to shake the hands of other
men who were standing about: other relatives from San Angelo,
Mason, San Antonio. It was the first of the many round-robins of
handshakings that my father entered before he left in the late afternoon – greeting still other men in hats who were gathered under the
shade of the many pecan trees, drinking coffee or iced tea out of paper
cups, standing in threes and fours and fives, periodically greeting
nephews and aunts and cousins as they made their way among the
tables before the reunion barbecue began.

My mother, paused in line, was immediately patted on the shoulder by a pleasant-faced, smiling woman in a cluster of other smiling,
graying, pleasant-faced women. The women smiled, my mother
smiled, there was more patting of arms and shoulders.

My brother – always popular at reunions because he seemed to
be a young man who was not just going to be another German relative, another rancher or insurance salesman or small-town grocery
store owner but someone headed up in the world, a headline maker,
perhaps: my brother had begun talking to a stocky young man from
Harper who had come over, a second or third cousin who ran a hardware store with his parents but whose main love was the fiddle, who
played in a Saturday night string band and liked more than anything
else to talk music and bands and drums to someone like my brother –
someone going to college, someone in touch with things.

I stood for a while, dutifully, as small boys with their parents at
family reunions were supposed to, waiting out the talk of the adults,
looking down self-consciously from time to time when the men –
through for a while with handshaking – finally asked my father, "Fred,
is that your boy?...I didn't recognize him he's grown so much." I looked
vaguely in the direction of the men, not speaking, then vaguely toward
the trees, until gradually I began to drift away from my family: to idle
along among the picnic tables and the many laughing, talking men and
women I had seen once a year for as long as I could remember. I wandered past the bowls of potato salad and smelled the barbecue smok-

ing in the pit and looked cautiously at boys my same age in clean
shirts and pants wandering among other bowls of potato salad – looking cautiously over at me – and I did not know if I liked them or disliked them: family reunions. They were awkward and strange and
familiar – and I was nine.

White shirts and ties, dresses and women's soft-fleshed arms,
laughter and cigar smoke and wrinkled old men in wheel chairs. I was
there under the tall pecan trees, it was Sunday, I wandered on.

# Chester Arndt

Sometimes in the vacant time just before supper I went up to the
elementary school playground near our house and fooled around. I
picked up acorns that had fallen underneath the oak trees and put
them in my pocket – just to feel them there, smooth and neat. I
watched the last of the smoke rising from the incinerator. I kicked dirt.
I wasn't thinking about anything; I was just being there in the emptiness of the grounds.

Chester Arndt would usually be there, too, standing beneath the
wooden football bleachers and smoking Kool cigarettes as the sun
went down. He was a lot bigger than I was – a huge guy for a sixth
grader. He usually wore a faded denim work shirt and brogans; a shock
of dark hair, like Li'l Abner's, hung down in his eyes. Chester was
always the one chosen first at recess and the last one chosen in a
spelling match.

I would go over and we would just stand around for a while in
the cave of the bleachers. We didn't have much to say. I was the
skinny kid who memorized the entire fifty lines of poetry Miss Sutton
required each semester, and Chester – well, his father was off in jail
somewhere and his mother took in washing in their little frame house
down on Quinlan Creek.

Chester never bothered to offer me one of his cigarettes. He knew I wouldn't know what to do with it if he did. I was a test passer, a book reader. He knew who I was.

We would watch people cross the school grounds, carrying groceries home from the Red and White. Cars would pass by. Dogs would bark. Then Chester would frown, spit, reach up with his thick fingers to pinch his cigarette and send it flying away into the grass, and stalk off across the field.

After I went on home for supper I would stay out in the front yard for a while, and sometimes Chester would pass by. I don't think he was ever going anywhere in particular. He would just be out there walking the rocky streets of the neighborhood – his hair bouncing against his forehead, his denim shirt stretched across his meaty back like a sausage skin, his eyes looking fiercely straight ahead.

# Church Service

## Sunday Morning

It is dreamlike, our slow progression through the front door of the First Methodist Church. I have yielded personal thought and will and once again am content to be part of a familiar whole: to be one among Sunday-morning Methodists, edging forward inch by inch. We are so intimate, so much of a common purpose that the coat sleeves of the men and the dresses of the women are an extension of my Sunday-morning self. I am their profiles, their perfumes.

I move along behind my parents and the others, entering a little deeper into the world of carpeted aisles and blue-back hymnals. I am part of a process and I accept it: These people next to me are the members of the church. They are entering while the pianist plays and the ushers move back and forth, nodding, indicating, retreating, advancing. I know that other church members are shutting their car doors along the street outside and will be coming up the steps soon. Still others are already seated – waiting, watching.

It is the way things are, have been, will be.

I fold my church bulletin longways and move another pace forward, my gaze more or less confined to the back of my father's old gray suit. I stand there, and he stands there, patiently, and it is as if I have been looking at the familiar spot on his coat forever, as if I have lived two separate sets of lives and in one of them I am always this half-step's distance behind him in the crowded church entrance.

Finally we are in our seats – my mother, my father, and I – and the feeling that we are no longer our Gilmer Street selves is even stronger. We are different from the people we were a moment ago when we climbed the steps: our spaces as persons – people with names, desires, memories – have been steadily blurred, have become intermingled with the spaces of those seated around us. There is a feeling that, as individuals, we have been reduced, shrunk – that we have become cells of a large Something gradually created out of piano music and decorous ushers and tall, stained-glass windows.

As I begin to draw idly on the Sunday bulletin I sink easily into the noise of the Great Church Non-Self: the huge intimidating sound of many people being quiet together – of people breathing, looking, sitting inches apart, row after row, waiting in a mindless commonality for that moment when the service begins.

## Sunday Night

By seven o'clock they have made their solitary ways up the wide, concrete steps and are settled in the front rows. They are the Sunday night faithfuls: white-haired women in silk dresses, wrinkle-faced men in long-sleeved white shirts and dark ties. They are old people mainly, women mainly, with a few loyal and lonely young ones scattered

about, all of them facing comfortably, passively, toward the empty pulpit and the lighted choir loft.

It is the gathering of late-August regulars, those who do not go
on summer vacations or have out-of-town relatives visiting them for
the day. For a while they exchange restrained nods and murmurings
among the rows, brief hand touchings; there is a general looking about
to see who is new and who is missing. Then the women adjust their
purses in their laps, the men cross their legs a final time, and they all
settle comfortably into the large, quiet emptiness of the church –
ready to end their week with the familiar rituals of a Sunday night
service.

In a few moments Brother Blalock enters through the side door
that leads to his office. He walks noiselessly across the stretch of dark-
wine carpet and takes his seat in his chair beside the pulpit. He slowly
crosses his legs, brings his hands together in his lap, looks down and
considers the air about his hands for a moment, then abruptly – almost
like a bird dog catching the scent of a quail – lifts his head to the congregation and confers upon them the confident greeting of The Gaze
– not recognizing any of them individually, not yet joining his official
pre-service privacy to their public restraint, but instead looking unsee-
ingly toward them, through them, beyond them, as if into the Holy
Spirit itself. Seated there, facing outward, he resembles, more than
anything else, a barber relaxing in his own barber chair on a slack
afternoon.

The woman pianist and the summer Youth Fellowship choir – six
girls and two tall boys – file through the opposite side door and take
their places in the choir loft. They stand solemnly – all of them full of
Youth Fellowship tuna sandwiches and Nehi orange – and look with
practiced reverence at the figures seated before them.

The choir leader for the night, a tall, red-haired girl with amber-
rimmed glasses, asks that everyone please rise and sing all four verses
of the hymn on page 231. The pianist begins playing the introductory
notes of "I Am Thine, O Lord" while the congregation rises and finds

the right page in the hymnal; then the voices in the church begin to drift out through the open windows toward the freshly mowed lawn, the darkening streets, the cooling early-evening air.

It is the chorus of the hymn that makes magic out of the Sunday night service. It is not the preacher sitting serenely in his chair – legs crossed, a long length of blue stretch-sock chastely exposed. It is not the young people's choir, dutifully acting out their roles as Good Methodist Youth. It is the hymn's repeated chorus, sung mainly by aging women – sung this particular night within the solid brick walls of the church but sung countless times before in tents, open-air taber-nacles, camp meeting pavilions – that would make a passerby stop for a moment on the sidewalk and listen: that would cause chill bumps to rise on his arms as he stands next to the faint watermelon smell of the grass and looks up to the windows above the shrubbery and listens and remembers:

"...Draw me near-er, near-er, near-er blessed Lo-o-or-rd
To thy pre-cious, ble-e-e-ding si-i-ide."

It would be that loud hypnotic wail of massed voices that affects him – that almost painful human simplicity and earnestness, that mournful high woman-whine of voices rising and falling, rising and falling.... And each time that the singers get to the word "near-er," it is as if they are almost there in the Promised Land, almost at rest: as if the constant ebb and flow of the chorus represents their repeated efforts to scale the peak where Jesus waits for them – and as if the final tapering cry is a long sigh of understanding that the peak cannot be reached tonight, that they will have to be content, once again, to stand together and let their voices die out peacefully on the mountain-side.

# Up above Hunt

On Sunday afternoons in fall Daddy would shut the front door of the house and we would get into the car and drive west of Kerrville along the pleasant Guadalupe River road toward Hunt. Mother would have put in a picnic lunch; I brought the thermos jug full of lemonade and parts of the Sunday paper. For the first few miles we just sat there in the Plymouth, uninvolved in the two o'clock sense of things, nursing the after-effects of a Sunday morning spent in church. We were still town people, reacting to the November countryside in stiff, town ways.

But after we got past Hunt, where the west branch of the Guadalupe grew small and more personal, Sunday began to lose its hold and the land took over. I would look out my window at the tall cypresses lining the stream, and at the brief flat fields and wooded hills, and I would almost become hypnotized by the texture of the land and the afternoon. It was as though the air itself was a blending of country essences – glints of sun, shadowed leaves, quietly feeding deer....

At a likely looking picnic spot – usually near a low-water bridge beneath tall, brown-and-yellow leafed trees – Daddy would stop the car and we would get out to stretch and walk around on the smooth creek-bed grass. I would eat my peanut butter sandwiches and listen to the crackling sound of the old Plymouth cooling beneath the sycamores, yet most of all I would look into the November stillness and think absolutely nothing – gazing out toward the bridge like a contented and mindless animal.

As we drove further up the river road names on the mailboxes became more picturesque – Lynx Haven, Panther Estates, Hodge Podge Lodge – and more expensive summer cottages rested against the sides of the hills. Occasionally Daddy would stop at a guest ranch, Wagon Wheel Inn, where his second-cousin worked as the foreman. The cousin would come out from his neat foreman's house and quiet his dogs and shake Daddy's hand, and he would show us once more through the elegant grounds.

Usually, however, we just kept on driving – the car straining a little as it climbed into the higher ranchland plateau above Hunt. And even though the west branch of the Guadalupe, for the most part, continued to be merely a pleasing and almost domesticated stream, there were places where it cut through stretches of high gray rock and became brooding and primitive. It would be right there, in the midst of the peaceful hill country, that the Guadalupe suddenly became timeless, as though it had just surfaced from the waters of a past geologic age. Swallows flew out of holes in the smooth gray cliffs, Biblical-looking rushes lined the shallow pools, and in the riverbed itself long ledges replaced the mud bottom. To me, it was as if the Guadalupe had gradually allowed the outside world, in all its strangeness, to break through the protective layers of Sunday blandness and loom awesomely around us. It was as if the old black Plymouth, rolling so innocently through the fall countryside, had finally been overtaken – and overwhelmed – by the afternoon's gigantic poetry.

# At the Magazine Rack

When I was thirteen I would go into the Rock Drug Store downtown and stand before the magazine rack, eating my ice cream cone and secretly staring at *Wink, Treat, Glamorous Models*. I would glance up every now and then to see where the clerks had wandered to and then I would casually lift up a *Sir* or *Pic* and begin to thumb through it – trying to look both studious and innocent; trying to seem, in case anybody was watching, as if I were merely undecided between *Scientific American* and *Boy's Life*.... I looked at smiling girls wearing boxing gloves who were paired off against other smiling girls with boxing gloves – the four of them in high heels, pants underwear, frilly brassieres; I

looked at girls who were leapfrogging one another, at girls in swim-
suits, girls brushing their hair before mirrors, girls sunbathing on boulders – their mouths open toward the camera, their tongues lolling in a
way that I knew was bound to be tempting even though I didn't know
exactly why.

I stood there, my ice cream cone melting down into its soggy
napkin, and hoped I was inconspicuous. I was hollow inside with the
guilt of my frantic, secret looking and with the rising urgency of my
thirteen-year-old lust. And although I continued to turn the pages with
an artful show of indifference, the thought never left me: some of
these people are bound to know me – are probably even customers of
Daddy's and have seen me at the feed store – and here I am staring at
women's half-naked bodies in the middle of the Rock Drug Store....
Finally the pressure of making a decision began to build: I couldn't
stand there all day, I would have to hurry up and buy a magazine – but
which one? There wasn't enough time to look at them all, even though
the *Cavalcade* at the end of the rack probably showed a model with
perfect legs, really astonishing breasts.

In desperation and trusting in the generosity of fate, I would buy
a *Titter* I had not ever looked at – along with a *Sports Afield* in order to
make me seem like a halfway regular fellow to the woman cashier –
then I would go outside and begin walking home. I would quickly scan
through the pictures and find, usually, to my immense disgust that I
had picked what was probably the dullest sex magazine ever printed. I
would flip through it – lingering a moment at a pretty fair shot of a
chorus girl putting nail polish on her toes – before I dropped it into a
trash barrel behind the Western Auto Store and opened my *Sports
Afield*.

# After the Parade

Every Friday afternoon during football season our high school band marched twelve blocks from the band hall to the main intersection in town and held a pep rally. We would stop in front of the Charles Schreiner Bank and the crowd of students and townspeople that had gathered around us would fall back to let each row of the band file out to make a big circle. Then the cheerleaders would burst through the circle to lead the yells, we would play the school fight song and alma mater, and it would be over.

I would wait at the edge of the crowd for three friends who lived in my neighborhood, and together we would begin our slow walk home – two with drums, one with a clarinet, me with my trombone. All four of us were tall, and as we moved along Water Street in our high, plumed hats we were like a troupe of Masai warriors returning from a celebration in Nairobi. We followed the same hot, Friday-afternoon sidewalks until we reached the Red and White grocery store across from the school. There we stopped to drink Pepsi-Colas and eat ice cream – our blue cylindrical hats parked on top of a candy counter, our hair plastered down with sweat, our voices cheerful and constant and loud with after-the-parade talk.

Outside the store I would leave the others and walk the two blocks home across the elementary school grounds. As I pulled open the door of the house – letting it slam after shouldering my way in with the trombone case in one hand and the remains of an ice cream bar in the other – I could expect Mother to come out of the kitchen and stand there in a moment of greeting in the living room dimness before going back into the kitchen to get me something to eat. (What was it about her being in the house after a Friday-afternoon parade?... Perhaps it was not only that she was always *there* – interested, friendly, waiting – but that she made me feel that I had done my duty, both as a son and as a student, and thus it was only natural that I should expect to be rewarded.)

After I had loosened my black tie and peeled off the sweat-circled coat of the band uniform – the air suddenly cool to my clinging,
sweat-soaked shirt – I would go over to the record player in the shadowed corner by the fireplace. I would put on some Stan Kenton
records – "Machito," "The Peanut Vendor," "Rika Jika Jack" – and let
the biting, flamboyant Kenton sounds fill the living room. By then
Mother would have brought in a bowl of fruit, and I would lean back
on the couch – unwinding, hugely relaxed, eating a pear or freshly
washed mustang grapes.

Later I would go into the kitchen and after getting another bunch
of grapes I would sit down by the window to read a while in *The Razor's
Edge* or *The Thurber Carnival*. The white cups that hung in the cabinet
shelves would be shining a little in the five o'clock autumn light, and
outside, in the narrow east yard, I could hear a Plymouth Rock hen
scratching around beneath the ligustrum bushes.

I would turn the pages and eat the grapes and smell the clean,
washed oilcloth on the table, and I would not be aware of when the
afternoon began to fade. But when I did look up I would see that the
cups were lost in shadow and that the ligustrum bushes had become a
blur in the darkening screen. I would stop reading and just sit there,
listening to the sounds coming in from the yard. Mother was outside
in the front flower bed, I knew – I could hear the water pipes running
underneath the house. And Daddy would be coming home from the
feed store pretty soon. We would have supper and then it would be
time to leave for the game....

At those moments, as I sat alone by the window, I would feel a
deep sense of peace – as if the world was a very good man and the two
of us had just shaken hands. I was that contented, and the mere passing of another day was that nice.

# Home Recalled

During my freshman year in college I walked the nighttime streets of Austin and looked into houses – those with lush lawns and gold door knockers and winding, polished staircases going to second floors – and the thoughts I had inside me burned so much like hot metal that all I wanted to do was yell out to the surrounding darkness:

"This is not my life here; I am not of this world. I am of a house that never had the proper thing, where closet doors never shut and faucets always dripped and dogs smelled a little like old grease – a place where eggs were gathered from the henhouse in a straw hat or a stewpot or a coffee can but never in a basket.

"I am of odd-shaped, inelegant yards: one in front that you used for visitors and Easter egg hunts because it alone had shrubs and flowers and bermuda grass; and a side yard that had cactus plants and dog bones and a chinning bar and once a colony of bees in small unpainted houses; and a yard in back that was not like the backyards in movies but was a sloping, grassless, weed-spotted place that was never fit for much except woodpiles and clotheslines and White Leghorn hens and birds and tree houses and gaunt caliche rocks that kept wearing away year after year in the steady washing rains.

"I am of oak tree roots running above the ground, big and friendly; of flagstone walks smelling fresh in a morning's dampness. I am of cold ashes carried from a solemn fireplace and dumped in the chicken yard for the hens to flutter and bathe in during gray November days. I am of loads of winter wood carried after dark to the woodbox on the long front porch, and a small, yellow-lit kitchen seen from the side yard through a cold-frosted windowpane, the two figures behind it frozen into portraits at the table: a nighttime kitchen so strangely intensified, so curiously abstract, that you, outside, always seemed to be looking at it through time instead of glass.

"I am of people living along the creek below the house: *creekers*, who grazed their cows in unfenced front yards and raised bantam

roosters and rabbits and tied hay on their fenders with baling wire
when they bought it at the feed store; who went to the Baptist Church
or the Assembly of God or the Church of the Nazarene and always
had a boy off somewhere studying to be a preacher; who would let
their children keep playing at a neighbor's house long after dark (hud-
dling there behind the dusty ligustrum bushes in games of hide-and-
seek, yelling and running for deeper cover in the yard as the fast creek-
er cars raced along the rocky streets and exposed them with their dim,
bouncing, yellowish lights).

"Yes" – I wanted to say, to myself, the night, the world – "and
there is so much more that's *me*, that I belong to, that I can't even begin
to think of it all now: afternoons so full of sparrows in the trees that
sometimes when you stopped thinking or playing they were all you
could hear, just them in the warm midafternoon, wildly busy, being the
actual heart and soul of the afternoon as far as you or they were concerned, almost boiling with sound inside the many green leaves; and

"'Stella Dallas' – the announcer, the organ music, the three
o'clock voices floating on waves of tears – coming out of the open
windows of the neighborhood houses, the whole block listening, the
houses tied together by the sound of the radios, and you as a boy of
ten or twelve moving idly from one playing-place in the yard to
another but still hearing the mournfulness of the program, from another angle, with another tone; and

"the BB gun – getting it as the sun went down and walking over
to the vacant lot across the street and standing beneath the cavernous
oaks that loomed about you like huge silent mothers; then moving
over the brown leaves and deepening shadows in order to hunt carefully for birds (never except once or twice actually killing one, and
never really caring to kill again after the first time, but always being
lured into forgetting how you felt when you buried it in the garden
and always wanting to feel as if you *could* kill again, at least); listening
with one detached part of your mind to a woodpecker knocking hol-

lowly against a nearby limb as you walked quietly, almost reverentially, through the many stilled trees; and

"climbing onto the roof of the house and sitting beside the chimney in the twilight: sitting on the warm wooden shingles, arms around your knees, watching as your mother worked in the flower beds and sent up to the roof the smell of watered earth; sitting in innocence and peace because at that time you did not know how memory would work – how it would intensify, how it would record the sight of the sun glowing against a tree and the scent of fresh-cut grass so that they would loom up again as things you have ripped yourself on, as things beginning to taunt: 'It was better that first time, it was better back then....'"

# Bode Feed and Hardware

It's a Monday morning at ten o'clock and I can visualize my father seated at the feed store behind his big dusty roll-top desk, examining the weekly ravages of his athlete's foot. He has his right shoe and sock off – very old-fashioned, high-top black shoe, very old black silk sock – and he is gingerly handling his toes so that the broken skin shows up more clearly in the light of the dangling overhead bulb. Without looking he reaches for his yellow can of Dr. Scholl's on the desk and gingerly pours and works in the powder between the toes.

My father does not hurry with his treatment, since this is no longer the kind of moment that is stolen out of the day's rush. Now some years back it used to be that on Monday mornings he would hardly have had time to answer the telephone, much less take time out to indulge an itching foot, in between the customers and the feed mixing in the back and making out orders for the salesmen due in the afternoon. But there is not that kind of rush any more at Bode Feed and Hardware, so my father has plenty of time to address himself, with complete concentration, to toe inspection or string collecting or just about any other little diversion that might show up during the course of a day.

I can see him peering down just a little more closely at his foot now, considering it further. He thinks he might try a little iodine on it, too.

He opens one of the side drawers of the desk – one of the many that have grown cluttered in recent years – and searches among the Pepsi-Cola empties and the old fried-pie wrappers and faded invoices until he finds his iodine. He looks down closely again as he touches the little glass applicator to the cracks in his toes. The iodine hurts, and he draws in his breath with a little hissing intake.

"Susss, dad *gum* the luck. *Ummmh!*" He winces and shakes his head a little at the pain.

My father hears the front door of the store opening. He closes up the iodine bottle and gives a glance to his foot before straightening up in his swivel chair to look out over the desk and see who has come in.

It is Frances Bouldin, the Negro woman who buys a quarter's worth of lime and a dime's worth of pigeon grit. As usual, she is carrying a couple of paper bags.

"Hello, Frances," my father says, looking at her briefly before turning back to survey his foot a final time. "Be with you in a minute."

"Oh, I ain't mindin, Mistah Bode. I been to town already this mornin and I'm just triflin now."

Frances generally fluctuates between two basic moods – she's either rather jaunty and carefree, or preoccupied with some personal gloominess: as she was, say, when her parakeet froze the very night after taxi fare went up to a quarter. Today she seems untroubled.

She soon notices my father's vacant sock and shoe beside the desk.

"Oh Mistah Bode, you havin feet troubles too? My, there's nothin meaner sometimes than just ole *feet* trouble." She hugs her two paper sacks a little closer, swaying, then cocks her head to one side in order to get the full scope of feet trouble in better focus. "Sometimes, I tell

you, my feets get to hurtin me so bad downtown I just want to stand
in that sidewalk and bawl like a *baby*. And I bet this ole feed store gets
you' feet the same way."

My father has his shoe on and rises from the swivel chair, clumping about experimentally to test the feeling in his doctored foot. He
puts away the Dr. Scholl's powder in a desk drawer, stands by the desk
to shuffle a paper or two, then turns to the cash register on the
counter. He makes a notation on the back of a check blank about
something he just remembered he wanted to take home after work.

Frances is reading items on the For Sale blackboard when he
finally steps behind the counter.

"Need some lime today, Frances?" my father asks.

Still reading, Frances answers in a vacant, singsong way: "Yassir,
Mistah Bode. I believe I'll take about a quarter's worth."

I can see my father moving on down behind the counter toward
the warehouse door – not leaving Frances with any noticeable rude-
ness, not moving with obvious, unlistening abruptness, but with just a
little grimness and a slight favoring of his stinging right foot. He has
never felt any deep fondness for Frances: back in the days when the
store still delivered she would call up for fifty cents' worth of rabbit
pellets and want it delivered "by five o'clock for sure, Mistah Bode,
'cause you know I always tries to be reg'lar in my feedin."

Frances stands firmly holding her two paper bags. Her small rimless glasses, that somehow are always glinting, blot out her eyes like a
pair of little silvery shields. My father goes through the middle door to
the back warehouse part where we used to keep feed. He fishes around
in an old wooden grain barrel full of papers and trash and finally
shakes the dust off a crumpled paper sack; then, after getting a scoop
from a nearby empty bin, he weighs out a quarter's worth of lime on
the scales. He lets fall a little extra jag of lime for good measure and
then twists the neck of the sack. He calls:

"You need some pigeon grit today, Frances?"

Frances always ends up buying pigeon grit when she comes to the store, but she never asks for it first. My father generally has to bring it up.

"Yassir, I suppose since I'm already in I might as well get some. How much is it a pound today, please?"

"Six cents," answers my father. It has been six cents forever, I think – it was six cents even when I worked at the store back in the forties. Frances knows that the chances of its still being six cents are pretty strong, but she always inquires just on principle.

"I suppose I'd just better have me a dime's worth today, then, Mistah Bode."

My father reaches down into the trash barrel for another sack, finds one, and gives it a shake to clear away the dust.

My father has owned Bode Feed and Hardware since 1937, and over the years it has seen, by and large, some pretty good days. It weathered several long, severe droughts, lasted out the war and family hospital bills. It never made my father prosperous but it made money enough to feed and clothe us all and to send my brother and me off to college. It hung on stubbornly and unspectacularly in the face of competitors who would open up in town, flourish mightily for a while, and then for some reason sicken and die or else settle down to being just ordinary business rivals.

I guess the store hung on for the simple reason that most people found out they liked to trade with my father. Many times, I know, they would continue to come up to the store even when they might be able to get feed cheaper some place else for a while or, in the case of out-of-towners, even buy closer to home. I suppose that over the years people came to believe that Fred Bode was that institution called A Good Man, and after they got that idea in their heads they just went on doing business with him, period. They found that he was honest, that he could be counted on to go out of his way to help a person, that he was never mean-acting or short-tempered. Too, he was a kind of amateur vet, in a way, and there were lots of times when someone with a bloated cow or sick chickens would phone up and say, "Fred, I got me a bunch of old Plymouth Rocks that are just drooping around, not laying, their old combs flopped over and turned bilious-looking: what d'you think I ought to do with them?" And my father, after giving his little preparatory, professional-sounding throat clearing, would ask a question or two further and then advise the caller about what ought to be done.

Sometimes when I get to thinking back on the pre-Frances Bouldin era and all the things the store used to be for people – for my father when he was making out of that big old warehouse not just a business but a way of life; for the ranch and town folks who came by to socialize as much as to buy feed; for me when I was growing up and helping out there in the afternoons – I can't help but hate it the way it is now. It's gone down hill so badly in the past few years I don't even like to go around it any more. It's just actually painful for me to look around at the empty, dusty shelves up front in the office and hardware part, or to walk around in the back warehouse where all the mashes and grain and hay used to be. Nowadays my father stores things for people instead of selling feed: he still keeps a few dabs of things for the likes of Frances Bouldin who just need a dime's worth of this or a quarter's worth of that, but his income now comes from renting out little squares of space in the warehouse for people who want to store air-conditioner units or cold drink cases or maybe old furniture. The last time I was in the store there were even some old bedsprings and a couple of rusted Maytag washing machines.

I wish the store could have kept on the way it was before my father lost his grip, or whatever it was, and began to back off into old age. Some of the relatives think it was his back operation that threw him for a loop: the VA doctors down in Houston scared him up pretty badly about ever lifting anything again and so for a long time afterward he just kind of sat around, not reordering any stock, hardly even noticing how the customers were drifting away because they couldn't get what they wanted any more. Maybe it was just simply that, the shock of the operation. Or maybe it was the last severe drought that came along about the same time and made a lot of people in the feed business uneasy and even put out of commission some of the best ranchers in the hill country. Maybe it was those things, and some others I don't even know about – things inside him, that only he knows – that caused my father almost overnight to take up the habits and thinking of an old man and caused things around the store to go to staves.

That old tin-roofed, sparrow-nesting warehouse had a loveliness about it, a peaceful sun-shining-on-a-warm-board contentment that made everybody who came there feel at home. Many an afternoon when I was working there I'd take a break and sit in the doorway on the steps, eating ice cream and watching the scenes around the block. Across the street to the west the sun would be catching itself in some of the tallest elms behind the bakery, haloing the trees and touching up the grass in a couple of the vacant lots around; and now and then you could get a whiff from the bakery of pastries and fresh bread; and there would be a hum of some kind of saw going in the metal shop right next door – not loud, but just a pleasant, afternoon sound, seeming as though the man running the saw might even be taking a good little pleasure out of the sound and feel of his work as well as knowing that he was doing something honorable and constructive in the world.

And sometimes the man who ran the secondhand shop on the other side of the bakery would be standing with his hat on underneath the shadowing eave of his store front, trying out the rod and reel someone had left with him to sell. He always seemed to get a genuine pleasure out of that reel: he'd cast out into the dusty, unpaved street between our place and his, reeling back his line in little jerky stops and starts – the way you do when you're trying to fool a fish – and the lead weight on the end of his line bouncing along over the dusty rocks somehow rather sad and lonesomely. Sometimes he would stand there for nearly half an hour or more, just casting and recasting, as if know-ing that was going to be the closest he would ever get to any actual fishing.

And over to the south of the store the Mexican kids would all be straggling up the tracks, coming home from school. There would usu-ally be an open railroad car along the tracks, and the guys from the lumberyard in town would be unloading Sheetrock. They would have their shirts open in front, streams of sweat shining on their stomachs but all of them joking around, not at all killing themselves with the work, and always laughing loudest and making remarks while the pret-tiest Mexican girls passed on slowly up the tracks. And catty-corner from us was the Jersey Lily beer joint, an old gray frame building with a high, square front and one lone hackberry tree outside the front door. For most of an afternoon there would just be one car or two parked in front and the occasional sound of some woman's high cackle in the big echoing hall, but when the painters and carpenters got off work about four-thirty or so the cars would begin to point in their noses all around the place and the jukebox would get going with all the slow, mournful hillbilly songs you ever heard.

Yes, when I get to thinking about it, there were lots of nice things about that old store. Back in the good old days of the thirties and for-ties when I was growing up – when the sign was still freshly painted in big letters along the side of the building and my father had sometimes two hired hands working for him – I remember I liked to watch how the big vans from the roller mills in San Antonio and other places brought us our feed. They would come backing up slowly to one of the warehouse doors, the driver twisted part ways out of the window of his cab, carefully jackknifing the van out of the street until the back end matched flush with the loading platform. Then the driver would let loose that big steaming sigh of his air brakes and he would lumber down out of the cab, taking off his black-billed driver's cap and mop-ping his big, white, sweating forehead with his bandanna. He would walk very slowly to the front part of the store and leave the sweat-stained invoice with my father and go on back into the small bath-room we had in the warehouse. He'd relieve himself, take several good long drinks from the gray-enameled tin cup that always hung by the water faucet, and come out still mopping his sweating hands on his white apron. He'd take off his billed cap again and wipe off more sweat with the back of his arm and then go to the loading platform doorway and stand in the breeze to light a cigarette. He'd stand there a while, resting and smoking, looking across the street to see what was going on there, and then finally he'd go to the back of his van and undo the big doors and begin to unload out of the pleasant, feed-sweetened darkness of the van his shipment of grain and mashes.  He would work for half an hour or more with his neat, well-balanced little loading truck, rolling his six-and-seven-feedsack-high stacks of cotton-seed meal and wheat bran and laying mash across the splintery ware-house floor and dumping them efficiently row after row along the walls. (Sometimes those great stacks of feed grew so temptingly high that small boys, if not watched by their customer fathers, would climb up sack by sack until they could touch the rafters. They were huge mountain ranges of feed, slanting gradually downward from the walls like miniature Alleghenies sloping toward the sea: maize, oats, wheat, corn, hundreds of pounds of each, sack upon sack, each a separate mountain system, each distinctive: Oat Ridge, Barley Butte, Rabbit Pellet Hill...and occasionally the small-boys-turned-alpinists would make their way from stack to stack, leaping deep chasms made where stock had dwindled low, striding boldly along high pleasant plateaus of alfalfa and peanut and Johnson grass hay, inching their way across knee-skinning, rough Siberian flats of sulfur block salt: sometimes being able to navigate the entire main rectangle of the warehouse without once touching the floor.)

During the good years some people came by as much to pass the time of day in the store as to buy feed. They felt comfortable sitting in one of the small, cane-bottomed chairs we had in front and looking out the south doorway down the railroad tracks. In summertime there was always a good breeze that swept up the long open clearing of the trackway into the store; it used to be people's favorite conversation opener. They'd rock back in their chair, maybe light up a cigarette, shove their hat back a little from their forehead, gaze down the tracks past the vacant lots and warehouses, and say to my father, "Fred, you've got the coolest place in town, right here."

And if there was a quiet two-o'clock lull in business, chances are the customer and my father would engage in the Great Feed Store Dialogue. My father, with his hat on, as always, would have stationed himself behind the counter just to the side of the cash register, his profile presented as a kind of offering of good listenership to the customer in the chair, his gaze directed vaguely, peacefully, and noncommittally somewhere in the neighborhood of the Burpee Seed Calendar on the south wall or the long crack beside it in the window glass. He was foremost a listener, an assentor, and that was what made the men who sat in the doorway comfortable, for they were usually talkers: small, sports-clothed retired colonels who found the informal atmosphere of the store to their liking since they had nothing more to do with their lives except to take care of their fine lawns and keep out red water for the hummingbirds and talk about their past military decisions; or wheezing, coughing, spitting old country men, barely able to make it up the front porch steps, who usually had spent most of their morning and afternoon across the street at the Jersey Lily: tough, leathery but nevertheless worn-out old men, soon to die of cancer if they didn't cough their asthmatic lungs out first or fall into a ditch and freeze to death on their way home some night from a beer joint: old men who had known my father when he was a boy living out on a ranch and liked him after he grew up and would still walk halfway across town to buy fifteen cents' worth of rape seed from him rather than buy it from a fancy-dan new Purina man in their neighborhood.

On occasion, though, the chair would be filled by one of the successful ranchers in the area who would come clomping up the front steps, his big boots polished to a T, his face pink and shiny from his fresh barbershop shave, his khaki pants and shirt smooth over his big stomach and thighs and still creased right: he would spread out in the chair with his legs apart and chew on a match stem and occasionally spit out the door and then in the middle of some trifling, general conversation about the weather would say abruptly, "Fred – what kind of price can you make me on a ton of range cubes?" And he'd spit again and chew on his match and look out the door while my father rustled around at his desk and found the back of an old envelope to figure on. If my father's price turned out to be all right, the rancher would slap his hands down hard on his thighs and hoist himself out of the chair and clomp on out the front door, hardly slowing down in passing to say, "All right, Fred, you go ahead and order me a ton and I'll send Joaquin in with the truck first part of next week," and down the wooden steps he'd go to his Buick, slamming the door hard and gunning out of the gravel and dust by the store to tend to his other business down the street.

(Those big income days, the ton of this, the carload of that: "Remember that $500 day, son?" my father recently asked me. I was at the store and somehow the conversation had turned to that Saturday back in the forties when all the first-of-the-month bills were being paid on time for once and when it had suddenly dawned on all of us that if business kept going as it had been up to three o'clock the cash register might surprise itself with a completely brand-new number by closing time. Customers were sometimes standing two and three deep during the afternoon and after any of us finished making a sale we would hurriedly lift up the lid on the cash register and see how far along we were toward $500. And it got to be a quarter to six and we were still forty-three dollars away from making it and dead tired – ready to close up and be content with being as close as we were – when an old man named Turner came driving up his box-square '20-something Ford and dug through his black coin purse until he found his monthly statement and then thumbed out $52.75 and slowly wadded up the receipt my father gave him and put it in his watch pocket and drove away.)

It's nearly closing time at the store, and I can see my father sitting on a stool in one of the warehouse doorways, finishing up a little job he started a while ago. He has a kerosene rag in his hand and he is bending over a Maxwell House coffee can full of old nails. He wipes each nail thoroughly, clearing away the rust. Every now and then he takes a bent nail and lays it on a wooden block he has nearby and taps it several times with his hammer to straighten it out.

A customer comes in, asking for a bushel of oats, and my father says he sure is sorry but he's out of oats right now. The man says he needs some to take home to a horse and asks where he could get some before six; my father says he might try the new place right down the street. My father doesn't rise from his bent-over, hammering position on the stool as he talks to the man. When the man leaves, my father turns back to his coffee can of nails. He scatters the nails about, searching out the ones that still need to be wiped clean. There are just a couple left. He pulls out his pocket watch and squints at it in the fading light of the doorway. There's still time to clean the last few before closing time. He puts his watch away and picks up his kerosene rag.

In the office the telephone is ringing but my father doesn't hear.

*For twenty years I lived, taught, and raised a family in sunny and serene El Paso. It was a good place, and I thrived on its desert air and desert clarities. But my personal Four Horsemen – Death, Divorce, Duty, and Despair – changed the rhythms of my life and thus at fifty, a year after my father died, I decided to leave nachos and margaritas and go back home for a while to Kerrville: to the cedars and live oaks of the hill country. My mother was there in a nursing home; my daughter was enrolled at the local college; my son, thirteen, lived nearby in San Antonio with my former wife.*

*What follows is part of a journal I kept as I camped in the old house I was born in and sifted among half-buried memories of my home town.*

# Gilmer Street Journal

## I

Incredible: I am in the Heavenly City, driving down Streets of Light. People move along the sidewalks of Water Street and do not see the strangeness of their town, of others' bodies. They think it is only another Monday – this awesome, sun-washed, sun-pierced day. They think they have seen it all before, many times, but of course they have seen none of it. It is as removed from them as Tibet.

...The light, the light, it is everywhere – on the sides of people's faces, the fronts of buildings, on the grass and ground and streets, under the blue-domed sky. Women carry packages, ranchers drive pickup trucks, children hold their mother's hand. They pass one another in this exotic, eternal, familiar place, and to them it is only double-stamp day at Super Save.

## II

The yards of the home place have turned into Brazil. Beggar's lice, ragweed, purple thistles, horehound are waist high where only rocks grew before. Hackberries and ligustrums sprawl, interlock, shut

out the sun. I get a saw and weed slinger and begin to win back the
territory. Then, resting, sweating, I look at the backyard and remember
where I sat as a child among the oak tree roots, playing cars. The
clothesline ran nearby – holding up my father's newly washed khaki
shirts and pants – and the back porch steps were behind me, still
splashed with the soapy dishwater my mother had just thrown out.

As a six-year-old, I scraped roadways among the roots. I sat in
dirt and found contentment there. I enjoyed being underneath the
trees, near random tin cans, near rocks, near chickens fluffing themselves in little dirt bathtubs, near the sound of the dogs barking in the
neighborhood.

I was small and I lived close to the ground and *lo, the ground was
good*. Those big, rough-barked, leisurely curving roots were my friends
– as the woodshed was, and the cow lot, and the oat field.

Childhood: that was when blueing bottles sat on the back porch
window sill and cane fishing poles lay across the rafters in the garage.
Childhood? Why, that meant scrapes on elbows and the Avon lady;
Sears catalogues and Big Little Books and flowered wallpaper and
vacant lots; quilts spread along the creek bank and the smell of burnt
tapioca on October nights.

...Yes, I fight the weeds of change and decay in the eighties, but
the thirties live on.

## III

Backyard, summer day: The locusts are here, of course, rising and
falling like Greek choruses within the trees.

After the summer rains the greenery is oceanic – weeds, grasses,
shrubbery; hackberries and oaks; they surround me like a sea. Above
me, the sun burns down like a friendly lamp fixed forever in the childlike blue of the sky.

Butterflies drift and swim across lantanas like girls picking flowers
in some Golden Age.

And in a neighbor's yard, beneath the shade of a pecan tree, a white tablecloth on a clothesline flows back and forth in the breeze: the tolerant metronome of a summer morning.

## IV

Ike Morrow walks knee-deep through weeds and flowers. I am behind him in the morning sun. As we walk along he grins at me, cigarette in the corner of his mouth. We are going fishing. I am seven years old.

That's all there is to it – this fragment of a scene – yet it has come to me and will not let me alone.

I seem to be passing through the heart of a physical sensation instead of the ordinary grasses of Turtle Creek. And Ike Morrow, my father's feed store delivery man: He is not just taking me to catch perch but is leading me mythically onward into some godly pleasure-place among the cypresses.

The sweep of the long, unbroken field below Mrs. Hall's farm – that is part of it. Trees are on the horizon, and fence posts and barns, but in the bottomland where I walk – small, bareheaded under the clear June sky – there is a delicious and intoxicating openness. I could not experience any greater sense of perpetual sky stretching over perpetual, bordering greenery if I were adventuring along a coastal plain in Bangladesh.

I carry a can of worms and a fishing pole and I am headed toward a clump of trees, but I do not know if I ever get there or if I ever fish. I remember only that lyric passage across the flatland: the romance of sweating and breathing and walking as a seven-year-old under the blaze of the sun; the sense of vistas – before me, around me, waiting for me; and – in the slouched khaki shoulders of Ike Morrow and the coiling blue smoke of his cigarette – the pleasure of a shared moment, of fishing-pal camaraderie on a hill country Saturday morning.

## V

After cutting weeds in the chicken yard I rest a while and look about at the back lot: yes, the home place has seen better days. The rabbit cages are in angles of collapse, their doors rotting in a mulch of hackberry leaves. Rusted rakes lean against the tool shed wall. In the cow lot weeds grow taller than my head. Everywhere I look there are old lanterns, paint cans, coffee pots, rolls of wire.

Yet the debris and neglect of recent years do not matter because the chicken yard this morning is a pageant in the sun. Ragweed towers elegantly beside the garden fence. The young pecan trees smell clean and bitter-fresh. Flies, wasps, bees sashay around in the mid-morning odysseys.

In the hen house a White Leghorn walks about within the shining rust of the screen wire. Her smooth white tail moves like a shark fin in the depths of the hen house light-and-dark: now gleaming, now gray. She is serene, effortless, perfect.

I sit sweating in the bright ten o'clock sun until I understand what the morning is all about. Everything in the chicken yard seems perfect simply because the human act of seeing is perfect. To see is to complete a perfect act.

The blade of Johnson grass against the cinder block wall, bending and tapering – is perfect. The red-brick chimney rising above the roof of the house, with the blue of the sky and the green of the trees behind and beside it – is perfect. The sun – shining, creating shadows and depths – makes each leaf, each flash of bird wings, each weathered board perfect.

The morning gives me intense visual delight simply because I am aware of what I am seeing at the moment I am seeing it. I see each object clearly, as if through a magnifying glass, and almost become the thing perceived, almost participate in its private being.

In the chicken yard everything dramatically *is* – every edge of board, every bug on the ground, every stem of every weed and plant. Ordinary backyard sights and surfaces exist superbly in the sun and I see them acutely – dish pan, broken flower pot, purple verbena – radiant with the presence of themselves.

# Mother

## I

I went to see my mother at the nursing home. I parked beneath the American flag whipping in a breeze above rows of bright sidewalk flowers and entered Hilltop Nursing Home. Old women, seated in the lobby, kept their faces turned toward me as I walked by, but I held no genuine interest for them. If I had been carrying an alligator under my arm or leading an elephant on a chain they would have continued to stare ahead with the same lack of curiosity or concern.

I entered Room 17, Wing D. My mother was sitting in her wheelchair, rocking slightly in the rhythm of her Parkinson's disease and clacking her false teeth. Her white hair was wilder than usual. As I leaned over to give her a bit of a hug I smelled her Hilltop odor of stale sweat and talcum powder. Her roommate, a stick of a woman hugging her knees, sat in the adjacent bed like a jaundiced praying mantis, staring at us with disapproval. She complained about the Hilltop meals, her stomach, television programs. Bitterness was oozing from her lips like tobacco juice as I wheeled my mother toward the door.

On our way to the home place my mother jerked and clacked and looked out the window. We made our small talk – and I tried to figure out why her words did not quite make sense anymore. It was as though the twisted flow of her thoughts was all that was left of a once-forceful river: one that for eighty years had been broad and smooth but during a storm had finally gone out of its banks. Rock slides had crashed down from overhanging cliffs, tree branches jammed the rapids, boulders filled in the bed. Now, as she talked, the stream that once carried her thoughts disappeared underground, reappeared, detoured suddenly around a hidden ledge, emerged, disappeared into a whirlpool only to reappear once more – a thin trickle among debris.

In the living room I guided her to a chair and leaned her crutch against the wall. I carefully pulled Tiger the cat from beneath the dining table and held him a few moments to calm him. I stroked his back – trying to prepare him for the ordeal ahead. I took him to my mother and placed him carefully in her lap.

Mother clacked and rocked and talked lovingly to Tiger. Then she started to pet him – banging at Tiger's body as if she were dusting a rug. Tiger squatted there for a while – stoically, drawing himself tighter, holding on.

I said, "Mother, Tiger is getting pretty cranky these days. I guess you'd better pet him a little easier."

I went over and tried to show her. I took her misshapen, arthritic hands and guided them slowly over Tiger's head and body, then went to the kitchen to fix her a glass of Coke with ice. When I returned she was banging away again. Tiger growled wildly, dug his claws into my mother's dress, jumped from her lap and ran beneath the couch.

Mother rubbed at the bleeding scratches on her hand and smiled up at me. "Tiger's still frisky as a jailbird," she said.

## II

She was being pushed along in her wheelchair by an aide. The hall was white, her face was white, and her hair, newly brushed, was so white and fine and shiny it looked artificial – a spun-glass wig. She came toward me, unsmiling, strapped in the chair. As I bent down to her I saw that someone, the aide perhaps, had touched lipstick lightly across her mouth in a gesture to encourage life.

It was a pleasant day and I wheeled her outside the nursing home to a porch that faced the sun. I rattled on to her about the hunting cabin, Kerrville traffic, my children, the weather – the useless ritual I went through each time I came to see her. Every now and then she would try to carry on her half of the conversation. She would open her mouth, struggle a bit to shape the sounds, and then speak. Her words were, as before, a Lewis Carroll jabberwocky that lacked meaning – like colored beads selected and strung by a deranged child.

As I stood beside her wheel chair and cut her fingernails I would glance down at her from time to time. She was staring ahead, her face set – and it was as if she were blind.... More than that: as if she were both unseeing and unseeable, as if she had disappeared: unreachable within the familiar outline of her body. "My mother" – the woman who had read *Anna Karenina* and Thomas Mann – was gone; yet, incomprehensibly, she was still there: a white-haired, white-faced, lip-daubed figure in a wheelchair: a stranger staring into a landscape she could not describe, thinking thoughts that had no language.

## III

In March I had given her a quiz. "Who am I?" I asked and gave her four names to choose from. To her, I was none of them. She was comfortable with the familiar sight and sound of me in the room, but I had become nameless. She was beyond motherhood, beyond the bonds of human attachment; she could no longer conceptualize me as her son. She lay on her incontinence pad, beginning to lapse into a coma – the final mystery close at hand.

In May, at age eighty-four, she died. At the funeral home where she lay in state family friends came by to sign the register and pay their respects. They solemnly shook my hand and said It Was For The Best, It Was A Blessing. I suppose they were right – about death being the proper thing for an old woman whose brain had slowly been degenerating. I had no better stance to take toward death as I stared at my mother in the casket. She was now a cadaver made ready for burial: artfully powdered and painted, bled and disemboweled and filled with formaldehyde. Her arthritic, knobby hands lay crossed on the funeral dress, her white hair gleamed, sprays of flowers were arranged about her in a semicircle. My mother, Maggie Mae, was ready to be placed in the ground.

Her funeral was at noon in Harper. As cars pulled off the single main street and parked on the grass of the small wood-framed church, a mockingbird sat on top of the church roof and poured out its dazzling sounds. The service began: the pianist played "In the Garden"; the soloist sang "Ramona" – the song my mother had sung to my brother and me when we were children; the minister recalled for us my mother's life and her virtues; another hymn was sung. The service ended.

We drove to the cemetery across the road, the minister said final words under the canopy, and my mother in her closed casket was poised over a hole that had been dug that morning next to my father's grave. We drove back to the hall behind the church and had sandwiches and iced tea.

...And I think about it: how I had stood looking at my mother's profile in that darkened mortuary room in Kerrville – faint organ music constantly playing – and half-expected to see her move; how people had walked decorously across the carpet toward the casket and looked at her and said "She's better off"; "She looks so peaceful"; "They certainly did a good job" – as if she were merely asleep or in suspended animation...how we, the living, carry our own life within us like an invisible candle flame that will never flicker out...how we live intimately with both life and death and do not understand either one.

## IV

I stood by the mound of my mother's grave in the small Harper cemetery. She was down there in the dirt. A week after the funeral she was still stretched out under ground.

"Hi, ma," I said.

I was properly erect on a June day, standing the way living humans do, and she was prone in her casket, getting ready for the bugs and worms.

Two feet away was my father's tombstone (1895-1981) and, beneath it, his skeleton. I looked around: I was in a community of gravestones with their carefully chiseled names and dates. And underneath, in their assigned portions of earth, were the Harper ranch people who once drank coffee on their screened-in porches and discussed the price of Johnson grass hay. My mother had just joined them – a newcomer in her dusty-rose burial dress and shiny green casket.

As I left her mound and walked past the grave sites toward my car, my legs and arms moved with automatic ease. They knew what they were doing. I was unquestionably alive – putting my familiar body into the familiar car so I could continue the familiar, normal business I had briefly interrupted by stopping at the cemetery. I was not dead; I was not under dirt.... As I drove down the lane toward the highway – past the Harper school building and the school buses dramatically yellow under the noon sun, past the shining oak trees, past the radiant roadside summer flowers – I could not fit the two together: being dead, being alive. There was no way that I could bridge the gap between the silent cemetery world and the sun-bathed morning. Those names carved in marble – Hopf...Bierschwale...Tatsch...Ahrens... Sageser – and the bone-people beneath: they simply did not belong to shining oaks and yellow school buses.

Cars kept passing me as I drove on slowly toward Fredericksburg, and I watched them disappear down the highway: all those people on the move, in a hurry, full of goals and purposes, with their children gazing blankly at me through their rear windows – children I would see once and never again.

What could I do about them: fire and ice, life and death, *I-thou*: always separate, never merging, never knowing the other?... I looked at the pasture trees: I would continue to spend my life next to them and not know how it was to be a tree. Or a dog. Or any other living thing.... We live in compartments – fractional, isolated. I will only know me and my life, and then, one day, I will be in a box in the ground and my son and daughter will stand there, six feet above me, in the sun, and say, "Hi, Dad" and I will not hear.

# II

# THE RANCH

# Zipper's Back Yard

We were there in the back yard on those many childhood mornings, all gathered beneath the tall and sober post oak tree: Gram – my
grandmother – in her faded bonnet, stirring soap in the washpot, bent
into the curve of her morning's work; myself, spraddle-legged on the
whitened, ash-packed ground, playing cars and war and ranch;
Grandpa – the sound of him – out in the west pasture on horseback
with Enselmo, the Mexican hand, yelling over and over in his peaceful
distant liturgy: "goooootie...goooootie," calling, driving, urging the
goats homeward to the pens; the big yellow mama cat, stretched out
on top of the washhouse with her chin hanging indolently over the
edge of the roof, her little pocket of a belly swelling out in its slow
meticulous rhythm, her long marble eyes nearly closed but still keeping a bare slitted watch; and our inquisitor, reporter, and clown:
Zipper, the collie, who made of every morning a dog-odyssey.

Except for Zipper we were all preoccupied in almost languorous
private concerns. The morning would wear on toward noon and Gram
continued to stir, Grandpa to call, the mama cat to doze and hang her
chin. I continued to make trim winding roads with my sardine-can
machinery and load and unload my acorn-cows and button-goats and
rock-sheep. But Zipper stayed on the move. He seemed to have an
artist's hankering to see everything that was going on and react to it.
As flies swarmed in the dense, mote-filled light of the washhouse doorway, he would pause to snap briskly at them, as if suddenly deciding to
take their swarming as a personal affront. He dealt with them in the
spirit of righteous reprisal, like Don Quixote engaging and vanquish-
ing a legion of small but dangerous windmills. You could hear his
teeth clicking and see the flesh curled out around his mouth. After a
while he would move on, immensely satisfied with his behavior.
Perhaps he would stand a moment in the coolness of the post oak,
going back over this most recent triumph or perhaps older and even
more enjoyable ones. Then, with no cause, he would suddenly and

violently decide to inspect himself. Wheeling his head down and stretching out his hind legs, he would scratch and gnaw until it seemed as if he had finally decided to scratch and gnaw himself to death.

Soon the spell would pass and he would rise, instantly alert, perhaps not pleased by a turkey gobbling too much out at the woodpile or by one of the baby yellow cats stealing with too much dramatic stealth across the yard and disappearing into the small fig tree just inside the garden. Sometimes he would be standing on the sidewalk that led across the backyard to the back gate and discover that several red Hereford cows were looking at him from where they stood at the water trough beyond the garden. Their looking and their chewing would seem so insolent that he would run to the end of the walk and be inspired to do some of his best barking of the day.

And sooner or later he would get around to his routine morning stunt: trying to take an unnoticed nap in the shady bed of four-o'clocks that bordered the back side of the house. He was never successful. Gram would always look up in time from beneath her bonnet and raise her long threatening soap stick and shout *Zipper!* And he would jump guiltily and dodge along the side of the house to the back screen door. He would sit there on his haunches for a while, quite chastised, gazing out toward the lots with the posed innocence of a well-mannered schoolboy waiting his turn at recitation. But gradually he regained his composure, and before long his shaky nonchalance had changed into a serene benevolence, like that of an elder statesman who found personality differences mere pettiness and not worth his long consideration.

# Flyswatting

Through the years Gram's primary concern was keeping the house neat and presentable for company, and daily she conquered the threats of dust, dirt, and wrinkled beds. But never was she wholly successful in mastering her arch-opponent: flies. As a boy I would see her start swooshing early in the morning, with a cup towel or the back of her hand – always in a general way at first, still restrained, as though hoping that if she did not fully admit their presence they would become discouraged and go away. But by ten o'clock coffee they had invaded the dining room in such numbers that she was forced to say, "I wish you would do a favor for Gram. Get that flyswatter down and kill some of these old *flies*. I declare, I don't know where they get in at but they just *take* over!"

As an incentive Gram always paid her grandchildren a penny a fly. I was glad to take the money but would willingly have worked for free. Prowling through the cool familiar rooms of the ranch house, waiting tensely for the flies to land, skillfully attacking, gathering up, carefully moving on – that was the real joy and lure for me. Sometimes I spent whole mornings in the kitchen-living-room-dining-room area, clutching the floppy wire swatter and an empty cracker box for disposal.

Flyswatting is an art, with different surfaces requiring different skills for killing. If flies landed on Gram's bed you stunned them, tangling their legs in the counterpane threads; then, with the edge of the swatter, you flicked them to the linoleum floor and finished them off in a businesslike way down there. A fly on a glass offered a different problem since you were unable to bring full power against something breakable. At best you could simply wave the fly away and follow it to another landing, always trying to coax it to some flat place – shooing, blocking, intimidating with your swatter, always feeling in yourself the stealth and cunning of an animal trainer moving a dangerous lion from stool to stool.

Generally, relatives made good surfaces but otherwise were not much help. When they wandered into the kitchen and attracted a few flies, they stood still enough while I crept onto a chair and swatted at their neck or arm or thigh, but on the whole they remained indifferent to the total drama involved and their chuckles at my kills were always a little forced and patronizing.

It was only Gram, of course, who understood my dedication to
The Cause. If I happened to see a fly on her while she was busy at the
sink, I would yell, "Gram, there's one on your head!" and she would
obediently freeze, bent over and waiting. She played her part without
the least bit of condescension and would have something laudatory to
say afterward – even if I had smashed the fly deep into her hairnet and
made her keep her pose while I picked it out carefully with a piece of
toilet paper.

After a good morning's work I would put my cracker box on the
cold woodstove and lay out the dead, usually around twenty or twenty-five. Gram would get her black silk coin purse from the dresser and
count out the pennies, saying, "My, you don't know what a help this is
to Gram. Everything just *feels* nicer without all those old flies around."

# After Dinner

Many times after the noon meal was over I would go sit in the
old green rocker on the front porch, my bare feet sticking out beyond
the porch railing into the warm sun. With the ranch settling itself for
the long afternoon, you could almost feel a curtain of rest drawing
itself closed across the land.

I would sit in the rocker, looking out to the big clearing beyond
the yard, then on past it to the low distant hills that on warm clear
days made a bright blue-and-silver rim on the horizon. You could see
far to the south from the porch, and on such resting summer days your
thoughts went moving out from your eyes in a great sense of ease and
freedom. You could just let your mind float comfortably on the afternoon and the scene before you.

Along the west ridges of the clearing beside the water trough the
sheep would be bedded together in deep live-oak shade. They chewed
and rested and let their ears flap occasionally at flies. Now and then
their bellies would contract awkwardly during an attack of sneezing or

wheezing and a head would shake itself violently from side to side, as though the sheep were saying, "Dang the luck! This old needlegrass sure does get up your nose and *stay* there." A few sheep always remained standing, chewing a little but mostly just staring out at the hot glare in the clearing, as if deeply puzzled at the need for so much heat and light at this time every day. Usually it happened, too, that one of the younger, more disenchanted ewes would decide to follow the impulse of some vague, private inspiration and would wander casually from the shadows into the harsh sunlight. Bemused, she would get a little way, then idly turn to look back at the rows of white, dispassionate faces chewing at her from their haven of shade. She would immediately realize her folly – like a swimmer out in mid-lake suddenly becoming aware of the distance back to the shore – and, panic-stricken, she would bleat wildly and run back to the safety of the shade and the mass of smooth, comforting bodies.

Inside the front yard red ants would be crawling slowly up the sidewalk toward the porch in the solid glare of the sun. You could see them pause now and then, as if to wipe their brows and glance up sharply at the hot and punishing sky. Then, barely rested, they would move on with a heavy air of martyrdom. They always gave the appearance of pioneers going west, facing each crack in the sidewalk as a new crossing of the Snake or North Platte. And under the shade of the salt cedar, next to the garden fence, Zipper rested his long black nose on his forefeet, the air from his nostrils tunneling steadily into the loose black dirt. During the main resting hours of the afternoon his slant eyes kept closing in an air of tired wisdom but never for long. He was always reopening them to keep a steady languid awareness of the yard, like a Chinese storekeeper watching his merchandise on a dull day.

There would be long stretches of time when life stopped and nothing seemed to move anymore. The yard itself, like someone finally rid of too many afternoon visitors, seemed to relax and take its long-delayed sun bath. Then, like shock troops, a squad of wasps would sail around the corner of the porch and land on the two hydrants in each side of the yard. They would walk with a great militaristic flourish around the pipes and you could almost see them whipping swagger sticks irritably against shiny black boots. Several of them, lesser in rank, made repeated forays into the darkness of the hydrant mouths and brought back reports. They would all make a few more investigations – some inspecting the nearby grass, others tabulating, conversing, exchanging estimates all along the pipes – until, on a given signal, they would peel off melodramatically and disappear from the yard.

After a while I would hear Gram come into her bedroom east of the porch and open the dresser drawer to get her Chapstick. I knew by that she was getting ready for her nap, for the first thing she did after finishing the dinner dishes was to come and open the old yellow dresser and reach in among the boxes of face powder and hairnets and packages of straight pins and get out the small green cylinder of mentholated ice. There always seemed to be a little fringe of roughness on her upper lip, and rubbing in the cool, soothing ice provided her with a moment of supreme self-indulgence. She would take the top off and hold it carefully in one hand as she rubbed; then, finished, she would replace the cap just as carefully and put the tube back into the drawer and walk away from the dresser still gratefully massaging her lip with her little finger.

This was all part of an after-dinner pattern on the ranch that remained the same, always, unless there happened to be company or it was Sunday. First the dinner table had to be cleared in the dining room and the dishes carried back to the kitchen, where they were washed and dried and put away in the big hanging cabinet; then the white tablecloth was taken to the back door and shaken free of crumbs; finally the broom was taken from behind the kitchen door and the dining-room linoleum was swept into shining blue cleanness again.

It was an easy matter for anyone on the front porch to keep track of the ritual by listening to the identifying sounds: the constant, monotoned ring of each dish placed solemnly on its proper shelf; the long empty whine of the screen door opening, the silence, the hard flat shutting; the broom knocking hollowly against the kitchen door as it was pulled from its quarters; and finally the strange, rather entrancing rhythm of Gram's feet: Moving chairs away from the path of her broom in a steady, precisioned way, with no wasted motion, she had a one, two, three pause-and-sweep routine that was the combination of a slow-motioned tango and the aggressive little waltz chickens engage in while scratching for food.

After dishes and sweeping and the mentholated ice, Gram was ready for her nap. She would get her glasses off the fireplace mantel in the front room and wipe them clean on her apron and gather up her magazines or *The Upper Room* and come back to her bedroom and lie down, hoping for a good breeze through the windows. She always made genuine first efforts toward getting her reading done, but it was never long until the glasses had slipped down her nose, her hand – palm upward – was limp at her side, and she was asleep, *The Upper Room* making a slowly rising and falling tent on her stomach.

And of course there was Grandpa.

At some point after the dishes had been put away I would hear him cough on the breezeway: the full-rattling, after-dinner cough that never failed to come after he had taken out his teeth and rinsed them in the kitchen sink and had begun to gather up newspapers to take to his room. Whenever I heard it, it never seemed just an ordinary cough of habit or from catarrh. In the silence of the house and the afternoon it seemed to take on a special and significant meaning: it was a pronouncement, a commentary, an act of assurance – all three. It said that this old man who had been head of his ranch for over half a century was still around and functioning. It said that once again a day had passed the halfway mark at the ranch and everything had gone off all right: once again Gram had strained the morning milk and it was sitting in cool crocks in the refrigerator; Enselmo had once again ridden the fences and chopped brush for the goats and doctored all the wormy stock in the pens; the hogs were fattening and the potatoes were growing in the garden and water was still coming up from the ground. It said that the dinner meal had been another good one and the little chores after it had been taken care of, and now once again the ranch deserved to relax until coffee time came at four. The cough went on to say that though drouths came and needlegrass persisted and windmills periodically broke down, there was no real reason for fear on the ranch. It said that even though Grandpa was getting old and was retelling his same familiar stories more frequently, he was still all right and thus the ranch was all right. And with hired help that was steady, and good whiskey toddies to warm up the blood, and a good nap each afternoon, everything would continue to be all right for a long while. Things could remain as they had always been.

I sat in the porch rocker on such afternoons, my feet out in the sun, listening to that cough and to Gram lightly snoring (*The Upper Room* going unread still another day) and to the Seth Thomas clock ticking gently from its place on the fireplace mantel. I could listen to all this, echoed in the steady creaking of the windmill behind the garden, and I could think: yes, the ranch, the other home of your life, is resting all around you now, with afternoon warmth and peace spread across it in thick slabs. And all you have to do is sit here, tranquilly, and just let the ranch come flowing into the heart of you and then, effortlessly, in return, let the love you have for it seep back out of you across the land, from your eyes and thoughts, from your very body. You can sit here and be privileged to know, definitely, right now, that there is something in life you love, something for which your love can be full and unqualified. You, the ranch, life, and love – a place, a person, and his emotions – all tied together and made simple, somehow, as simple and complete as a hummingbird that is poised for a suspended moment in time and space to spear a drop of water from a hydrant's mouth.

# Summer Nights

When the supper dishes were washed and put away and Grandpa had set the pie pan full of scraps out the back door for Zipper, we sat on the front porch and looked south to the darkness and the stars. Gram sat in the rocker, combing out her hair from its tight braids, and Grandpa and I shared the curved-back double seat.

Everything out in the night would be in an orderly flux and simmer. A bullfrog croaked now and then from the fish pond, and crickets sang in the garden. Katydids flashed peaceful electric signals to each other in the trees.

There would be stretches when no one spoke, when each of us seemed to be tempering himself more strongly in the night and silence. Grandpa became just the red glow of his cigarette and Gram the steady crackling of her rocker against the cement floor. Sometimes after one especially long silence Grandpa would cough deeply and lean forward over the railing and spit into the flower bed. Then he would settle back to say, "I remember one time in the lower country when Paw and I went up to Cuero to sell some hogs," and the tale of Old Times that had been growing on him in the dark would begin.

If it was a familiar and often-told story Gram would begin to rock faster until she would finally interrupt brusquely: "George! We've all heard that old story a hundred times!" And Grandpa, never insulted but instead quite mild and unruffled, would say, "Well, I reckon one more time won't hurt nobody then," and would continue. It would never be a self-glorifying story. It would be pure reminiscence, reclaiming the era of his boyhood when he and Gram grew up together on neighboring farms and touched either on the gently humorous or the gently vulgar or a balanced combination of both.

As Grandpa would weave his way through long-past scenes and revive shadowy, forgotten figures out of the turn of the century, it never failed that Gram slowed her brisk censuring rock and was lured back into the vaguely sweet years of her girlhood and early marriage.

She brushed her hair slowly in the darkness and forgot she was supposed to be aloof from the tale. Many times, if Grandpa failed to wrest up a date from memory or got a fact wrong, Gram was right there immediately to say, "Lem's *cousin*, George; it was Lem's *cousin*, not his *sister*." Grandpa would pause to consider, agree, and then be off again on the rest of his story.

# Goat Killing

When Enselmo threw the other end of the rope over a live oak tree the goat gave a long, desperate, strangulated Bluaaaahhhh, but Enselmo did not even seem to hear it. He went right on stringing the goat up by his hind feet and tying the rope around the trunk of the tree while Grandpa stood beside him, chewing on his tobacco. Then Grandpa got out his pocket knife and after turning to spit to one side and wiping his sleeve along his mouth he placed the tip of the finely whetted blade against the goat's neck and jabbed it deep and across the throat. When he pulled away the jugular vein gave its first big rush of blood.

After the knife blade disappeared into the white taut neck and the cry broke and gurgled away with the splashing of blood to the ground, the four of us waited there in the woodlot beneath the huge oak tree: Enselmo and Grandpa were waiting for the neck to stop draining so they could skin the goat and hang pieces of the carcass in the smokehouse; Zipper was waiting for the hot intestines to be thrown over against the garden fence so he could begin to chew and gnaw and worry them for the rest of the morning. And I was waiting because it was my first goat killing.

With his knife hand still held out wide from his side Grandpa chewed fast and methodically on his wad of tobacco, watching the goat empty himself of blood. Finally, when the bleeding had slowed to a steady drip, he and Enselmo went to work. Enselmo began to skin the goat with quick, slashing strokes of his own sharp pocket knife, peeling back the hide and revealing layers of shining, globular fat; and Grandpa, after first dipping his hand in a bucket of water beside the tree, reached into the cavity of the goat and started bringing out the heart, the sweetbread, the pink spongy lights. With both of them slashing and peeling it wasn't long before the goat stopped looking like an animal to me: it seemed more like a piece of strange, muscular sculpture that someone had hung up inside a suit of long-handled underwear.

Later in the day I went into the smokehouse and stood beneath the sections of meat. They swung gently, almost contentedly, from the dark rafters, as if already adjusted to their new home. I tried to visualize how they had been early that morning – all of them connected inside the hide of the goat, all of them working together so that the goat walked and snorted and bleated with the mysterious fullness of life – but I could not. It seemed as if there never had been such a goat; he had merely been a dream. There had always been just these smooth, white-streaked slabs in the smokehouse gloom: silent tombstones of meat.

# The Mulberry Tree

Standing in the corner of the peach orchard beside the rock water tank, the mulberry tree at the ranch was a friendly temple of summer shade. Many mornings I climbed within its branches and lived for long, secluded, blissful hours. Idle as a king, I ate handfuls of white and purple mulberries and swung my legs and spied on the outer world. I saw spring lambs run against their mothers' bags and jab at them furiously until they found the teats – while the mothers stood there placidly, as if pleased by the attack. I watched horses move slowly out of the lots and into the back pastures, their heads bobbing, their tails flicking, their smooth coats glistening under the nine o'clock sun.

I saw Gram open the back door of the ranch house, first to shake out the crumbs from the tablecloth and then just to stand there a while, gazing out at the morning.

Sometimes I watched hummingbirds flash across the tank to get a drink from the windmill pipe: They would quiver at the mouth of the pipe, immensely cautious, making sure that things were peaceful and right; then they would thrust their long needle-beaks into a hanging drop of water and peel off into the sky – curving away from the tank so swiftly and elegantly that they seemed like small, beautifully shaped ornaments swung at the end of invisible strings.

As I stayed buried within the greenery of the mulberry leaves there were just two realities: myself and the long morning; the perceiver and the perceived. I did not think of losses or gains, of future or past; I was concerned only with the profound pleasures of being alive – bearing my own private witness to the truth that the pursuit of happiness was not a pursuit at all but a witnessing, an embracing.

# Sunday Afternoons

At four o'clock the families always reassembled around the dining room table for coffee. The grownups, just arisen from afternoon naps, sat woodenly at the table and spoke with level, sober voices – as though they were all joined in a sorrowful wake for their dear friend Sleep who had just departed. They moved their arms and bodies with almost painful care, as if during sleep their muscles had not only hardened into hinges but had rusted as well. Periodically they would lift slow coffee cups, suspend them a moment near their mouths while making some mild affirmative or negative grunt to a question, tilt the cups mechanically to pursed lips, then carefully settle them down onto the saucer rings with a bare polite sound.  After each separate rite of drinking, their bodies seemed to settle and sag a little in the chairs, as if waiting to indulge more fully, like indolent lovers, in the voluptuous caresses of Folger's coffee that would ultimately woo and awaken them from their long passiveness.

No one moved or spoke excessively for half an hour or more. During long silences perhaps a sheep would bleat outdoors in the distance or maybe the windmill would give a creaking turn. Both the silence and the sounds made the world of the ranch seem very simple and still. Shadows had begun to form noticeably in the dining room, softening and deepening the corners, and the room took on a rich subdued tone, like that of a mahogany cave. The men covered their yawns and idly drummed thick, work-toughened fingers on the tablecloth while their cigarettes sent up hazes of smoke that hung in the darkening air like thick trails of phosphorous.

Finally, at some unspoken moment of agreement, a chair was scraped back, a coffee cup was touched to its saucer a final time, someone laughed, someone left the room – and coffee time was over. The four o'clock spell was broken, there was movement, the dining room became lived in again. Doors slammed, someone was coughing and clearing his throat out on the front porch, someone was flushing the commode in the bathroom. The small sounds of the mantel clock and the sheep outdoors were lost. There was movement outward into all the rooms of the house, into the yard, and soon the chairs around the dining table were pushed back and empty.

Usually it was at coffee time that we grandchildren suddenly remembered that each Sunday at the ranch inevitably came to an end. Up till that moment we had not stopped long enough in our play to think about it. We had forgotten everything – that we did not really live there on the ranch, that we only visited sometimes, that we would all have to leave and go our separate ways at nightfall. When four o'clock came, it was like being drunk on play and being forced to sober up at the dining table on the grownups' coffee fumes.

After leaving the dining room we would usually wander out to the lots for a last look around, realizing that everything was gradually being geared toward leaving, that pretty soon one of our parents would seek us out to say, "You'd better start getting your things together; we've got to be going soon." We prowled through the goat pens and loading chutes and tried to recapture the wild, eager delights of the morning, but it was never any use. We would be leaving soon and we knew it and there wasn't enough time to start up old enthusiasms again. So we just walked along, touching fence posts and dragging our hands along the sides of barns, more or less summarizing the look and feel of things at the lot, fixing them in our minds until the next time we would be back again.

We threw rocks at trees and cans. We chunked at roosters but even when we hit them, we did not feel elated. The roosters seemed to understand our lack of malice, and they made little insolent, threatening advances at us behind our backs as we walked away. We went to the clump of small shin oaks beside the chicken pen and rode the springy limbs for a while, making them arc down toward the ground like horses' necks. They bent obediently and we galloped up and down, but they too lacked their old morning joy and we jumped off, leaving them to quiver awkwardly behind us.

We walked the edges of the dipping vat beside the hog pen, trying to generate a thrill at the thought of falling in and getting the disinfectant all over us and in our eyes and maybe even swallowing some. We dug at things half-buried in the ground: small amber-colored bottles full of dirt and with old-fashioned small-necked shapes; a rusted ice-cream dasher; half a croquet ball. We walked out into the maize field beside the hired hand's little house and looked a long while at the sky and remembered the time that we flew a kite so high in spring. We circled through the lots again, throwing rocks at the hollow, orange-rusted water tank beside the corn crib just to see who could make it sound the hollowest and oldest and most deserted. We stood on one another's shoulders and lifted up one of the tin windows on the shearing barn and stuck our heads inside and looked at the quiet gloom and smelled the onions spread out along the floor and listened to our voices made strange by the emptiness around them.

Sometimes, as a last resort, we climbed on top of the shearing barn and looked west across the many oak trees and watched the milk cows trailing in. Out in the clearing doves sat on smooth oak tree limbs, calling in their gentlest, late-afternoon way, and there would still be a few sheep by the water troughs who had not gone on to eat in the pastures. Everything we could see and hear – the peaceful doves, the sheep, the rocks scattered in the clearing, the trees themselves – seemed to be marooned in a special stillness and quiet. The sun would nearly be down in the west and the yellow light of it was coming wildly through the trees, haloing their tops and scattering gold and red so harshly along the trunks that the bark actually seemed to be burning.

We would sit there, our arms around our knees, until the power of the scene had passed and the sun had disappeared below the horizon. Then we would climb off the roof and start toward the house, walking silently with our heads lowered and our thoughts turned inward, looking down at our curiously loyal legs and feet that had kept moving all day long without our ever knowing it.

When it got almost full dark we would load things into our car and turn around in the front clearing so that we could wave a last goodbye to Gram and Grandpa standing together at the gate. We would see them still looking at us long after we had started up the road – until they finally accepted us as gone; then they would turn and start back up the walk together toward the house.

Inside the car everyone would be full of that big special silence that always settled on us after a day at the ranch. We would all look straight ahead, staring into the glare of the headlights on the road as if we were looking into a mild sun and trying to sear over the wound of our late Sunday emptiness and letdown. We listened to the sound of the motor the way bone-chilled people would seek out the warmth of a fire, letting it draw us together and comfort us in a way we could not do ourselves.

# Enselmo and the Triplets

Enselmo was the strongest man I ever knew. He could carry a
sack of oats on each shoulder from the front-yard gate around to the
cow lot and do it walking straight. He enjoyed doing things like that —
carrying or pushing or pulling; he liked putting his strength to work.
And he liked it best of all when he lifted cars out of ruts after a big
rain. He would be milking or working around the lots when Gram
would send some of us grandchildren after him to go pull an uncle or
neighbor out of the mud. We would follow him down to the long
black mud flat below the house where everyone usually got stuck and
we would watch him grab the back bumper and begin to strain himself
with the lifting. We stood back under the live oak trees out of the mist
and drizzle and chanted, "Come onnn, Enselmo...we're betting on you,
Enselmo...come onnn, Enselmo," and we would grunt and breathe
heavily and get down low and pretend to strain along with him. And
Enselmo would start shaking his head from side to side to show that if
we didn't stop we were going to make him laugh and lose his hold.
Then with the loose strap of his old aviator's cap flapping from side to
side and the rain streaking down the smooth glistening black rubber
into his face, he would set the back wheel down beside us on the grass
and let out his roar of pent-up laughter. For a long time he would
stand there, shin-deep in mud, leaning back and laughing and showing
his big yellow buckteeth, looking as if he wanted to laugh so hard and
so long that he would have to sit down backwards in the mud, too
weak to stand, and give us all a chance to laugh that much harder.

Enselmo was about thirty when the triplets were born; Angelita,
his wife, was just eighteen. They had been married four years and
although both of them were crazy to have children, for some reason
Angelita never could get pregnant. That was the year I was twelve and
was staying out at the ranch on weekends, and I remember that at
night when they would sit with us on the front porch of the ranch
house Enselmo would say to Gram, "Oh, Miss Maggie, I sure do wish I

had me a little boy – oh, I sure do," and he would put his big arm
around Angelita and pat her to let her know that she was not to blame
– that he was just sad she could not give him any little ones.

Then, as it sometimes happens, there was a shift in chemistry, a
breaking of the spell – however such things are explained – and
Angelita became pregnant. She was sick in the mornings, Gram said,
and I know that whenever I saw her, her eyes looked large and very
black and tired. As the months passed and Angelita got bigger
Enselmo would bring back little things from the pastures to cheer her
up – a hummingbird's nest, shiny pieces of quartz, wild grapes. He was
gentle with her, always opening gates and doors before her very carefully – even trying to walk a little more softly around in the house. But
when he was out working around the ranch he was as excited as a little
boy. Sometimes I sat on the corral fence and listened to him talk to the
cows as he milked them. "Hey, old cow," he would say "don't you wish
you going to have yourself a nice big boy, or maybe a pretty little
*chamaca?*" When the cow would just go on eating in her feed box, paying him no mind, Enselmo would strip one of her teats extra hard and
laugh – and after he was through milking he would kiss each cow
lightly on the ear and then turn them loose into the lots with a terrific
hand-smack on the rump.

The day the triplets were born Angelita's kinfolks came out from
Kerrville and parked along the fence line between Enselmo's little
house and the cornfield. Gram and Grandpa wanted to take Angelita
in to the hospital, but the old women smiled and said something to
the effect that they were very familiar with babies. I don't remember
when the first one came – I was out hunting squirrels in the front pasture – but about nine that night Grandpa came back from Enselmo's
house and told Gram and me that the dam had broken – Angelita and
Enselmo were parents of triplets, all girls. The next morning when I
went up to see, they were laid out on a quilt, looking like three big
shriveled acorns. Each had a thick wad of black hair – as though they
even had on little dark acorn caps.

I don't recall exactly what it was that went wrong with the triplets – some sort of infection or respiratory trouble, or maybe they were just too small – but within a week all three of them had died. When the first baby got sick Grandpa wanted to take it in to town, but the old women just kept on fussing over them and making some kind of herb tea and saying the *niñas* would be all right. After the first one died Grandpa got a doctor to come out but it was too late; the other two died the same afternoon. The doctor told us that the old women just sat huddled over their knees, shaking their heads and saying it was God's will.

The funeral was held in Kerrville the following afternoon at three o'clock. Maybe Enselmo and Angelita didn't belong to any church, or maybe they were actually Methodists – but instead of being held at the neat Catholic cemetery near the Mexican settlement, the funeral took place at the small, run-down Protestant graveyard on the east side of town. It was Sunday and when we got there a big crowd was already gathering. There was a row of Mexican men dressed in dark suits and they were standing beside their cars, holding cigarettes down by their sides and talking quietly. As Grandpa drove up they all turned to face us and the talking died away. I remember getting out of the car and noticing how still everything was – and how you could hear the short, almost polite sound of car doors being shut up and down the dusty country road.

The cemetery was full of weeds and yellow June flowers and dark places where the tombstones were hidden. We all walked through a gap cut in the wire fence and headed toward the middle of the field where a hole had been dug that morning. The Mexican women were dressed in black and seemed unusually small – strung out across the cemetery like little dolls of coal. The men had dropped their cigarettes and they walked along together. Some of them touched their hats every now and then to pull them down a little more the way they wanted them. We gathered around the hole and then turned sideways to watch the men who were bringing the small home-made coffin through the gap. When they got to the grave the men set the coffin down and then stepped back into the crowd. They carefully dusted their hands away from their suits and looked at the minister, waiting for him to begin.

Reverend Rodriguez talked first in Spanish, then in English, but I don't think I heard much of what he said. I kept watching Enselmo out of the corner of my eye. He stood there next to Angelita with the front half of each shoe disappearing into the caliche dirt and his body jerking as though he were standing on top of some kind of throbbing machinery. His eyes were squeezed shut and a row of big yellow front teeth was clamped down over his bottom lip. Every now and then little pouches of skin on each side of his mouth would puff in and out as air forced past them in explosions of crying.

The services ended and the casket was lowered and before I knew it we were making our way back to the cars outside the fence. I remember thinking as we walked along that the whole east side of town would have been quiet that afternoon if Enselmo had not been crying. He staggered along through the knee-deep weeds with Angelita gathered under his big right arm, and it was like a shambling bear being led along by a child trainer. When they got to Grandpa's car Angelita opened the back door and helped Enselmo inside. They sat there together while Grandpa made his way around to the driver's seat. Enselmo had his arm in the window, holding on to the side strap, and you could see his big wrist sticking far out of Grandpa's old blue suit. When I got in the front seat he was starting to let low broken screams crawl around in his throat.

Grandpa asked Enselmo if he and Angelita wanted to stay in town a day or two with some of Angelita's relatives. But Enselmo shook his head and said, "No, Mr. George, we go on home." So we started on the twenty-mile drive through the heat — Gram, Grandpa, and I solemn and quiet in the front, Enselmo moaning to himself and his window in the back. Angelita just kept on being numb — almost wilted down inside herself, whimpering a little and twisting and retwisting a white lace handkerchief around her thumb.

Since it was Sunday and there was no work to do except the chores later on, after we got back to the ranch Enselmo and Angelita went up to their house and I had coffee with Gram and Grandpa out on the breezeway. They sat in the green wicker chairs and began talking over everything again – going back to when Angelita was pregnant and how no one thought that a frail little person like her would ever have triplets, even though she did get so big; and how small and wrinkled the girls were when they were born – "just like little old possums," Gram said. And they talked about how pleased Enselmo had been all that spring, laughing and shaking his head in the happiness of Angelita's having a baby. Then Grandpa told again – though it was the first time I had heard it – how he and Enselmo had been out in the pasture riding fences back in April and Enselmo had spotted two baby cottontails in some brush and got off his horse and put them inside his denim jacket and carried them back for Angelita. Gram said that Angelita had laughed and held them out for her to see and called them her babies.

And we were still talking along there on the breezeway – we hadn't even reached the midwives and funeral part yet – when we heard Angelita yelling as she came tearing through the back gate. Grandpa had got up – he was barefooted and was walking gingerly across the concrete floor toward the kitchen – and Gram was pushing herself up slowly from her chair when Angelita rounded the corner of the sleeping porch, waving her arms. She came inside the breezeway and fell on Gram as though she were a crying post and could hardly stop crying long enough to say that Enselmo had gone, had left the house and walked straight across the cornfield and disappeared into the west pasture.

I wanted to go with Grandpa but he told me to stay there with the Gram and Angelita. He said he didn't think Enselmo would do anything "bad" – he paused a little before saying the word – but he ought to go take a look. He saddled up and rode off from the pens and stayed gone the rest of the afternoon. Angelita cried a while but gradually she settled into long after-crying hiccups. Gram made some strong iced tea and got her to lie down. Then Gram and I went out on the front porch where we could see the pastures better, and we waited. We listened to the cows beginning to low in the fields and watched the cardinals sail into the yard for their late afternoon dips in the bird bath, but there wasn't a sign of Enselmo.

When Grandpa came back to the house it was after dark. He said he had ridden all over the west and south pastures, calling Enselmo, but he didn't see a thing. Angelita broke down again and Gram got her to say she would spend the night at the ranch house so she wouldn't be so lonely. We all had a little supper and after doing the dishes sat out on the porch a while. Nobody cared much about talking so pretty soon we came inside and went to bed.

We were eating breakfast the next morning when Angelita sort of yelled and then stopped herself with her hand at her mouth. We looked out the front door and saw Enselmo walking up the road from town. He was still a good way off but we could tell he was carrying something on his shoulder – some kind of box. I guess we all knew what it was the moment we saw it but no one said anything – we were pushing back chairs and heading for the porch.

Enselmo carried the coffin as if it were just a short two-by-four – both shoulders were perfectly straight and level. When he reached the yard gate he bent his knees a little and opened the latch with his free hand and after carefully shutting it behind him came on up the front walk. He looked first at Angelita, then let his eyes slide on past Gram and me until he was facing Grandpa.

"I heard you, Mr. George," he said, "and I saw you, but I was scared you stop me. I was scared Angelita try to stop me too." And after getting a little better hold on the coffin he went around the corner of the porch. We heard the back gate slam and the cows bawl as he walked up past the lots toward his house.

We watched him off and on throughout the morning. He picked out a clump of live oaks down the fence line from his house and there he dug the grave. He covered it with wild flowers and then chipped out a small tombstone from a smooth caliche rock and engraved three crosses on it and placed it solidly in the ground. When he was finished he knelt down and cried a final time and then he went on back to the lots in his sweat-circled blue suit to help Grandpa with the chores.

# The Ranch: An Ending

The ranch is going now, as any living thing must go, and I am not sure what will come along to take its place. I believed, once, that such a passing would be entirely bad, and I raged and mourned in the same breath, just thinking about it. But now, with Grandpa three years in his grave and Gram sitting hollow-faced before the fire, I cannot truthfully say what I feel, for my grandparents were the heart of the ranch when I loved it most, and once both of them are gone I will not care, perhaps, to know it again.

During my childhood the ranch was many sights and sounds and smells, all in their proper places and never in excess – balanced, as the days themselves were balanced between work and eating and talking and rest. There were always the sharp yells of the hired hand working with goats out at the pens, and the hard bumps of the goats themselves as they ran frantically against the tin sides of the shed. There was the strong smell of soap cooking in the washpot under the back yard post oak tree, and the scent of wet laundry in the peach orchard – coming faintly on the breeze like a clean-smelling bloom. There was Grandpa, with only the top of his old Stetson visible as he moved along past the board fences at the lots; and Gram, walking back and forth between the kitchen and the screened-in porch, humming fragments of a hymn as she set the dinner table.

The ranch was where life relaxed – seemed willing to breathe. It was where, in summertime, the mockingbirds sat on telephone poles like kings, and heat lay across the green rows of the garden in loving, shimmering waves. It was where I could be day after day without having a secret, gnawing desire to go to some other place. For whatever I needed was right at hand: a cool front porch to sit on if I grew tired or lazy, a slice of watermelon to eat if hunger spoke up too loudly before dinner time, back lots to roam through if I felt in need of mild adventure.

In summer, too, there was earth to touch – plowed clumps to pick up in a field, to crumple idly in your hand until they satisfied you by turning into warm, trickling dirt. There was a windmill to climb, wild sage to smell, an old truck to look at west of the house (seeming good, somehow – as though having a rusting green cab and worn upholstery and a scarred bed with wooden sideboards was actually a virtue). Sometimes after wandering across bright midday ground you went into the luring brownness of an open-faced shed and explored the strange and intimate dark. You could usually find a hen stealing out her nest in a corner and the remains of an old broken plow.

And then always following the heat and exploring, a bath. You washed leisurely – the scent of Palmolive soap rich in the room – and afterwards, as you dried, you stood listening to the bathtub draining itself with its familiar Lewis Carroll words and voices: *barl, blouk* – the water went belching down through the old pipes; *platt, platt,* the faucet began a steady drip. And at two o'clock, as you listened closer, the whole ranch would seem to be moving at just such a *plern...dar lunk* bathroom rhythm, as though the very boards of the house were yawning and stretching in the lazy elegance of a summer afternoon. The peaches in the basket on the breezeway seemed to be sitting there at just this kind of pace. And Grandpa snoring peacefully through the wall; the fan slowly oscillating in Gram's bedroom past the kitchen; sheep snorting loudly and abruptly under the live oaks in the front clearing – all were in the same obscure but patterned ranch tempo, and all gave you a sighing contentment deep in your bones.

Grandpa never spoke about his own love for the ranch – not directly. But sometimes on Sunday mornings, while Gram finished getting ready for church and Grandpa and I waited on the porch, we talked casually and gently about things of the land.

You never talked hard or overly long with Grandpa. You simply stood there on the edge of the porch, looking out with him across the yard, and touched the outline of a subject with familiar, comfortable words. You drew topics from the interests of his world – rain or drouth or animals or how the pastures were holding up – and never tried to prove a point or uphold some idea you had about truth. For such conversations were not a flexing of egos. They were the rare opportunity you had to renew your covenant with the past, to take part in the simple ritual of bridging the years through old and tested words.

If it happened that Gram was still not ready after our survey of the yard and the times and the weather, Grandpa would stand silent for a moment and then slip into the groove of old memories. He would usually duck his head a little to one side – in a kind of involuntary twinge of delight as he previewed his tale – and then begin, almost shyly: "There was a feller who got married down near Nopal once and he still had trouble with wettin' the bed...."

(I stood with a friend the other day, looking out into the pastures of the ranch, and as we talked we spoke of the dying-out of the old men who had lived on the land and of who was going to replace them. "Who is going to tell the tales now," he wanted to know; "who will tell the young ones of the traditions?" And it was true: that our fathers, born on the land, had long before moved to the city and had then in turn caused us to be city raised; and that the old men who talked at night on the front-porch swings and who handed on the family heritages to whoever would listen – they had passed now. And there was not anyone left to take their place; their century was finally over. "Why," my friend went on, "already the people in my family are turning to me and saying, 'You were with Uncle Seth a lot; you heard him tell about the cattle drives, and the feuds, and the James River place. What was it that he said; what are some of the old tales?'" And there was genuine anguish in my friend's voice as he blamed himself: "I didn't ask enough or learn enough when I had the chance; I didn't listen to all I should. And with the old ones gone now the young ones are asking me – *me* – to make the connection.")

Grandpa always showed, openly and plainly, that the ranch was his life. But Gram had a pose of only being wearily tolerant of her lot and always managed somehow to find a little list of grievances and discontents. Partly she was just following the country woman's code that said you must, out of good manners, tend to belittle your own: your cooking, the cleanliness of your house, the temperature of your porch, the state of your affairs in general. Partly she was indulging in the petty grumbling that all rural people are subject to when they get to feeling cut off from the world and a little lonely. If possible, she would want to gain whatever sympathy she could from the visitor who – in finding the meal wonderfully cooked, the house airy and spotless, the porch unbelievably restful and cool – might thereby miss the hidden bothers that Gram felt were her daily crosses ("these old *flies*...I could just kill that fool pup for laying in my flower bed...listen to that icebox: it makes more noise than a thrasher...").

And partly she was always being caught in the bind which developed when her natural desire for praise ran headlong into the country ethic that demanded modesty in all accounts of one's doings (I remember the many suppertime conversations in which she and Grandpa passed in review the foibles of their various neighbors: no one ever came in for as much scorn as the "blowjack" – the pompous, overweening braggart). So many times she was forced to fish for compliments – to say, "I sure made a bust on my ol' cobbler; don't eat any of it if you don't want to" – in order that everyone at the table would immediately look up from a second dish of excellent peach cobbler and deluge her with protests – would declare stoutly and at great length that not only the cobbler but indeed the whole meal was good, grand, sumptuous, out of this world.

I supposed the closest Gram came to being completely honest – emotionally, personally honest – was when she watered her flowers along the front-yard fence. She always watered in the late afternoon, just before supper – leaving the greens and potatoes to finish cooking themselves in the kitchen while she took up the water hose she had laid aside the previous day. I will see her there always in my memory, fixed in a kind of tableau: a full-fleshed, compact figure in a flour-sack apron and torn canvas shoes; her back to the rest of the yard, her head bent slightly forward in an attitude of close attention and thought. Every now and then, with a quick, determined pull of her shoulders and waist, she would jerk the hose loose from its tangled coil near the faucet. But even then she never really turned about. She kept on watching the little forced stream of water as it sprayed out from underneath her thumb and battered against the flowers.

She remained for long stretches at a time, unmoving, gripping the hose almost like some kind of weapon. She was obviously watering her flowers, giving them life, but all the while she seemed to be doing something for herself, too, something private: it was as if at the end of another long day on the ranch she was letting the vigor of the stream pull out her deepest thoughts in order to let them disintegrate harmlessly against the cannas and four o'clocks. Yet all that I, or anyone, ever needed to do was come outside the house and call Gram! – and she would turn around, instantly the familiar figure of a person just getting her watering done. Many times, however, I have wondered what might have been on the other side of that steady, tranquil-looking back while I was growing up – and who that woman might have been that so often faced her flowers in moments of privacy and yet always turned around to us simply as Gram.

Emotions: for years they have been circling above the ranch in a quite predictable way: serenely at first, in childhood, like the pleasant wings that float lazily high above you on a cloudless day; then, later, with more dark distinctness, clearly not mere wings but obviously birds of bone and feathers; finally – recognizably – buzzards....

I remember one Sunday morning when I watched Gram and Grandpa get into their car and move off in a thin cloud of dust to church. I was standing on the ranch-house porch, seeing the old green Buick get smaller and smaller as it made the familiar curve around the big oat field and then finally disappeared into the line of shin oaks that marked the eastern horizon of the ranch. Long after Zipper had come back from the gate to lie on the steps, and long after the dust had drifted slowly southward over the front pasture, I stared down that curve of road, telling myself: You had better get ready. Someday there will be no gray heads framed in a Buick window – no gray heads, and no more reason for the ranch. Someday this corner of the earth will heave in an invisible little spasm, surrendering its old folks and its claim to glory.

I knew then, as I know now, the facts: that the windmills would find no reason to stop their turning just because one set of owners had gone; that the pecan and post oak trees would keep on towering above the yards. Even the back gate would go on slamming with the old collapsing sound, no matter whose hand grasped it and let it go.

But the emotions – I knew them even better. I knew that they were deeply and unreasonably committed to the hundred and fifty years' worth of pioneer life that had just driven off to church. So, on the porch, I strove for a little wisdom. I told myself: All right, mourn this unhappened thing now; maybe that will help you later. Break the big dose into smaller ones and make it easier to swallow.

But I knew that was foolishness. I could not mourn on the installment plan; I could not get the jump on future sorrows. I had to just stand there – with Zipper at my feet and wisdom nowhere in sight – and do what I had done so many times before: look out across the ranch, searching it, hoping that something in the land itself would shift around and balance the uncomfortable weights I found within me.

Grandpa had a heart attack not too long after that (the same week my daughter was born: rhythm, balance? – such words have a way of coming around again to haunt you). He was in his eighties then and had broken almost overnight – his hearing, memory, and eyesight failing; his contact with the world suddenly becoming tentative and unsure. It was hard to watch him in his decline....

There was one scene just before Grandpa died: I had driven him from the ranch up to Harper so he could get some drench for his sheep; and afterwards before starting back, we stopped at a grocery store-cafe to have a bottle of beer. That was one of the pleasant rituals he observed after the grandsons were grown: to stop in after "tending to business" and treat his company to a Budweiser or Jax. And it would have been fine again this time – despite his stumbling gait, his cane, his air of not quite seeming to know where he was or what was going on – except that he spilled his beer. Grandpa just couldn't see any more through his thick glasses, couldn't judge distance, and as he reached for his bottle he knocked it from the table. The woman behind the counter came over with her dustpan and mop and in her deliberate singsong way told him, "That's all-l-l right, Mr. George" – trying not to show what her mind was actually saying: "Umm, umhh, that old man...still drinkin' his beer when he can't see no more how to hold it or even hear the bottle when it breaks." I knew all the people in Harper could remember Grandpa from better days – before he had become so awkwardly old – but that didn't keep my insides from crawling as the woman patiently mopped the floor and Grandpa, his eyes hugely grotesque through the Coke-bottle lenses of his glasses, smiled foolishly and apologetically and tried to tug his wallet out to pay extra for the trouble he had caused. I kept wanting the woman to remember Grandpa as he had been in his younger days – as I had seen him in the family albums. And as we drove home I kept wishing he could have yielded to posterity like that too. For with his Stetson hat, his black solid boots, his blunt toughened hands, it had always seemed to me – looking at him over and over in those old snapshots – that he would have needed only a slight injection of marble or steel to become immortalized into a monument: to become permanently transformed into the hard-creased prototype of Hill Country Rancher.

It is spring now at the ranch — not a traditional time of ending. Yet the ranch as I have known it, as it has known itself, keeps slipping away from the old forms into something new.

Even the habits of grass are changed. After Grandpa died and Gram sold off most of the stock, there were few hoofs left to beat the ground, so the grass started to grow where it had never dreamed of growing before. The woodlot back of the house — a place pounded for decades by milling herds of goats and sheep — has suddenly found itself covered by a spread of green. Looking at it, tender and quite beautiful — and remembering the woodpile and the great bare spots and the goats that would stretch all morning long trying to reach a single weed through the garden fence — I cannot help wondering where the lushness will stop now that it has begun. For it is not just in the woodlot. It is everywhere, and seemingly full of purpose — as if part of nature's silent reconquest of an old domain. It is like a graceful fungus, sweeping steadily out of the pastures, through the yards, over the house....

Gram — she is merely sitting now in one place or another: when it is cold, before the fireplace in the living room; when it is pleasant outdoors, in the front-porch chair. I see her that way quite frequently: a small, gray-headed woman with her hands in her lap, letting her thumb flick back and forth against the rough, cracked skin of a worn finger.

I see her watching the sheep out in the clearing as they move toward the shade of the live oaks. She looks at them the way she has always looked at things — with her same old absorbing keenness, with that superb willingness to engage herself in any act of seeing or hearing. But though she does not miss a movement of the sheep as they walk, head down, toward the shade, she doesn't really see them any more. She looks intently in their direction and then straight on through to where her thoughts are. And it is no feat to imagine what she is thinking – to know that she is saying to herself, as she has often said aloud: I want to see George.

As her thumb moves idly against her finger she brings to mind those mornings when Grandpa stood there in the clearing, studying the sheep – his boots dusty, his hat pulled low against the sun, his jaws working hard with the tobacco in his mouth.

George – the name hangs in front of her all the time now, a veil that prevents her from noticing things clearly any more; that keeps her saying over and over: I want to see him; I want to talk to him again. This old place....

# III

# THE HILL COUNTRY

# A Visit Home

My folks still lived in Kerrville, and in the summertime I liked to go back there and stay a while. I liked it when the camps along the river were open and tourists were around town and things were generally relaxed and green and summery. I liked just being around home, too, getting some August sun and doing a little work in the yards. It seemed to clean me out good and help get my mind straight to be able to use my hands again, to swing a hammer against a broken gate or pull weeds or paint a strip of weathered boards. And my folks, of course, were always glad when I was back. The three of us got along well together. We didn't get on each other's nerves.

Some of the mornings after breakfast I got into my old clothes and gathered up rags and a turpentine jar and cans of paint and I painted on the house or maybe a section of fence. I liked painting: the easy, mindless stroking of brush against wood, the slow erasing of old surfaces and the friendly spread of new ones. And I liked it best of all when I worked on the front fence next to the street. It was pleasant there on my knees in the cool bermuda grass, making the old palings grow clean and white. The oaks and young hackberries along the fence waved light summer shadows and the paint and turpentine smelled pungent and clean. Locusts were in the trees along the street, and doors throughout the neighborhood slammed casually back and forth during the long mornings. Sometimes I heard an ice-cream wagon moving slowly and peacefully by, ringing its bell.

After working all morning I would scrub up a little with kerosene and change clothes and walk down to a small neighborhood grocery store to buy a bottle of beer. It was a familiar walk, past many of the same old houses I knew as a child – the same deep yards, the same high, dust-covered trees, the same noontime angles of shade covering the porches and cement walks. I enjoyed walking straight down the middle of the dusty, unpaved streets, bareheaded and in the sun, watching the dogs run to bark at me through their picket fences – the same way dogs of my childhood did.

Usually during summertime one street or another in the neighborhood would be under repair – paving or grading or maybe oiling – and the smell of hot tar or oil or even just the huge shiny metal bulk of road machinery would make the noonday of such a street abnormally hot. But I didn't mind; I even liked it. Being hot, thoroughly and brutally hot – that was as good during summertime as being cool. I felt a kind of private stoic joy at the heat burning into my face and arms and the sweat prickling in my skin. There was something beautiful and exciting about the heat of a summer noontime – about the locusts singing long and wildly in sidewalk trees and the sun almost seeming to eat down through the sky with its terrific glare and the white frame houses sitting very tidy and modest and subdued behind their yards, as though intimidated a little by the rough vigor of such a masculine noon.

After I bought the beer and a package of Fritos and walked back home, I sat on the front porch and rested a little before dinner. I tilted the beer bottle slowly – the dark brown kind with the tall neck – and looked out to the oaks and grass of the yard. Down the street a neighbor had the radio on, getting the noon weather report and livestock market news. That was always a comfortable program for me to listen to. I knew that all across the hill country ranch families were sitting around their dinner tables now, tuned in to hear how many points of rain fell overnight in San Angelo or Luling and where the low-pressure systems were over the state and what the chances were for rain in the next couple of days. I didn't care myself about low-pressure systems or rain in Luling, but somehow it pleased me to think about how much the ranch people cared for such things, how they would be including the weatherman's comments in their party-line conversations that afternoon: "...yes, well, old Henry Howe said at noon there might be a chance for a few late-afternoon thundershowers, but I'm not going to hold my breath none." I would sit there on the porch, not really listening to the actual words of the weatherman but rather to the sound of them; and when Henry Howe began his long wrap-up of feed and cattle quotations, using all the special, singsong phrases – "sheep: 600; active, mostly steady; ewes strong to 50 cents higher...good and choice stocker calves $22.50 to $28.00" – such words and figures went beyond language and became a kind of lulling, dreamlike chant of noon folk music, a kind of casual and inviting vocal guitar.

In the evenings after supper, when my mother would be out watering in the dusky shadows of the yard and my father would be out back working in the garden, I would get into my car and drive off slowly toward town. Summer nights were always the same in Kerrville but that was their lure and even their peace. I drove out by the Dairy Queen on the north highway to see the people waiting patiently on the smooth gravel in front of the small window screen – just as they had waited the previous night and the many nights before that. I would drive to the other edge of town and then slowly back along the main street to see what was on at the show, passing the other lone, slowly cruising cars and the other lone drivers. Sometimes I would park and buy a Dallas or San Antonio paper at the newsstand and with it folded underneath my arm I would walk along past the dark storefronts, seeing how they all felt and looked at night with their doors locked and their merchandise silent and inaccessible behind glass. At the side of the Robert E. Lee, the main hotel in town, a bellboy in his faded blue uniform would be standing at the curb, taking an eight-o'clock smoke and idly keeping tab on the cars that kept wandering by.

Occasionally I drove up the river road past the summer camps, the small hillside farms, the spacious summer homes of the well-to-do that would be lit by strings of yellow lights stretched among many somber yard trees. Nighttime along the river was always nice in the summer, and I sometimes stopped for a while at a low-water crossing and turned off the lights. I would sit listening to the pleasant river sounds – the many frogs, the katydids and crickets – and I would smell the refreshing cleanness of the river air. Lightning bugs were usually off in the distance, directly over the water or perhaps deep among the tall cypress trees, almost hidden. Sometimes a small waterfall would be downriver just within hearing. I sat in the car, tired from the day's work, listening to the strong, lulling rhythm of the frogs and the heavy sounds of the big tourist cars that passed over the bridge and then lunged away up the opposite slope toward town. Usually I grew sleepy, my mind and body sagging into the peaceful dark of the river and the night, and I would have to wrench myself into the notion of going back home. For the first few miles I opened the small window wing and let the cool summer air off the hay fields and the river flow hard into my face, bathing it back to taut alertness.

We owned a piece of ranch land north of town, a wooded, rocky place passed on to us from my grandfather. There was no house on it, just an old hunter's cabin that my father kept working on little by little during the summertime. Several times a week I took my lunch and worked out there all day. In addition to the cabin improvements, fences were always in need of repair and the livestock needed to be seen after.

It was a nice thirty-minute drive out from town. For about ten miles the highway kept close to the north fork of the river, with a heavy green line of sycamores always in sight beyond the small bordering fields of grain and hay. Then a farm-to-market road turned off the highway and after winding first through a close little walnut valley it gradually rose upward to the higher plateau of ranch country. Some of the land there was free of timber, and the sheep and goats and cattle grazed in open stretches of grass within sight of the road. Most of the land, however, was wooded with live oaks and cedars and the small shin oak trees that goats like to eat on. Country lanes turned off the road every so often, gently bending around a line of fence and going to the neat ranch homes set off in the distance in a clump of trees. Sometimes one of them could be seen from the road – perhaps a cool-

looking flagstone house with a curving archway in front of its porch
and a border of tall, red-topped cannas along either side.

Near the top of the plateau I would leave the farm-to-market
road and drive about a mile through our place down to the cabin – a
rock-and-tin building set in the low center of several sloping hills, with
pens and water tanks and small clearings all around. There was a little
dry hollow that ran south from the pens under a trail of Spanish oak
and walnut trees, and along it were rocky shelves and ledges where a
stream once made its way into the lower flat land of the pastures.

It was never lonely working out there in the country. Everything
was friendly – the sun on the grass, the flint and caliche rocks scattered about under the trees, the coiled strand of smooth tie-wire hanging here and there around the tops of fence posts. Sheep were always
bleating and calling from the ridges; heavy-bellied red Hereford cows
wandered in from the pastures to get water and lie up under the shade.
Black squirrels dashed from secret tunnels beneath the cabin to their
homes down beyond the corral. Sometimes bumblebees got down in
the thick, sweet-smelling sage along the fences and moved across the
blossoms like clumsy old men with knotty canes. And ever so often, in
a sudden intense blaze of color and noise, there appeared pairs of small
reddish birds that suspended themselves in the sky: With their tail
feathers fluffed and spread out like miniature turkey gobblers' and their
small red wings waving frantically for support, for minutes on end they
would hang there and sing little shrill, wild, quarrelsome melodies
directly into each other's face.

After dinner, when the sun was overhead and the day had settled
into its long afternoon exercise in heat, I stretched out for a while
along the shaded ravine on top of a cool rocky shelf. As I lay there
under the Spanish oaks I would sometimes hear from a hillside the single, idle tinkling of a sheep's bell. And with the day so explosively dry
and hot it was almost as though the hot air itself out in the pastures
had made a small crystalline sound, a single comment about itself to
the afternoon. Somehow this would make me restless, would stir up a

desire to be out deeper within the pastures and the heat; so I would gather up an armload of small cedar staves from out at the corral and go along one of the fence lines that led away from the cabin, wiring a stave against the fence here and there where it sagged. It was a simple chore, just taking pliers and short pieces of smooth tie-wire and securing the small slim cedar poles against the fence so it would have a little added strength. But out there in the pasture in the long afternoon, among the trees and grass and steady heat, wiring staves was somehow a handsome thing to do. It was good to be in a place where you could fix something like a fence and wipe away sweat now and then with the back of a sleeve and afterward stand looking out across the ground to your rocks and your trees, knowing that you were where you should be, knowing you were home.

Occasionally my father would take an afternoon off from the feed store in town and would come out with me to work at the cabin. He was not a big man but he was used to working long, hard hours. The two of us always worked steadily and well together.

It never failed that when we were out there at the cabin – working, say, at repairing the roof – my father would look up from driving a nail to squint at the sun and say, "What about it, son, you ready for some of that good studhorse coffee?" I would nod, saying I guessed it was about that time, and together we would lay aside our hammers and climb down from the roof and go around to the east side of the cabin where there was a little shade. Usually it would be just about the right time for coffee – between four and five, when the main burden of the afternoon heat had begun to lift and the sun was already deeply committed toward the line of oak trees rimming the west. My father liked strong coffee – studhorse strong, as he called it – and he especially liked it during the summertime when he and I worked together out at the cabin.

He would begin chopping sticks for kindling and building a small fire while I took the big smoke-blackened coffee pot around to the windmill and washed it out. Then, after the fire was made and the cof-

fee pot was steadied on top of the crossed burning sticks, and a pair of
washed tin cups were set in the open cabin window, the two of us sat
on an old bench in the shade of the cabin to watch the fire grow hot-
ter and to look out at the gradually settling afternoon. Both of us had
our straw hats off, and both of our khaki shirts were darkened from
heavy sweating. We sagged forward a little on our knees.

As we sat there I knew my father was content, knew that it was a
pleasure for him to be there sitting on the bench beside me while the
two of us waited for the coffee to boil. I could feel the pleasure. My
father didn't show it openly: he just sat chewing his small wad of
tobacco and squinting off into the pastures beyond the corral. We did-
n't talk much; we waited on the coffee and rested. But I knew that my
father usually didn't chew tobacco except when he was off somewhere
by himself – maybe late in the afternoon when he worked in the garden or early in the mornings while doing up the chores in back of the
house. Chewing there on the bench with me was a sign of his ease and
comradeship. Even just gazing into the pastures – I knew that was
something, too. My father was not a person to spend his idle time gazing; he was one to be fixing a loose board in a porch floor or rehang-
ing a gate so it would swing better. To sit down and lean over on his
hunkers a little and cast even the most casually interested eye outward:
actually to get close to ruminating on the scene before him – that was
something rare and revealing.

I knew that I had not shared much time with him after growing
up. I remembered how often we had gone fishing together when I was
a boy, how the two of us would sit on the riverbank during the long
Sunday afternoons. We had done a lot of that kind of sharing and
being together – not really talking about anything, just the two of us
joined by the act of fishing and made content by it. But after high
school, after I left home and began living in other towns and just visited back with my parents now and then, there hadn't seemed to be
anything to join us together again except words. We would talk in the
front room at home on holidays or while driving someplace to visit

relatives with my mother. But it would just be fact-talk, an exchange of news and family happenings. It was only when words weren't needed – like at the cabin, working outdoors and waiting for coffee, or like the Sundays years before along the river – that the two of us could bridge the awkward gap of words and come to a kind of union again.

As I thought about it I knew it was worth coming home just to give my father a moment of old companionship, for us to be able to sit down together, both sweating, both in the same kind of old worn clothes, both tired and waiting for the hard clean smell of coffee to rouse our spirits a little. It was worth having my father sit there beside me without awkwardness or strain: for him to enjoy the knowledge that I was indeed his son, had not gradually and subtly evaporated beyond reach but was still someone to be close to, someone he could still look at and call his own.

And once, as my father rose from the bench to see how the coffee was coming along, I looked at him and thought, with sudden amazement: Why, my God, I'm still this man's flesh and blood and he has never forgotten it, not for a moment, even though I haven't given him anything of myself except news for the last fifteen years. I watched my father carefully take the pot off the fire with his handkerchief and begin to pour into the cups on the window sill. I thought: How easy it is never to know how a father would feel about a son; how easy to overlook that a man would go right on feeling he was someone's father long after the son had gone away, had gathered up his life like a neat bundle of clothes so that nothing was left of it around home any more except the empty hangers in a closet – old reminders and memories.

And so the two of us sat with cups in our hands, sometimes drinking briefly, mostly waiting for the coffee to cool: an aging man with false teeth and a chew of tobacco in his jaw; a younger man, his son, just home for a while, visiting.

# Crider's

Probably no one in the hill country – certainly not old man Crider – thought you could take a slab of cement, add some benches and a wire fence, and end up with a gold mine. Yet he did exactly that. And it turned out to be the best kind of gold mine, actually, not dependent on limited veins of ore but on unlimited human beings – on the twenty-five cents they will pay for a can of beer and the dollar bill admission they will dig up for Saturday night. So far, there is no indication that people or their money will ever play out, and Crider's seems destined to remain as solvent as any hill country bank.

There seem to be at least two Crider's – the one you go to, say, on a Saturday night and the one you might see the following day. A tourist, going for a Sunday drive along the river road west of Kerrville and suddenly coming upon Crider's at three o'clock in the afternoon, will most probably pull his Oldsmobile off the pavement and ask his wife, incredulously, "You mean this is where we went to last night?" For daytime Crider's, minus the acres of parked cars, the blaring music, the sight and sense of people dancing and drinking and milling around, is wholly unprepossessing. Its essentials stand out sharply in all their bare country homeliness: the empty field of smooth cement, the small covered bandstand down at one end, the green tables and benches and a big drooping oak leading at the opposite end into the two-room cafe-kitchen. In the glare of a hot three o'clock Crider's looks quite deserted and forlorn – the kind of place to buy a Coke in maybe or a package of cigarettes and then move on past.

But as the day softens – as the sun fades behind the cedar-covered hills and the nearby river greenery darkens into a long, lush stage backdrop – Crider's gradually reveals its virtues like a brilliant night flower starting to bloom. It becomes a fine place to rest from the day's labors. You can get yourself a cold can of beer from the cafe and come outside under the oak trees and sit down at one of the tables, and everything – the hill country, the river, the coming to an end of another summer afternoon – seems very right and pleasant. And if it happens to be a Saturday you can look out past the dance floor and see that already a couple of cars with horse trailers are parked down at the large, bleachered corral, unloading for the Crider's rodeo.

It's entirely pleasing at dusk – but just let night fall and the whole visual world lie dead and buried beneath the Central Texas blackness. Let eight o'clock, eight-thirty, nine o'clock come. Let the summer camp bugles finally sound taps up and down the river and the off-duty counselors start for their cars; and the tourists from Houston and Dallas and Port Arthur begin to get bored with the quietness of their summer lodges; and high school kids from Kerrville get tired of driving back and forth along the same familiar streets; and the cedar choppers from Hunt and Ingram start rattling down country roads toward the main highways and home. Let darkness cover the land and people begin to feel the need for a place of light, a place to gather and drink a beer or two or more, a place to be private within yourself if you want it or be unrestrainedly lively but nevertheless a place to be in the midst of others. Let these conditions exist and Crider's becomes a thing beyond the sum of its benches, trees, and strings of colored lights. It becomes The Good Place Up The River, the yellow-bulbed oasis in a vast black desert of night.

Saturday night is always the big night, of course. There is a string band – sometimes a local, inexperienced group from Kerrville or Fredericksburg, usually a more professional outfit from Austin or San Antonio – and extra counters set up for beer and cold drinks and the customary dollar admission charge. There are always several members of the Crider family working at the gate – one collecting the dollar bills in a cigar box and the other stamping a black circular receipt on the back of each customer's hand: "Crider's, Since 1925."

Crider's has no specialized clientele. Indeed, the whole charm of it lies in the unselfconscious mingling of people who would ordinarily never rub shoulders except in a movie script – rustic and sophisticate, oil man and groundskeeper, college drama instructor and high school majorette. Where else would an aging Houston dowager hold tightly to the muscular arm of a young six-foot-six horse wrangler from a sum-mer girls' camp as they make their way to the dance floor to try a German *schottische*? Where could the son of a Leakey truck driver order a Bireley's orange for the daughter of a Dallas banker? Where would the female lead of "Finian's Rainbow" – the summer stock "Finian" showing nightly down river at the Arts Foundation – slap her delec-table thigh in such unrestrained laughter at the tales of a Rocksprings bachelor who raises Poland China hogs? Where, also, could a balding little man climb on a tabletop and do a prolonged, yogi-like headstand to the cheers and handclappings of the onlookers – or chin himself half a dozen times from an overhanging limb – and then, his nightly ritual over, grab the arm of some pretty woman forty years his junior and go strutting off to the dance floor to put-his-little-foot?

The peak time of Saturday night is from ten o'clock until one. The rodeo at the corral is generally over by ten, and the crowd and performers from it begin to drift in along with late-comers who first went to a show in town or a private party. Since the few tables under the oaks are always taken early, the overflow has to distribute itself about in little standing groups or on the narrow wooden benches scat-tered along the fence. The phalanx of young stags that rather loosely blocks one end of the dance floor early in the evening begins to edge solidly forward – like a school of curious fish intent on observing more closely a band of deep sea divers. And in the anonymity of the flow-ing, shifting crowd a highly reserved doctor from Kerrville may find himself throwing aloofness to the winds and dancing a very loose-legged polka with his eleven-year-old daughter; or a hard-swallowing young camp counselor may finally approach the table of a tanned, beautiful woman twice his age – the mother of one of his "boys" – and ask her to dance and have her smile up at him with a very definite and pleased yes. It never seems to matter particularly who does what; it's just accepted that you come to Crider's to let your hair down.

But even if most people come to Crider's to be in the big middle of things – the dancing, the jostling back and forth to reach tables or the beer counter, the laughing, the flirting – there are some who are content just to remain outside and watch. They sit on the fenders of their cars, holding babies, smoking, chewing on matches. Primarily they are family folks who can't afford a dollar for themselves and their kids so they come early and park along the fence and look. Now and then a few of the men will saunter down the line of cars to the outside beer counter and hunker outside the rim of bright lights. They exchange handshakes – the single, brief little respectful jerk of country and ranch people – and then join in with the gazing toward the noise and music and lights. Perhaps before long a barefooted boy will slide out of the darkness and stand next to his father – not saying anything at first, just watching and listening to the quiet steady talk of the men, then finally speaking down to his father: Mama wants you. The man nods and reaches a slow arm around the boy's legs. He says, All right, run along; I'll be there in a minute – and after a while he rises and nods toward the group and moves on back toward his car.

As the hours slip on by toward one o'clock and the cars begin to circle out of the big dusty parking area, one of the hill country's unsolved puzzles reoccurs. By all logic, the high-geared, drink-laden drivers of so many fast-moving cars along such a narrow, twisting, up-and-down river road should provide accident headlines each Sunday morning. Yet despite curves, beer, and one-arm-around-the-girl driving the road in from Crider's has remained incredibly accident-free. It's as though some kind of special, pilot-light shrewdness remains lit even in the most bleary-eyed of drivers, saying, "Look, just keep your wits about you and you can make it – you got to be up here again next week, you know." And like a flock of tipsy homing pigeons they all go racing back through the darkness into town.

# At the Ewell House

On fall Sundays my parents and I turned off the Bandera highway and went down the rocky, winding dirt road that led through the Ewell pastures. When we came to the pens we parked the car in the grassy shade of a big live oak and walked down the slope of a small bluff to the creek. We crossed it on flat rocks placed there as a bridge and when we got to the other side we were once again beneath the strange canopy of towering pecan trees. Once again we were walking across fallen leaves through a great still space of subdued light.

Mary and Forrest Ewell lived in a small, unpainted house that sat in the perpetual shade of the many pecan trees. It was like a private, bypassed little world down there – a gigantic cave, with cave-horses rubbing against the wire fence of the yard, with Forrest Ewell standing on the front porch, welcoming us with his quiet, cave-dweller's smile.

It was as if the Ewells lived in a mountain cabin of Kentucky or Tennessee: the rooms of the house were small and dark, and a bucket of spring water and a dipper were always on a stool beside the back door. There was a banjo and a guitar and a violin hanging on the bed-room wall and in the late afternoon Mary and the two children would get their instruments down and play hymns and country songs out on the porch. Forrest would spit tobacco juice over the railing into the flower bed and the juice would splatter near his collie dog. The dog would lift an eyelid for a moment and then go on sleeping while the violin scraped and Mary sang "The Old Rugged Cross."

The Ewell children, Billie Jean and Talbert, were my age and we played long hours down at the creek. It was narrow and grassy-banked and curved pleasantly out of one wooded pasture into another while small, light-brown frogs sat beside it on the sand. A spring came out of the ground beneath a big walnut tree and made a clear pool between its roots. Watercress and mint grew along the side of the pool and the round, clean rocks on the bottom looked as if they were right beneath the surface of the water – as if your nose would touch them when you lay down at the pool's edge to get a drink.

Standing beside the creek, my stomach full of fresh-tasting spring water, I would look up the bluff to where palomino horses were lazily switching their tails in the sun. Up there, at the lots, it was an ordinary fall afternoon; down along the creek, in the deep pecan-tree shadow, it was no definite time or place. It was like looking out from a dream, or a children's storybook – where life never moved or changed but stayed deep inside itself, content to remain within its own pleasing depths.

# Camp Meeting

The big thing on the congregation's mind is the preacher – will he look good, does he sing, is he impressive? To be in the tradition of the best ones of the past, he should have traveled from a respectably far-off place like Houston or Dallas or Brownsville. He should wear white shoes, still be somewhat young but with a quietly firm jaw. It helps if he is brunette and has an executive tan. Of course he must have a beautiful young wife and small child, and they must sit on the front bench near the pulpit where he can nod and smile in their direction during the opening remarks of his sermon (remarks designed to show how warmly human he is; to demonstrate, charmingly, his own personal fallibility). Both the wife and child must wear nice starched clothes and both must appear as an obviously rich reward and blessing for a favored man of God.

Yet he cannot have these qualifications and fail to be high-powered; he cannot lead the people into the big open-air tabernacle with his calmly commanding air and soulfully sunken eyes and then stand on the speaker's platform and be somebody they all could have heard in town. Above all else he must bring the message of power they have filed in to hear. He must stand there with a fist leveled in their faces and shame them; he must catalogue their many sins and have them

look nakedly into the deep moral abyss of their souls; he must shake
them with his words as a dog would shake rabbits until they sit in
purged passivity. He must thunder down at them and then be dynami-
cally silent; he must thunder and be silent once again. Then he must
become a prowling lion of Jesus, slashing at sin with his righteous
claws. And at the proper moment, just before the roars lose their
power and their weight and their credibility, he must suddenly be a
lion no more; he must gradually regain the quietly elegant form of
God's humble and moral man. He must taper to the hush of the
Garden, and then be still.

All of this he must do in exactly thirty minutes – from 11:30 until
12:00 – for evangelical gusto is a two-edged sword that must be skillfully handled, especially at camp meetings. He must always remember,
even in the supreme moments of his oratorical splendor, that twelve
noon is the witching hour for men who would come before their fellows to tell them what to do for everlasting grace. He must remember
that the three main reasons for a summer camp meeting – preaching
and eating and visiting – are championed with equal stoutness; and
should he happen to succumb to the glory of his own voice and edge
the gospel over into lunchtime, such an act of intemperance will go
hard on him and the pure image of him in the people's mind will be
badly smudged. He must realize that, to the rows of captive men who
have sat out their dutiful hour, after-twelve preaching is always a
breach of camp-meeting code and that although they agreeably suspend their personalities for a while in the expectation of winning the
community's salvation, at twelve o'clock they automatically switch
their reasons back on. He must be shrewd enough to know that it is
not possible for any preacher – regardless of his pretty smiling wife
and his white shoes and his years along the Amazon – to retain full
status among such a group of men if he takes lightly their hour's sacri-
fice and thereby implies that grace, in the long run, is more important
than barbecue.

These men, these husbands in stiff Sunday clothes, sitting erect on the hard, splintery benches, holding babies straight in their laps with both hands around them as if they were dolls or flower vases – they demonstrate in this camp meeting hour a strange stoic quality which they do not show anywhere else. They manage an almost saintly composure. While their womenfolk begin to fan briskly in the August heat and comment tersely behind their fans about covered dishes getting cold out in the car and how they never did get to go to the bathroom at home because they had been in such a rush, these men sit as though they had totally suspended reason and judgment and attention, as though they had silently attached their minds to small balloons and let them rise to the roof of the tabernacle. And content to be free of them for the duration of the sermon, the men simply sit and look polite. When the whole business is finally over and the crowd begins to rise and loosen itself for dinner, the men know that they will have plenty of time then to summon their thoughts down from the roof and begin formulating congratulatory words for the preacher.

Always at such gatherings there are old women with moles on their chins and white-turning-to-yellow hair full of old-fashioned combs. There are small harelipped boys who stay close to their mothers' skirts in the barbecue line and stare out at the crowd with fearful eyes. Sometimes there is an old toothless man who after the service makes his headquarters beside the water tank where the other men come to stand in the shade and drink from the dipper and talk. He generally finds himself shaking hands every now and then with men from town who are surprised to see him there – they were under the impression he had died some years before. ("Well," one of the men will ask him, "who *was* it I thought died, then?") And nearly always there will be at least one small boy listening behind a blue hymnal to old women too crippled to leave the tabernacle at dinner – old women talking of "tumors" and "an aching uterus" and using other compelling

and magical terms that the little boy vows to use on his friends when
he gets back home.

# Two O'clock and Red Flowers

Every day a hill country ranchman is up before six, moving about
in the coolness milking and scattering hay in the back pens and looking out across the maize and oat fields lying quiet in the bare early
light. Sometimes after breakfast he takes a quick run into town in his
pickup to get some washers for a windmill or a couple of jars of sheep
drench, but he's usually back before nine. And then, well, there is riding to be done along the fences in the pastures, and wormy sheep to
be tended to, and maybe even the rods in the windmill to be pulled.
With his wife it is the same thing: going steady from before sunup,
getting breakfast and straining the milk and cleaning up the house and
dampening the clothes and gathering and silking the corn from the
garden and in general getting things moving along in the right way
toward dinner time.

But when it finally gets to be two o'clock – that's when it is a
ranchman's nap-time. To him there is nothing more sensible and necessary after dinner than to have his shoes off and be stretched out sound
asleep in the back bedroom next to an open window – his white-cot-
ton-socked feet resting one on top of the other, neatly, his mouth open
and slightly pooching and pouting with each long, relaxing escape of
breath.

If you would happen to drive up to this ranchman's house right at
two, you would be struck by the quietness of it, the complete sense of
rest nurtured by an almost friendly heat. The house would be set off
from the road on a slight rise of ground and surrounded by oak and
pecan trees that would be very green and calm and somehow almost
domesticated. You would notice a windmill behind the house – just the
top of it, the fan, visible above the roof – and then, looking about, you

would see the scattering of pens and barns and water troughs and a cement tank or two.

You would notice that the house itself is neat, in good repair, with new white paint on the window frames and underneath the eaves. The front-yard fence would be the kind most ranchmen have in the hill country: the tight, strong-looking, smooth-wire kind, with the top wire going along in little regular, arcing waves. The yard would be in two sections on either side of the flagstone walk; perhaps it would be recently mowed, with faint, gently curving patches of confetti-like grass still trailing here and there. On the porch – which would by now be caught in a mild afternoon shadow – the chairs and the rocker would seem inviting and open and still full of greeting, as if the ranch-man and his wife had at that very moment risen out of them and stepped indoors.

These are the things your glance would take in at first – the obvious, simple pleasures of the resting house and its surroundings. Yet there would be something else there, too – something perhaps not too noticeable as you drive up, something seemingly quite innocent and even uninvolved in the scene.

It would be the row of red, long-stemmed flowers that the ranch people call old maids, standing in their clean, well-tended bed next to the small porch. Standing there, just at that time of day, with so much silence and heat and rest in the air, they would gradually seem more than just themselves, more than just flowers: they would seem like a round-faced, heat-flushed, well-behaved children's chorus. They would seem almost to be smiling, as though they neither sweated nor wilted nor were in the least way affected by the great heat. Dry-stemmed, hardy, very much at ease, they would look out contentedly on two o'clock – as if a ranch afternoon were one long, held breath and they could hold their breath longer than anyone. And if you would happen to look their way, they would seem to be nodding and wobbling a greeting to you just slightly, as if saying with an immensely subdued but genuine courtesy: "Well, *hello*...the rest of the folks are asleep right now but won't you come in, anyway? We're sure they'll be glad to see you." And with another nod they would withdraw from the conversation and stand in their red, poised hardiness – like sensible domestics who had attended to the social amenities and then retired into respectful silence.

# A Day at Palo Alto

## Teddy Mudge

He did not want to come so high. While the other boys yelled and dug wildly into the side of the cliff for fossils, Teddy Mudge sat in jumbled leaves under a wild cherry tree and sniffled. Yellow-haired, blue-eyed, his pale legs scratched from the hard climbing, he looked down at the dirtied laces of his new tennis shoes and gave another little sudden sniff of crying. His canteen had spilled on his new Palo Alto T-shirt and the pocket of his short pants had ripped on a persimmon limb. And he had dust in his nose. He sniffed and looked between his legs at the leaves: he did not see the point of climbing a mountain if your legs got skinned and dirt got in your eyes and nose – especially if you hated climbing anyway.

He touched his newly scraped knee where it was sticky and wanted very badly to go back down into camp. He wanted to go into his cool cabin and blow soap bubbles through his hands in the bathroom, or listen to his tennis shoes as he flopped around in them across the cabin floor. He wanted to scratch a nail file across one of the rusty window screens and watch the dust puff away outside. He wanted to go to the tennis court and run after tennis balls for a counselor – and then get tired and bored and go around to the back door of the dining hall to see if Jennie Mae had any cookies.

Teddy Mudge looked down through the tree tops to the camp grounds and wished he were there. He wished he did not take nature study. He wished his knee were not skinned and his shorts weren't torn.

Then, as he was wishing, he saw a spider's web shining in a crooked cedar tree. At the center a big green spider with a hump on its back was coming out of its spider hole with slow, watchful steps. For a while the spider simply clung there to its gently rocking web – casually, contentedly, like an acrobat riding a safety net after dropping from a trapeze bar. Then something happened: maybe there was a shift in the morning breeze, or a cedar branch swaying across the sunlight. Maybe it was just some mysterious and instinctive skittishness aroused inside the spider itself. Anyway, whatever the cause, it was enough, and just as the big green spider with the hump on its back was beginning to rock most gracefully in its web, it suddenly turned tail and ran. It lunged backward into its hole like a flustered old woman throwing up her hands and fleeing from the sound of a squeaking mouse. And Teddy Mudge, watching the spider disappear, rubbed his arm across his nose and threw back his head – and giggled, through dangling tears.

## White Butterflies

The ten o'clock sky was a hard blue and the sun was burning down through a magnifying glass of clear shining air as the nature counselor led his class into the walnut flat along the river. Here small walnut trees grew thickly and a long stretch of clean, sun-bleached rocks lay in the old dry-branch fork of the river bed.

The counselor stopped and sat down on a cypress stump and let the boys explore for a while. A killdeer soon ran crying across the rocks and the boys started after it, making shrill piping sounds like the killdeer and laughing. There was brown debris from the last flood still lodged in the top branches of the walnuts, and as the boys passed by they stopped and raised their hands above their heads toward the matted sticks and leaves – marveling that they were actually standing on the spot where a flood once was. They quickly forgot the killdeer and began turning over big rocks to see what was underneath. As they looked they found a mother scorpion with many small amber children huddled on her back, and one small cool-black snake, and occasionally trap-door spiders who rushed out of their holes to see what was the matter.

It did not take long for the boys to become lost from time and from themselves. They strung out along the flat, poking and prying and feeling rough things with their hands. The blood went to their heads from so much bending, and with the close heady smells coming from the walnut blooms and the damp river bank and the hot sun on the rocks, they soon became a little drunk. Whenever they would finish exploring under a tree they would start off suddenly in brief half-dazed runs, hearing nothing but the sound of the smooth rocks crunching together beneath their shoes, seeing only the bright glare of the sun.

It was in such a condition – their mouths open from unformed, excited thoughts and sweat circling neatly beneath their eyes – that they suddenly saw jerk into view out of the trees a pair of white butterflies. Perhaps it was simply the heat of the morning and the dizziness of too much running about along the old river bed, but as the butterflies danced together above their heads in elaborate and tantalizing wildness the boys saw right through the wings and their delicate motion into forgotten dreams and imaginings – into pictures of clipper ships, smoke trails, dancing elves. They watched, fascinated, and then before their eyes the fragile wisps of their dreams scattered off in a little white zigzag trail above the jungle of walnuts, disappearing like bits of morning vapor into the wide blueness of the sky.

## Eight Boys

It is after lunch and eight boys lie on cots in their cabin, reading funny books. Although they suck thumbs and dig idly into their noses and now and then pinch or pull at their tight bathing suits, they never take their eyes from their reading. They lie passive and content, dressed for the free swim period that will come when rest hour is over.

Eight boys, resting – very lean and satiny-brown now in mid-July but not obvious in their growth, not even having definite rear ends yet. They are still developing with the clean, embryonic lines of childhood. Their bodies do not shout strength and hairiness as they will later; calves and biceps are not yet bunched in muscularity. There is no awkward excess. Every line is still the simple straight line of a boy.

Eight boys, with only their little washboard chests rising and falling to give testimony of the tireless motors inside. They are soon to yawn and stretch and let the funny books slide from their cots to the floor. Then, just as effortlessly, they themselves will slide into two o'clock drowsiness, the silence of the cabin continuing to float on their slow and even breaths.

Eight boys, nine years old, more attuned to the pulse of a warm afternoon than they ever will be again – for they are still part of it. Some unseen placenta of the day still gives them nourishment, preparing them for that disconcerting moment in the future when they will be born, wild-eyed and awkward, into adolescence.

## Mountain Top

Only an hour ago the smiling-eyed riding instructor had shifted his buttocks on the patio chair – skillfully, as though they were instruments he had mastered – and generously using his friendly smile, with its many obedient wrinkles, he had assured the mother that the camp horses were good ones and gentle and that Luanne would be perfectly safe. And the mother on her cool summerhouse patio had jangled the white bracelets on her slim brown arms and poured more ice in her glass and sat smiling: she was obviously pleased. She had watched through the patio screen as the two of them rode across the low-water bridge back into Camp Palo Alto and on up the mountain trail: he, suntanned and authentically western-looking, with an orange plastic lanyard hung around his neck and his muscular legs sausage-tight in

his jeans; and her girl, slim and blonde, with caliche dust from the
road already beginning to powder her expensive riding boots.

And now they were riding along the mountain ridge above camp.
Below them, in the white cabins, it was still rest hour. The camp area,
from above, was mainly a thick covering of oak and cedar trees, but
they could catch a glimpse of flag and a few white patches of the tennis court and gravel drives. They stilled their horses at the rim and the
riding instructor pointed out across the bare grounds of the baseball
fields to the long line of cypress trees that meant the river. Sighting
along his out-stretched arm, the girl searched for her summer home
among the many similar squares of rambling lawns. As he gradually
lowered his arm she saw the riding stables north of camp and the horses looking small and toy-like there. "We'll try to get back down before
rest period's over," he said. He looked at his watch. "But we still have
time to see the rifle range." He took off his big-brimmed Stetson and
dragged his sweating forearm across the red hat-line on his brow, then
replaced the Stetson firmly at exactly its old slant. He grinned his
broad, friendly grin and slapped Luanne's knee and said to his horse,
"Let's go, Jiggs!"

They turned away from the ridge and headed straight across the
top of the mountain. To reach the rifle range they would have to turn
right and go down into a long shaded hollow. But they didn't make it
to the rifle range. A little way down the trail the riding instructor
reined up, dismounted, and tied both horses loosely to the branch of a
cedar tree. He helped his girl get down and kissed her a long time as
they stood there beside the horses – and then he took her to the
ground. Without words being passed, the brown riding instructor
asked and the mother's blonde daughter said yes and the two of them
were down in the leaves and hot needlegrass, in a whole mountain top
of quiet, in a whole afternoon of pulsing July fever.

(As the minutes passed grasshoppers flew out of the grass, sailed
along in a fierce brittle snapping, then dropped back into the grass
again, as though felled suddenly by the great heat

(Long thin leaves of mesquite trees hung in a plumb-straight
greenness, like socks on a line or many bats sleeping: hanging as if trying to remain cool through sheer inactivity

(Lizards waited on the tops of big flint mounds – suspicious,
watchful, their necks frozen to one side: looking as if they had stopped
in all the stillness and heat to catch a faint hollow voice from deep
inside the earth, perhaps one of God's left over from eons past

(Purple wine cups wobbled along the trail as little breezes
touched them, and out in the clearings small yellow daisies shook
almost all the time, making a yellow shimmer in the bright afternoon
air

(Unseen insects on the mountain top kept up their steady drone,
occasionally a dove would call in its lonely detached way out of some
distant hollow

(And it was not long before the horses, straining forward a little
after grass, pulled their reins free from the branch of the cedar tree and
began eating their way, unhurriedly, back toward the ridge).

Sometime during the afternoon one of the camp cooks gave four
quick strokes on the dining hall gong, signaling the end of rest hour.
On the mountain top a cricket heard the sounds coming faintly across
the ridge, and he quickly gave one single short answer from his home
under a rock. Grazing along through the alternate patches of shade
and brightness among the Spanish oak trees, the two riderless horses
raised their heads once as if they might have heard the sounds too, but
went on chewing. Farther back on the mountain top, stretched side by
side in the leaves and shade, the riding instructor and his girl heard the
sounds. They listened a moment, then somehow found gongs as good
a reason as any to smile at one another again and touch each other's
hands and kiss.

# Aunt Annie

After turning the dinner glasses upside down to drain on the white tablecloth, Aunt Annie would get her bonnet from the nail by the wood stove and leave her cool dark ranch kitchen and go work outside in her garden in the hot afternoon sun. She would gather snap beans with her German police dog, Tom, who moved along behind her in the rows like a detached but loyal honor guard. They both enjoyed the garden: Aunt Annie could do the small steady job of picking or gathering with her hands and still have her mind free to play among old memories (her mouth pooching out nervously, quickly, as it tried to match the inner rhythm of her thoughts, the many wrinkles around it working like a dozen drawstrings closing and loosening a tobacco sack). And Tom, though dutiful and companionable, could still sport along in the sun and find his own idle amusements in clumps of vines and good-smelling dirt.

They liked it there in the garden very well, even after Uncle Newt had died. They liked the sound of the windmill's endless and comforting afternoon music, the long tranquil calls of the doves sitting in the green pecan trees beside the garage, the sun glinting along the smooth top loops of the garden fence in a friendly intimacy.

That was a few years ago. Today Aunt Annie lives in a rest home in Fredericksburg, on a side street that is quiet and still. But the stillness is not like the kind on the ranch. It does not calm and surround a person with peace but isolates and makes lonely. It lacks an essential warmth. Aunt Annie knows this, but there is nothing she can do because her children decided she was too old to stay on the ranch by herself. (Their constant cry: "But Mother, what if you broke your hip or got sick? You won't even let us get a hired girl to live with you.") So chances are she will spend the rest of her life on that quiet street, sitting on the front porch under a light blanket and watching occasional cars go by.

It would have been better if she could have died out there along Johnson Creek, in her garden, on some warm and friendly day after dinner when the cool water from the windmill pipe was flowing down the potato rows and she had her apron full of squash or okra or peas. Then she would not have died among strangers but in her rightful place, still at work and useful, still alert to all the small magics she had known from her girlhood days: the breeze moving through the sycamore trees down along the creek, making their lazy, papery sound; the old brindle cat licking itself in the sun with long untiring sweeps; the single small distant sound of a sheep's bell coming from across the creek in the west pasture. And in dying out there, on some bright July or August day, Aunt Annie could have had the funeral she deserved: the mockingbird to sing a tireless, flamboyant song from its corner fence post, the windmill to turn out somber benedictive sighs all afternoon long, and Tom to lie down quietly at her side and mourn.

# Places

There are certain places encountered in childhood that are best left unexplored, unknown, so they can remain one's personal Everests, shrouded in mists.

I am talking of those half-glimpsed houses, buildings, pastures, towns – quite ordinary sights and scenes – that a child happens to notice from a car window on family outings. Whether they are seen once or a hundred times does not matter; they are remembered. They remain preserved in a special ambiance of memory, hinting at curious depths and mysteries. The stone archway of a ranch-house porch, a dirt road curving through prickly pear, a rust-stained water tank hidden among oaks – such unspectacular features of a landscape assume mythic proportions in one's mind. They look like answers to important questions that are never quite asked.

For over thirty years I have thought, off and on, of a wooden church near Fredericksburg. I have seen it in all weathers, usually on Sunday trips from Kerrville to Austin: a Lutheran church for German farm families, a gray, narrow, austere wooden building set among trees.... Out of all the churches I have seen, why has this one persisted in my consciousness so long? Is it mainly that serene stretch of highway I am aware of – that gently curving hill country road with peach orchards and hay fields on either side and the meandering Pedernales River always somewhere nearby: with stone farmhouses a hundred years old still standing, still lived in by descendants of the farmers who first built them? Is it the contrast of the warm-toned, Breughel-like countryside – deer grazing in the pastures, sun bright on the green fields – and the severe, single-spired church on its aloof little rise of ground? Is it that the traditional shape and purpose of the church not only seems out of place but is, indeed, less important than the post oaks, the barns, the windmills, the fireplaces of the Steinfelds and Kounzes and Bierschwales who worship there – that is, less *godly* than those fields and barns? Or is it something else: mere curiosity about those unseen German families who come each Sunday to a church-among-trees: who disappear solemnly through that narrow doorway and reappear – purged – an hour later into sun and shadow: who need a stern Sunday focus, a formal churchliness, to add proper weight to their lives?

I have thought, too, of a green-trimmed, two-storied white house at Castell, up above Mason. My father was born on a farm near there and one Sunday, on a visit to relatives, my family drove by. A gas station-post office and the house – that was Castell: half-a-handful of buildings above the Llano River on a pleasant June day, nothing more.

But what a house it seemed to be, with its wrap-around, bannistered porch, towering pecan trees, wide green yard without fences, huge garden: a bright, sun-bathed house with second-story window curtains moving in the noon air and rocking chairs sitting on the porch and children racing in the pecan-tree shade: a house seen leisurely but

only once as our car eased down the slope toward the low-water
bridge over the Llano. Fixed there on its breeze-swept hill, the Castell
house has gradually become for me a blur of fact and fancy – a
Thomas Mann creation, country home of the Buddenbrooks, where
girls in straw hats and summer dresses pack picnic baskets and swing
down familiar trails to shaded grasses bordering the Llano: where families gather in nineteenth-century leisure and innocence for Sunday dinner, the men smoking cigars on the porch, the children chasing one
another, the women putting heaping platters on the dining table....

   They are timeless, these places – dreamlike, yet indestructible.
They are, quite simply, friezes: intrusions of immortality into the random flow of daily life. They should not matter, but they do. And, once
perceived, they glow, stubbornly, like hoarded treasures, in the attic of
the mind.

# Rabbit at Sundown

   Once, just at dark, a rabbit fell down and a man saw him. The
man, a rancher, was seated behind an oak tree near a windmill in his
pasture. He had been working on the mill that afternoon and had sat
down to rest a few moments when the jack rabbit came scooting along
a trail through a group of cedar trees. Daylight had almost completely
faded and the rabbit was simply doing what it did many afternoons –
come in to get water and nibble in the hay that was scattered around
the mill for cattle. The rancher was looking off into space – not moving – so everything seemed quite safe and ordinary to the rabbit. But
just as he got clear of the cedar trees and into the open area around
the mill, he saw the rancher looking straight at him. He braked,
became confused, and fell, all within an instant, tripping over himself
and his long feet in the dust. As he went down the rabbit looked
across at the man – not with fear or concern for his safety but in simple amazement at what he, a wholly nimble and healthy rabbit, was

allowing himself to do. He was down only a fraction of a moment, just long enough to know beyond doubt that he had truly fallen and there had truly been a witness – that he had not dreamed it all – and then he was up and gone, zigzagging in furious shame across the clearing and into a clump of shin oaks and out of sight.

# Betty Lee

Each fall afternoon she changed from her starched school dress to clean blue jeans and a flannel shirt and went outside to do the chores. She gathered eggs from the barn, watered the rabbits in their cages beside the garage, scattered corn in the woodlot for the guineas – and all the while kept whistling and scuffing her shoes and listening to my uncle call "gooooatie, gooooatie, gooooatie" down below the hill in the creek pasture.

I remember her best that way – growing up so easily at her ranch home among chickens and horses and cedar trees. She was my cousin Betty Lee: a pretty, soft-faced girl with brown hair and a small childish voice who liked to sit at dusk on the back porch and shell pecans while my uncle chopped wood for the fireplace. She was always happy in these long early years – did not once realize that life could ever be more than raising fawns and baking fudge and sewing dresses for the FHA.

Then, out of the blue, things happened to Betty Lee: she got married, moved away, had a baby, became sick. It all seemed too much, too sudden – at seventeen she knew nothing about Los Angeles or husbands or polio. She knew quite a bit less about iron lungs and dying. She was simply not prepared.

I kept asking myself afterwards: What would you have her do – stay out there forever along that cedar ridge, whistling "Red Wing" and trailing corn to the guineas? Would you keep her permanently thirteen, prevent her from meeting her fate?

No, I would say...but I still find it hard to drive to her house any more. In my mind it has always stayed November along the Harper Road, and Betty Lee is always there in her blue jeans and plaid shirt – calling out in her clear, innocent, childish voice to the animals, to me.

# Nora and Fayrene

In the fall Nora, the madame, and Fayrene, her red-haired girl, liked to drive about the Fredericksburg countryside on Sunday after-noons, gathering branches of Spanish oak leaves to put over the nick-elodeon in their farmhouse parlor. The rich oranges and deep reds brought out the new pine paneling and added a rustic touch to the room. Nora was always thinking of new ways to brighten the place. She bought throw rugs for the upstairs rooms and painted the hallway blue; she kept the parlor floor waxed to a shine. She took pride in the old farmhouse and was glad she had bought it instead of the house in Dallas. She had come to like the tall lonesome post oaks and the rolling farmland – even the red sandy soil. When she and Fayrene sat on the porch in the late afternoons after doing the outside chores, she felt that she had a fine place to live and do business.

Fayrene had been with Nora for almost two years, and Nora liked her. She was sensible – someone she could trust. She didn't try to push herself like most of the transient girls who passed through from Galveston and Houston. And even though she wasn't pretty she dressed well and was friendly with the customers. Sometimes the older ones just liked to come out and sit in the parlor with her and pass the time of day.

So Nora and Fayrene enjoyed their warm fall afternoons together, occasionally driving around in Nora's new Cadillac and soaking up the lazy farm countryside, sometimes just puttering around out back in the chicken pens. They were raising a few ducks and guineas but Nora thought she might buy some Rhode Island Reds a little later on. She would have to ask Alton Kahn, the Purina dealer, how the prices were the next time he was out.

# The Sun Children

When the day finally reaches its deepest mood in the hill country and begins to rest a little in preparation for night, it always gives a signal to the sun that she, too, can relax a few minutes from her long duty in the sky. She can settle out in the west and give her children a little freedom – twelve hours is a long time to be confined in that small bright circle.

So the sun pauses just before night and lets her horde of slender yellow children creep in from the horizon and spread out over the land. They come silently and joyfully, slanting their lean bodies across rocks and weeds and tree branches like long marine animals hunting food. They clasp the faces of barns and picket fences, hanging on in a silent fierce yellowness, and for a few sustained minutes the land is their playground.

Then their mother calls. It is getting twilight, she says; time to go. Obediently, on a soundless cue, the yellow children slip from their leaves and posts and hurry westward. There, on the horizon – in a hushed moment that the land strains to hear – they get back inside their mother and disappear below the rim of the earth, leaving the world drained of its color for another day and feeling very old and still.

# Melvin Oehler

He haunts me.

I walk by his small white house on Hermann Street, with the green garden hose coiled neatly in the chinaberry shade, and I want to veer from the sidewalk and stride up on the porch and stalk inside. I want to confront him in his lair – counting sacks of gold in the bedroom, or smoking opium in a closet, or reading John D. MacDonald detective novels in an arm chair, or sitting in the bathtub, bouncing a finger across his lips, making blubbering sounds of insanity.

But I will never go in because it is no use: I know there isn't anything bizarre or revealing or interesting that I would discover. And that's what inflames me. I cannot accept the fact that nothing whatsoever goes on in the house – or life – of Melvin Oehler.

Sometimes I see him in the porch swing in the late afternoon, reading the newspaper – hat, white shirt, tie, dress pants, as if he had been on the job all day and now, like any man home from work, was scanning the headlines in a moment of well-earned rest. Or I will look down the driveway into his garage: empty. Melvin Oehler is out, though I cannot imagine where.

But mainly he is in the house, out of sight – the same house he has lived in for forty-five years, the house where his children grew up and his wife lived and died. The Melvin Oehlers of Hermann Street – small-town people, stay-at-home people; people who lived on a shady street and sent their kids to school a block away and went to the Methodist church and watered their lawn and sat on the porch after supper and let the days slip by until half a century had disappeared....

Back then, before he was by himself in the house – when his sons were in school with me and he went every day to work – I suppose he and Leona must have left the house to go somewhere besides the Red and White grocery store or the Methodist church – must have got into the Chevrolet and driven to a movie at the Rialto or gone to a Fourth of July parade or taken a Sunday afternoon drive. But in all my growing-up days I never saw them going places, never even thought of them as being part of the life of the town. Melvin and Leona – they seemed to belong right there in the swing, looking out at the cars passing by.

He is still in that house – Leona died five years ago; his sons are married and have moved away – and I cannot conceive of his daily routine. He is not a reader. He does not drink. He is retired from his bakery job at the VA hospital and has not taken another job. He is a seventy-year-old man with no hobbies and no passions, no problems and no concerns – more like a rubber band, a pane of glass, a postage stamp than a human complexity of nerves and urges and memories. He is something that holds a shirt together; he is something beneath a hat.

Melvin Oehler has no job, no family, no commitments. He does not go to the Methodist church any more. He apparently eats and sleeps and drives his car at a modest speed to undisclosed places. I assume he has a TV. Conceivably he is in the living room watching it every daylight and nighttime hour of every week of every year – but I doubt it. I believe that he is content to put on his shirt and tie and dress pants and do absolutely nothing at all from breakfast till dark. I believe he exists like a fungus in the airy dimness of his house, and that he is neither bored nor un-bored – that it has never occurred to him that he might be one or the other.

I think Melvin Oehler gets up every morning the way mercury rises in a thermometer – mindlessly, effortlessly. If someone planted him in a pot and set him there in the front window, I doubt he would mind too much. Just let him have his hat.

# Afternoon Wine

One hot August afternoon an old buck sheep stood on a high ledge overlooking a stream. He stood motionless and intent, with his massive head and horns turned slightly to one side. He seemed curious about something in the scene below – perhaps the glint of silver minnows in the water, or a cluster of wild canaries flashing dramatically by. Maybe it was just a mirage, a vagary in the heat-charged valley air that arrested him. But regardless, he stood there on the narrow ledge while long minutes passed, his head turned, his legs planted solidly, his big unblinking eyes still staring.

Yet who can say, really, what such a stream and its surroundings might mean to an old buck on a hillside – a stream lying in the midst of so much bright sun and afternoon peace, a stream that spoke with such a melodic gurgle and bubble from its small waterfall? Perhaps to the sheep, isolated on his ledge, the stream was like a skilled country winemaster, gathering out of the valley all the tender grapes of sight and sound and smell. The damp pungencies of watercress and cool river shade, the papery touchings and retouchings of the cottonwood leaves in the wind, the sound of distant mourning doves – the river gathered them, crushed them into its dark steady flow, and then, magically, released them back to the afternoon in the form of champagne – a sparkling afternoon wine that the old buck sheep could hear tumbling and bubbling downstream.

No one knows much about the emotional constitution of sheep – maybe they are just not made for such things as wine on hot August days. In the case of the buck on the ledge, it is probably safe to say that he overreached himself in his moment of contemplation and became heady. For after standing and looking and listening a while, he suddenly gave a deep buck-sheep cry of surprise and fell from the ledge into a deep ravine. It was exactly as though he had fainted. Tree limbs cracked and there was a scattering of leaves, and then – a long silence. Nothing could be heard except the river, still speaking quietly at its waterfall. Minutes passed, and finally the old buck arose from his thick bed of Spanish oak leaves. With a huge snorting and shaking of horns he slowly made his way out of the ravine and climbed back into the hills.

# Home Country

It starts at Ozona, with flowers along the roadside and the desert turning to tree-covered hills.  Home territory – that Stephen Vincent Benét-place: "bone of my bone"....

I came back to it one summer from the west – in June, after a month of soaking rains. Through Pecos, Fort Stockton, all the Texas desert towns, I had been content with sunlight and great quantities of space: I was still pleased by the western absence of things. But at Ozona the mesquites began – miles of them, fresh and green and shiny as silk, with the white-ivory blooms of Spanish daggers scattered through them like cannon bursts – and it was there, at the sight of greenery and hills, that I knew I was home.

For home country does not mean relatives, or city streets, or friends of the past. That is something else again: a world made by people, complex and painful. Home country is *country* – a place of rocks and trees and goats and sheep: of mourning doves and cypress-lined rivers; of hay-fields; of pastures.

(Pastures: To go into them as a boy – into the grass, the scattered flint and limestone rocks, the shadows, the leaves and dirt on the sides of ravines, the bare clearings, the green thickets – was to enter a beautiful clarity, a great sense of what was pure and real. I would walk through tall needlegrass – stumbling now and then over half-buried rocks – and when I rested in the shade of a live oak tree it always seemed that each limb was hugely intimate, like a thought, and the tree itself like a family. I came to love trees – and summer glare, and fence lines, and cedar posts – the same way you come to love people.)

Home country, hill country, the whole stretch of familiar land: I drove past shin oaks standing in the heat like demure tree maidens, heads together, their feet lost in a pool of mid-afternoon shadow; and a rancher in a beat-up hat and faded blue denims, reaching down from his horse to loosen a goat from a wire fence; and a highway workman resting in the roadside shade. Closer and closer, a sweet-sinking into familiar things – and pondering them in the leisure of the passing miles....

A windmill, say: There it was, mounted on its commanding knoll. How many years had it turned like an all-seeing eye above that same clump of ranch-house trees – a constant symbol of possessions and home to the ranchman riding horseback across his land?

Or rocks. Lying there, white as tombs, they represented all that was timeless and impersonal – geologic upheavals, erosion by wind and water – yet they did so in an entirely pleasant way. A rock in a pasture was not like a galaxy suspended in eternal night; it was a *human*-sized thing fit for both the hand and the mind. A rock, in summertime, was one of the beatitudes of earth – enduring as the trees, pleasing as grass.

Toward Sonora the mesquites gave way to live oaks and cedars – the tops of distant oaks looking smoky-blue in the four-o'clock heat – and the land was alive with the sound of birds. Occasionally a deer arched over a fence and an armadillo moved through masses of shadows and leaves. A white butterfly jitterbugged its way among wild flowers and across the green roadside.

Passing still another wooden pasture gate, another windmill, another rancher on horseback, I remembered a similar-looking pasture on my grandparents' ranch and a similar afternoon. It had been in early summer, with a breeze drifting in from the south, and Grandpa and I were out hunting the last of the goats to be driven home and sheared. I had gone on ahead down a long draw, and Grandpa had circled around by the fence. And I remembered coming out of the live oaks

and deep shade and seeing Grandpa riding along the top of the ridge
with the goats. They were a subdued little bunch for goats, following
fairly well the trail to the pens. Grandpa was jogging easily behind –
not exactly smiling, but it amounted to that: his hat was pushed back
and there was a pleased set to his face. His free hand rested on his hip
and a curl of sweated gray hair was plastered above his eye.

And although Grandpa was then in his sixties and had never
before, to my knowledge, tried to whistle or sing a tune, he hummed
all the way across that live oak ridge.  With the goats wagging agreeably along the trail and the shadows coming long and deep out of the
trees and the sun lighting the tops of the yellow needlegrass, Grandpa
sat on his own horse driving his own livestock toward his own home
lots – and was a very contented man.

Near Junction the highway cascaded through great stretches of
blasted rock – naked white gashes of exposed limestone – and entered
the Llano River valley. The Llano, first of the home-country streams
going east, first to create its meandering Babylon of towering pecan
trees and deep-green fields....

I thought: Now I know why I am not a revolutionary – have
never had the desire to kick over old, established things. It's because
the hill country does not teach you the need for change. The land is
always so satisfying that you want it to remain the same forever as a
kind of handy immortality.

I watched a pickup speed around me and then turn down a narrow farm-to-market road. It sailed past sumacs and fence line and
Indian paintbrush and was almost like a fish sporting along in a sunlit
bay: trim, assured, wholly beautiful in its own calm surroundings, it
obviously *belonged*.

Sure, I thought, that's the way it is: you stay next to the land long
enough and you can't help but develop a natural kinship with it: you
blend together. It's like the piles of brush out in the pastures: you look
at them rotting there – simply, with a kind of bare, stoic dignity – and

you begin to feel that somehow even they add to you, complement you, are an actual part of your life and meaning.

As I passed a house a blond, bushy-browed rancher's son was getting letters out of the roadside mailbox. He was still dusty from working with stock and I could almost see him as he had looked stomping around in a crowded pen: yelling and waving his hat at the bawling, milling cows, the dust thick and swirling and clinging to his eyebrows until they finally shone in the sunlight like the hairy legs of bees clustered with pollen.

...The lazy, hazy poetic sense of fading heat as the road curved leisurely through the hills.  Small neat houses, butane cylinders, water tanks: they were stuck here and there in the green countryside like currants in a rich pudding. And everywhere the pleasant unobtrusive handiwork of people – gateposts, barns, small bypassed bridges from simpler times.

At Ingram I decided to leave the highway and cut across to my grandparents' empty ranch house before going on into town. It was getting dark, and the Black Angus cattle feeding on a distant hill looked like hatchet blades driven solidly into the ground. The road dipped first into low-water crossings, full of the smell of walnuts and sycamores, and then climbed back again to the wide ranch-land plateau.

I was just starting to open the gate to the west pasture of the ranch when I stopped and listened: a neighbor's horse across the road was moving slowly through a sudan patch, the bell at its neck jingling casually. It was just an ordinary hardware store bell, and the horse was a bony-ribbed old mare; but for a moment, with the land quietening, it was like the Angelus as I had always imagined it would sound in the countryside of France or Spain: patient and solitary, a reminder for those within hearing that day was about through, that people should lay down their work and start gathering close to home.

The porch of the ranch house faces south toward Kerrville and a line of faint blue hills. As I sat there in the early darkness, listening to katydids pulse back and forth in the surrounding trees, I tried to think a little about Grandpa and couldn't. I knew the *alive* George Duderstadt – the shape of his head underneath a hat, his gait in the worn, run-over boots as he half-walked, half-stumbled across the back lots. But this new one, the one over in the Harper grave, the one barely three years old: I found we had nothing to say.

And Gram, sitting in town in her lifeless little room, a small gray-haired refugee from the country adapting, at eighty, to new town ways: she had surrendered the ranch too.

They were both gone now – the human trustees had finally loosened their grip – so what would happen to the land? What exactly *was* a piece of land anyway, I wondered – did it ultimately belong to itself? Should earth always return to earth after a while – for a period of silence and private growth? Did anyone ever have the right to claim a hill or a clump of trees as his own?

I thought of these things for a while – sitting where I used to sit so often as a child, where I had listened to the big gray doves as they perched in the live oaks west of the house and soothed the air with their gentle calls: I thought about them and then got into the car again and began driving toward home.

It was clear that people had caught up with me – had gradually begun to nudge the country aside. For five hundred miles I had been loose on the land and now it seemed only fair that I yield to the demands of my own kind: to family, duties, memories. After all, I was due at a house, not at one of the pastures. So as I topped the last hill I opened all the windows and barreled on down – the cool sweet cedar air in my face, the familiar lights of Kerrville shining below.

# Clayton Weatherby

I think frequently of a man I've never met. His name is Clayton Weatherby and he lives alone in a house across the valley from my Uncle Doug. I keep forgetting that he must be in his sixties now. In my mind he is still that strange young man who turned his back on people – who returned from World War II and lived with his parents until they died and then just kept on ranching and living alone among the cedar and Spanish oak trees of Central Texas.

I have sat out on my uncle's porch on summer nights and looked across the darkness of the valley to the Weatherby house. Sometimes I can see a light, sometimes not. And if I hear the rattle of a pickup and see dim headlights bouncing along Indian Creek Road, my uncle will say, "Well, I guess ole Clayton has been in to see his woman."

If I were around him a while maybe I could learn something useful – how to do without city lights, city distractions, how to back off from the world. But I couldn't live alone for thirty years: Get up each morning and stay there on the ranch during the day doing whatever needs to be done and then after night begins to settle – whippoorwills calling from the pastures and the bullbats gliding though the pens – sit alone on the porch for a while listening to the katydids before going inside to bed. I could do that for a week at a time but not for thirty years. It wouldn't be enough for me – a trip now and then for groceries or to see a widow.

I think of Clayton's light across the valley. I think of him sitting there on his porch – looking over to the distant light of other homes – and I wonder if he is content with being who he is and with what he is doing, or if he is simply another cripple unable to endure the stress of human give-and-take. I wonder if he is serene or nearly mad with loneliness. I wonder if he is aware that people wonder about him.

Chances are I will never talk to Clayton Weatherby – never sit with him in the early evening – and that is perhaps a good thing. He

will remain an unsolved, and thus unforgettable, mystery: another dim
porch light burning enigmatically in the unending human dark.

# At the Hunting Cabin

### I

I reclaimed, last summer, a personal territory, a place to call home
for a while. I lived at the family hunting cabin among the trees – wanting nothing more than what I saw before me each day: pastures, sunlight, hillsides. My cup was empty when I went there in June, but by
August it was full.

Nothing flashy or dramatic happened: no meteors dropped from
the sky. I simply lived as though I were seated on the front row of the
First Day, watching Creation. The countryside was my Book of
Knowledge.

When I woke on those overcast mornings in June I had to adjust
to my new reality. It was 7:30 by my watch, time to be headed glumly
to work on a conveyor belt of cars, but I was no longer on Loop 410
in San Antonio. I was lying on my sleeping bag with a delicate south
breeze bathing me through the cabin doorway.

I had no plans to follow, no obligations to meet. The day was
simply what unfolded: read in the shade of one of the oaks, look at
gourds growing so pleasingly striped and round and green among their
vines, watch a buzzard soar, a cow chew. I could cut cedar if I wanted
to be productive; I could drink cool water from the windmill if I wanted to feel contentedly alive. It didn't matter what I did or did not do.
Human *doing* was not on the hunting cabin agenda. It was the natural
world that was on display there, and I was ready to be its dedicated
observer.

After luxuriating in the breeze that touched my face and arms as
tenderly as a geisha, I made coffee on the Coleman stove and sat in

the doorway in my bare feet. I drank coffee while a wasp investigated the window screen and lone doves sat on the bare limbs of a dying oak – as if resting in the somber branches of time. I looked at lichen-covered rocks by the cabin gate, then at the liver spots on my hands: unnoticeably, we had been aging together like country cousins.

## II

Each morning the cows came into the water lot. They convened slowly from the various draws and hillsides in a carnival of calls and bellows. They announced themselves without preamble or niceties, their sounds abrupt, strangled, imperious: *"I'm here; where are you?"*

One of the Herefords stood beneath the huge water lot oak, the peaceful captain of her ship – while her calf, a big one, sucked and jabbed with abandon. After finishing his assault the calf drew his head back and stayed there at the mother's side, nose to hip, facing west. The mother remained motionless, facing east. As other cows drifted past, mother and calf stood side by side, solidly content, as if in harmony not only with each other but with the earth itself – indeed, with all heavenly bodies.

One morning three cows came down the arroyo, around the corral fence, into the water lot – slowly making their way through the tree shadows like late arrivals at a camp meeting. They stopped at the water lot gate, looking distracted; then they raised their chins and bellowed fiercely toward the pastures. They were bereft, you see. Their owner, Talbot Garven, had come to the cabin the day before, sprayed the herd for summer flies, and afterwards had loaded eight calves into his trailer and taken them off to market. The three cows at the gate were several of the disconsolate mothers, wandering separately – grazing their way through the early morning, stopping, staring, calling out.

The cows at the gate were studies in depression, unwilling, even, to lean down and pull off the inviting top of a nearby purple thistle while they waited. One of them finally shook free of the mood and tentatively began to graze. But in a moment she raised her head – not

caring that she looked wild-eyed and dumb as a stump, with slobber
and runners of mesquite grass dangling from her mouth.

In the late afternoon I sometimes opened the gate of the cabin lot
and let a few of the cows in to graze on the thicker, greener grass. It
was like a summer lawn party, with the invited guests on their best
behavior: ten Hereford cows, all in red, and Bull, their dehorned, plod-
ding companion. Several cowbirds always flew down to join them, and
like small French serving maids moved briskly among the hoofs and
heads, sometimes even busybodying their way beneath a cow to get to
the grass on the other side – as if hurrying beneath an arch on a familiar Paris street. The cows, unconcerned, grazed along in their green
commons – past the outhouse, the rolls of wire, the discarded harrow,
their tails making a casual swinging ballet in the bright four o'clock air.

## III

At noon I sat in the sun, my body hot with life, and I wanted to
sing the summer as a song, the way the locusts did. I wanted to turn
the day into words, but everything important was being said: the sun
and the earth were saying it all.

Beneath the big oak in the water lot cows licked salt blocks; others stood at the water trough, drinking in long smooth throatfuls.
Finally, through with licking and drinking, they stood in the shade,
chewing, looking out.

The cows and I were witnesses of that midday hour: We saw yellow butterflies sit delicately on moist manure piles – like trim Chinese
sailboats becalmed on muddy flats of the Yangtze.

We saw the weathered boards of the cabin lot gate gradually
darken as the trees drew shadows over them as smoothly as a curtain.

We saw the sun gloss the smooth poles of the corral fence, making them shine like the calluses of a worker's hand.

We saw great sagacious trees hold private conferences along the
hillsides – the sun scattering highlights on their loose green robes that
flowed and lifted in the noon wind.

We were witnesses and I was awed, even if the cows were not. I waited patiently for meaning to emerge from the stillness of the rusted oil drum and the cedar posts in the fence. I expected no less of them than Buddha might under his banyan tree.

I was trying to slip past nature's guard, you see. I looked and listened – I was attentive to the processes going on in every square and cubic yard of my cabin world – and I wanted to get a glimpse of what was happening, so relentlessly.... How did it work, this incredible earth? I wanted to solve the mystery of the commonplace – come to grips, at last, with the tantalizing oak tree shade that lay like an eternal hieroglyphic against the rocks of the hunting cabin wall.

I looked at the sky through the burning glass of midday and thought of Greece: didn't it have the same heat, the same locusts singing from hidden places, the same bare, white rocks and caliche roads? When I walked up the arroyo in the late afternoons to my favorite shelf of rocks and sat beneath the gigantic oak among its bare, Medusa-like roots, didn't I ask it my unanswerable questions and didn't it, like a hill country temple of Delphi, offer its silent replies?

## IV

The Spanish goats started coming by in the early afternoon, browsing their way north through the fences, across pastures. They belonged, apparently, to a neighbor near the interstate.

On the first day they appeared the cows were taking their ease in the front clearing. I was reading in the cabin doorway. The goats, nine of them, simply materialized in the patch of purple thistles by the molasses wheel.

I watched them: nicely brown and black and white, a pleasant and unexpected plus on the landscape. But since Spanish goats are generally a standoffish and independent breed – gypsies of the pastures – I assumed they would just give me a look of casual disdain and move on about their business. In a moment, however, the smallest goat, a black kid with a white face and lank belly, came bleating up the

fence line. He headed toward my outstretched hand and began sucking away at my thumb. He had definitely been a bottle goat but I had
no milk for him, not much of anything store-bought except carrots. I
got one from a cellophane sack in my cooler and offered it to him, but
he was not interested. He wanted milk.

It was then that I met the black billy. He had started up the fence
line too: his smell, like a pennant, announced him. The kid dodged to
one side as the billy, with his steady black eyes and dramatic goat
smell, walked forthrightly to the cabin. He regarded, circumspectly,
the carrot in my hand; then, satisfied it posed no threat and might,
indeed, be as interesting to eat as to look at, he leaned forward, his
upper lip curved outward like a black pseudopod of flesh. I cut the carrot in two and offered him a half. He took it: bit it and chewed it
solidly, and waited. I offered him the second half. He crunched it too.

That was that – like the first hit of heroin. The black billy was
hooked.

The next day, at noon, when the goats were back again among
the thistles, the billy licked at the molasses wheel a while – then bleated. I was out of sight inside the cabin. He licked and looked toward
the cabin and bleated some more.

I was bending over the cooler when I smelled him. He loomed in
the doorway like an apparition from a child's nursery book and
watched as I cut slices longways from a carrot. We went outside. I fed
him two carrots, slice by slice, and then shooed him back to the water
lot and closed the gate. He reared up, put his forelegs on the wire
fence – leaning toward me as far as he could. He stretched forward,
the tip of his tongue reaching out in shameless little quivering, searching thrusts. He was a goat dangerously close to losing his dignity. I
had one carrot left in the cooler and I gave it to him. He chewed it
while still leaning awkwardly over the fence.

When the rest of the goats began to ease around the corral and
on through the trees, the billy lingered. He stayed there with the cows
during the midday heat – nibbling thistles. The Herefords moved out

to graze in the late afternoon, but the billy remained. At five o'clock, when I began to make coffee, I could still hear his tentative bleat: the half-hearted cry of a cold-carrot junkie, desolate and alone on his hillside.

## V

At nine o'clock the ranch land was still covered by low morning clouds, but the birds were singing away as if already drunk on sunshine. Small black squirrels strayed from their home in a walnut tree and climbed within the squares of the cabin lot's wire fence: squirrel children taking turns on backyard monkey bars. On a nearby knoll a deer and a fawn stood like light-brown statuary placed overnight among the trees.

In the clearing a cow licked her calf – newly born, with some of the new still on it. The cow licked along one side of the head, then along the other; along the top of the head and then under an ear. When the cow finished with her own calf she turned and started in democratically on a nearby yearling, who stood luxuriating in the rhythm, the touch, as the licking went on and on.

The wind rose, the windmill turned, the leaves of the Spanish oaks – pale green and papery and delicate – jiggled and rustled for a while. The wind was like a surf among the trees.

A long spear of pasture grass waved and bent in the air – a yellow-tipped metronome – and the cabin lot could have been a Dakota prairie in the 1800s or an African savannah with small, pre-human hunters stalking game with pointed sticks. The land seemed as young as the morning, coeval with the rabbits and black squirrels and the birds.

I knew I would accomplish very little that day. Yet, I wondered, what was the proper measurement to use in gauging work? If it took nature 500 million years to lay down a new stratum of rocks in the Grand Canyon, what should nature – or I – be doing on a Tuesday?

I looked at a weed in the water lot. It was an ordinary weed but nicely shaped, as weeds go, with several yellow flowers. I could chop it down and feel productive or let it remain there in its bare space.... I looked at it closely: it had a nice completeness, one might even say style – certainly a context among the grasses and animals.

I did not touch the weed. It belonged in its spot of ground as much as I belonged in the cabin doorway.

## VI

As I read on the front porch slab a mouse came out from a crack in the wall. He was a wee beastie, as Robert Burns would have said – about half the size of my thumb – and his long trailing tail looked like the queue of hair that young men wear at the back of the neck.

At first I thought he was just looking for adventure; a mild, baby-mouse kind of exploration along the side of the shaded tin wall. But after watching him a while I understood his mission. He had eaten my Decon-poisoned grain and was on his death march.

The field mice had been invading the cabin at night and I had finally decided enough was enough: I had put Decon paper trays under a table and waited. The mice had been making themselves far too comfortable in my sack of groceries – one had even become a fan of chocolate chip cookies. (I would lie on my sleeping bag in the dark and listen as he rattled around in the sack – gorging himself. When I would shine my flashlight across the cabin he would appear for a moment at the top of the sack – hanging there with a kind of bemused, tolerant expression – then go right back down to his mid-night feast.)

I put my book aside and bent down to look closer at my porch visitor. The little guy would move and stop, move and stop, not know-ing what the devil was giving him such a bellyache (..."Is this the nor-mal way to grow up and be a field mouse, Ma, or *what*?"). Not mouse-like yet in shape – not sleek, not ready for climbing and cavorting – he was still just a hump-and-tail, a kind of tadpole-mouse edging himself along the cabin wall.

When I got down on my knees I could see that his eyes were closed – either he had shut them against the death agony or had not yet opened them after birth: he had never seen the world he was going to die in. He had begun to tremble and twitch, like a little old man with bad dreams nodding in a chair. As the sow bugs – gray, relentless eighteen-wheelers on their personal interstate across the concrete floor – passed over his tail, the mouse would flinch, blindly, then face in another direction and sink back into his private quivers. Every now and then he would get an itch and would scratch himself with his perfectly shaped little field mouse feet – lightning fast, it seemed to me, for so comatose a creature.

After a while I got up and went about my business – patching a few holes in the cabin roof, straightening up a wire fence. I checked on Mouse once to see how he was doing, but he was gone – had bumped his way back into a crack in the wall, I assumed, and was somewhere beneath the cabin.

At noon I went to the windmill in the cabin lot, got a long drink of well water, and put out salt blocks for the cows. When I came back the mouse was lying on his side in the sun. A very still little body on the hot porch slab, he had been made dead by me. I had sowed my seeds and reaped this small harvest. He had taken the poison-dusted grain that his mother – good provider that she was – had brought back to her children and – good son that he was – had dutifully eaten it.

Somehow, stretched out on his side he looked larger – more mouse-like in shape – and had an impressive kind of mouse dignity: front feet formally together, touching one another; ears flattened; fur neat; tail curved down in a proper symmetry. And of course the eyes were still closed: Mouse's brief span of days had been completed in darkness, and he was unaware that he cast no shadow in the blazing summer noon.

## VII

I grappled with my problem of the moment: how to interpret a cow's stare. That is, how could I get down on paper the essence of a Hereford's stare as she lifted her head at midmorning, turned slightly, and regarded me from within her solid cow center? How to convey that deep cow-superiority and cow-indifference, that all-seeing and unseeing gaze-and-drool? The Hereford's look – apparently so guileless, so impersonal, so much like a blank pane of glass in an empty house – seemed, suddenly, to contain an awesome, cryptic message coming to me across the chasm of evolution.

The Hereford, drinking at the trough, dripped and stared, and I waited for a breakthrough. I demanded communication: I wanted to see past her pink comedian's nose into a hidden First Cause.

I moved towards her. I walked slowly, stopped a moment, talked to her quietly, came closer, stopped again. I was within six feet of those childish, towheaded swirls and curls above the blunt plain between her eyes.  She continued to stare at me from beneath the awnings of her long, white, girlish lashes and then – convinced that I was not hiding feed for her behind my back – moved off heavily to the salt blocks, imperturbable as Nero.

## VIII

We were together in the heat, the cows and I. We were under our respective trees, looking out together toward the bright August afternoon. A buzzard drifted overhead, a deer crossed the road at the top of the hill, flies angled about, bees settled and lifted from the water troughs. In the rock tank frogs sucked their throats like small contented boys rubbing balloons.

It was hot under my oak tree, but I did not abandon it. I breathed, I existed, I rested like the other creatures of the earth. There was no hierarchy among us. We shared the given moment.

In the late afternoon, as if welling out of the heat and the waning sunlight, a dove began calling. It was like an escaped breath from the land itself, an unobtrusive, suggestive voice saying "Do you remember? Do you still care?" Like a tide coming in to shore, the dove call flowed so evenly through the trees it was as if I had thought the call rather than heard it.

I followed the call, somewhat. I walked toward it down the dry creek bed west of the pens, then I looked back to the clearing of the cabin and the remains of my father's old feed store truck there beside it. As I stood beneath the walnut trees, on the layer of smooth rock where we had once had family picnics, I thought: How do you repay a pasture, a clump of trees, the sun? What can you give them for making your life worthwhile?

The dove called, again and again, taking me deeper into the mood of the silent rocks and lengthening shadows. As night fell, it seemed to me that the only way to give a proper thanks – to the earth – was to keep on paying it close attention. To keep looking hard and saying: Yes, I see.

## IX

"Chi-ink. Chi-ink."
Gregorio was digging post holes in a layer of rock.
"Chi-ink. Chi-ink."
I saw him on the fence line morning and afternoon – blue cap, red shirt in the sunshine-and-shade. He maintained a smooth, swaying little rhythm, almost a dance step: feet in place, swinging a bit from side to side as he sent the crowbar twisting down.

Each morning he got up at six, made breakfast in his tent, and was there at the fence line as I rolled over in my sleeping bag outside the hunting cabin door.
"Chi-ink. Chi-ink. Chi-ink. Chi-ink."
At noon he would stop and come back slowly toward the pens, walking past his row of cedar posts gleaming ivory-and-brown in the sunlight. He would eat and rest in the tent, then walk back to his crowbar and gloves.

"Chi-ink. Chi-ink."

The afternoon shadows deepened, the sun lost its glare, doves scouted above the walnut-tree arroyo, and Gregorio worked at the fence line, cutting cedar trees, stripping and shaping posts – aligning, tamping them until they were solidly in place: as if made of rock themselves.

He would stop working just before dark and come to the water lot to fill his bucket at the windmill pipe. Sometimes he pushed back his cap – at fifty-three, his hair remarkably full and black – and smoked a Bugler cigarette and we talked about the cows, or cedar ticks, or the spread of purple thistles in the pastures. He spoke deliberate and carefully enunciated Spanish.

Once, when we were talking about sports, I mentioned that my son had become a cross-country runner at his high school. Gregorio talked at length – almost didactically – about fitness programs for athletes and the Olympic trials he had watched on Mexican television. He said his sons had also been runners in school. When our conversation died away and he finally lifted his bucket and headed toward his tent, the bullbats had begun to sweep over the water lot and katydids were flashing their messages in the darkening trees.

...Gregorio: I think of him and the other lives he might have led. I see him seated behind a desk, an investment broker giving measured, articulate advice to a client. I see him in the dugout of a semiprofessional baseball team, his silk manager's shirt fitting tightly over his thick chest and muscular arms.

As I drive down a city street or have coffee in a cafe, I hear his crowbar biting into rock; I see oak tree shadows sliding across his blue cap and sweat-circled red shirt. A cardinal flashes through the cedars, a buzzard coasts in the midsummer sky, and Gregorio makes another envelope of dollars he can send to his sister in Piedras Negras.

"Chi-ink. Chi-ink. Chi-ink. Chi-ink."

Alone in the pasture, from daylight till dark, Gregorio digs through hill country rock. I listen, and he is like a myth that keeps growing in my mind.

# IV

# ACROSS
# THE STATE

# A Saturday Visitor

It was Saturday morning in Austin and the day of the big football game. We had got up late at the boarding house, my brother and his two college roommates and I, and had gone around the corner to a drugstore for cups of coffee. We sat for a while – the three of them talking and smoking and drinking coffee while I sipped at a glass of water – then we started off on a casual tour of the campus area that lasted until dinnertime.

Although I was just ten or eleven at the time, it was as though I had already read *Ulysses* and could thus recognize in my brother and his two friends a little troupe of sober, serious Buck Mulligans, leisurely strolling about the Dublinesque streets and talking to one another in their incomprehensible jargon. At first I tried listening to the strange, interminable words: "bourgeoisie...Dostoevski...Dos Passos." But I soon gave up, accepting the sound of them as a kind of verbal ferris wheel that was to turn continually above my head.

I remember that once during the morning I spoke tentatively of breakfast, but there was no reaction so afterward I remained quiet. We continued to drift on down the many tree-lined campus streets, in and out of boarding houses and conversations with tousle-haired young men still bedded in dark rooms. I soon lost any desire to enjoy this, my first trip around a college; I was getting too tired and too hungry. I was no longer even concerned about walking – about where and when to direct my steps. I simply wanted to remain true to my one last conscious need: to follow the long crack between my brother's right arm and his body and finally end up at a place where I could sit down.

As the quarter and half hours passed by, the reality of the morning gradually smudged and faded. My brother and his friends, and even the streets and the buildings, began to take on a kind of depthless, cardboard quality, like scenery in a play. It was as though we had walked so much and so far that we had finally walked straight out of reality and into a dream.

(I remember standing once on the corner of a busy intersection at the bottom of a hill. As I waited, the street before me ceased to be an ordinary street of concrete and stoplights and curbs, and became, somehow, a stretch of light gray water. Cars were racing past each other out in midstream like boats in a weird regatta, all with flags and streamers and the arms of white-shirted young men hanging in the windows. And as I glanced up at the three companions of my dream who were standing beside me – looking tranquilly out across the water – they appeared perfectly at home, as though it were simply their habit to stroll together each morning as we had done and ultimately wind up there to muse a while beside the small inland bay.)

It was sometime after twelve when we entered our last boarding house. At the sound of the opening front door heads of young men slid out from behind the pages of newspapers like those of mechanical dummies. They were out at all angles, watching us file across the living room toward the kitchen. As we passed they receded one by one behind the pages – like puppet heads drawn slowly offstage.

In the kitchen a small woman with white hair and a flowered apron patted me on the shoulder while my brother spoke some words to her about breakfast. She seated me at a long table with a clean tablecloth, and after a while the Negro cook brought me sausage and eggs. I remember how strange the food on the plate looked at dinner-time – as if it were not food at all but miniature lifeless figures stretched out on a round china slab: the three dark-brown Brookfield sausages resembling shriveled, bald-headed slaves and the two white-frilled fried eggs their heat-prostrated mistresses. I looked at the plate a long time, and the more I looked the more I began to remember how desperately I had wanted breakfast all morning long – until finally I was so overwhelmed by hunger that I could not eat.

I asked the cook where the bathroom was, and she very kindly pointed the way down the hall. But when I reached it I was out of luck there too: it was not just an ordinary bathroom, like the kind I used back home, but a holy temple of cleanliness, with sweet-smelling soaps and deodorizers and powders spread around like incense. It seemed out of the question to violate the sanctity of the commode so I closed the door quietly and left without doing my business. I went back to the living room. The young men were standing around in twos and threes, or sitting in front of windows, looking out, or lounging on the sofa behind the walls of their newspapers. Almost all were holding coffee cups now, some loudly discussing the afternoon game, some talking in the manner of my brother and his two friends – oblivious to everything except the steady sounds of their serious mouths.

For a while I sat and watched the shoe polish can on the fireplace mantel, and ties hanging on the backs of chairs. I smelled the bitterness of the sofa – a smell like a number of old unwashed dogs. The gas burning in the wall grates clung heavily and oppressively to the air, as though trying to wear it down and finally displace it so that no one could breathe. Newspapers turned incessantly in the room, their steady crackling like the popping of distant siege guns. And outside there were heavy cars that kept lunging uphill toward the football stadium.

It was here, in this heightened, close, unreal place, that I began trying to remember something that seemed important: who, or what had I been all those mornings before I started out on this one? What had happened to that person I had always known so familiarly as Me? Almost frantically I worked for an answer – right up to the moment when my head grew lighter and things began to swim in the room and I passed out cold under the whatnot stand.

# Raymond

He was doomed. He rode around town in his parents' blue Dodge, appearing for all the world aloof, untouchable, secure. But those who knew Raymond were not fooled by this old pose. They watched him drive past on his daily, pointless tours of his home town and they knew. They pitied him, yet they knew.

Sometimes pals of his high school days would come back to Kerrville on weekends or holidays, and they would try to re-create the bluff, hearty encounters of the past: "Say, man, how's it going...still closing up The Big Drive-In every night?" – then ingratiatingly, falsely confidential: "Say, Raymond, you gettin' any tail off these little high school gals?" With their token gestures of friendship they tried to establish continuity for Raymond from the high school days, tried to build a structure of people and events for him to cling to. But it didn't do any good. Raymond was lost. At twenty-six he was jobless, unmarried, still driving around the streets at night in his parents' car.

Raymond always seemed to be doomed, though for a while after he returned home from Korea his folks had a legitimate-sounding apology for him: "Raymond was ruined by the war. He just can't seem to pick up things again after being over there. So we just told him to take his time and feel his way around. He served his country, and that's more than a lot of these other boys can say." It was good Raymond's mother had that crutch for a while. It blotted out the old haunting notion of failure; it removed the guilt. Raymond had been to Korea, she could say, and it ruined him.

But to those who knew Raymond, living at home at twenty-six was just another predictable event in the long sad series. He had never done well in school – had just sort of sat in his chair with a freshly sharpened yellow pencil, looking puzzled. He was not popular with girls – too skinny, too shy – and he couldn't dribble a basketball more than twice or catch a pass.

The main reason Raymond got along in high school was because he could play the trumpet. Those rich, clear tones – they were his sole call to glory, the rock upon which his life was based. He played in the school dance band and got to wear a white coat with a purple boutonniere and use jazzman's lingo with his friends. And every afternoon he could go into his bedroom and practice his scales and imagine himself talking a chorus with Harry James or Billy Butterfield.

So at seventeen Raymond was still okay; he wasn't backed against a wall. He could still pretend to laugh when he read out the D's and F's on his report card. He could still ride around at night with the boys in his crowd and be the butt of their jokes because at least he was counted as one of them – as part of the group.

The deep strains of failure opened later – and of course people wondered if they were caused by his hearing loss. It was just a slight impairment at first, a kind of fuzziness in Raymond's left ear, but it was enough to discourage him from going on with his music. It provided him a good excuse for not auditioning with dance bands after he came back from Korea. Yes, a battlefield explosion might have caused Raymond to lose part of his hearing – as his mother maintained – or it could have been as the family doctor said: that Raymond's ear trouble had been coming on for years.

At any rate, Raymond never touched his horn again and stopped buying records. He just rode around town, not doing much of anything besides drinking beer and getting fat. Those who knew him watched and shook their heads and said, Jesus, how long can something like this go on?

# Saturday Night Dances

Outside is the West Texas darkness – bigger and blacker and emptier than any darkness has the right to be.  Inside is a Saturday night dance.

Call it Rob's Place, or The Hut, or The Highway Inn – it doesn't matter; such places are always the same in West Texas. The great dark dance floor is there, with tables scattered along the walls in red-checkered tablecloths. The string band is down at one end on a small stage, the players wearing elaborate Western dress. Quick-moving waitresses

– like white-aproned bees pollinating their customers with spore-filled bottles of beer – constantly thread their way through the surges of laughter and talk and dancing bodies.

The night has reached eleven o'clock and Little Leon is singing again. A small wiry man in a big Stetson, he stands close to the microphone and sings, "Slowly, I'm Fallin'," a favorite Webb Pierce recording. It's a lonesome tune, and as the dancers glide and pump across the floor they know it to be another of Their Songs, the kind that describes the loves and disappointments of their lives exactly as they happened – the way they themselves would tell about them if they only could find the words. The more Little Leon sings in his high mournful tenor, the more it seems to the dancing couples that they have at last died and gone to hillbilly heaven. They clutch one another in even greater embraces – the woman with her hand high and tight against her partner's neck, the man with his arm angled deep along a blue-jeaned hip and thigh – and they are satisfied that they hear the gospel and feel the glory.

But the tune finally ends, the spell breaks, and arm in arm the couples walk back to their table. Perhaps for a short distance a head of hair rests gratefully, peacefully, against a broad shoulder, and the man's circling arm is content around the warm, sweating waist. Then – like a tray of glasses being dashed to the floor – there are sudden bursts of laughter, and the heads pop erect and the circling arms fall away. For as the couples begin to rejoin their friends they find that the ritual of Table Hijinks is still in progress: ice cubes are still finding their way into shirt collars; gin bottles are still being knocked over; giggles and hoo-raws and shoulder slappings are still the lifeblood of dance-hall camaraderie. And as the dancers settle themselves before the familiar rows of beer cans and liquor bottles and ashtrays, the sweet-sad heaven of Webb Pierce fades into the surrounding night – replaced once again by the oh-so-solid earth of Rob's Place.

# My Uncle Mitch

Every kid should have an Uncle Mitch. He was what kids and uncles are all about.

Mitch met my Aunt Geneva – Neva, to the family – when he was working as an oil field roustabout in the early 1930s. My aunt was teaching school in Texon, a little West Texas oil field town. For two years she was undecided about Mitch – there were other beaus, other plans and possibilities. For two years they rattled along dusty oil field roads into San Angelo, down across the border to night spots in Villa Acuña. Then she decided yes – and it was a twosome, a team, for life. (I've looked at them dozens of times in the family photograph albums: Neva, the heart-faced beauty with plucked, arched eyebrows – a dead-ringer for Clara Bow, the "It Girl" of the silent movies; and Mitch, the big, blond, smiling Irishman: the man's man.)

Soon after they married Mitch was transferred by Plymouth Oil to Sinton, thirty miles from Corpus Christi on the South Texas coast. They lived in a little white frame house with crushed shell in the driveway and oleanders in the yard. They had no children those first years of marriage and it seemed as if they never would. They had, instead, each other – and Jerry, their Airedale. (Jerry: they stood him on his hind legs between them in the black-and-white Kodak photographs: Jerry at the beach, Jerry in the front seat of their old Plymouth: Jerry, grinning, between the handsome young Mitch and the pretty young Geneva: Jerry, their substitute child.)

Then, as it happens, after years had passed, a child was born: beautiful, by all accounts, as his parents were beautiful: Michael Lanier, who was born on a cold January morning and who lived six days.

Mitch loved to fish, and so did I. When I would visit them he would load Dr. Peppers in his huge ice chest and get his tackle box with the two levered trays filled with hooks and lures and lines and weights, and we would take off for Port Aransas. We would walk out on the pier and Mitch would establish our spot. I would stay with him all day without complaint, casting and casting, as if nothing else mattered in the world except watching my cork on the blue-gray water and listening to the swells as they lapped beneath us against the pilings.

I think that big men, when they are patient and kind, are the kindest and most patient men of all. Mitch never lost his temper at some miscue of mine. If I accidentally kicked our sack of bait shrimps off the pier, Mitch would laugh and lumber off down the pier in his old Stetson and khakis to buy some more. Since he had no son to show things to, Mitch showed them to me. He took pleasure in my pleasure instead of his own. He showed me how to fix my line for salt water fishing (the weight is placed lower, the triple hook is up above); how to peel shrimp and what part to use as bait (not the head); how to cast and when to reel in; how to clean fish and gut them; what to do when I caught a scavenger catfish and it jabbed me with its toxic gaff as I took it off the hook (put some of Mitch's wet tobacco chew on it).

Mitch talked to me in the same easy way he talked to everyone else: the filling station attendant in Sinton, the grocery store clerk, the cafe owner. He liked people and liked talking to them; he liked to tell jokes and anecdotes and stories. He liked to explain how things worked. When he would take me out with him to the oil leases, he would point with his cigar out the window at a new oil well pumping in a clearing of mesquites and then spend the next fifteen minutes telling me how deep it was, who drilled it, how many barrels a day it would bring. He never talked down to me just because I was eleven years old.

Sure, I didn't stay a kid forever and he didn't always have to sell milk and eggs on weekends to supplement his income. He began to get into the oil business a bit himself and gravitated toward big cars, a big house, big money. And sure, life caught up with him: cataracts, eye surgery, and finally cancer (I would call his hospital room and talk to his nurse and would listen over 600 miles of long distance as he screamed with pain that morphine no longer eased).

My aunt lives alone now in a two-story house with her twelve dogs, television set, and reclining chair. All the big money is long gone. During my last visit to see her she said she still wasn't ready to "go," but if she did it was all right. She had her cemetery plot paid for right next to Mitch.

# Waiting for Dinner

It is Sunday dinner time on the farm near Robstown, and while the women finish getting the meal ready in the house the men bring their chairs outside and put them on the pale-green carpet grass underneath the front-yard mesquites. They sit there for an hour or more, smoking, looking out into the bright South Texas noon, talking country talk in the mesquite shade.

In one corner of the yard several young cousins stand a good way apart, playing catch. They face each other rather stiffly, with the special, sober formality of family get-togethers. They don't throw or catch nearly as well as they can at more natural times. They miss frequently and have to chase the ball over to where the men are sitting in the chairs. When this happens one of the men casually moves his leg or tilts back his chair and then, giving but one brief uninvolved glance downward to where the boy's hand is reaching, he goes ahead to scratch himself gently in the crotch or ribs and settle himself again to the easy mesquite-shaded talk.

Next to the porch steps on the concrete front walk a small, pretty, fat baby sits spraddled before a fox terrier, playing. He waves his hands vaguely in the air before his face like antennae, and the fox terrier occasionally ventures bold yet shyly self-conscious licks into the baby's face — very careful, tender licks, as though he knows exactly what a strange and marvelous and helpless thing a human baby is.

Outside the yard, on the top of a telephone pole, a mockingbird lets bright twisting scraps of song flow from his throat. He is almost like a vocal kaleidoscope, using snatches of varied and colored sound in place of glass. Sometimes when the mood strikes him he rises above the pole in high elegant jumps, sustaining himself in the air on balancing wings almost like an African ceremonial dancer strutting and leaping grandly about in ostrich feathers.

Away from the house, cotton fields are spread out like mild green lakes, and midday heat hovers closely about them in an almost masculine anxiety – as if the green planted rows are harems of vulnerable women to be guarded fiercely from an enemy world.

The noon wears on, and in the yard the men continue to speak their dinnertime words about cotton prices and Mexican laborers and politics with the same measured ease as the mesquite limbs above them move their long yellowish beans in the mild May breeze. They sit with comfortably crossed legs, their polished boots curving up in solid and restful arcs like dark shining scimitars. Those who smoke continue to hold their cigarettes and cigars down close to their chairs – and periodically, like indolent spiders moving about on a web, their fingers perform a kind of tentative dance as they join for a moment to idly flick the ashes away.

# Sanctuary

That little concrete porch at the front of a Baptist church in a small Texas town – I think about it, wondering what it really meant. At three o'clock on a July afternoon, when the sun had finally moved its fierceness toward the west and left the porch in an elegant shadow, what truth did the porch suggest that somehow made it memorable?

I try thinking of the little knots of faithful Baptist men and women who gather there every Sunday, in the hot times of the morning and in the cool of the afternoon. I can see them on that modest and smooth concrete, finding comfort not only as Baptists but as Baptists-joining-together-in-a-very-small-town.... I think of the young, untried boys in dress pants and white shirts ( – indeed, Baptist Boys, soon to take on their special role as Baptist Men) who talk among themselves in the long Sunday twilights: who gather on their pants the white dust of summer from straggling clumps of Johnson grass beside the porch as they speak knowingly of things they do not understand.

Yet as I consider the porch – the way it was one hot weekday afternoon – I remember that the strong Baptist feeling was absent. It was just an ordinary square of shade – a porch offering relief to anyone who might be walking by and finding himself in need of a place to rest.... And that, I suppose, was at the root of the emotion I felt: The knowledge that such a small white wooden church, sitting so staunchly on its dusty side street, was actually irrelevant to the town except for the aesthetics of its cement porch. *Aesthetics*...a Baptist church having as its only real claim to glory a pleasant bit of shade: having its porch become what the church itself had tried futilely to become for everyone, at all times and in all weathers, yet never succeeded in becoming: a refuge, a sanctuary.

# No

It was a typical South Texas night – vacant and huge, with darkness and heavy warmth drawn like a languid curtain across the land – and a few cars had stopped for beers at a small highway cafe. Several men sat inside at the tables, talking; a couple of Mexican braceros in old hats and denim jackets stood in front of the doorway, smoking and waiting for the bus to come along from the valley.

A young man and his girl remained parked in their car outside the cafe. They were not talking. The young man drank coffee while the girl sat slumped against her door, looking out at a mimosa tree that grew at the corner of the cafe. She reached her hand out the window once toward the tree, as though to touch it, but the tree was too far away. She let her arm die slowly against the side of the car.

The young man watched her as he drank his coffee. Finally he lowered his cup and looked out his own window at the highway.

"Look," he said, "you want to split a beer? Just one very small beer? This really is rotten coffee. And I promise: only one this time. One and no more."

He looked at her and waited, but the girl didn't make a reply. She still faced out her window, toward the mimosa tree. Finally she turned and looked at him and then she let her head drop back against the seat. She began to shake her head no, rolling on her neck back and forth across the top of the seat. It seemed the last and only thing in the world she wanted to do.

The young man looked at her and left the car with his coffee cup and went inside the cafe. When he returned to the car the girl was huddled down against her door, quiet but not crying. She still had not put her lipstick back on.

The young man did not look at her anymore. He tilted his beer bottle, taking very small sips, and watched the summer bugs crowd against the one lone bulb above the door of the cafe. Across the highway in the bar ditches, crickets sang steadily from their weeds. And every now and then the heavy monotony of the night was broken by a car passing by, going south in the darkness toward Mexico.

# Virility: Bewitchment

The young South Texas rancher waited with his trained fighting cocks, one under each arm, until his friends from Alice and Kingsville had gathered around him in a circle beside the barn. Then he put the cocks on the ground and stepped back.

As they fought he moved about them with his muscular, unhurried step — casually, the way a rodeo performer walks away dusting his hat after he has successfully ridden a Brahma bull, or the way a high-school football hero leaves the downtown drugstore on the Saturday

morning after a big game. He moved as though his body were a hugely estimable thing – comparable to a cloud moving along in the sky or
one of the seasons changing.

He stood there in the clearing, saying nothing, charging the cock
fight with the tension of his bullish silence, using it almost as a tangible force the way someone else would use fists or words. And though
his manner bordered on a kind of laziness, it was the restrained laziness of a well-fed lion moving idly about. His heavy shoulders and
thighs seemed to swagger inside his body, in a careless sloshing about
of weight and bulk. He had a match in his mouth, and as he watched
the two cocks he lolled it vacantly with his tongue. He was so full of
nonchalance and self-assurance that he seemed ready at any moment
to lift up his boot and rest it against thin air, the way he would indoors
against a chair rung or the railing of a bar.

Suddenly, without any apparent cause, he spat away his match
and reached down and grabbed both cocks, mastering and quietening
them in the same instant. Neither of them had decisively beaten the
other – perhaps he was just piqued at some flaw in their performance.
He opened the barn door with a single quick movement of his knee,
went inside, and then pulled the door shut after him by reaching back
and hooking it with his boot.

Maybe what seemed to happen next did not really occur at all. It
had been a long hot Sunday afternoon, with the drifting hours falling
away into a kind of lazy vagueness and unreality – so maybe the group
of friends just imagined it. Maybe they just succumbed to an August
illusion created by too much heat and Carta Blanca beer. But several of
them swore it happened: that they were staring straight at the closed
door when they saw the whole barn begin to tremble and rise from its
foundation – like the cyclone-lifted farmhouse in *The Wizard of Oz* –
and then fly with theatrical slowness out of sight beyond the trees.

Those who were bewitched the strongest say that they could not
only follow the barn out of sight but could also see right through the
door – could see him standing there behind it, one cock resting under

each arm, a new match lolling under his tongue. He seemed wholly unconcerned, just waiting patiently for the barn to land.

Well, they say, it did land – far off toward the Gulf in a mesquite and chaparral clearing. But when the barn door opened and the young rancher stepped out, he emerged not with the two cocks but with two beautiful young women – each of his huge arms circling their slim and graceful waists. And though his friends at the ranch kept straining their eyes eastward, that was all they could see – just the three figures walking away into the brush with the coastal twilight beginning to settle about them in an almost magical swirl.

# Out-of-town Game

Since it was Friday and the day of the first out-of-town game, Harvey Adkins closed his hardware store earlier than usual and drove home along the narrow, familiar, hometown streets, thinking about his kids. Buddy, his oldest boy, had already left with the team in midafternoon: The big yellow school bus had come lumbering through the center of town and Harvey had managed to get a glimpse of it as it headed south down the highway. His daughter Jenevelyn – well, if things were going along as they should, Harvey figured the band buses ought to be pulling away from the school parking lot any minute now. He hoped she wouldn't forget her clarinet in the bleachers like she did the week before. And Carl – Harvey smiled as he eased his Plymouth into the driveway because sure enough, there was his nine-year-old waiting for him on the front porch steps. He looked well scrubbed and had his tan windbreaker lying across his knee.

Stepping out of the car Harvey Adkins noticed that a light breeze had sprung up – not much of one for September, not even anything strong enough to be called a breeze, really; just a kind of cool edge to the air that was drifting in from the north.  But it was air enough, he thought, plenty to make you think about fall and football on a warm South Texas afternoon. And with his front yard smelling fresh the way it was — why, he seemed there already, in the stands, breathing in the night air and the grass of the football field.

Harvey squeezed between the car and the hedge and winked at Carl waiting for him on the steps. Harvey knew how his boy felt — knew he wasn't in the mood to jump around and pull on you and yell Daddy-hurry-up, the way Carl usually did. He was just sitting there quietly, feeling the excitement of the game in the air — that little something extra added to a Friday afternoon.

Harvey was almost to the porch before he saw the Neismiths backing out of their driveway, leaving for the game. Harvey waved and called out, "Think we got much of a chance, Bill?" The man dipped his head and hat expressively in the window and called back, "Boyyy, Harvey, it's gonna be *rough*." He smiled, then let his hand dangle outside his window in a trailing, spraddle-fingered good-bye while he carefully guided his car into the street. Harvey exchanged a final wave with Bill's wife and two girls before turning and starting into the house. On the steps he squeezed Carl's shoulder and said, "Well, now...looks like I might have to take *somebody* to a *football* game."

The game was eighty miles away in Freer, a little South Texas oil town. By leaving right at five-thirty Harvey could get on down there by about six forty-five, have time for a bite to eat, and still get out to the field before the teams started warming up. It was a straight new highway and by just keeping on sixty and sixty-five he could make good time.

He put on a clean white shirt and his brown-checked sport coat and kept on the tie he wore to work; Harvey's wife got the same blanket to sit on she had been carrying to ball games for no telling how long — and with a final round of shutting windows and locking doors they were off. Carl sat in the back seat by the window, ready to look out at the oil wells and mesquites that stretched into the distance.

Harvey's town was a strong one for supporting its football team so the road to an out-of-town game was always crowded. High school kids soon began to pass Harvey and the slower traffic – their horns blaring, the maroon-and-white crepe paper streamers whipping around from their aerials and bumpers – and as they waved and yelled Harvey smiled and waved a little in return. But he shook his head to himself after they passed. He knew most of their parents – some of them had been good customers of his for over fifteen years – and he wondered how grown, sensible people could let their kids out loose like that. Harvey remarked about it to his wife; she listened and agreed, and both of them watched with concern as the fast cars scooted on down the road.

Freer was not a big game – just the second one of the season – and it didn't have any of the real tenseness that went along with the last games at Laredo and Corpus Christi. So as the afternoon faded into a long twilight Harvey let his thoughts slip away from football for a while. His wife wanted to know how the new water sprinklers were selling and if the tall woman with the lisp ever came back after her dozen horseshoes. Mrs. Adkins kept books part time at the store and she always liked to stay in touch with things.  She and Harvey talked while the miles slid by.

The only towns Harvey passed on the way down were two small gas-and-cafe places. Going through them he spotted familiar cars pulled in at filling stations with small clusters of people standing around drinking Cokes and eating candy bars and gazing vacantly toward the road. A large man in a brown suit recognized Harvey's Plymouth as it went by and the man lifted his Coke bottle in a wave.

The closer Harvey got to Freer the stronger the gas smells became – the horizon on both sides of the highway glowing here and there with orange oil well flares – and the more the darkening land settled into the peace of a warm South Texas night. Harvey and his family sat for a while without talking, just enjoying the nice close feeling of being together on a trip. Harvey began to slow down to a comfortable fifty-five as the lights of Freer grew steadily larger, and he opened his window wing to let in more cool air. At the outskirts of town a roadrunner darted in front of the headlights and sailed a little way before disappearing into the darkness and mesquites.

The B-and-B Cafe in Freer was crowded so Harvey and his family had to stand until a table was cleared. As he waited Harvey saw people from his home town studying menus, sipping ice water, eating chicken fried steaks – and looking around every once in a while to see who else had come in. Newcomers kept arriving as others were leaving, and everyone tried to get in a little quick, casual visiting – laying a hand on a shoulder, giving a short loud laugh before moving on toward the cash register with parting waves. Harvey finally slipped his family over to a table, and by seven-thirty they had their hamburgers eaten and were starting out to the football field.

Both the school parking lot and the road leading to it from the cafe were unpaved so the air was filled with a big cloud of white caliche dust. But if there was one thing Harvey didn't mind on a mild September night, it was a little caliche dust.  No matter where he smelled it during the year, it always reminded him of fall nights like this one – when the cars were streaming into the parking lot with their headlights long and bouncing; when the late band kids were running toward the gate carrying an instrument and their wobbly plumed hat in one hand and no telling what else in the other; when the big yellow school buses from Harvey's home town were lined up side by side next to the stadium fence and somehow making him have a nice full feeling of pride (making him think: Well, there they are, part of our town.... They made it all right, like they always do; and after the game they'll make it back home carrying my boy.... Funny: on my way to work in the morning I'll drive by and see those buses sitting there back of the gym and it'll seem like they never moved – as if this whole business tonight was just another one of my dreams).

So he couldn't help it: when Harvey bought his tickets from the teacher seated in the lighted booth and ushered his wife and son in front of him through the gate, he couldn't help but feel good. Buddy was going to be on the field in a little while – on the second team, of

course, and without much chance of playing very often, but still playing. And Jenevelyn was in the band that was going to do some kind of
high-stepping business at halftime. And with the rest of his family
there next to him contented and waiting – well, it was just not a bad
feeling at all. Right at that moment Harvey guessed he wouldn't trade
places with any other man in the world.

For one thing, Harvey Adkins simply *liked* football games – not
only the game itself but the feeling of companionship or whatever it
was he had by just being with all the people there in the stands. He
liked the yells of the Boy Scouts as they worked up and down the
aisles with their buckets of cold drinks, and the smell of cigar smoke
and popcorn and hot coffee in the pleasant night air. He liked watching the calisthenics on the field – the boys out in a big circle going
"One!...two!...three!...four!" in their hoarse way while they did push-
ups and side-straddle-hops. And when game time finally arrived –
when everyone stood up and the band played the national anthem –
he liked to feel Carl's hand edge over and take hold of his coat sleeve.
His hand always stayed there while the starting whistle blew and the
two teams scattered through each other on the kickoff and the ball
carrier was finally tackled; then, as the roar of the crowd faded and
everyone sat back down and began to get settled, his son's hand
slipped away.

It was a good, close game. Harvey's home town held its lone
touchdown lead throughout both halves and when the final gun
sounded and the cheerleaders and students rushed on the field Harvey
felt that his team had played pretty fair ball but was also pretty lucky.
Freer seemed to have the better team a lot of the time.

As the crowd began to file out of the bleachers Harvey and his
family moved along with it – slowly, patiently, advancing one step at a
time, just kind of attaching themselves to a little piece of space and letting it do the drifting forward. Harvey's eyes rested comfortably on
familiar sights – broken Coke bottles underneath the wooden bleachers; ticket stubs lying in the gravel; lone persons standing off to the

side, watching intently for someone in the crowd. Mrs. Adkins walked
in front and Harvey rested his hand easily on Carl's shoulder.

Going through the gate Harvey saw the Neismiths headed
toward their car. Harvey called out: "Well, we sure had to have us a little luck with this one, didn't we, Bill?" The Neismiths turned, smiling.
Bill said he was sure glad to hear that final gun; he didn't know how
much longer one touchdown was going to hold out: "...That
Hesseltine, number 12, I'm sure glad he never got loose. He was a *fast*
little booger, wasn't he?" He shook his head, remembering Hesseltine
and his short wild runs; then he raised his hand, showing Harvey and
his family his flat palm in a friendly goodnight.

Harvey waited a while and finally was able to ease his Plymouth
out of its parking place and into a line of cars leaving a side exit. He
went the half mile or so back to the center of town, turned at the
highway, and headed north for the drive back home. Looking out his
window he caught a final glimpse of the high rows of field lights dimly
bright above the horizon, then he and Mrs. Adkins began talking over
the game – the people they saw; Buddy and Jenevelyn. Mrs. Adkins
wondered if Buddy should keep on with football, as small as he was
and as little as he got to play. Harvey said Well, he didn't think it hurt
him any; and besides, all his friends went out so the boy felt like he
almost had to.

The two of them talked, staring ahead at the road and the passing cars that kept disappearing into the darkness. At first Carl sat forward on the back seat, listening, but soon he fixed his jacket into a pillow and went to sleep. And, as always, Mrs. Adkins tried to stay awake
to make conversation – feeling it was her duty to help keep Harvey
from getting drowsy when he drove late at night. But the silences
between them grew longer, and before many miles passed Harvey saw
her head begin to drop slowly forward and then snap back – until it
finally steadied itself against the door.

Harvey shifted about at the wheel, hunching his shoulders several
times and stretching his leg muscles. He yawned once – a long, slow-

motioned yawn that made him rear his head back, close his eyes, and spread his mouth widely into a kind of teeth-clenching, sober grin. Immediately after the yawn he felt very tired and very relaxed. He took himself a comfortable new hold on the steering wheel, his hands grasped firmly around it and spread farther apart than usual. As the familiar roadside park glided by on the left he looked at his watch and thought: Well, we ought to be home a little after twelve if I don't have to stop for coffee. And with his family asleep and the night dark around him, Harvey Adkins kept his car moving steadily on down the road.

# Suzy

Suzy wasn't beautiful – not the way boys think college girls ought to be beautiful. She wore her hair cut short and brushed to the back of her neck in a kind of ducktail, she was skinnyish and she had freckles scattered across her forehead and underneath her eyes. But somehow you never got around to thinking about classic features when you looked at Suzy; you never remembered to see anything except her fluid grace, or cloudy blue eyes, or that childlike, almost beatific smile that curved up just enough – a smile as fresh and pure as morning.

I met her one afternoon at a park near the campus, on a day that was falling all over itself with spring. Children were yelling "Annie-Over" far across the baseball field, the trees were bursting with lush-ness – almost screaming inside themselves, *"We're green! We're green!"* – and black grackles were everywhere, wheezing and gliding through the clean dampness coming up from the creek.

I was lying on the grass, trying to study, when I glanced up and saw her standing on the narrow wooden bridge that arched across the creek. She was looking at me – her arms folded over her breast, hold-ing her books – and she was smiling. Maybe it was that smile, or the way her head was tilted back, with a long pencil angled through her hair, or the shine of her pink sweater in the sunlight; maybe it was just me, feeling lonesome. Maybe it was the deep-green afternoon. Whatever it was, it was enough to make me brush the grass off my pants and walk over to her.

We talked for a little while casually, and then, holding her books with one arm, she carefully began to pick grass off my shirt. Maybe that was part of it too – her touching me so easily and naturally, almost intimately, as if she were reaching over and straightening her husband's collar at a train-station farewell. I asked her if she wanted to swing on the swings, the afternoon being so pleasant and all. She laughed and nodded yes, and together we strolled off across the shadowed, four-o'clock grass.

That's how it was in the beginning – the two of us just walking along through those great, dimmed spaces of cathedral light, saying half-cautious, half-excited words. We let our hands trail idly against the trees in passing, and when we got to the swings Suzy put her books on the ground with a pleasing and exact efficiency – as though she had long before rehearsed and mastered the minor physical business of how to place books – and then she sat on one of the boards and I began to push her. She made a lovely sight: her slim legs pointed toward the surrounding trees, her head dropped back into a kind of wild-Indian pose, her laughter drifting behind her like a banner in the lazy air of the park.

There was no real sequence to the days that followed. Time became a kaleidoscopic present, with days and places revolving around us like fragments of pastel-colored glass. We took prodigious walks, roaming across town in the long, spacious afternoons. We found snake-spit cones glistening like snow in the weeds of the vacant lots, and tire swings filled with birds' nests in people's yards. We watched small boys sitting alone in wagons, crying, while their older sisters left them on the sidewalk and ran inside the house and never came out; and in a downtown alley a small, amber Pekingese stared down at us from a dirty second-story window with sad, squinting eyes. And once we found a fat green caterpillar with orange stripes curled on the glossy leaf of a magnolia tree. We put him in an empty jar and carried him with us — lying on his piece of leaf like a small, indolent Buddha.

Sometimes we went to a vacant lot behind Suzy's dormitory, where brush and boards were piled high in the tall grass. I would first poke around to see about snakes and then both of us would crawl deep into the grass. The afternoon sunlight just barely filtered through, and the heavy, rotting smells of lumber and grass sent up a heady incense. We would sit there side by side, doing some of our best talking — about jazz, and Thurber, and how good the smell of shrimp was on your hands when you went fishing down on the Gulf coast.

And I think it was there, in that snug brush cave, that Suzy told me about the time she broke her arm — how she had dressed up in a black robe and floppy hat and jumped out her window one night into a fraternity pinning party on the lawn, yelling that she was Cyrano de Bergerac falling from the moon. I can still hear that laugh of hers when she was tickled by her own tales. It always seemed to touch her inside and excite something deep and sensitive and almost sexual. She would laugh and tighten her body and bring her elbows in close to her sides, as if wanting to keep the laughter within her as long as possible and enjoy its exquisite richness.

Love? Well, yes, but not at first — not when we were just barreling along across the days. I don't think I loved anything in the beginning except my own sense of freedom, my own joy. We were too delighted in the sense and touch of each other, too pleased with ourselves and the days.

Then one afternoon something happened — not much, really, just an inevitable refocusing on familiar things. We met as usual after our last class, went walking, and on our way back to the campus stopped at a drugstore. It was a hot day and the ceiling fan was going lazily around, blowing a little Dr. Pepper sign at the end of a string. We were just sitting there in a booth, spooning away at our ice cream, when we happened to glance over at the sign and then back at each other. I don't know what it was, exactly, but at that moment we seemed to *perceive* each other – to understand in a split second how strange and awesome another person actually is.

I remember that we glanced back down and began eating again in our first self-conscious silence. We knew a curious thing had happened – as though we had accidentally seen each other naked – so we toyed with our paper napkins and pretended to watch people passing by on the sidewalk. We kept sneaking glances across the table and always caught the other watching. Even after we left the drugstore the new awkwardness persisted, and as we walked back to Suzy's dormitory we spoke to each other with shy, almost courteous words.

It was later the same week, I think, the night we went to hear Louis Armstrong at a dance over on the east side of town, that I first realized what Suzy meant to me. It was during intermission when I left our table and went to find the men's room. I had put my hand on the restroom door and turned around to look back at Suzy – and just seeing her made my heart jump. I guess it was her being there alone, in the middle of all the cigarette haze and white tablecloths and surging bodies. She was holding her glass in that special way of hers – not casually or idly, but almost earnestly, clasping it tightly the way a child would. Perhaps it was simply that – her looking so isolated, so incomplete without me there beside her; or maybe it was her sitting so erect and motionless, as if suddenly fixed in time and space. I don't know what I saw or what it meant, but right then I felt the first strange stir of love.

Afterward we walked down the moonlit streets. We swung our hands and sang loud bars of foolish songs while dogs ran out to the fences and barked. I remember that I could just barely make out the figures of people sitting on their dark front porches, talking about us in low voices. And I remember too that we finally stopped somewhere in a vacant lot beneath a lone, shadowing tree, and while cars with bouncing headlights rattled by and the lush spring night throbbed around us, we held each other as if the only reality in the world were made of lips and hands and warm, moist skin.

It was about the middle of May, with final exams right on us, that we decided to study out at the lake on the edge of town. I was going to borrow my cousin's car so we could start out early and make a day of it. But when I got to her dormitory the house-mother told me Suzy was feeling sick and probably didn't want to go out. Suzy was in the kitchen, she said, if I wanted to talk to her.

I found her perched on a little kitchen serving table, peeling an orange. She had on blue jeans and a man's long-sleeved shirt with the tail hanging out. Her face was pale and the freckles on her forehead stood out like little scabs. She looked worn and thin and pitiful and ugly. At first she started to smile – to make some kind of joke of it all – then suddenly she jumped off the table and ran to the sink and vomited. I held her, bracing her shoulders and putting my hand across her forehead, and after a while she shuddered and sank against me. I got a dish towel and wiped her face. (Looking back on it now, it seems almost like a kind of primitive marriage ceremony: holding her tightly, vowing without words to protect her, in sickness and in health.)

Suzy went to bed after that, but when I went back in the afternoon she was feeling better. She got her books and we drove out toward the lake. It was a fine, warm afternoon, and as we drove past the new subdivision houses their crushed-tile roofs were blazing in the sun. We turned onto a partly graded road and stopped in front of a long ravine that ran down to the edge of the lake. There were a lot of Spanish oaks and sycamores rimming the ravine, and when I turned off the motor we sat for a long while listening to the leaves moving in the breeze coming off the water. Suzy wanted the sound up close so I got out and cut some branches from the trees and then stuck them around the car. For the rest of the afternoon we listened to leaves scraping lazily across the windshield while we studied.

When it was dusk we walked down into the ravine. The air was heavy and chilled, and birds on the hillsides made frantic little settling noises for a while; then, as if finally smothered by the dampness and gathering silence, they were still. There was an immense quiet, and as we walked across the floor of the ravine the twigs broke beneath our feet with intimate, brittle sounds.

After it became fully dark we sat on the ground against a log, Suzy's arms around my legs and her head in my lap. I ran my hand slowly over her face and lips and across her hair, and I began to tell her how it would be when we were married. I don't remember all the words, but I told her how we would get a cabin on some mountainside out West, and how we would go down every morning to the lake below and watch some old fisherman give us his toothless, bless-you-young-folks smile. I told her how we would speak to everybody along the bank and examine all the early catches, and how every now and then we would look at each other and want to touch so badly we couldn't stand it. I told her how in the afternoons, about dark, we would go outside our cabin and put our arms around each other and watch the lights blinking on down below.

And I was just getting started, actually – telling how later on we would have children, a couple of really terrific kids – when I felt the wetness of her face on my arm and her moving away from me, saying, "Oh, honey, stop, please stop, I can't stand it any more," and heard her crying hard against the ground.

I did not know, of course, that for four years she had been engaged – that in June she was to be married to a West Point cadet beneath crossed swords. She had never mentioned this home-town boyfriend of hers, and I had never bothered to ask if there was anyone else. Maybe she had kept stalling for time, hoping to find an easy way to tell me – or perhaps, as her roommate insisted later, she was actually going to break off the engagement. I can't say. All I know is that the afternoon at the lake was our last day together. Before the week was out she flew to New York, leaving her books and a closet half full of clothes. She didn't take her exams or even say good-bye.

I have never quite figured out that long intimate spring; it has remained an unfinished chapter in my life. And although I gradually came to accept the end of it, and Suzy, I am even now, ten years later, strongly susceptible to memories of her. Whenever I walk down some fresh-smelling, tree-lined street I can almost hear, once again, Joe Mooney singing "Nina Never Knew" on a car radio and feel Suzy's slim, taut body swinging along close to mine. I can still visualize the way her hair strung down across her cheeks as she waited for me on a street corner in a pouring rain – can almost see her fingertips as she took my face in her hands because it was April and life was good and we were in love.

# An Excursion into Mr. Reade

We can begin almost anywhere with Mr. Reade. Let's catch him at the movies. There he is, at the side, by himself. He's unmistakable, even in the dark. Hear his little strained "huh-um," that fast automatic clearing of the throat? And now watch how he handles what is for most of us the rather routine business of sitting. First, there are the legs: should they be kept crossed, or perhaps firmly straight down? Or how about buckling them under and sitting on them, yogi style? See, he tries each position for a while, finds it...what – unsuitable? uncomfortable? Who can say, except that it is all a matter of nerves – and indeed, what else *is* Mr. Reade than a matter of nerves? And arms: what shall they be: crossed, or a bit akimbo? Or, as a compromise, how about each hand gripping a knee?

You see, it doesn't really matter where we start our excursion – at his school, in a movie, at the zoo. Mr. Reade will be the same quiet, hoarse-voiced, throat-clearing, arms-akimbo young man in all places, staring out at the world from his body-prison with his unblinking, sometimes frightened eyes.

Mr. Reade – twenty-nine, unmarried, rather solidly built – directed the Davy Crockett Junior High School Band in San Antonio, Texas.
Back in his college days in Iowa he had seriously considered the trumpet as a career and he would sit for long hours practicing, his feet
squarely on the floor, his elbows out at proper angles. He would have
looked very good had he gone on with his plans: perhaps a little too
tense for supper-club combos but excellent with the serious Young
School of a Kenton-type group or even the Cities Service Band of
America. With his fine posture, his solid frame, the green-and-white
trim-fitting Cities Service uniform, he could have stood up with the
Trumpet Trio and made precisioned, biting flashes of sound.

Yet he found he did not want the trumpet as a career and lost
faith in a traveling musician's life.

"Nuts!" he said quietly to himself one day, and ended up after
graduation in the public schools.

As a teacher Mr. Reade was a good man and very kind and
patient. But he was hard to get to know. His students and fellow teachers considered him too formal and private. And besides, he had grown
a small, tufted, reddish beard.

But we must get deeper than this into Mr. Reade. We must find
the essence of the man. Is there some catch phrase, some easy summa-
ry that can focus our attention on the basics of Mr. Reade? Well, let's
say this: Mr. Reade was, above everything else, a highly conscious
man. There was no sluggishness in him. Awareness resided in him like
a jeweler's polishing rag, and it kept shining the facets of his percep-
tions until they stood illumined in his mind like rows of quiet, glistening gems. But also he was a human chameleon, responding not to
color changes but to every emotional nuance that touched his atmosphere. Thus, Mr. Reade had become over the years a very much ill-at-
ease man, highly *self*-conscious, sensitized to himself and his surroundings the way a blind man is to the various surfaces of his room.

Mr. Reade, being not merely a charged set of wires and pulleys
and controlling neurons but human flesh as well, had habits and tastes

in addition to a high intelligence. But they too marked him and set him aside as a nineteenth-century man obligated to find a suitable niche in the modern jet age. He was – to cite examples – a ten-dollar-leatherbound-volume man surrounded by thirty-five-cent paperbacks; a Haydn-and-Beethoven man confronted on all sides by Fats Domino and Little Richard. He was an onion-soup, green-salad, and an hour-or-so-for-lunch man faced with swallowing the sixty-nine-cent Walgreen special. He was even a straight-razor-and-leather-strop man in an electric-razor bathroom.

Mr. Reade became, then, a study in control, in self-discipline, and this is what made him tense. The constant rub of himself against the world – both surfaces greased by the clear light fluid of his awareness – caused Mr. Reade to stand before life as a knotted fist.

What was he obligated to control – his mind? that smoothly-operating machine? No, it obviously controlled him. It was his body, his public image, that he had to beware of.

His body was of a rather stout frame, giving no indication to a casual onlooker either of neurasthenic heightening or of animal grace. Mr. Reade knew this, had felt his body move awkwardly in tennis and basketball, had known that only its bulk had made it serviceable as a guard on the high school football team. Mr. Reade, from a child, knew about bodies.

The head – what of it? Well, the body had been saddled with a rather grim one, a Java man's head, which, to the same casual onlooker, might seem more interesting for its construction than for its contents. It looked as though the skull's framework had been wire ribs covered with papier-mâché. Then, apparently, rough freckled skin had been stretched tightly across the dried, protruding mâché bones. Finally, both the top of the skull and the chin had been seeded with brownish-red hair. The top hairs, upon growing out, were trimmed off to make a flat field of skull-bristles. The chin ones, a poor crop, were allowed to remain in a straggling force.

Where, in such surroundings, did the consciousness of Mr. Reade greet the outer world? Where could one hope to find the soul of this complex young man?

In the eyes. Only the eyes were not subjected to the forces of Mr. Reade's control and discipline, and they seemed to stare out at the world like the images of two forgotten children locked high in some prison tower. They not only watched but seemed to listen, too, as if over the years the burden of alertness and concern had become so acute that they could not afford to trust the ears any more than they could the body. Sometimes, if the light was in them just right, they seemed like the eyes of a stallion locked in a barn who is constantly smelling smoke but has no possible way to escape if a fire should break out.

In the late fall of his first school year a thing happened to Mr. Reade, and it was all brought on by Delilah Barrera. Delilah was a shy Mexican-American girl who played second clarinet in the junior high band. She always wore her black hair in a neat, bouncing ponytail, and her round serious Indian face was a truly happy moon when she smiled. She wore neat starched dresses, carried her clarinet home each night to practice, and always tried to please Mr. Reade.

At the first of school Delilah had been afraid of Mr. Reade and his small reddish beard. He never seemed to smile like the other teachers and he spoke so quietly and pronounced his words so surely that Delilah did not ever want to do a wrong thing in band and get Mr. Reade angry at her. Sometimes when he went through the sections and asked members to play a line from a march for him, Delilah's heart would beat so hard she could not get anything but squeaks from her clarinet. Mr. Reade would never scold her but spoke to her quietly and kindly, and after a while she could make the notes come out as they should.

As the months passed Delilah began to be less afraid of Mr. Reade, and she looked back on that day in October when Mr. Reade had said in his quiet, hoarse voice before band practice started,

"Delilah, will you pass out the folders for me, please. I have to go upstairs to the office a moment." And Delilah, who had come in early and was getting out her clarinet, looked up at Mr. Reade out of her wildest, blackest, most nearly frightened eyes and managed a little dodging jerk of her head that meant yes. That had been the first day Delilah helped Mr. Reade, and thereafter he asked her to do occasional band-room tasks. But just arranging folders on the stands or chalking notices on the board did not seem all that she should do for Mr. Reade. Sometimes when he stood on the little wooden platform and looked out over the band with his almost listening eyes, Delilah felt that he was sad, somehow. She never told this to any of her girl friends because they would laugh at her; they did not understand Mr. Reade. But all that fall Delilah wondered what she could do for Mr. Reade that he would be indebted to her for – something big, something he would remember her for all the rest of his life.

It was during the Christmas holidays that Mr. Reade made a visit to the city zoo. He wore his green-and-red golf cap, dark sunglasses, and gray houndstooth coat. His small beard was shining wirily in the sun. He was, as always, monumentally ill at ease.

He walked slowly, stopping to study the signs on the cages and to review the genus of the animal or bird. He was somewhat pleased by the flamingos and a bit disgusted with the Australian wild dog.

When Mr. Reade came to the Bengal tiger, he paused and, with his arms crossed and one foot slightly forward, stood regarding the long body stretched out in the dimness of its cage. Many long moments passed – Mr. Reade watching the tiger, the tiger looking back at Mr. Reade. Neither of them made any noticeable movement or sound until Mr. Reade, with his little pronounced jerk of arms and shoulders, cleared his throat. It was an ordinary hawking sound, with no unusual embellishments, yet another zoo visitor strolling past the cage at this moment would have been so struck by it that he would have walked on down the way a piece and turned around sharply to

stare. It would not be anything he could put his finger on exactly –
just a rather stiff-figured young man in a golf cap and a small beard
coughing in front of a cage. But there was, nevertheless, an extra
dimension to the scene.

It was not like someone clearing his throat *before* a tiger: Mr.
Reade definitely seemed to be clearing his throat *at* the tiger.

And, knowing Mr. Reade, perhaps he was. Perhaps he had suddenly felt violently embarrassed at having stood there so long, silently
appraising the tiger in his cage, and, in typical Mr. Reade fashion, was
trying somehow to make amends. Mr. Reade knew exactly how he
would feel if *he* were in a cage and someone came up and stood with
his arms folded and stared, uninvited, at *him*. So perhaps the throat
clearing was a sudden act of attempted politeness, a lame but sincere
acknowledgment of the tiger's presence.

Or perhaps Mr. Reade was embarrassed at suddenly realizing that
he represented to the tiger the same sort of blank-faced, baldly staring
person who came by day after day to look in at the tiger as if it were
some true curiosity or freak. There *he* was, Mr. Reade, with his arms
folded critically and staring, as if he were like all the others who sauntered by, stopped and thought idly, "Hump, damned *tiger*...." And Mr.
Reade was not thinking that at all. As a matter of fact, he had stood
there and slowly realized how much he and the tiger were really alike,
in many ways, locked in the circumstances of their lives.

Perhaps it was having such thoughts as these in mind and suddenly, impulsively, wanting simply to say hello to the tiger and greet it
on equal terms, as one fellow-animal on earth greeting another, that
caused Mr. Reade unconsciously to clear his throat and release himself.

But his thoughts could get no farther, for at that moment someone called out, "Hello, Mr. Reade!"

Mr. Reade turned and there, in front of the cheetah, was Delilah
Barrera. She had her hand raised just slightly to show that it was
indeed she, Delilah, who had called.

"Good day, Delilah," said Mr. Reade in his stiff-sounding voice. "Zoos are good to come to on holidays. I'm glad you know about such places."

"Oh, I come to the zoo all the time, Mr. Reade," said Delilah. Suddenly she exclaimed, "And guess what: yesterday the hippopotamus had a baby! I bet you can't guess what it weighed!" Delilah was very excited that she had thought about the hippopotamus and could make Mr. Reade guess.

Now the approximate weight of a newborn hippopotamus was exactly the sort of thing that Mr. Reade would happen to know. He also knew how long the pregnancy period was and how much a grown hippo weighed.

But Mr. Reade held his chin and beard thoughtfully and said quietly, "Well, let me think. I shall say...two hundred pounds."

By now Delilah's pupils were so round and black and shining that it seemed they would have to pop from her eyes out of sheer buoyancy.

"Oh, no, Mr. Reade, not *near* so much. Not *near*. It weighed *sixty* pounds. Not *two hundred!*" And she ducked her head and tried to hide some of her laughter from Mr. Reade. She was very pleased at asking him and having him miss so far.

"Well, now," said Mr. Reade, clearing his throat, "I must not be very good at hippos." He tried looking a while at the cheetah and so did Delilah. They were both suddenly self-conscious. "But I think there *is* something that I know," said Mr. Reade, and Delilah looked up a little more directly into his face. "I know that without much trouble we should be able to find ourselves a vinegaroon."

"A *what*, Mr. Reade?"

Mr. Reade held up his forefinger, cautioning Delilah to ask no further but to trust him and she would see. And together they walked, rather formally, with Mr. Reade leading and Delilah just a bit to the side and following, to the reptile garden and the vinegaroon.

So it was that Mr. Reade, the band director, after a period of fall
gestation, found himself the following spring developing a tender
place inside his heart for Delilah Barrera of the eighth grade. It was a
quiet little feeling, much like a father's love, but it warmed him and
made looking at her and her shy ways a pleasure.

Of course Delilah, in her wildest dreams, could not, did not, conceive that such a thing as love, in either its raw or transmuted form,
could lie within the bosom of such a man as Mr. Reade. Mr. Reade was
grown, a teacher, and these facts alone were enough to eliminate him
from even the imagined role of paramour.

And true to this very incontestability – of his *being* no one other
than that formal public figure of himself – Mr. Reade contained his little pastel-colored feeling of love within him and merely stared out a
little more awarely from his already most cognizant eyes. No stitch of
propriety was dropped, and he continued to talk to Delilah that spring
in his same kind and gentle way. But he ended up with torticollis.

If you don't happen to know about torticollis, the dictionary says
it is "an affection causing twisting of the neck and an unnatural position of the head; wryneck." That was Delilah's big gift to Mr. Reade,
for him to remember her by.

It was during the second semester that Raul Hernández transferred to Davy Crockett Junior High and enrolled in band. He had all
the appealing features that Mexican boys can have – stocky build,
thick black hair that glistened like bristles on a new paintbrush, good
strong teeth, a ready wit. He played the trumpet with undeniable skill
and by the end of April had captured the heart of Delilah Barrera.

The result, of course, was Mr. Reade's torticollis.

It came about slowly enough. Each day Mr. Reade came to his
band class after lunch and there was no Delilah to pass out folders.
Each day there was no Delilah to tell him how the grass got up her little baby brother's nose when she mowed the lawn or how she was paying out a set of encyclopedias by buying coupons at the Piggly
Wiggly. No, there was no more early Delilah. She was outside by the

drinking fountain with Raul. Sometimes there was even a late Delilah, and Mr. Reade had to send her and Raul to the principal's office for tardy slips.

Each day Mr. Reade dreaded to go to his after-lunch class and see his shy Delilah in her new lipstick and permanent wave. Each day he dreaded catching her making eyes at her trumpeter. Each day he felt more ashamed of his attitude: "You're the one who is behaving abnormally, not Delilah," he told himself.

Nevertheless, one Tuesday afternoon in late April Mr. Reade raised his baton to direct a Palestrina chorale, stole a glance at Delilah, and saw her new jade earrings, and was seized with his torticollis. His head was drawn irresistibly toward his right shoulder, and his right shoulder rose to greet it. The muscles locked and Mr. Reade was left sitting on the platform stool with his baton raised and his head at a forty-five-degree angle.

"Excuse me," he said hoarsely to the class and made his way unsteadily from the room.

"It's all nerves, Mr. Reade," the psychiatrist told him. "You are too nervous for your own good. You read too many books. You should go to more ball games." And for ten days Mr. Reade lay in the hospital, taking insulin and orange juice and untying his nerves. He lay for long hours on his narrow bed, many times just at the borderline between consciousness and sleep. He rarely thought of Delilah. He rarely was able to think at all. But sometimes it seemed that he could see standing in the doorway a tiger dressed up as a nurse, staring in at him on his white-sheeted slab and periodically clearing its throat.

# V

# ON THE BORDER: EL PASO/JUÁREZ

# Spring in the Plaza

In March, when the mornings begin to lose their chill and the elm trees begin to bud, the downtown plaza in El Paso ceases to be the bleak, windswept bus stop of wintertime and once again resumes its rightful character as the heart of the city.

The first of the religious orators take up their positions near the center alligator pond – usually in pairs, one speaking in English, the other following in Spanish. Both revolve slowly, arms outstretched, facing little groups of onlookers who watch them as they would a fist fight or the attack of an epileptic – with the same detached curiosity.

Old men in mismatched clothes – the regular park idlers, the swappers of tales about ailments and travels and philosophies – are joined by secretaries and businessmen taking a few moments from lunch hours and coffee breaks; by college students, soldiers, and tourists; by school children on their way home; by maids waiting for their bus; by all the downtown strollers who wander through to watch the people and take a look at the alligator and in general keep up with what's going on.

The alligator crawls out of the cold, blue-tinted water and lies on the gravel pathway, his chin resting on the edge of the pool. Cigarette butts, small rocks, matches – such things soon accumulate on his back, thrown by bored and idle young men who would like to see the alligator awaken from his torpor and amuse them with a yawning display of jaws.

Off to one side of the plaza a small hunchbacked man in a double-breasted blue suit and with severely parted, smooth black hair talks to a group of men – explaining Marx's theory, the life of Mary Baker Eddy: who knows? But he is very articulate and evidently quite persuasive. The men listen to him gravely, nodding in agreement now and then – as though just on the verge of professing Judaism or agreeing to some new labor-management arbitration.

Thin little Mexican women – who have probably spent more time walking than most people have spent sitting – come briskly into the plaza from the north, make the half-circle detour around the alligator pond, and pass on to the south toward the *tranvía* stop and Juárez: looking neither right nor left and never slowing down, the knotted calf muscles in their wiry legs flexing with each step like small mechanical instruments constantly changing gear (while at the same moment their younger, prettier sisters – girls with hairdos like great fluffy clumps of black cotton candy – loiter through numerous slow circles around the alligator pond: laughing, slapping one another's shoulders and arms in artificial glee as they let themselves be consumed by the eyes of lounging, match-chewing young men).

And all the while – as the alligator sleeps and the strollers amble and the old men sit with their feet wide apart telling how it was in Guatemala in the thirties – there is contentment in the air. It is as if peaceful alliances have finally been reached between the forces of nature. Morning passes on into afternoon and no discordant note jangles the air – the pigeons coast and wheel above the grass, the flag waves imperially from its small granite monument, and the buildings on surrounding streets continue to jut up in pleasant alternations with cloudless blue sky.

# The Room

Watch Maria clean my room, watch her open all the east windows and let in the morning light. Watch her as she shakes my counterpane and smiles at the lint as it swims in the sunrays in a yellow aquatic ease.

For young Maria it is glorious to be in this big and airy room in the morning – in this room where the *americano* lives, where the green curtains suck in and out of the windows and make little brief pockets against the screens. She dusts with care, as if the room is a holy place, wiping the bottles and little boxes on the dresser tenderly and always setting them down again in their exact former places. She works surely and with dedication, progressing from the bed to the dresser to the desk with an accustomed rhythm, almost like that of an organist bending over familiar keys in an empty church.

As she works, things tempt her. She moves her dust rag over my typewriter and pauses to think how it would be to touch one of the white letters within the circles – touch it hard enough to make it jump inside the machine. My books tempt her. Each morning she takes them one by one from the shelf and wipes their covers, sometimes tracing the letters in the titles with her finger. Many times she has wanted to sit in the big chair by the window and open one of the books and look a long while at the words, but she is always afraid that she would somehow, unknowingly, cause some kind of damage – the way she was afraid that the typewriter was broken when her rag got caught in the keys once and made the little bell ring.

Sometimes, alone in the room, she wants to lean her head and shoulders out one of the big windows and call down into the courtyard and say, "Antonio, I'm up in the *americano's* room – see?" She wants the old gardener to look up and shake his head at her as if to say, Such a girl, such a girl. And she wants to go right on smiling down at him and pull up her shoulders in a great intake of fresh air. She wants to throw out her hands and sing to the big pink mountains to the east.

When Maria daydreams she suddenly stops, a little ashamed, and hurries to finish her work. And after the room is clean, she stands holding her hands about her broom and gives one final glance around the bed and desk and books. Then, upon leaving, she closes the door behind her as gently as she can, as if it might be possible that I could hear her and be pleased.

# Milady

I saw a woman in a parking lot – a very slim and fashionably dressed woman – and for a long moment just the sight of her caused me to balance between outrage and a kind of giddy despair. Not that she and her midday elegance were at all outrageous in themselves: it was just that such a chic dash of noontime femininity, such a pretty little human frill, juxtaposed itself too sharply, too incongruously, against past scenes of the morning.

For I had left behind, in south El Paso, other women – those in the alleys and doorways and patios of dirty red-brick apartment houses: women with dark roomsful of children, women bent over washing clothes, women carrying heavy bundles, women with babies on their hips staring out through screened doorways. There was no sign of elegance there – only the cheerless concerns of people fighting the daily battles of poverty and survival.

To leave those women and walk north toward the business district just in time to see Milady get out of her small foreign car – to see so slim and twisty-tailed a trick emerge like a butterfly from the shiny red cocoon of her Jaguar – made me lose all perspective about life and human nature. My first impulse was simply to shout at the woman: Lady, how can you – how *dare* you – exist in such splendid isolation from your sister humans? How can you be so oblivious of the lives they lead, their constant burdens? Who are you to be exempt from washboards and hungry bellies?

But my quixotic indignation gradually melted and I realized there was nothing to be gained by being upset. Indeed, asking such a woman to be concerned about social injustices and inequalities would be like asking a peacock to give up its feathers to make pillows for the Salvation Army. So I withdrew my demands of her and just watched, for she made an undeniably pretty sight moving along with her small rapid steps toward the Citizens' National Bank. With one black-gloved hand she would touch, automatically and very lightly, her stunning little rear to check the smoothness of her beautifully tailored yellow dress ( – a wholly useless gesture; the dress, as she well knew, hugged her slim hips like a silky banana skin). And with the other gloved hand reaching up to her hat – a tall upside-down felt chamberpot with white brim and bow – and constantly glancing about little-girlishly through her dark glasses, she let the small arcs of her shiny black shoes carry her through the side entrance of the bank.

There she is, I thought, the slim society matron going about the routines of her nicely appointed day: a pop-in at the bank, a green-salad lunch with similarly sheathed and bedecked young friends, a shopping tour through the best department stores followed by an executive meeting of the Garden Club. Considering her, I couldn't help wondering: Did she inhabit the same earth and breathe the same air as the women of south El Paso? Was she truly their human kin, or of an entirely different species? Would the camel pass through the nee-dle's eye before Milady of the Parking Lot understood that life was more than a very dry martini?

# Nut

She was dressed the way eccentric old Apple Annies usually are: tennis shoes without socks; a long shabby coat full of tatters and holes; a worn scarf that did very little to control the dry wisps of hair that strung out above her forehead.

I watched her in the downtown El Paso plaza as she walked about and wrote in a small blue spiral notebook. Standing perfectly still and cradling the notebook in one hand, she would write for ten minutes at a stretch; then after walking a short way she would stop – the heel of one tennis shoe arrested in mid-step – and bending her head down toward her notebook she would write some more.

Most of the bench idlers took her in stride, not paying her much attention. Perhaps they accepted her as one of themselves, only in just a little worse shape. But one grizzle-bearded ex-New Yorker with a huge paunch and a yachtsman's cap seemed bothered by her: "Look at dat nut," he would say to whoever was seated beside him. "She oughtta be locked up, runnin off like dat at da mout. It just don't sound good, somebody talkin like dat in da pahk." And he would frown, shaking his head and big belly, and then breathe a little harder with his asthma.

I was in the park only once when she started on a talking spree, and her pacing was as curious as her monologue: it was as though she were declaiming inside a zoo cage, moving back and forth in a constrained and tireless prowl. She never acknowledged the presence of a passerby, and even when she would halt to specifically address an empty bench or a building across the street she never really seemed to focus on it. She just seemed to be musing violently to herself in the private world of her little blue notebook and her hates.

It was not quite clear what her total complaint was – she stopped too often in the middle of one tirade to begin another – but primarily she was down on Mrs. Roosevelt and the Catholics. She paced along, first talking to her tennis shoes or the pigeons on the grass about "Catholic abominations," then sliding right on into "old Eleanor Roosevelt" and the New Deal. At one point she enumerated a long list of peoples of the world – Ethiopians, Senegalese, Chileans, Koreans, Vietnamese – and though I did not get the connection between the list and Eleanor Roosevelt I was surprised at how knowledgeably she rattled off the names. She spoke in a rich, throaty, drawling voice that would have been rather pleasant to listen to if she had not been using it as a vent for such venom and hate. She had a crooked front tooth and a kind of Humphrey Bogart slant to her jaw when she spoke, and they helped to give her words an added spit and snarl.

She was tanned from years of walking about outdoors, and from a distance her face seemed rather vague – nondescript brown parts sewed together with wrinkles. She resembled, as much as anything, some kind of mad monk whose face is always kept hidden within the shadow of his dark cowl. Yet when I finally saw her face up close, and clearly, it was not that of an old woman at all.

She had paused right next to my bench, not to write in her notebook but just to stare off into her special corridor of space. I looked up, and instead of her face being truly old, it seemed more like a movie starlet's that had been made up rather poorly to resemble a Bowery grandmother. Somehow the wrinkles were not part of the skin but seemed superimposed – almost extraneous to it, like smudges of dirt. And despite the lines and roughening effect of years in the sun, the features were still astonishingly soft and somehow even innocent. The lips were like those of a young girl – very tender and full – and the eyes were clear and well defined, without any wrinkles or pouches.

I was in the midst of an urge to take a cloth and wash the tan and dirt and wrinkles away – to see what she really looked like underneath – when suddenly she moved on. She reached inside her coat, scratched fiercely along her collarbone and underneath her arm, then began walking out of the plaza in her bobbing, long-gaited stride – looking down to the cracks in the sidewalk and giving Old Eleanor hell.

# Morning and Life

In Juárez the world seems very much lived in. It is good just to walk down a street there in the mornings and see the dust, the bits of orange peel, the stray rocks scattered beside the curbs. Children sit cross-legged on the sidewalks, playing games, and women hurry along carrying sacks and pails. Life is a stuff, an essence in the air, heady and strong – like the smell of fresh laundry borne on a good morning breeze.

Parrots have it as they shift about petulantly in their bamboo cages in the cool dark front windows. The boys on the sidewalk have it in their black watching eyes as they pull back a bare unwashed foot to let you pass by. Old street-cleaning men pushing slow brooms have it as they move down the curbs with their little dabs of trash going toward the next shady chinaberry tree on the corner where they can stop and rest. Women have it in the very swelling tight firmness of their breasts. They step along with a strong carriage, and their legs, used to much walking, are as tightly rounded and firm in the calf as their breasts are. Watching them, you get the feeling that they are carrying life around invisibly on their heads, with the same deliberate ease that their Indian mothers once had when they carried baskets along the trails of the distant mountains.

Life, the forms of it, the tempo — how indelibly it is there each morning, as noticeable and unrelenting as the albino chow dogs who sit in the shade of doorways and level their amber eyes at familiar interests out in the bright sunlight.

# Willows

South of Juárez the farmland stretches flatly out of sight, and the single highway that passes across it provides the lure of Other Worlds. A man sitting beside the highway and thinking loose thoughts on a warm day could be led to consider fanciful or strange things. He might stare at the hazy line of the horizon or up into the heart of a willow tree and get notions.

Such a man, a laborer, sits now beneath a group of tall willows that arch down thickly around him at the edge of a cotton field. He is eating tortillas and resting. His lunch is spread out between his legs on the old paper sack he has torn to make a plate. He takes a long time to chew his food, his temples flexing in a steady contented rhythm. He has put his straw hat on his knee and it rides there while he eats.

As he chews in the noon shade the man obligingly notices all things around him. He watches cars as they pass on the highway. He looks to the east where the thick, pinkish mountains are. Sometimes he is aware of the clouds, and studies them. But mainly he is concerned with the tall willows and their wild elegant limbs that have tumbled down about him in a green cascade. As he chews, his eyes keep scanning upward into their deep fountain of greenery. He finishes his lunch and leans back comfortably on his arm and dozes. Perhaps he dreams.

He is just an ordinary field hand, this man, and does not easily come down with a vagabond's fever from a little quiet noon relaxing. So there is no apparent change in him as he yawns after a while and picks up his straw hat and returns to his rows of cotton. Nevertheless, when the day ends and he leaves the field and returns to his little brown sunbaked hut on the edge of town, I'll bet you one thing: I'll bet he carried those willows with him. He'll speak to his wife and children in his usual unconcerned way and go about old after-work routines as always. But I'll bet those willows will be working on him. I'll bet in the hot, dry landscape of his mind there will be growing an intimate green scene – perhaps not one with words or even objects in it but instead just a gentle green lure, a willow-colored cast to his thoughts.

For it's just such innocent things that can affect the simplest man sometimes: a sense of space, some green trees, a little rumination.

# Club Tin Tan

It is a bar on Calle 16 de Septiembre. You enter the big airy room and there painted on the wall in his white zoot suit, white hat, and wide white smile is Tin Tan, the Mexican comic, his hand raised to you in greeting. If you are in a gloomy mood, you only have to look at the looping key chain, the thin elegant moustache – at Tin Tan's whole palm beach salutary air – to end up smiling a little inside. You can't help being lightened by this man who obviously doesn't take life quite as seriously as you do. So you relax and take your place at the bar and enjoy an after-dinner bottle of Carta Blanca.

It is pleasant there in the early afternoon. There is lots of natural soft light slanting down through the high windows facing the street, and the conversation of scattered twos and threes at the tables is always background mood music. No sound is ever hurried; even laughter rises and fades easily, without being forced. And whenever the jukebox plays the loud, slow, melodramatic Mexican tunes, the men sitting at the bar in their hats pour their beer a little more slowly and carefully and look steadily ahead into the mirror behind the bar, as though studying themselves briefly and finding contentment in their images.

Sometimes a man, the owner perhaps, will open a small second-story window and look down into the bar from some hidden office. The little hole is just larger than his face – barely big enough to frame the smooth dark hair, the strongly hooked nose, the pale narrow face and its sleepy, heavy-lidded eyes. It is a shock each time to see the face: it is like looking up suddenly at the sad face of Manolete gazing down from heaven. The face usually lasts only a moment or two before the man draws back his head and closes the little door smoothly into the wall again.

If you stay long enough you watch the appearance of the big woman with oversized breasts. She comes out from a back room and stands with a great display of stateliness at the far end of the bar. She wears her hair upon her head and constantly touches the loose unruly strands that flow out at the back of her neck. She stands talking to the nearby men on the stools, occasionally accepting drinks, always blowing smoke from her cigarette toward her watching face in the mirror. Sometimes, when she shifts her weight about, her breasts sway in their great fluid whiteness almost like separate living things, making her seem no longer One but Three: a living Trinity of Flesh.

# Conquistador

He is just a shoeshine man, but he moves along Calle Mariscal with the air of a Spanish explorer. He is monumentally dirtied and almost as monumentally haired. His beard, black and wiry, coils and juts about his face with a debonair boldness.

He wears a tasseled hat – not an ordinary straw, but a kind of Aussie campaign hat, with the gold tassel looped around the crown and hanging in double strands down the back.

He doesn't have on a shirt; he wears a short maroon jacket with an Eisenhower cut, very dirty, yet fitting trimly and militarily around his waist. His pants, once white, are full and pegged at the bottom and much too short – there are wide stretches of dirty ankle above his shoes. The pants are held up by a cotton rope, tied in a knot to one side.

He makes his rounds from bar to bar, the shoeshine box strapped diagonally across his back with two jointed leather belts – like a carbine. He enters each pair of swinging doors, makes his questing little tour inside, then emerges again a few moments later – wholly unperturbed at not finding a customer, still swinging jauntily along the sidewalk like an alpinist making his way toward the Matterhorn.

If you got just a glimpse of him from a distance you might think he was one of Captain Kidd's men striding down the back street of some Caribbean village. He maintains that easy, swashbuckling gait. And you feel, too, that whenever he does find someone willing to have his shoes shined, he will give the customer a single confident nod, swing his wooden box off his shoulder, and begin making preparatory swipes with his brush the same way a fencer loosens up with initial thrusts of his foil – with the same gracefully bold assurance.

Obviously this is a man of parts, of prominence, a man cast in the mold of Cyrano de Bergerac and Lafitte and D'Artagnan. It was simply his fate to be born in the wrong era and the wrong circumstances so that instead of approaching life with rapier and arquebus he must content himself with the weapons of Calle Mariscal: polishing rags and a can of Shinola.

# Summer Days

At five o'clock men just off from work stretch out along the banks of the Juárez canal like Steinbeck *paisanos*. They lie sprawled and dirty underneath the cottonwoods, their greasy hats rolled to one side, their legs jackknifed into angles of collapsing rest, their arms flung out on the grass or across their eyes. A few of them lean back on their elbows, chewing grass and looking across the canal into the nearby streets. They talk some, even manage a couple of short-lived lazy laughs, but before long they too succumb to the heat and their tiredness. They roll over – facedown on the grass – and sleep while the crows flap and call above them in the trees.

Across the canal, inside small wooden stands, vendors sell cool drinks from big, open-mouthed jars – beautifully pale lemon-and-orange-ade, with chunks of fruit rind floating languidly on top. Customers gathered around the stands drink slowly, taking only small swallows. They seem not to be drinking to quench their thirst as much as to simply be part of a nice social act – to engage in a street corner summer ritual.

Nearby, in the shadows of low adobe buildings barefooted and long-haired Indian girls from nearby mountains stand in their little islands of solitude, their dark legs powdered almost to the knee with dust from the road and the Juárez streets, their many layers of once-white skirts uniformly darkened – as though they had been carefully washed and rewashed in dirt. The girls press their hands and faces upward toward the passersby, begging in small, faint, fiercely mono-toned voices while behind them old Indian women sit against the buildings and stare into the street – seeing nothing, saying nothing, sunk into the silent caves of their long black shawls.

# Old Women; Prostitutes

As the heat begins to go out of the air and the walls of the adobe buildings allow their shadows to creep out across the sidewalks, you can see old women crossing the side streets of Juárez in black head-wraps and maroon shawls. They move tirelessly and fast, not limping down curbs the way you think old women should but hardly even stopping for them or noticing them. They are on errands, or coming home from work across the river, or out for a moment to scavenge in garbage cans. But they are all hurrying, all skimming along the dusty streets in their black moccasins like Chinese coolies pulling light invisible rickshaws, all with buckets in their hands or paper sacks, all finally disappearing suddenly around corners or into dark passageways.

The prostitutes do not hurry. They clatter along in their high heels and shiny black dresses, taking their time, not caring to get to the bars where they work any sooner than necessary. They do not solicit on the streets; they are working girls with a place of business and do not need to fool around on the sidewalks. At night, inside the bars, they sit perched on their stools like small bored gulls and call to the young American boys and lay their arms across the boys' shoulders and ask for a drink. But now they are among their own people who know what it is to have to do such things for a living. The Mexican men who pass them now will not be the ones who come to see them later in the bars; they will be selling hot dogs on a corner or trying to take pictures of tourists in the clubs or helping to park cars. It is only the Americans who mill in and out of the swinging bar doors at night, who go upstairs. It is only the Americans who have money.

Americans, sex, money – these are the prostitutes' three fates pulling the young women slowly and inevitably down the old narrow streets in their wobbling heels and loud-smelling Woolworth perfume.

# West Juárez

Stretching away from the hidden banks of the Rio Grande toward the dusty mountains in the south, West Juárez seems part of another hemisphere. It is like some lonely desert city of Asia Minor, a primitive hill town of Berbers or Arabs.

From a distance – from across the river in El Paso – nothing seems to move. Of course, now and then a boy can be seen running along a dune; a brief section of laundry will flap on a line; occasionally there is the figure of a man, a sign of smoke, a dog. But they are not really noticeable; they do not constitute the scene. What is there is the array of adobe cubes sitting implacably in the sun – the solid rectangles and squares scattered aimlessly across the sand like hundreds of small brown boxes.

A place of squatters, it has no visible trees, no yards, no streets – just trails here and there, eroded ridges and bluffs, arroyos. Silence, rather than a community of people, seems to live there – it, and poverty and space: elements and the elemental.

# Darkness and the Canal

After night has settled you move away from the neon streets near the international bridge and you go to the parts of town where there are no tourists. You go to where Juárez lies waiting as a true Mexican town, as a place of darkness.

There, among shadowed walkers and silhouetted trees, you learn that no one tries to conquer the night as they try to do so often in other places. Night exists in its own blackness; it is not contested by great commercial areas of pseudo-day. Night is accepted on its own terms and is responded to with welcome. People move within it comfortably, easily, as fish move through deep silent seas. And if lights are used, they are used as means of temporary relief from an acknowledged greater power. They are used as shade is during the day – to assuage, a bit, the main reality.

To be sure, small dim bulbs are lit on scattered street corners, and children gather near them to snatch a few last scenes out of the day. They run in and out of the pale yellow circle on the dusty street, shouting excited cries, dragging behind them everywhere their long quivering shadows. But even the children don't believe that the bulbs are doing battle with the night. They know that they are just staunch little islands of light, serving only to accentuate the vast waters of the dark.

After walking a while – after entering deeply into this town of walls and darkened streets and medieval air – you come to sit beside the dry, crumbling canal that winds through the west part of town. There, resting, you hear others like yourself passing by in the muffling dust. You hear lone dogs barking in the distance, somehow sounding right on the very edge of the night. You hear low voices of lovers from a building's shadow, and voices of people walking home down in the dry bed of the canal – hollow voices, yet strangely heightened, as though coming from a cave or filtering up through the crust of the earth. Sometimes there is the sound of old cars gunning in second gear for long distances on nearby streets, going across the night with wildness, then returning along a parallel street a few moments later, again in second gear, still gunning – sounding like mechanical racing dogs who have gone mad or been fed ground glass, running violently everywhere and nowhere, trying desperately to find relief.

And then, when it is very late and all the old men's feet seem to have passed in the dust for the last time and all the doors across town are finally quieting, you look across the canal to where a young girl sits reading in a vendor's stand. She is hunched over in the stall, reading a magazine by candlelight, and is barely visible above the counter top. A row of red and orange soft drinks stands on the counter before her, and magazines hang diagonally about the stand.

You wonder how long the girl has been there, so still, and how long she will remain. It is past midnight. You look at her hair, shining a rich glossy Indian black in the candlelight. You look about once more at the night, so encompassing, so total, except for that small glow of light within the stand. Finally you fall to watching the candle on the counter top: despite the breezes that fitfully scatter the dust along the banks of the canal, not once does the flame of the candle waver. It bores up through the darkness in the full rigid form of a classic flame. It sits there, pointed and clean, as though subject to no temptation.

And it almost makes a believer of you, here in Catholic Mexico – almost makes you ready to believe it possible that an angel of purity could descend and invest herself in a candle flame just so a little vendor girl might have the steadying hint of God to comfort her on dark and lonesome nights.

# Waiting Room

It was late afternoon and I was waiting in the El Paso railroad station to meet a friend. I had started reading an article in a magazine, killing time, but after a while I laid the magazine aside and sat there reveling in the building and its cathedral peace.

I listened as the voices of station employees filtered in from unseen passageways – pleasant, casual, contenting. I heard the shoes of slow old men passing over the tiles in a kind of muted, rhythmic litany. A typewriter pecked somewhere in an office, a train released its swish of steam far down the tracks, a janitor's broom knocked hollowly against the porcelain in the men's washroom. And subtly connecting them – all the muffled, echoing, unhurried sounds – were the smells of cleaning compounds and a faint, immemorial dust.

While I waited there, musing, very much at ease, a Negro woman with her three granddaughters took seats down the bench from me. The girls wore starched pink dresses and had their hair neatly plaited.

At first, before they got restless, they remained solemn and quiet and looked around carefully at their surroundings: at the roof arcing high above, the big supporting beams, the wide slabs of white-tiled stairs going up to the second floor. But finally one of the girls began to scoot along on the bench – just to hear the noise that her bare thighs made against the smooth wood. Then the others began to slide, and to look at each other and giggle, until their grandmother was forced to raise her hand warningly and say in a loud whisper: "Shhh, girls; not here."

As the three granddaughters composed themselves again and as figures from the entrances continued to move almost soundlessly by, I wondered what it was that seemed to affect us as we waited in the huge room. I looked at the high doors and walls, the great imperious dome: Was it sheer size that intimidated us, the sense of almost Olympian dignity? Yes, that seemed part of it – the natural awe a person has for physical majesty and grace. But for me there was something else too: a feeling that the waiting room was somehow a *good* place, a place that year after year had borne the constant touch of human beings and in the process had not been defiled. Whatever urge men have always had, in their emptiness, to scratch Me on the sides of monuments and on restroom walls – it was absent here. The waiting room seemed to touch something deep in the human spirit, making it bow to the simple elegance of silence and air and stone.

# Heaven

If there were a Heaven, I would want it to be the Florida Club on a summer afternoon.

I would have been walking the back streets of Juárez, you see – at peace with things, with myself: ready to nod at dogs and smile at yellow walls – and finally I would have come to Avenida Juárez and the Florida Club. My cave. My home away from all other homes. My sanctuary.

...Ah, to be very much with the world – to be walking on sun-and-shadowed streets, to be physically part of cigarette vendors and begging children and shopkeepers eternally reading in their doorways – and then to step bouyantly inside, to almost swing into the cool dimness of the Florida and slide onto a bar stool and wait there, comfortably, for the bartender to come toward you – already searching for a glass as he asks, *"Cuba libre, señor?"* – and you to nod and smile and say yes and then just to remain there, at ease, receptive: savoring the sense of homecoming, of belonging: knowing that if the mood strikes you after a drink or two you can go across to the dining room where a waiter will signal to you: where, after he professionally slaps his towel across the bottom of a chair as he offers the table, you can sit at the clean expanse of white tablecloth and consider the menu: deciding, perhaps, on Boquilla black bass with baked potato.... To be there, too: to dip a tostada into the chili sauce and sip a Gibson and await the arrival of soup and salad and perhaps see across the room, under the arced mounted sailfish, a familiar face – another patron who, like you, has taken his ease in the Florida Club over the last fifteen years or so; to listen to the brief touch of dish against dish, a rise of laughter; to feel, by God, that it is certainly fine to be in this stable and familiar place and know that life at this moment is touching you lightly, casually – to know that in a world where all things go bust a person can still have a measure of eternity on his own terms: with a Gibson, a white tablecloth and Boquilla black bass.

# Drew

He was laughing – but not really. He had merely recoiled slightly from the force of a social chuckle, holding a beer glass lightly in his thin fingers and looking past the head and shoulders of his companion to the other dancing, talking, gesticulating young men.

I had hoped that I would not find him there – that he would be holed up in an apartment, painting again, or had gone on into Mexico, perhaps, to struggle in solitude with his demon, or had even driven on back to Dallas in his shiny new Porsche to live with his mother.

But there he was, head reared back, glass in the air, joining the bursts of high-pitched male laughter up and down the bar. He had come back home to Mr. Larry's.

I had not known Drew very well at first. Although we taught at the same school in El Paso he always seemed more comfortable around my wife – laughed more genuinely when she was around, talked more freely. He would drop by our house in the late afternoon and say, "Come on, Judy, let's go driving. I've found a really cute place with dormer windows and it has a wonderful view." He was always house hunting. Sometimes I would stop whatever I was doing and go with them. We would drive across town, park at the bottom of a hill, then after climbing a weed-sprouting path we would stand before the red-brick, turn-of-the-century colossus that Drew had discovered. "Well," he would say, looking at Judy, then at me, "how do you like it? It has a lot of possibilities, don't you think? Of course it would take some fixing up...."

Drew was not meant to live in the twentieth century with all its stresses and upheavals. Slight, fair-skinned, surprisingly agile and poised, he was an Elizabethan, an Etonian of the 1890s, a medievalist. He loved gardening, musical comedies, beautiful cars (once, in a movie, Sophia Loren kicked the side of a Rolls Royce. Drew, sitting next to me, immediately stiffened, began making uneasy hand and body motions; I thought he was going to rise and attack the screen). He could refer almost casually to his nervous breakdown in New York, but he never did like to talk about his father – a man cursed, apparently, by a life-long need to get-rich-quick but who was always in debt, always on the move. Drew's mother had been the stabilizing force in his life; she still taught high school English and speech.

At thirty-two Drew was witty, a good artist, invariably pleasant company. He was also a homosexual and, from what I could gather, enormously lonely.

During the three or four years I knew him he seemed to waver between gay and straight life styles – that is, he kept trying to decide if he should finally plunge into the gay world and not look back.

For months at a time he would teach his art classes, work on his own paintings, go to movies and plays and parties with his married friends. He took no male lovers, stayed away from gay bars.

Then he would disappear – a trip to Albuquerque, a weekend in Phoenix. (He once rode 150 miles on a Harley-Davidson in the sun, bareheaded, clutching to the leather-jacketed body of his hustler friend who had entered motorcycle races in Carlsbad; stayed all day at the track while his lover-of-the-weekend competed; returned the following day, again in the sun and searing desert wind. His delicate skin blistered, burned, peeled and he missed a week of school.) For a while he lived with a young man named Bob, who worked in the drapery department at Sears, and they moved into a large, expensive apartment. Drew seemed at peace. He had a place for his oriental rugs, a pitcher of screwdrivers in the mauve-colored refrigerator, a circle of companionable gay friends.

But it didn't work out – as the previous alliances had not worked out. Too many young men flowed in and out of the apartment, overstayed their welcome, borrowed money they never paid back.

Finally Drew quit teaching and left town. He was gone for a year or more – working, I think, for a state agency in Austin. It was midsummer when a mutual friend of ours hailed me on the street one day and said Drew was back in town driving a new Porsche. I waited for him to call, but he didn't. So I went looking for him one night at his old hangout.

Mr. Larry was tending bar – a dyed-blond satyr surveying his domain. On the go-go stage in the corner a small, barefooted male dancer, dressed in blue denim shorts and a leather jerkin, was doing muscular bumps and grinds.

I didn't see Drew when I sat down – it was Friday night and the go-go boy had drawn a crowd. But I soon heard his laugh from the end of the bar – his light, David Niven chuckle.

He had lost weight and looked worn out – devastated. He was not only beginning to lose his hair in front but he had cut what was left almost to a burr. His face was sunburned; the tops of his ears were peeling. His head looked like the reddish knob of a walking stick.

He saw me once. He had tapped his cigarette into the ash tray and let his eyes drift past his motorcycle companion in visored cap and dark glasses, and he focused on me. I tilted my beer glass, just slightly, in his direction, and I nodded. He made no sign of recognition.

As I drove home I kept seeing Drew's head at the end of the bar: a death's head, a solitary, skull-shaped periscope sinking into the smoky deeps of Mr. Larry's.

# The Day the Earth Stood Still

If there had been a declaration of war, or an earthquake, or perhaps some shocking new turn of political events, people in El Paso would have felt that they had a reason to remember Sunday, November 11. Editorial writers would have pounded out editorials. Commentators would have commented. News analysts would have analyzed. And people would have agreed that something significant had happened in their lives that day.

Something did happen in El Paso on November 11: it was a day the earth stood still. But no history book will ever record the fact that it did. That particular Sunday passed unheralded by headlines on Monday morning.

Yet it was as important a day as ever comes in a person's life, even though that's all it was – a day. A non-historic, non-newsmaking day.

If you were alive, you surely remember it – that perfect, rare, autumn Sunday when the earth stood still and let men and women and children and animals and all other breathing and crawling and flying things move about in the sun as if they were eternal creatures of the universe and would never die.... That day, surely you recall it: how the sun came casually down and the afternoon shadows gathered like old friends and the air touched the skin like a lover.

That day: when boys ran and cats curled in the warmth of the afternoon grass and couples walked about and there was no sense of tragedy, of excess, of unmet needs anywhere.

That day, that impossibly friendly and lovely El Paso day – just right for human living – stayed a perfect day all day long and then it ended.

But such a day – a day worthy of gods and editorials – will not go down in the history books because nothing happened. It did not make any news; it only made life worth living.

# A Man

Nine o'clock at night and a man was seated on a bench, leaning over on his knees. He was drunk, tired, worn out, and he was also very sick. The flu, perhaps. From time to time he dropped his head and coughed between his knees in a weak, soft way.

He seemed quite alone in the world. Perhaps he wanted to get back to Los Angeles – mother city of the West for castoffs, strays – but was out of money. Perhaps he was stranded in El Paso on the bus station bench.

...You looked at the man and tried to imagine him as he once might have been: strong and capable. You thought of him back in his home town during the 1940s: a strapping Robert Stack of a fellow in his blue and gold football uniform: smiling, the helmet held casually underneath his arm, the dark hair curled with afternoon sweat, his sunken blue eyes steady and direct and full of the knowledge that he was not just handsome and tough but also exceptionally shrewd in getting what he wanted from people. And then you imagined him a bit later, after a hitch in the navy, say: back home again, still aggressive and dashing but his eyes not quite as direct: for he had a family now – two kids and a blond-haired, thin-mouthed wife – and he was getting a reputation as a drinker. He was still reliable, though: was still a steady worker during the day on his bread truck route....

The man on the bench rallied a bit, coughed, managed to bring up his head. He reached unsteadily toward his pants pocket, struggled in it a moment, found his dirty gray wad of a handkerchief. He feebly tried to blow his nose into it; missed; tried again; missed; continued to blow past it into his fingers.

For a while the man sat straightened up, working hard to keep his eyes from closing. He batted them slowly, above the great sagging pouches of wrinkled skin, and they were like fish mouths gulping for air. The red eyelids strained, the eyeballs rolled.

He searched and found a cigarette in his right front pocket, then held it in his fingers for a while as he tried to master himself. After wobbling his head for a bit, and blinking, he managed to turn a little toward the man sitting in the row of benches behind him. He opened his mouth, hoped he was saying it – Hey, buddy, you got a light? – but the words blurred and faded and the man behind him went on reading. The sick man lost control of his neck muscles and his head swung back. His eyes closed again, his chin sank to his chest.

The man sat that way, bent over, beaten.

*And so worn out.* That was what struck you most about him. His virility gone. His spirit leaked away. The stench from his body like a wolf's breath.... You looked at the jacket stained with vomit, the wrinkled black pants caked with mud. You looked at the creases in his neck and face: they were like the deep slashes of a turtle's mouth. This man – you thought it in a kind of wonder and disbelief: this man was destroyed; at forty-five he had blown himself out. It was as though time had moved across his body like a strong electric current and had crumpled him.

Suddenly the man stirred and got awkwardly to his feet. He balanced himself for a moment, then began to stagger toward the baggage counter. He just got a step or two before he lurched into the metal trash container at the end of the aisle. He knocked it to the floor with a loud clatter and sprawled across it. As the passengers from the 9:15 bus began to enter the waiting room the man lay there among the scattered paper and orange peels – Robert Stack just short of the goal line, his eyes gulping, his unlit cigarette still jutting from between his fingers.

# They Should Have Been There

They ought to have been there.

They ought to have been walking down the streets of Juárez and come within a block of their parked cars – ready to return across the bridge to middle-class America – and they ought to have looked down at the sidewalk. They ought to have stopped, as I did, in the head-pounding July sun and seen the mother begin to unwrap the bundle of rags she was holding as she sat there beside a building, moaning. That was what it looked like, at least – just a bundle of gray woolens picked up from a *ropa usada* store.

And then as the woman in her old scarf and faded skirt and gray wool coat gradually pulled aside the rags of her bundle, they ought to have been looking down over my shoulder. They would not have minded the heat any longer or for that matter remembered where they were going, or what country they were in, or whose politics they preferred: they would not have even cared to remember what their names were.

Because all they could have thought about was this human *something* that the woman had just laid bare.... A child? Surely not; their

minds would not have accepted that. Surely that wizened little creature with its gnome-like head – that skull of stretched skin and scattered hair: surely one could not possibly call that a *girl*, or a *baby*....
And that little vine of a body: surely that length of grotesquely shrunk-
en chest and legs was a skinned rabbit or squirrel. That could not be a
– what had someone once called it: a fleshly temple of the immortal
soul?

Yes, indeed, they should have been there. Because if they had,
they might have accomplished much more than I. For at first all I did
was stand there and stare. Then, finally, I turned to a man sitting nearby on a curb and asked in my poor Spanish, Is it dead? The man
shrugged and said he didn't think so. When two shoeshine boys came
up I put out my hand and asked them: Is it dead?... I kept thinking that
the woman, in her grief, was simply carrying the child around, wrap-
ping and unwrapping it with her rags, refusing to admit that the baby
had died.

But no, the boys said, it was alive. It was two months old and
needed milk and medicines, and the woman had no money. She had
other children at home, but she was too poor to buy things for any of
them.

Well, what would others have done? They would have perhaps
taken charge in a more effective way, would have managed things better: indeed, would have so completely discharged their moral responsibilities to that woman and her dying little girl that later, whenever
they took a bite of food or relaxed in a movie or smiled at a clever
joke they would not automatically have that child appear before their
eyes – lying there on the sidewalk looking a hundred years old and
with its mouth finally beginning to work in a soundless cry; with its
mother, bent over, moaning, wiping its excrement away with its own
covering rags.

Me? I just did things in the usual American way: I took out my
wallet and gave the boys some money.... Sure, I was upset, concerned,
and I explained to the boys that the mother must go to a doctor and

that she must do exactly what he said. And after the boys gave the money to the woman she slowly gathered up the child and the three of them started off toward a doctor's office two blocks away. I stood there on the street corner and watched until she went through the doctor's door.

I got into my car and drove on across the bridge, thinking about my own child. She was four years old – firm-legged, cheerful, healthy. She was taking ballet once a week at the YWCA, and sometimes at night she would fly around the living room in little sweeping ballet prancings. She was beautifully alive and vibrant.

When I got home I looked at her and could not help feeling guilty as the guiltiest dog. For not three miles away still another ruined little fragment of a human being (one of how many: a dozen? a hundred? a thousand?) was probably lying in its bundle of rough rags.

What I wanted to know was: Who was to blame? Did you blame Mexico as a country; God as a Creator; Juárez as a poverty-filled town? The man sitting on the curb? the shoeshine boys? the father? the mother: should you blame her for being poor and perhaps ignorant and out of work? Or the child: maybe blame it for not being born stronger? Or blame me, for not staying there and doing more?... *Nobody?...* Don't blame anyone – just say, Well, that's life?

...They just should have been there, that's all – those who always have an answer for the world's problems. Then maybe I could have learned how you deal with poverty.

# Compatriot

A small Mexican man in his sixties, he sat down beside me on a park bench and read a while from his Spanish-language newspaper. He was wearing a dark brown suit and narrow, square-toed black shoes – shoes abrupt on the end like the nose of an old Ford. His hat was the black, creased-down-the-middle kind you could have seen on a

Mexican doctor during the days of the Revolution: indeed, he looked like a movie extra from *Viva Zapata* who was relaxing before his next scene – perhaps a trusted friend of Madero, waiting for his chief there in the El Paso plaza with a message from the States.

Everything about the man suggested alertness and orderly habits. He had a recent haircut, squared in the back, and there was still a fresh, youthful line arching above the ears. Except for a few straggling hairs on his neck and chin his face was clean and almost Indian smooth – as though he no longer shaved and the pores of his skin had thus neatly sealed themselves over with wax. Only his sunken temples were those of an aging man; the earpieces of his steel-rimmed glasses went across them like miniature railroad tracks spanning deep brown gorges.

It was a warm day in June and after a while – without ever looking up from his newspaper – the man removed his coat and laid it carefully across his knee. I could see that his light-blue pin stripe shirt was frayed a little at the collar, but it looked freshly washed and ironed. The sleeves were kept precisely at wristbone level by two rubber bands around his upper arms.

For a quarter of an hour the man read his paper, thoroughly and capably – never moving his lips or using his finger to steady a line of print, never bringing the paper closer to his face. Occasionally he gazed off into the elms, as if reflecting on the significance of a paragraph.

Finally it was time for him to leave. He pulled out a round gold watch from his shirt pocket, checked the hour, and after slipping the watch back into his pocket put on his coat. He folded his newspaper several times so that it would fit easily into his hand, then began walking across the plaza. I couldn't be sure, but I thought I recognized Francisco Madero alighting from a Juárez street car just across the way.

# Alien

One morning in mid-August I decided to take a stroll along Rim Road. It was impressive, as usual – the sweep of streets-and-sky that blended so easily into both time and space. I stood for a long while at the rim's edge, trying to take it all in: two cities sprawled in the sun, spread from horizon to horizon, century to century.... My, my, I thought – looking out, looking down – such a place of perspectives, this El Paso; such a city of hillsides and vistas, of flatlands and heights, of neighborhoods that climb and wind and slope.... Yessir, a fine place, always interesting to the eye.

I turned away and began walking along the streets north of Rim Road – Blacker, Hague, Campbell. I passed homes of the well-to-do with their smooth hedges and manicured lawns. A quiet neighborhood on a quiet mesa, it was like a museum of tastefully maintained houses and orderly lives – deserted, now, at ten o'clock except for occasional yard men and maids. Down the street a man in a straw hat and blue bandanna hanging down his neck was cutting the grass. On a back porch a young woman in a white apron slowly dusted a rug. Locust sounds soared and then fell dramatically in the trees. A mockingbird sailed down on graceful, outstretched wings and began to sport about in the shining grass near a water sprinkler.

At an intersection I stopped and stared – I couldn't help it. I wanted to absorb the sights of this summer morning into the very tissues of my body. I looked west, and the homes dipped in a smooth, rhythmic line as the Juárez mountains slowly rose in the distance – making a neat and pleasing balance. Overhead, the sky was a cloudless blue saucer, swept clean by an early-fall breeze that kept bathing my face and making a tall sycamore on the corner move its leaves in a continuous sycamore dance. Tree shadows had spread themselves across deep-green yards and into the streets.

Standing there, I couldn't resist the temptation to put something down on paper – to record the moment and the place. I pulled a small notebook from my pocket and began to write – turning here and there, trying to soak up the essence of a morning and a neighborhood so blessed with sunlit, El Paso serenity.

It was then that I saw him – the white-haired man who was crossing the street from his yard behind me.

"Who are you?" he demanded. "What do you want?"

At first I did not answer. I finished making a note. Finally, half-turning, I said, "I'm a citizen of this town and I am standing in a public street." I smiled a bit and looked at him more directly, hoping he would appreciate my reply – would take it as an appeal to his basic good sense and back off from his aggressive stance.

But he would have none of it. With his head and shoulders bent at a slight angle he stared at me and came a step closer – a man in his sixties not used, I thought, to verbal sparring matches in the middle of a street.

"What are you writing?" he asked next. It was not a question; it was a command.

Now I have to tell you: I was in no mood to give him satisfaction. If he had bothered to introduce himself and make some kind of courteous inquiry, I would have probably indulged the man: told him right off I was a teacher, that I wrote. I would have humored the guy. But his tight-lipped and blunt interrogation was a patrician's demand that his questions be answered by a lesser mortal: in his mind we were not equals, socially or any other way. By pausing there on the street I had become the accused and he the accuser, judge, and jury.

"Look," I said. "It's a nice day and I don't want to ruin it.... If I had thrown a rock through the window of that house over there, or sprawled out on your lawn, then you would have a right to ask me questions. But this is not your neighborhood; you don't own it and – "

"It is my neighborhood," he shot back. "I've lived here for thirty years. And I want to know what you're doing."

We were less than a foot apart. He stood peering into my face, his mouth slightly quivering. He was definitely worked up – wanting to know exactly what kind of strange fish he was dealing with.

It was a stalemate. I felt no obligation to satisfy the curiosity of a man who suddenly appears before me and demands: Identify yourself. Justify yourself. Explain yourself.

The man turned on his heel and went over to stand on his lawn. He continued to glare at me. I walked away. I had almost reached my car when it hit me: So that's what a Mexican-American, minding his own business, feels when he is stopped by the Border Patrol: that instant rage, flush of anger, stubborn refusal to cooperate when asked to Identify, Justify, Explain simply because he is on an El Paso street and has a brown skin. Sure, I knew the role of the Border Patrol: illegal aliens pour into El Paso and it is the job of the men in green vans to find them. And sure, I understood where the white-haired man was coming from: he felt protective about "his" neighborhood and had seen a guy in old tennis shoes staring at things – a guy who was writing something down. Certainly a suspicious character. Better check him out.

I believe that if I had stayed there much longer – undocumented – the white-haired man would have gone inside his house and called the police. They would have probably answered his call and – to satisfy this worthy and allay his fears – would have asked me to Identify myself. And I think I would have refused to do so – would have bowed up indignantly as I did when accosted by the Concerned Citizen; would have stood there and asked, steadfastly: Why?

I wish now that I had tested my rights – found out if I would have actually been arrested in my favorite city for pausing too long to look at the sky.

# Back Road to Las Cruces

I drove to Old Mesilla — seeing ahead of me the jagged Las
Cruces mountains rising to meet the summer-noon haze, seeing to the
east the reddish Franklins stretched along the horizon like a gigantic
statement from the past that had been preserved in granite.

I looked out at the day — just that: the day — and it was there in
the summer light as I first saw it as a child: when I was profoundly
innocent of adult knowledges, when a single day was the same as life
itself, when each morning and afternoon meant possibility and
promise.

That kind of day — full of shining surfaces, breezes, pleasing rural
sounds — was outside my car window. The beckoning lure of life was in
the upward thrust of the mountains, in the midday gleam of irrigation
water that ran beside the lettuce and alfalfa fields, in the globe willows
standing at the curve of the road and the *whurr* of blackbirds riding on
springy salt cedars. The green fields and brown shining earth carried a
simple message of renewal, and the sun spread it across each weed and
child and dog and rose bush and orange crate. It was free for the asking — which was to say: for the seeing, the knowing, the understanding.

Just before La Union I took a walk down one of the canals,
through a pecan orchard, and it was like a park beneath the trees: cool
and shadowed and still. I stood there, the sun on my back, the pecan
trees gracious in their immobility and deep shade. I took a green pecan
from a limb, scraped my fingernail across it, and smelled the rich, tart
smell. It was a little thing to do — to smell a pecan — but that is what
the road to Old Mesilla is all about.

I drove on, slowly. From time to time I pulled over to the shoulder and let faster cars and trucks go by. I was in no hurry.

At Chamberino I passed an adobe house with washing on the
line, a dog sleeping by a door, a boy playing with a stick in the small

dirt yard. It was like a Platonic Idea framed in the car window: Boy, Shaded Yard, Smooth Packed Earth, Timeless Summertime.

At La Mesa I got out again, stood beside the car, looked, turned, looked some more, turned again.... What a remarkable strip of earth I was standing on. The cotton fields were spread out like gigantic green quilts sewed with yellow thread, and above them the clouds sat on a dish of deep blue. And the sun: it shone and cleansed and illuminated and made perfect every leaf on every tree. It was the land's antiseptic and sustainer, beautifier and companion.

And the mountains: at four o'clock they were solemn intermediaries to distance, to the sky.

And the afternoon silence: it was not something separate but somehow consisted of the fields and mountains and sun-washed space. Birds on the wing seemed to know this secret, could thrive on it like an elixir.

In Las Cruces I ordered a hamburger and fries at a Lota Burger and sat outside at a small table, reading. I ate and I read.

Then I looked up, looked east, and once again I understood why I had eyes, why I drew breath, why I live in the West.

The sky had turned overcast, there had been late afternoon showers, and now, just before sundown, rain was in the sawtooth Organ Mountains.

My table offered a wide-open view. In front of me was a low line of brick and adobe houses shining in the sun. Beyond them the Organs lay behind a film of sunlit gauze, and violet-colored cloud islands stretched out in long archipelagoes.

To the left of the main peak a red-yellow-and-green gash – a dramatically flung segment of a rainbow – arched downward into the mountain mist and upward into the overhanging clouds.

The sky was a monumental palette of pastels, and the bright multicolored connective arc an almost metaphysical slash: an otherworldly signature.

A breeze moved the pages of my book, the sky was still an ocean awash with summer blues and grays, and the solid, purplish Organ range loomed like Olympus, taking as its due the moment of sundown grandeur. Shadows lay in the gorges; the mountain tips were tinged with rose and pink: desert cosmetics the gods allowed themselves from time to time.

Suddenly, before I could take the next bite of fries, the rainbow gash extended itself into a gigantic arch from the horizon in the north to the horizon in the south: an all-encompassing Metro-Goldwyn-Mayer extravaganza across and above the sky, framing all in sight: mountains, clouds, rain, sky.

And just as suddenly – behind me – the sun went down, the east turned bruised and faded, became private and withdrawn. Day died in an instant, and the Lota Burger sign began to put forth its pale attempt at neon glory.

# Irmalinda

Irmalinda steals, and I will have to let her go. But I cannot say to her, "Irmalinda, you steal" – just like that. First of all, I have never caught her taking anything: I have no proof. Things are simply missing from the house – a little money, a few towels, my wife's hairpins, a couple of diapers. They are all small things, things that would fit easily into Irmalinda's purse when she leaves each afternoon and returns to Juárez.

It is the principle, of course – you don't want to have a maid you can't trust. She will just keep on taking things until you can't afford to ignore it. And besides, if she steals, perhaps she isn't to be trusted with the baby. You just can't tell....

"Irmalinda, there is something I must tell you. You are stealing from us; therefore I must let you go" – is that how to do it: abruptly, the Master of the House informing the Pilfering Servant Girl she must leave? I would be perfectly within my rights. I have no proof, true, but things are definitely missing – and it is a situation which can only grow worse. How could I possibly keep on calmly greeting her each day, saying, "Good morning, Irmalinda; is it very cold out?" and then wondering what she was going to carry away in the afternoon – a comb, perhaps, or a pair of my wife's earrings, or one of the baby's dresses?

Yet I keep saying to myself: maybe I ought to drop this righteous attitude. For I have been to Juárez. I know how the people are forced to live there. I have walked those streets and seen the old women scavenging in garbage cans; I have seen the poverty and have felt the pangs of guilt at my having so much when they have so little. And I have read enough and seen enough to realize that morality is generally no more than a point of view: I, the white Protestant college graduate living in my air-conditioned house, can look upon life with a purity and idealism that a black man in Mississippi or a Mexican in Juárez does not share. (Steal? rob a supermarket? Ah, no, the moral one says: I would not. Or is it only that I need not?)

All right, I say: what if I simply accept the fact that a few pins, a diaper here and there, twenty cents bus fare twice a week are things I can well afford to lose to my little splintery-legged Irmalinda. Aren't they small contributions indeed to a sixteen-year-old girl whose mother not only works but is pregnant again as well – a girl with seven smaller sisters at home ready to join the Juárez labor force whenever they can get their permits? Isn't life hard enough, unfair enough, to someone like Irmalinda – who should still be in school instead of washing clothes and sweeping floors – without my having to play the role of the godly American *patrón?*

Yes – and my inner dialogue turns still another corner: doesn't she actually expect to get caught? When she works up to canned goods and silverware – as undoubtedly she will if I let her – how can she hope not to be confronted one day and asked to leave? Even as young as she is, isn't she simply being fatalistic, knowing she has to take whatever she can before the inevitable dismissal?

I pursue my questions, and can only come to one sad conclusion: I will have to let her go. Despite knowing that Irmalinda, like the underprivileged everywhere, simply regards stealing as one of the weapons of the Have Nots in their long silent war with the Haves, I must hold her accountable. To understand why she steals does not excuse me from doing what I think is right.

Somehow, though I'm not sure why, I have the feeling that Irmalinda will take her dismissal perfectly in stride – with a slight shrug and a nod and an "All right, sir, if that is your wish." She will gather her few personal things out of the closet and then, smiling one last childish but already professional smile, she will leave the house, closing the door firmly and quietly behind her and walking with her bare, lonely Mexican dignity down the street toward the bus stop.

# On Sunset Road

I

We live in the Upper Valley near the greenery of the Rio Grande. We thrive near elms and cotton fields. I am content. My half acre on Sunset Road is my private island in the universe bathed by a radiant desert light. It is a place of trees and animals, children and stabilities. As I water the front grass I can watch the cars go by; when I finish I can sit on the porch and watch the cars some more. Time flows evenly in measured, human-sized amounts.

I enjoy simple, sensory pleasures. I walk around drinking tall glasses of iced tea flavored with mint from the yard. I smell beans cooking on the stove. On Saturday mornings I stand with a cup of coffee in the kitchen doorway, thinking pleasurably, "It's Saturday morning" – and it is as if we have all been rewarded or blessed.

I go outside and stand a while looking at Fellini, our sheep, grazing the back lot. I visit the quail in their cages and the pigeons sitting
in the low branches of the elms. I look at their watchful pigeon eyes as
they sit there looking back at me, and I know I am glad to be living in
my peaceable kingdom.

On late afternoons I watch our black rabbit leave the shrubs of
the church rectory across Sunset Road and come down our long plank
fence. He is returning home from the Great World before dark – coming back to the security of the other animals after having ventured
abroad to St. Matthew's during the day. He noses under the fence and
goes to his accustomed place under the big elm. He eats his alfalfa pellets, cleans himself a bit, then sprawls out beside his bowl.

Sometimes I go outside after dark to walk around. Neighborhood
kids are still riding their bikes along side streets, offering a few last-
ditch yells before surrendering to the demands of bedtime. Stars are
out. I listen to the night as I sit for a while on an overturned bucket
beside the rabbit. He never seems to think I am intruding. He just flat-
tens his ears and stretches out a bit more comfortably. It is a good
moment, I think, for both of us.

## II

At five o'clock Byron is up from his nap and comes outside in his
red tennis shoes and undershorts to play in the irrigation water. The
ducks have moved from the cool shaded ditch where they have been
swimming and diving since noon and are now nuzzling loudly in the
sunny, flooded grass in the middle of the lot. They seem giddy, almost
overcome by this sudden wealth of water, and give frantic accordion
wheezes of delight.

The turkeys walking nearby go perk, the ducks continue to suck
noisily in the shallow pool of water-and-light, the huge Rhode Island
Reds plod about in the wet grassy strangeness.

At supper I eat with my daughter – just the two of us at the
kitchen table. I fix ham sandwiches, and then after peeling a couple of

peaches I put sugar on them and serve them in a dish. There are a couple of leftover pancakes from breakfast, and jam, and half a pear, and orange drink.

I look across the table at Deborah and consider her future. I watch her eat the inside of her sandwich – leaving, as usual, the outer edge – and try to imagine her as she will be later on in school, and married, and with children of her own. I sit there, knowing that nothing I can ever do will save her from pain, or disappointments, or the whims of fate. I watch her, sitting in the green curved-back chair, and listen to her shrewd eight-year-old's questions that make chills go up my back: innocence-in-pigtails starting to unfurl her sail, beginning her long drifting out to sea....

I leave the children, and their unknown future – Byron in the bedroom with his coloring book, Deborah still swinging her legs at the table – and go stand for a while in the back lot. It is the Saturday after a week of rain and the scattered patches of grass are a confident, paint-can green in the sandy soil, and the garden tomatoes hang rich-red on their vines. The afternoon thundershowers have moved on and left the clouds and the mountains in a sweeping display of heroic desert sky. In the vacant lot beyond the fence the sun glows like varnish on the new lumber of a half-built house. There is a barnyard mellowness under the nearby trees as the chickens and turkeys and pigeons settle in their cages for the night. High above the Upper Valley a hawk coasts in the currents of a sweetened west wind.

## III

I sit in the living room looking out, and the afternoon is framed within the window. Just that: a window scene, an everyday moment. But momentous. Summer light, like invisible acid, is etching trees and houses and grasses. It is a timelessness that I see – a moment of eternity under the sun – and it burns in the creosote depths of a telephone pole, in the gleam of a mailbox.

The radiance of the ordinary is what I am talking about.

Everything just is, yes, but *supremely*. There is a drama in the undramatic, an awesomeness in the commonplace.

Creation happened today, if we can see it. Not to see it is to rob the earth of its mystery and depth.

So I sit and I look and I say: I would not trade lives with anyone. I like, too much, the way I see the days – the earthly paradise of sun and greenery, of rocks in a field and fences standing in the shade. I take too much pleasure in a patch of dirt, a weed; in flies in the air and buildings at rest and mountains jutting through the morning haze; in a wheelbarrow, a gum wrapper in the grass.

To be sure, there is nothing grandiose about a beetle or a gourd, yet any living thing, seen clearly, is stunning. I look about me and I see sacred substances, for wherever we walk is holy ground.

## IV

This summer I have a job to do. I watch thirty elms, large and small, as the elm leaf beetles try to destroy them.

I don't really have to watch them – watch as the beetles eat the leaves, watch as the leaves grow brown and brittle and begin to blow across the yards in the wind – but I do it anyway.

I seem to have no better thing to do with my time than water patches of grass, fix a sagging gate, watch the elms. (And the mountains beyond. And sunlight in the air.)

I am only fit for this kind of thing. Day watching. Tree watching. Watching the two thin-legged, inelegant white turkeys as they walk about in the heat.

And I do not know if it is a summer of sickness or supreme health: sitting in a chair, looking out.

## V

I have with me a clipboard, pencil, paper. I am sitting on an old chair beneath five small elms that make a nice canopy of green. It is the long moment after sundown.

I am in the back lot where the garden used to be. Byron is batting dirt clods with a stick. Fellini is nosing through islands of grass that are smooth from her daily grazing. The pigeons walk nearby on another stretch of grass.

...Eight-thirty on a late July afternoon. All cells are in equilibrium, all pulses are serenely beating. The sheep, my son, the pigeons, the neighbor's quiet yard: We are in the calm eye of creation's daily hurricane.

Thus I can say, in this green-leaf cave: I am totally, consciously alive, and I have no wants. There are no mountains to climb, no metaphysical puzzles to solve. Whatever is absolute is here before my eyes in the back lot, in this ordinary moment before dark.

Creation is this time-and-place — invisible as the roots of trees, relentless as a dirt clod falling.

## VI

I hear Byron in the back yard, feeding Sniffles. He is in his green-and-white tennis shoes, carrying a bag of Purina Dog Chow. He brings the dog food back into the house and replaces it in the bottom of the kitchen cabinet. It is 7:30 in the morning, the sun is beginning to slant strongly through the elms — and he is whistling. Moving about rather jauntily as he does so. Going to the change jar on the buffet and getting out his school lunch money. As he puts fifty cents in his blue jeans he sees his balsa-wood airplane on the couch — still upended against the spelling book from the crash landing of the night before. He goes to it, straightens the wings, examines a chipped spot in the tail, and then experimentally sails it toward the living room — still whistling, still mildly bouncing.

The whistle: it is mainly tuneless. There is possibly an intent to duplicate the theme from "Star Wars," but no matter: reproducing a recognizable melody is incidental. It is the spirit of the whistling that counts: the lilt, the verve, the mindless morning nonchalance of finding yourself rather on top of things: of being a nine-year-old and feeling no pain, of having done your chores without being asked, of having seen Junior the cat yawn luxuriously from his bed in the honeysuckle vine, of having heard the red gate slam familiarly behind you as you carry the coffee can of grain around to the chickens, of having listened to your own footsteps cross wooden floors of the house, of having seen the front door standing there beyond the breakfast table, opening toward your day: of having felt your striped T-shirt against your skin and your lunch money in your jeans as you walk about through the shadowy light of the rooms.

My son whistles, shrilly, easily, monotonously. He does not smile or speak, but he has no need to. Whistling at 7:30 on a school morning: that's quite enough.

## VII

I live alone. My children visit me.

Byron, eleven, half-runs across the back yard, heading past me toward the gate. He does not run full speed because there is no sense of urgency: He is luxuriating in the knowledge that he is home again for the summer. Yet he runs instead of merely walking because he is in fact here at home after a three months' absence.

He bangs through the gate, scattering ducks and causing Fellini to rise awkwardly in alarm from her bed beneath the chinaberry tree.

"Dad," Byron calls, "what's wrong with the duck?"

"I don't know," I say, and come over to look at one of the females. Her left eye is shut and crusted.

Byron half-turns toward the pigeon and turkey pens – still on the move, still checking out the territory. He is pleased at his discovery of the duck's eye – pleased that he is once again part of the life of the house and yard, noticing things, telling me about them. It is almost as if he has never been away – as if there has been no divorce, as if nothing has changed, as if running across the back lot to his buddy Steve's house is something he has been doing all spring.

I tell Byron we will certainly have to watch that eye for the next few days — purposely saying we, wanting the casual sound of it in the air; wanting, like Byron, to establish old routines.

I go back to raking the lawn. After a while I hear voices, then see them, on bicycles, riding out of the Dahill garage. It is a familiar sight: Byron in front, his legs pumping briskly, Steve behind, both heading toward the church parking lot.

As I watch Byron calls out: "Hi, Dad," he says, not slowing, legs still pumping, blond hair shining in the sun.

Just two words, said in passing — unnecessary words, really, because he had left me in the yard not five minutes before.

But they are not a greeting. They are Byron's final affirmation of his return, of his being once more in the long vacant lot beneath the trees. He is comfortable, he is where he wants to be for the summer, and he cannot contain himself. "Hi, Dad," he says, instead of "Look at me: I'm here, I'm home."

# VI

# ANAIS

## I

A day seldom passes that I do not think of Anais Brautigan. She is dead now – her ashes in a jar – but I cannot leave her alone. She haunts me dead as she haunted me alive, and I have a need to tell about her: to reach back and re-examine the summer we were together on River Road and the time that followed.

It was May and I was at loose ends, recovering from a divorce after eighteen years of marriage. A friend said, "Hey, why don't you look up Anais. She's...*different*, and terribly bright. She's had more things happen to her than the law allows, but she paints and writes poetry and raises greyhounds – I bet you'd like her."

I was teaching then in San Antonio, and with school nearly out – and a bleak-looking summer ahead – I thought, okay, why not, I've got nothing to lose. So I called her up one Sunday. We talked a bit and Anais told me how to get to her place south of town.

I followed her directions and drove through San Antonio to the city limits. I turned off the interstate onto a paved road that went past heat-seared fields, roadside junk piles, occasional oil rigs pumping among mesquites. I bounced onto a dusty, unpaved road and kept going past yellowing gourd vines and cactuses. It was depressing flat-land under a hot South Texas sky.

When the road came to a T, I saw a small handwritten sign on a board – River Road, No Trespassing – and turned right toward a line of tall trees. I drove through a natural archway made by two huge oaks, entered a shadowy tunnel of druidic-looking elms, and there it was: a brief clearing in the river-bottom jungle and a small white frame house within a new chainlink fence: Anais Brautigan's hideaway acre.

I drove up to her gate, and before I had time to wonder if I should honk she was coming out the front door. She walked towards the gate, smiling, smoking a cigarette and holding a smooth black greyhound on a leash. She wore dark glasses, tight blue-jean short-shorts, a man's white dress hat, and high heels.

"Do-you-have-your-toothbrush?" she asked in a Germanic drawl, still smiling, looking at me above her dark glasses as I got out of the car.

And that was that: The next weekend I moved in with Anais, her greyhounds, paintings, radio tuned twenty-four hours a day to low-volume Beethoven and Pavarotti, and I stayed until the end of August.

I must be clear about this: I felt no love for Anais in the beginning. I don't fall in love easily. But there was an immediate companionship between us — an automatic ease. When we started talking that Sunday afternoon it was as if we were picking up a conversation we had stopped temporarily a few days before.

Those first summer days: they were like a ball of string that just kept casually unwinding. We talked, and ate, and drank coffee; we made love, and read, and did chores around the place. We sat in the side yard under the tall, interlocking elms and drank beer and talked and then made love and held each other in the dark. Another day would begin and our routine would start all over again.

Sometimes in the afternoon I would go for a walk or a run down the road. Sometimes — rarely — a friend of hers stopped by. And sometimes we would drive in to a shopping area at the south edge of town. We bounced along, the two of us in her truck, past the dust-covered hackberries standing in the blazing heat, and we were in our exact, proper places: as if we had spent the first fifty years of our lives getting ready to sit together in a Mazda cab at 3:30 on a summer afternoon. We would go into a liquor store next to the Value Club and walk around among the bottles. Anais would get a fifth of Jack Daniels and a carton of Marlboros; I would get a bottle of white wine. As we stood together at the check-out counter I would look up into the small TV screen of the surveillance camera and see her there beside me: the curiously diminished Anais in her small gangster hat smoking her small cigarette ( — as though already miniaturized into memory, into a photograph). We would get back into the truck, drive the lackluster south-side roads past the drab subdivision houses, go back under the interstate – and it was as if we had been off on an extended vacation: the connection between us was that calm, that close. It felt like a married-life homecoming to be heading toward Anais' little house with the trumpet vines growing across the west wall and circling down over the butane tank; with the two greyhounds asleep inside the house on the front room rug; with the summer sun bearing down and the rusty air conditioner roaring in the bedroom window as we pulled up next to the gate.

(When I woke on the first Sunday in June the windows were open and Anais was curled next to me, still asleep. I lay there a while, my arm beneath her waist, my face touching her hair. Then I raised up carefully and sat against the headboard with a pillow behind my back.

It was 8:30 and the house was still. I looked at the shadowed corners of the room, the wood stove, the clothes hanging across the tops of doors. I looked through the window screen at the trunks of the elms. I heard the doves at the river. It was like the first morning of the world, and I was content.

I sat there in the bed and thought of the Sundays of my adult life – the days that shriveled my spirit, the days I always had to kill, hour by vacant hour – and then I looked down at the evenly rising and falling shoulders of Anais and smiled: It would be a River Road Sunday all day long.)

There were only the two greyhounds that summer: Cleopatra, the regal black queen mother, and Apollo, the tawny son that Anais planned to race in the fall. I would stand in the front room, drinking coffee, and look at River Road royalty stretched out in their chairs. They were dozing or sleeping – who could tell. Their chins were slung off the edge of the two big chairs almost to the floor. If I had fired a cannon over their heads they would not have moved an eyelid.

One afternoon when Anais and I were giving them a little exercise in the back lot, I decided to sprint ahead toward the river and invited them to join me. "Come on!" I yelled over my shoulder to Apollo, and he took off toward me like a shot.

I didn't know anything about greyhounds – gazehounds, as they are called. I didn't know that they do not swerve to avoid humans as other dogs do. They keep coming, gazing ahead, gazing beyond.... Apollo did just that. He ran into me and across me and kept on going. It was while I was on my knees in the dirt, with Apollo blazing toward the river in his incredible rocket lope, that I remembered the story Anais had told me: A farm friend had come visiting one afternoon and had yelled, "Oh, Apollo!... Cleopatra!" as I had done, motioning to them from below the garden. They had bolted toward her, doubling, tripling their speed in an instant, and while she stood there in the field – this kindly, smiling, white-haired grandmother – Apollo had flattened her like a white-tasseled stalk of corn.

Several mornings we meandered through the county in her truck. We listened to her tapes – Wailin' Waylon, Madonna, Kitaro – and drove past junky trailer houses with half a dozen cars pulled nose-in toward the trailer door, past faded curve-of-the-road beer joints and abandoned old houses half-visible among vines and weeds and drooping tree limbs. Sometimes we would stop and make our way past the dumped debris of old sofas with the stuffing coming out and pick bucketsful of wild grapes that grew along the fences. Or we would end up at Braunig Lake and Anais would get out her paints and do a few watercolors while I wandered along the shore. At dusk the wind would get up and the little waves would come washing in. Men in worn tennis shoes and with toothless, sunken jaws would stand next to their tents, beer in hand, and tell us about the red fish they would be catching after dark.

On the way back from the lake one night we started talking about cornbread – good, satisfying, red-beans-and-butter cornbread: family recipe, flaky, made-with-buttermilk cornbread. We worked up an enthusiasm and an appetite for cornbread we did not know we had. I pulled off the highway at the next stop-and-shop, bought buttermilk, and for supper Anais made a panful of cornbread that we ate like cake.

(I don't think Anais ever hurried in her life. She had an inner
metronome that measured her stride, and she moved the way a cat
would move walking upright. It was both a physical mannerism and a
philosophical statement. I am in control, the walk said. I do not plan
on being seriously deterred or surprised or thwarted, but, if I should
be, it does not matter.

It was good to watch her anywhere – drifting along the aisles of a
supermarket, looking for a three-way electrical plug or a can of mush-
rooms, or coming out the front door of her house to greet a visitor:
With the screen door shutting gently in her wake, she would pass
through the affectionate front-yard lunges of the greyhounds like
Faulkner's barefooted boy moving obliviously through the maelstrom
of hurtling, wild-eyed spotted horses.

I liked her best, though, when she was prowling the side of a
pool table when we went over to the Friendly Tavern. With her black-
and-white gangster hat pulled low and at an angle, with her constant
cigarette at its downward slant, she circled the table in the subdued
bar light. She would chalk her cue stick and lift her gaze slightly to
look over at me above her dark glasses, then look back down, slide a
few steps along the table in her narrow black boots, make her shot,
keep on moving in her cat-like way – already preparing for her next
shot as the ball rattled down through the chute.)

One night she fixed rainbow trout with brown rice and white
wine. She put on a dress and earrings and high heels. The light was
dim, just a candle on the kitchen table. After supper we sat outside in
the dark, talking. The trees loomed about us and from time to time a
strange hidden bird at the river – almost like a manic jungle-bird in a
movie – gave out its screaming teakettle calls. We talked and listened
to the bird and finished off the bottle of wine.

Anais took the wine glasses inside; I went around to the back of
the house to bring in the laundry from the line. She took off her shoes
and went back outside to water her marigolds by the front porch. I
had an armful of shirts and was reaching for the socks when I heard

her yell out my name. I ran inside and found Anais holding on to a chair in the front room, her bare foot raised. "Something bit me," she said. She had turned off the hose and started toward the porch, she said, when she felt a stab – sharp and hard.

I made her sit down, and after I tilted the lamp for better light examined her foot. I couldn't see the sign of a sting or any swelling. There didn't seem to be any mark at all. I told her it was probably a scorpion, but she was shaking her head no: she had stepped on scorpions before. This was different. I said, well, maybe it was a tree asp. They were around and they could hurt.

Anais was one to downplay discomforts and pains – almost to belittle them as being beneath her – but it was obvious she was hurting. "I need to lie down," she said, and I helped her into the bedroom.

She kept getting worse.

"I think...it might have been a water moccasin," she said. "Maybe a little one." At first I didn't think that was a possibility – the house was fifty yards from the river. But she said – her voice barely audible – water moccasins were known to breed that far from water. She thought maybe they had made a den under the house.

I called Southwest Baptist Hospital and told them we were coming.

"Let's go," I said, and I half-supported, half-carried her to my car.

As I was driving fiercely through the southside San Antonio streets, Anais asked me for a piece of paper and I tore a page from a little notebook I carried in my shirt pocket. I turned on the dome light and she began to write as she leaned against her door. "What are you doing?" I asked as we hurtled along. "Writing my will.... I don't think I'm going to make it to the hospital." She wrote her holistic will, as she called it, on the little sheet – stating in one sentence that she was leaving all her earthly goods to me. She signed it, handed it to me, and sagged further against the door.

At the hospital the doctor on duty gave her a shot of Benedril as she lay on an emergency room bed. He could find no fang marks, he said, and he could not explain her symptoms. Maybe a snake bite; maybe not. After we waited another hour or so Anais said she felt she could make the drive back home.

She remained sick the rest of the week. She would get up for a while but would soon go back to bed. Her ankle was swollen a bit but not too much. She kept running a degree of fever, off and on, and had a general sense of malaise.

One night I heard Apollo barking out in front. I turned on the porch light and went outside. About a yard beyond the porch, in a coil, was a small, grayish-green snake. I yelled at Apollo to get away and carefully reached for the hoe that was leaning against an elm tree. I struck the snake a good lick and killed it. Then I called through the bedroom window to Anais. She came to the front door and I showed her the snake draped over the hoe. "Well, that's one," she drawled. "The brothers are waiting for you under the house, I suspect."

The next morning I got a flashlight and peered through an opening in the tin bottom that ran along the side of the house. There certainly could be a snake den under there, but I wasn't too keen about searching for it. I walked gingerly around in the yard, thinking about the problem. It might have been just the one little moccasin that had bitten Anais – the one that I had draped across the chainlink fence and was now shriveling in the sun – or there could be more.

Each night for several nights I went on snake hunts in the yard with a flashlight and a hoe. I walked carefully, slowly. The first night I found another small, gray-green moccasin and I racked him smartly with the hoe. I killed a third one the next night. Then no more.

Anais had heard, somewhere, of a pro-life organization called Save-a-Snake. They were conservation-minded folks who would come to your house or farm and catch – and save – any snakes you didn't want around. We agreed they were just the ones to go crawling around under her house. We gave them a call, and the young woman on the phone said they would try to be out within the week and thank-you-folks-a-lot.

Anais slowly returned to good health and, as the workaday world kept on going beyond the rim of the river trees, we did nothing that did not please us. We joked about being so unrepentantly white-trash sorry. At noon, after pouring glasses of white wine, we would fix cheese-and-jalapeño nachos and put them in the microwave; then we crunched on them as we sat at the big cluttered kitchen table and listened to Ella Fitzgerald tapes – watching Sarah, the small gray cat that sat on the microwave and watched us back.

If Anais would go into the bedroom afterward to fold laundry, I would come to the doorway, lean against the frame, and say that the bed certainly did look nice in its two o'clock shadow. And with the sun blazing down and the air-conditioner whirring – and the dogs asleep on the front room rug and the chorus of elm-tree locusts rising and falling outside like evangelicals of summer heat – we would take off our clothes and once again be as luxuriously, as deliciously sorry as we had been all the days before.

It was on one such afternoon that the Save-a-Snake couple drove out. Anais and I were in bed. She was in her climax, yelling out her curious cry, "Oh, God-dy, oh God-dy!" when the dusty, beat-up brown van stopped in front. I had finished – was arched back, almost ready to collapse and fall across Anais – when I saw them through the window. "Be with you in a minute!" I yelled as the door of the van opened and a tall, rawbony young man in overalls and a painter's cap got out. I held Anais, telling her in a rush, "The snake people are here!" and rolled off to my feet. I put on my shorts while Anais lay there grinning up at me ( – grinning the way I liked to see her best, without lipstick, stretching the sensitive skin of her full and beautifully symmetrical lips). She eased off the bed, put on a shift and sandals, and we went out to meet the snake couple at the gate.

The rawbony hunter crawled around underneath the house to his heart's content but did not find any snakes. Anais and his plump companion talked about canning tomatoes.

One early morning in July we took our coffee cups and sat on a bench in the back yard beneath the trees, watching our bantams – the six we had bought at a flea market near the interstate. The garden we had started was now burned to a crisp, but in the little chicken run we had our six bantams to look at and enjoy and it was like money in the bank. The dogs roamed about in the yard, crapping huge craps; the river sycamores loomed against the sky. Anais and I sat close on the bench, drinking our coffee, watching the chickens go after bugs as we would have indulgently watched children at play.

At night we sometimes played Scrabble on the front room rug. Typically, I would find myself staring at one of the strange-looking words she had just made. She would casually slide each square into place on the board; then not smiling but almost, she would lower her head and look at me over the top of her glasses: "Care-to-look-it-up?" she would ask. I would reach over and get her huge brown Oxford dictionary from behind the chair. I knew it was useless to check, but surely – surely once she would be bluffing. But there it was: a three-letter word meaning "Japanese urn." Or maybe she had made a two-letter word: "si." It would of course turn out to be the fifth note on some obscure scale or other. Through her curling cigarette smoke she would watch me close the dictionary, shake my head, and write down her points.

We played half a dozen games during the summer – each time at her suggestion, of course – and she won them all.

Despite Scrabble, I felt very much at home in the little white house. I did nothing in particular – write a little, read a little – and doing nothing was quite enough. Just being there with Anais was satisfying.

Yet there were times when I felt cut off from much of who and what I had been before I met her. I felt torn between the old framework of my life and this new, separate, almost hermetic world along the river: the flat, coastal southside with its fields, sunflowers, mesquites, dust-layered weeds; the canopied twilight mood along

River Road; the river-bottom greenery, the almost undersea shadow-
and-depth of trees, trees, more trees.... I had wandered into a strange
and compelling oasis – with the sky, the familiar world outside seeming vaguely unreal – and I could not quite decide how to feel about it.

Sunk into the privateness of myself, I would rake leaves in the
side yard – the mindless raking letting my thoughts unwind. It was
obvious that Anais wanted me but I did not – so soon after my divorce
– want to be wanted quite that much. I liked to be with her, but on my
own terms. It was as if we were two boats that had drifted together
and were rocking side by side in a pleasant inland bay – with a rope
flung loosely from one deck to the other to keep us from ebbing apart.
I was definitely glad to have dropped anchor for a while, but I wanted
to keep my freedom: to be able to pull up my anchor if necessary.

So I kept resisting, for the first month and a half, being pulled out
of my own separate space. Anais was magnetic, but there were things
about her that gave me the willies. I just couldn't cross the last hurdle
of commitment until I knew, for sure, that I loved her.

Late one afternoon I asked her if she wanted to leave the house
for a while – go have a drink some place, just get out. No, she said,
she was feeling tired – running a 99.9 temperature again. I said, I think
I'll go on the southside for a while, be back after a bit.

I left, bought a few home-grown tomatoes and a newspaper at a
little roadside store, read the paper in the car under a tree. I drove in
past the interstate and had a beer in a tavern that had a long, uncrowd-
ed bar and played conjunto music on the jukebox. Afterwards I sat in
my car in the dusk: just sat, like a rock enjoying its own inertia. I
looked at cars passing, at the night falling. I decided that Anais would
not want to fool with supper – she would just want to sleep as she had
the afternoon before – so I got a bite to eat at a nearby cafe.

About ten o'clock I went back to River Road. Anais was wild. She
was walking her slow walk in the front room, and smoking. She wanted to know who She was – this woman I had gone in to see. I told her
– tried to tell her – that I hadn't seen anyone, that I just needed to get

away for a little solitude and self. I opened the sack from the car and handed her the three glossy tomatoes. She threw them back at me and turned away.

It took two more hours of constant talk before finally – or so she said – she believed me.

## II

Nagging problems had been there all along but they were in the background – small stuff, I thought.

For one thing I could not stop feeling like a guest. It was Anais' house, her dogs, her lifestyle, her repair work that needed to be done, her friends that we went to see occasionally. It was her this and her that, and I understood it should be that way. I could not presume that I should walk into her life and take over what was hers. I did not want to act like the male chauvinist that she so stridently disliked. Things might have turned out differently – might, I say – if she had come to live at my house, in my town, among my friends; or if we had gone off to some neutral area to our house and started our life together. But the River Road dynamics were loaded: she was in her element and I was not. Thus at times I knew I came across to her as a guy who didn't seem to have much to offer or to say.

The truth is, I simply liked to listen while Anais talked. I listened because she was interesting to listen to. I was also more passive than usual that summer because at age fifty-two I felt that I did not have a whole lot more I wanted to say to people. I still said on paper what I wanted to say, and for nine months of the year in school classrooms I talked more than enough. And I enjoyed talking to my friends back home. But there on River Road, in the presence of someone like Anais, I was content to listen in the same way I would be content to look at Rio de Janeiro: simply because Anais was fascinating, perhaps the most unique person I had ever met.

So I listened and learned. I was a spectator at her show. (Not once, however, did I get the impression she was interested in learning about me or about anyone else. She was basically self-absorbed.) In a way Anais was always on stage – for an audience of one or for a roomful. She liked being witty and having eyes turned toward her. She was delighted to be delightful – and unconventional – and she knew how good she was at impressing people. That was what was so disconcerting about the "Damn I'm Good" button she would sometimes pin on her longsleeved work shirt and wear around the house. As a Renaissance Woman who could do almost anything she set her mind to – from learning Latin to changing the oil in her truck – she was the last one who needed to announce – to proclaim – her worth. Yet, as I began to see, beneath her bold air of female liberation and self-assurance was a person who did not seem to believe in herself at all.

(She was mechanically inclined, like her father. In contrast, I am not handy with my hands, have no ability to construct things. She could look at a schematic drawing – "Place Gadget C through Flange 12..." – and it was as clear as spring water to her. In early June we – that is, she – put together a portable typing table she had ordered for my birthday. We sat on the living room rug among the screws and bolts and from time to time she would glance at me through her curling cigarette smoke – smiling at my discomfort. No Leonardo, I.)

As the weeks went by on River Road I learned a little about her childhood, somewhat more about her teenage years, significantly more about her marriages and male involvements. Her family, of course, cast the shape of her life. Anais' mother – a gifted mathematician who endured, with great bitterness, years of teaching high school algebra in San Antonio instead of doing research in higher mathematics at Berkeley – felt she had married beneath her. Anais' father, a solid citizen from a German farm family, apparently agreed with his wife's assessment. He preferred working long hours as the head mechanic at a car agency to facing silent accusations at home. But it was Donald, Anais' mildly retarded older brother, who turned family drama toward tragedy. In his mother's eyes Donald was not lesser but more; flawed and thus more deserving; the one male in the house who could do no

wrong. Anais? She threatened her sullen, aggressive brother by her
very existence. Fiercely, the mother gave Donald her attention, protec-
tion, encouragement, love. Anais, like a Cinderella, was denied them
all: Mother punished daughter for the sin of being so conspicuously
bright. (Anais would go through life cowering before the private image
of a disapproving mother; the future Mensa member would never be
good enough for Mama....)

At sixteen Anais, who was brainy and pretty and trying desperately to look and act and be sophisticated, met a fellow who was stationed in San Antonio with the air force. He was in his late thirties,
bored, heir to a family fortune back in Pennsylvania. He took Anais –
smoking her first cigarettes, wearing her first high heels, winning her
first prize in an art show for a brooding self-portrait – and did his own
Professor Higgins on her: giving her a bored gentleman's culture
course while also getting her pregnant. Later that year she had her first
abortion. (Needless to say, it did not please Mother, and Daddy never
found out.)

At seventeen she had graduated from high school, entered college and tried out the first of her four marriages. ("I had almost forgotten about him," Anais said as she talked about her college days. After a
freshman history class a tall fellow from the back row came up to her
and asked if she wanted to get married. "I told him, 'why not?'" and
they went across the border to Mexico for a quick ceremony in Piedras
Negras. They stayed together for six months before divorcing. She
taught him fencing.)

She was twenty, working for an advertising agency, when she
married Ted, who was older and – by her assessment – brighter than
she was: perhaps, she thought, the only man she ever met who was.
That seemed to be his hold on her: he could treat her any way he
wanted to and she would take it because he was brilliant. And handsome. And also homosexual, or bisexual, except she did not realize it
for a while. They remained married for twenty-five years even though
he was gone much of the time – he did some kind of secret work for

the government – and even though he treated her with a kind of grand indifference. They lived in Miami and Nebraska and for a while in the Philippines. Much of the time she was alone so she painted watercolors and wrote haikus.

While they were living in California she did advertising work for a business concern – apartment complexes, shopping centers – that she later found out was controlled by the Mafia. (I have, in a box, her 200-page manuscript about that experience.) She also entered law school and took classes for a year.

Her classes and her marriage to Ted came to an end one weekend, she said, when he tried to kill her. He hit her from behind in their living room and then left, assuming she was dead. "Unfortunately for Ted," she told me as she worked on a crossword puzzle, "I have a German's hard head." She suffered blackouts and spells of amnesia and ended up in the hospital. Ted had moved to an apartment in another part of San Francisco. When she got out of the hospital she recuperated at home after first stealing back from Ted's garage their red Porsche she now considered hers. She phoned Ted, telling him what she had done and daring him to do anything about it. I could never understand why she had not pressed charges for assault or attempted murder. She was never clear on that point. I think she granted Ted-the-genius the right to do whatever he wanted to do – up to a point.

A few weeks later a girl in her twenties was found dead of a drug overdose along the shore below Anais' house. The girl's father, Clarence, lived alone across the street from Anais, and they were soon offering each other consolations for their various losses. Kindly Clarence seemed a good-enough sort to Anais – he was quite good at crossword puzzles and knew a lot about the stock market and investments. She was without money or resources – and still had blackouts, severe headaches, memory loss – so they decided to get married. They sold the Porsche, bought a second-hand trailer house, and hit the road to Texas. She lived with him in the trailer house for a year – on family farm property about thirty miles south of San Antonio – before learning the bad news: both Clarence and his brother Eugene, who lived in Atlanta, were con artists who operated throughout the South and Southwest and were wanted by federal authorities. (They were part of Chapter 10 in a book about swindlers that someone sent to Anais. I read about their remarkable exploits as I sat out under the elms.)

End of Marriage #3: Anais divorced kindly Clarence and moved to River Road.

(I do not know what the male sexual organ meant to Anais, but apparently she needed the presence of it, as she got older, in a way that was excessive; yet at the same time she was constantly on guard against it: it meaning male domination.

Everything about her was contradictory. She seemed to seek out brutalizing encounters – hitchhiking in California after her divorce from Ted she was picked up by two men who almost dutifully raped her. But she was constantly on the lookout for sexism: she saw it lurking everywhere and was ready to defend herself against it. And I can understand why. I can visualize her years in the advertising world when she had to defend herself against the crudest of male bosses and clients: defending herself with the formidable array of her tongue and intelligence; defending herself as she had been doing since childhood. A lesser person, a lesser defender, would have soon gone under. But she had obviously paid a price. She looked for offenses against her where none existed. She was suspicious, volatile, accusatory, wrongheaded. I can't recall a single time when she admitted that she had misjudged or erred.

I read once about Bubu de Montparnasse, a prostitute in Paris who submitted to men who beat her because, she said, they were like a "strong government" who could also protect her.... I suppose Anais, more than anything else – despite her bold, intimidating posture before the world – wanted to be protected: wanted security as she began to look down the barrel of her own mortality.

I cannot believe Anais was true-blue to Ted for twenty-five years, but she said she was. They seldom had sex and then not lovingly; they often stayed in separate rooms of their house.... After her marriage to Clarence ended she said she would go into a highway dance place near the farm, sit in a booth while she drank a beer and looked over the available males. When she had finally picked out a suitable-looking candidate, she would signal the waitress who would then take over a drink to the prospect with Anais' compliments. He would come sit in the booth with her for a while, then off they went to the trailer house for the next several hours or for the night.

I learned that until I came to River Road she had lovers from all over the county who made her little white house in the elms their pit stop at least once a week. Usually, she told me, she couldn't wait until they were gone: after the sex was over they bored her.

...Need them, then cast them out. It was as though sex to her was a way for her emptiness to be filled up, a way to be reassured she was still wanted, still desirable.)

In early August we went back to the flea market and got six more bantam chickens. Then Anais decided she wanted milk goats, too, so we went back and got three Nubians. We already had cats, and fish, and a small rabbit I found one night in the yard. And greyhounds.

When Anais started planning the construction of a back-yard room for the prospective greyhound pups, she got the name of a guy who did part-time construction work on the southside – a Ray some-body. He came by one afternoon – smallish, dark-haired, a smoker – and gave her an estimate. She walked around the proposed back-yard plot – coughing, feverish again – and discussed cement mixers and window spaces while I tried to get some materials ready for new class-es I would soon be teaching.

And suddenly we were out of sync. She was increasingly hostile; weekly confrontations were becoming more and more destructive. I thought: it's going to be this way forever; there will be no change. Rather than live like strangers under the same roof, arguing, I left.

Twice I packed my stuff in my car and left River Road. And twice, at a hot 7-11 telephone booth on a hot San Antonio street, I called

Anais and we talked and afterwards I drove back beneath the arch of trees and unpacked and hoped that it was the end of the quarreling. Each time I was glad to be back, each time the prospects looked okay, and each time the peace only lasted a week.

By then I knew I loved her. I also knew that what was waiting for me outside her hidden acre was the chaos of my mid-fifties with all my personal bridges washed away. I had found a little island of satisfaction by the river, a place and a person that suited me, and I did not want to leave.

I kept thinking: Maybe if we just take our time, going slow over the recognizable rapids we now know are here, we can make it into October and watch the leaves fall; and then into winter and watch the outside world from within the snugness of the house, sitting by the bedroom stove and sipping rum-and-Coke. We'll make us a contract – a commitment – to stay together at least until spring and then we'll see....

But in late August, for the third time in three weeks, I left and did not return. I got an apartment on the north side and started living – if it could be called that – away from River Road.

(I had walked across the bedroom to where she was watching me pack. She stood by the wall in her tight blue jeans and boots, smoking. I put my arms around her and held her. Her body was stiff, unyielding; her skin was cold. When she finally spoke it was like a statue talking: "All I'm good for, you know, is a lay."

She only half meant it, but the half she did mean was a terrible summing up.)

I called her in September on the first day of school. She talked a bit about the construction of the room, about Apollo and Cleopatra. Then she told me – almost casually mentioning it in passing – that she was probably going to get married the following weekend.

Married?

Yes, she drawled. To Ray.

(Random snapshots of River Road:

– The second day after I had moved in she walked behind me in the kitchen, ran her finger down the back of my shirt and said, "You-wanna-get-married?" I remember thinking: My God, I don't even know you.... I *want* to know you, but *marriage*? After just a *day*? You're crazy.

– "I've never wanted to fix breakfast for anyone before," she said one morning as we washed the breakfast dishes.

– She would drift by the kitchen table where I was reading or writing and leave me a note on a piece of paper: "Thou swell."

– One night after a reconciliation we stopped at a Whataburger. I went inside, stood by the counter, and waited. I would look out to the cab of the pickup where Anais – wearing her gangster hat – sat with her friend's monster-sized dog, Lewis, that we were keeping for the weekend. Lewis filled up almost the entire front seat and drooled. We went down a back street, parked, ate our hamburgers on a grassy rise of ground. The night wind was blowing in from the coast, and tree shadows flowed back and forth across the sides of houses behind tall street lights. Anais smiled at me as she sucked her milk shake through a straw and Lewis moaned in the cab.)

### III

I tried to write lesson plans for school, to read, to put away in the apartment the few odds and ends I had brought with me from River Road, but during the long hours of the weekend I couldn't concentrate on any one task for very long. So I sat down at the typewriter and started a letter to a friend of mine who had visited River Road during the summer. Ostensibly it was a letter, but it was actually just a chance for me to analyze and reanalyze on paper what had gone wrong: excusing Anais, then blaming her:

"...One afternoon in late July, when we were making love, I told her, 'Don't look now, but, by God, I *love* you.' It came out easily, spontaneously; the words were just there in my mouth. And I was so damn glad it was finally over – the long waiting for some kind of genuine, gut-level acceptance of this strange and amazing woman.

"It's weird, but if I had to point to a single moment during the summer when our relationship started to go sour – when Anais began to pull away from me – I think it would be that one: when I finally told her that I loved her. It was as if I was no longer someone who had 'power' over her. She had got her own power back – her own self-pos-session – and I was like one of the guys at the dark restaurant place I mentioned: someone to experience and throw away.

"You see, I think Anais has been hurt so many times before – plus five miscarriages – and tried so hard to find some kind of happiness that by the time I met her she was no longer interested in Romance. She wants marriage – the badge, the official seal and permanence of it. It would be fine to have it again with someone she could respect, but if not, well, so be it: she'll take it any way she can get it.

"I keep wondering at what cost she maintains her air of unflap-pable self-assurance: the cost of her life? She would rather break than bend. She will never say, 'Help me, I'm messed up like everybody else; my whole life is a testimony to being messed up.' Because she refuses to be like anyone else. And she refuses to quit smoking. She coughs and lights another cigarette and coughs and smiles sort of coquettishly and coughs some more.

"And how about this: All during the summer we would each buy groceries and stuff when we were in town, but we had agreed that at the end of the month we would settle up the other expenses – phone, electricity – and split the costs. And I did that for June and July. But when I was leaving, finally, a couple of weeks ago Anais sat at the table, smoking up her Marlboro storm, and she totalled up my 'August and final bill.' She charged me an additional $600 rent for the three months – my 'half' of a 'typical $400-a-month rent.' That's Anais for you: charging her ex-boyfriend and ex-lover summer rent.

"She's supposed to get married this weekend to a guy who is building a back-yard room. She's known him a total of two weeks.

(The first afternoon that he came out, slouching around in the back yard with his measuring tape, Anais told me as she watched from the window: 'I could have him if I wanted him.' Sexually, she meant. I didn't even bother to answer. It was just more of her bad-ass bluster.) What I think is this: she doesn't want to go back, now, to the side-of-the-road restaurant stuff – the casual whoredom of past times. So she's going to turn herself over to this Ray joker and have him keep her life from destroying her. Something like that.

"I'm here in San Antonio at the edge of Alamo Heights and the edge of my self-control. It's Sunday afternoon and that's not a good day any more."

I intended to mail it but got sidetracked and put it in a folder with some pictures of Anais. I remember thinking, finally, that it really wasn't a letter but just an exercise in writing-it-out therapy for me – and certainly not anything I should send on to my friend Carl, who was having his own problems that year. I decided to write him a less personal, more upbeat report when I could summon up the energy.

I moped my way through the fall, avoiding southside streets and trying not to think of Anais and Ray.... I didn't see how anyone could last much longer with her than I had – before she drove him away for reasons too complicated for mere mortals to unravel. I figured Ray for an opportunist out for any bird's nest on the ground.

I gave them until New Year's.

My estimate was off, but not by much. I got a call from her in early March. It was Sunday about two o'clock and I was lying around the apartment trying to get rid of a cold. The telephone rang, and Anais offered her "What's-going-on" as nonchalantly as if we had just had a buddy-buddy chat the week before. "Not much," I said, "and you?" "Getting by," she said.

After a few more preliminaries about dogs and ailments – she had been sick with a bad case of pneumonia in January – I finally asked her about Ray. He had gone back to Michigan in February, she said, and good riddance.

We maintained our low-key oh-yeah?-is-that-right? casualness until it gradually gave way to a Well-if-you-want-to-I-want-to honesty. Meaning, now that six months have passed, what have we learned and what do we want?

I told her I had a cold but I would meet her for coffee some place near the interstate.

When I got to Cap'n Jim's Cafe Anais was waiting in her truck with Cleopatra. She looked pale and thin. We talked for an hour or so in the cafe, and I listened hard – alert to every nuance of her manner and voice, almost trying to read the very air around her. She was agreeable, forthright, complaisant – as if properly tempered by her last marital adventure although not humbled or apologetic. It was as if the Good Anais had been in battle with the Bad Anais and had won.

We talked about the idea of my coming back to River Road and we both seemed to say:  All right, but no need to rush. We can take it slow. We've been through trying times.

And Ray? I finally asked.

A reprobate, she drawled. She said she had already filed papers for divorce. I didn't press further. (Later, after I had moved back to River Road, Anais went on binges of Ray-bashing, ridiculing every-thing about him from his belief in reincarnation to his taste in socks. He had gone off for weeks at a time without letting her know where he was. She had advanced him money when they married and he had never paid her back. She had also bought him a new Jeep because his Pontiac was junk and he needed, he said, something to drive while he looked for work. He never found a job. "Sounds like he really *was* 'sorry'," I said, catching her eye, and she giggled – actually giggled.)

Each afternoon during the following week I drove south to River Road after school. Anais and I would walk down to the river, hand in hand; then I would drive back to my apartment for the night. I was determined to take things slow, do the job right. I kept on the lookout for any sign that might show a return to "August tendencies" – the suspicion and paranoia of those intolerable weeks. I found nothing but pleasure and delight.

In mid-March I moved back with Anais, and we had one good week of almost honeymoon-like tranquility. We took baths in the old tub together. She gave me a haircut out under the trees. I bought her a baby orchid corsage – "just on general, middle-class principles," I said – and she told me it was the first flowers she had been given since high school.

She called me several times at school to update me on the latest escapades of the greyhound pups. At night I would be grading papers at the kitchen table and I would feel the urge to call out to Anais: "I love you." Maybe an hour later, or the following night, she would appear in the doorway, light a cigarillo, and say it too, nice and spontaneous: "I-love-you."

And then her sickness started. First it was fever and a hurting in her chest. We went to a southside doctor who gave her antibiotics. She stayed in bed almost all day every day. She kept running a temperature and began feeling worse.

I checked her into Humana Hospital, where doctors took X-rays and ran tests. A specialist thought she might have a rare lung fungus, desert fever, which is difficult to treat. After a week Anais was released with watch-carefully-and-wait precautions.

That was in early April. She got up each morning for a while, went back to bed and stayed for the rest of the day.

In mid-April I got a whiff of it: "the August tendency." I heard it one morning in her voice at breakfast before I left for school.

(Anais had three voices. She used one voice when she was attentive, modest, cooperative. It was light, somewhat breathy, almost excitable and girlish. Her second voice was the drawling, hypnotic one: low and slow. It was her resonant telephone voice to friends, lovers, strangers she wanted to impress. It contained a trace of the Germanic brogue of her childhood. Her third voice was lower than the other two – throaty, hard-edged, and with a longer drawl. It was her In Command voice, and chilling to hear. She would have used it had she been a queen or a despot.

All three voices reflected the inner Anaises.)

At breakfast I refused to believe that anything was wrong. Anais was sick – and sick of feeling sick. That was all. I fed the dogs and drove off to school. In the afternoon, I remember, I spent an hour or so going to three different record shops on the southside trying to find a new Pavarotti tape she would like. I bought juices and dog food and hurried home.

She was sitting in the front room when I got there. She was smoking and staring out past the butane tank toward the river. I put the grocery sacks down, went over to show her the Pavarotti tape I had bought.

"I read the letter," she said and kept looking out the window.

"What letter?" I stood there with the tape in my hand.

"Your newsy letter to your friend Carl."

Then I saw the folder on the rug and understood. She had been prowling through a box of mine and came across the unmailed letter I had written in September. I didn't remember all that was in it but I knew it couldn't have made very pleasant reading for Anais.

I could have told her, "You had no right to go through my personal stuff" or "That was when we were both upset" or "My God, it hasn't got anything to do with us now." I could have said a lot of things. But I kept standing there with the tape, trying to recall the words I had poured out that Sunday afternoon, and looking at Anais, who was drawn and tired. Just at that moment a car stopped out front: friends of Anais who had heard she was sick and came to cheer her up with fruit and flowers.

Somehow I got through the amenities of greeting the friends and listening to Anais charming them from her chair – between coughing attacks – with funny stories. They stayed a couple of hours and I fidgeted around the house and in the yard.

After they had gone Anais went to the bedroom. I cleaned up the kitchen and went to clean up the uglier mess of the letter.

Except that the bedroom door was closed. I tried to open it, and it was locked.

"What...." – is as far as I got.

"If you try to open that door," came her voice from the other side, "I'll shoot."

I had seen the gun. She kept it in a drawer by the bed. The previous summer she had taken it out in the yard and showed me how proficient she had become in using it. "Any son-of-a-bitch who comes around when he shouldn't will soon be a dead son-of-a-bitch," she said, shooting four or five rounds at a tomato soup can on a post.

"Anais," I said, "open the door and quit being ridiculous."

"You try to force your way in here, and this 'whore' will see to it that it is both your entrance and your exit."

I frankly didn't know if she would shoot or not. I spent the night on the living room rug.

When I drove off to school the next morning the bedroom door was still locked. I called at noon, but she hung up on me. When I came back that afternoon Ray was hanging out clothes on the back clothesline. The Jeep was parked out front.

To her, her position was clear: I had insulted her and she was righteously incensed. But I knew better: it was just a convenient excuse. My reading of the "August tendencies" at the breakfast table had been correct and she had grown tired of me, needed a change in male scenery, whatever. She had obviously been telephoning Ray – for how many days before? – and was waiting for the opportunity to invite him back.

...It was a grim late-afternoon: Anais sat in the front room chair, smoking, her gun in her lap; Ray shuffled about. During the hour it took me to load my belongings into my car I did not speak to either of them, and they did not speak to me. They murmured now and then to each other.

With a final paper sack of odds and ends in my hand I stopped in front of Anais on my way out the front door. I looked at this woman that I loved and said the only words I could think of that seemed appropriate: "You're not 'sorry,'" I said, "you're scum."

She did not look at me or make a reply. I drove off, and it was the last time I ever saw her.

## IV

What I know of Anais' final days is based on random reports from friends of mine and acquaintances of hers. In June the Humana doctors removed part of her left lung. She had cancer, not desert fever. Apparently she then became addicted to the morphine which she took during and after the operation and spent most of August in a drug rehabilitation clinic in the cedar hills north of San Antonio. Ray was either dismissed from further service or left of his own accord – interpretations varied. He might have been understandably miffed when Anais took up with Burton, a fellow patient at the rehabilitation clinic. Burton, an alcoholic, was a huge man who wore a speech-assistance device and ran a salvage yard in Austin. Anais found him sexy and amusing and during September he was the next caretaker for her dogs on River Road. But he stayed drunk and proved to be a man with a violent and uncontrollable temper. Anais, finally scared, called the sheriff, who had a peace bond placed on him.

The ever-lurking Ray showed up again and Anais hired him to take care of her and the place – no bedroom privileges. He was with her when she died the following April. Her body was cremated.

## V

It hadn't mattered, for a while, if Anais was *lovable* or not. She was like a gyroscope, a fixed center, and she had drawn me to her.

Somehow she had seemed unassailable: no matter which way she was thrown by adversity, she kept landing on her feet.

"Death," too, should have been just another of her bizarre but temporary setbacks. She should have reapppeared out of a back room, paler than usual but no worse off: smiling with that knowing look of hers, head lowered, peering over her glasses.

...Several years after she died I came through San Antonio and went by River Road. I drove through the arched oaks, got out of my car, and stared in the midsummer heat at what remained of her hide-away acre. It was like revisiting a battlefield after the war was over. Her house had burned down and the yards had turned to trash and weeds. A few straggly sunflowers grew where the front room used to be, and broken limbs lay in the square of the bedroom area. A tin strip bordered the kitchen foundation.

The locusts whirred wildly from the line of river trees, and they were like a chorus of destruction: Now both Anais and her little white house were ashes.

# VII

# COMMENTARY

# Requiem for a WASP School
## (1970)

They stand in their tall, glassed-in picture frames, looking out from the uncomplicated 1940s to the crowded main hallway of El Paso's Austin High School. Small gold plates beneath the frames give the identifications: Walter Driver, State Champion, Boy's Single Tennis 1940; Billy Pitts, State Championship, Declamation 1942; Robert Goodman, First in State, Slide Rule 1948. Holding their rackets and winners' cups, wearing their double-breasted suits with wide lapels and wide pants that sag around their shoes, they are reminders of the Days That Were: the days of Admiral Nimitz and General Patton and Ernie Pyle; of Glenn Miller and the Andrews Sisters and "Kokomo, Indiana"; of Jarrin' John Kimbrough and Betty Grable and "One Man's Family." They remain there behind glass, representing the Jack Armstrong-Henry Aldrich-Elm Street America that is gone forever.

It is easy, of course, to understand how rich in memories, how painfully nostalgic, these and other hallway pictures are to an old-timer at Austin High. Why, to him the 1940s mean – well, just about everything that was decent and sensible in American life. They mean kids who weren't perfect, of course, but who nonetheless respected rules and obeyed adults and knew how a human being cuts his hair; they mean jukeboxes and soda fountains and hayrides on Saturday night. They mean getting a lump in your throat listening to a glee club sing "The Halls of Ivy" because even if you weren't Ronald Colman standing before a fireplace in college you understood exactly what that kind of song was saying: it was saying that Our Country Was a Grand 'n Glorious Place and Our Youth Were the Hope of Tomorrow.... And such an old-timer only has to turn from the pictures on the wall and gaze about him to feel an even greater sense of pride, and of loss. For can't he look at thirteen showcases full of cups, plaques, statues, medals that have been earned by the hard-working students of Austin over the

years? And over there – although no one ever stops to read them anymore – aren't those still the bronzed words of Theodore Roosevelt:
"What we have a right to expect of the American boy is that he shall
turn out to be a good American man"?

...'The American boy," the old-timer can muse: that's the key to
the glory that once belonged to Austin, and to our country. And now
look who we have filling these sacred halls: Mexicans.

Austin High School – the name is rich with associations for many
El Pasoans. Over the past forty years it has been a symbol of quality
education, of good students from good homes, of traditions to be
proud of. Students in nearby elementary and junior high schools
looked forward to their freshman year at Austin with a certain amount
of trembling, respect, and awe, for Austin meant everything a high
school was supposed to mean: a long, elegant, two-story stone building for unsure freshmen to get lost in; teachers who presided over difficult courses that "prepared you for college"; a Panther football team
that everyone could get excited about in the fall; homecoming assemblies and class officers and DAR essays and clubs and honors and pres-
tige. Austin was the kind of all-around good school that lawyers, archi-
tects, businessmen wanted their sons and daughters to attend.

And then it happened. The forties and fifties wandered innocently into the explosive  sixties, and Austin High found itself with a problem on its hands: social change. The image of an old Anglo-American,
college-oriented student body began blurring into the image of a
racially mixed, academically varied student body that was more than
half Mexican-American. A highly regarded middle-class WASP high
school was becoming a gathering place for *chicanos*.

To understand this change it is necessary to know something
about the geography of El Paso and the location of its high schools.
Juárez, Mexico, lies south of the Rio Grande from El Paso; thus tradi-
tionally the heaviest concentration of Mexican-Americans has always
been on the South Side. Jefferson and Bowie High Schools, located in
South El Paso, have for years been made up mainly of Mexican-

American students. In contrast, El Paso and Austin High Schools, located in the central part of town, have largely had Anglo enrollment along with a scattering of typically middle-class Mexican-American students. The newer suburban high schools – Andress, Irvin, Burges, and Coronado – have also had, with the exception of Burges, relatively few Mexican-Americans. Technical High School, in the center of town, was changed this year to Technical Center – a school which next year will no longer offer academic courses or a high school diploma. Thus, since regular classes were being phased out, a number of students – largely Mexican-Americans from South El Paso wanting to enter "la Tech" – were forced into the halls of Austin High School last September even though they wanted to go elsewhere.

Here they came, the slow-walking girls of the freshman class. They moved along sidewalks toward a building which they had always considered "the gringo school on the hill," the snob school with its fancy golden dome, the school that – so rumor had it – didn't really like Mexicans. They came with their dukes up, not willing, in 1969, to let anyone put them down. They ate lunch in groups, they shouted in Spanish at boys from crowded doorways in groups, they waited in groups for whatever action might develop at the nearby Dairy Queen. And they were not Americans, in their own minds: they were Mexicans, they were La Raza. Their ties were to Mexico – its language, its culture, its dress and mannerisms.

They were the first class ever to enter Austin High expressing openly the attitudes and behavior patterns of a subculture world (and there seems to be little reason for their younger sisters and brothers to be thinking any differently in '71 and '72). They were not concerned with their "future," these stubborn, defensive South Side girls. Why should they be? They had on their block-heeled shoes; a transistor radio was pressed against their ear; their hair was hanging long and black and loose past their shoulders. Their skirts – brief triangles and handkerchiefs of color – revealed a long, mod stretch of legs halfway up the body.

They were like aliens in a hostile territory, not bothering to care about Austin's Most Beautiful Girl ( – it certainly won't be a Mexican, they told one another) or the Select Scholars list or the "Let's Really Yell It Now, Y'All" that the blond cheerleader was getting red in the face about down on the gym floor. And they didn't care when they were warned during the morning p.a. announcements that they would "seriously jeopardize future freshman assemblies unless their conduct was more in line with what Austin expected of its student body."

They weren't interested in what Austin expected of them any more than they were interested in diagraming sentences or reading *The Odyssey*. They were simply prisoners being held in an Anglo jail and they would continue to stare out sullenly through their granny glasses until the sentence was lifted.

It has long been the custom of school boards to select principals and other administrators from the ranks of coaches. It is not unusual, therefore, that the principal of Austin High is a former football coach; that the coordinator of instruction and guidance – presumed by many to be the successor to the principal when he retires – is an ex-coach also; and that the counselor most influential with the Austin administration is a former basketball coach. (Indeed, Austin is such a sports-and-coach oriented school that teachers in the good graces of the administrators are likely to be addressed by them as "coach." Thus the most unathletic math or government teacher finds himself being called "coach" as he requests an overhead projector or discusses a class load, for *coach* is the official password, the casual sign of camaraderie, the measuring stick of status.)

It is safe to say that the principal and the coordinator love Austin High School – that they consider it to be the core of their life's work. It is also safe to say that both are sincere, intelligent men who are doing their jobs as they see them and who want perhaps more than anything else to keep Austin's image as a Good School from being damaged.

But sincerity, intelligence, and love-of-school – certainly adequate equipment for administrators during the less complex era of the forties – are not enough to cope with the unsettling seventies. What is also needed is a high degree of flexibility in responding to potentially explosive situations which did not exist thirty years ago; a willingness to understand and trust student leaders who ask for change; and perhaps more than anything else, empathy with persons of minority groups – especially, in El Paso, Mexican-Americans.

High school administrations are generally conservative by nature; Austin's administration is perhaps more conservative than most. It thus views hippies, Reies Tijerina, César Chávez, black militants, antiwar demonstrators, college longhairs, etc., with a wholly unfriendly eye. The faculty, however, shares in large part this same conservative view. (Austin's Teacher of the Year for 1969-70 – selected by Austin teachers – had a sticker on his car reading "Register Communists, Not Firearms.") Whether the teachers' conservatism is directly related to age is conjectural, but the fact that out of a staff of over one hundred probably less than half are under the age of forty does suggest that the majority of the faculty is far from being attuned to the strident harmonies of today – especially those voiced with a Spanish accent.

During the past year there was mild racial tension – mainly in September when a *chicano* walkout was threatened and Mexican and Anglo groups fought several afternoons after school; there was an awareness that the "melting pot" togetherness which Austin had begun priding itself on during the last few years had gradually begun to disappear; there was a feeling among many of the Mexican-American students – not just the reluctant freshmen – that they were the Unseen and Ignored Majority as far as honors, offices, awards, etc., were concerned. There was also a grim little war concerning censorship of the student newspaper, the *Pioneer*.

At the beginning of the year an administrative staff member had been assigned the extra duty of censoring the *Pioneer*. (Such censorship by an administrator rather than the journalism teacher was a citywide policy.) In October the administrator censored a letter to the editor by junior journalism student Cecilia Rodriguez. The letter, which dealt honestly with Mexican-American experiences and attitudes in typical school situations, was subsequently printed in the University of Texas at El Paso (UTEP) newspaper, the *Prospector*.

In April, a group on the *Pioneer* staff wanted to devote an entire issue to the concerns, problems, and culture of Mexican-American high school students. After much discussion – in which a few of the more secure Mexican-American students themselves balked at being singled out for special attention ("We're all Americans, aren't we?") – it was agreed that a single page of Mexican-American features would be run. When copy was submitted to the administrator, he cut the four lead articles: "Brown Misery"; "La Huelga," an article about César Chávez and the California farm workers' grape strike; an article on the origin and significance of the term *chicano*; and "The Race United," an article on the newly formed political party in Texas for Mexican-Americans.

It was a typical student-administration conflict. The administrator, in keeping out of the *Pioneer* what he considered to be extremist or inappropriate material, felt, one can be sure, that he was fulfilling his role as censor and was doing what was best for Austin High. What he did also, of course, was frustrate – once again – the efforts of some of the most creative, conscientious, and morally sensitive students at Austin – both Anglo and Mexican-American. ("Change this school?" said one depressed student afterward. "Never. You see how much trouble we had getting just one lousy, watered-down page in the *Pioneer*." Another student added: "They say their doors are always open – yet every time you go to see them their minds are always closed. You can see *No* staring at you before you even open your mouth.")

Thus the staff member added another footnote to an already familiar tale: high school administrators ironically helping to create the very college radicals whom they dislike, as well as stimulating the possibilities for an underground press. For the students finally end up believing what they really, at first, do not want to believe: that the administration *doesn't* really care to understand what they are trying to say, *doesn't* realize that times have drastically changed, *doesn't* care about the quality of people's lives if those lives are led by blacks or browns; *doesn't* care to admit to the reality of a world which exists right outside the classroom doors in the streets, on the television sets, in the books available at every drugstore. Such students who try to express their idealism, and fail, simply resign themselves rather bitterly to their high school fate and wait for college – when they feel they can get rid of all their pent-up frustrations in orgies of action.

Thus, at a crucial moment in its history, Austin seems to be maintaining a steady course of drift. Apparently, the official policy is: Business as usual. Don't rock the boat if you want to be considered a good fellow. And don't stir up any trouble about problems which you feel are mounting – wait and see if they don't go away as they always have in the past.

But what is buried at the heart of the problem? Why *should* Austin teachers sigh at the prospect of their high school being filled with Mexican-Americans? Why, really, should Mexican-Americans be less academically capable than Anglos? Who is to blame?

The problem is many-rooted and complex, of course. Yet if there is an answer to the question, Who has been at fault, it should be arrived at after considering these points:

1. For too long Mexican-Americans have been offered the least and the worst of everything that is available in Texas, from jobs to housing to education to social status. They have been forced to live on the bottom rung of society and adopt the survival rules of what Daniel Moynihan has called the "underclass." They learn at a very early age not to believe in the "better tomorrow" of America's Protestant ethic. They learn not to believe they will get ahead by merely studying hard and saying yes-sir and going by all the rules. They learn not to hope,

or to save up nickels for a rainy day. They learn not to be open and trusting and optimistic. Indeed, they learn many things which do not help them get A's in government or spelling.

2. A study of underprivileged children, by Norma Radin (condensed in the September-October 1968 issue of *Children*), has this to say about the "hidden curriculum" which is available in middle-class homes but which is generally absent from homes of the disadvantaged: "Shapes, colors, numbers, names of objects, words on signs, etc., are part of the continuous input to the child.... Books are read, stories are told, intellectual curiosity is rewarded, and efforts perceived as school-oriented are praised. These activities are not part of the mother's role in the lower-class home." The study also states: "A large fraction of the intelligence of a child is already fixed by the age of five. No amount of environmental change beyond that point can affect the intellectual capacity to any significant extent."

3. Granting the difficulty of trying to do alone what society as a whole should do, and granting the possibility that some Mexican-American children by age five are already too severely handicapped to compete on an equal basis with Anglos, the public school administrators of El Paso should nevertheless be held accountable for failing to implement – years ago – a program of bilingual education for elementary grade Mexican-American children. Chances are the school system will not remedy these children's needs until officials decide to give them massive assistance and the highest priority: until they decide that not only the bright Debbies and Bills from middle-class homes have the right to become surgeons and bankers and civil engineers but also the Rogelios and Alicias from south of Paisano Street who have typically grown up not able to read and not seeing much point in learning how to anyway.

The school system must try bold new approaches in order to break the miserable chain of failure which has linked each successive wave of Spanish-speaking students. The traditional methods have not worked, and Head Start – which gets children after the first crucial five years – is simply not enough. Therefore, if the school system does not wish to perpetually deny children from Spanish-speaking homes a chance at the greatest possible success our society offers, then it must implement programs which will allow a child who speaks no English in the first grade to nevertheless become proficient in writing and reading English in a reasonably short time.

4. The voting public bears part of the blame for school ills: One group generally wants "safe" school board members – those who will go slow – instead of concerned, progressive individuals who understand the need for change. The other group refuses to vote at all: it always lets conservatives have their way at the polls and determine important elections with a few hundred votes.

5. Many nervous parents transfer their children from the inner-city schools to those in the suburbs – leaving the inner-city schools to become, finally, all Mexican-American. This happens because the typical middle-class Anglo parent is unwilling to run the risk of having his child receive less than what he conceives to be the best education – that is, the parent refuses to let his child pay the penalty for society's failure to educate Mexican-American children so that they are on a par with Anglos. Thus he sends his son to the suburbs – hoping the kid won't get on pot or acid – and leaves such schools as Austin and El Paso High to sink or swim with the many black eyes and brown skins. (Classic example: For many years El Paso High School was attended by students from the affluent Kern Place and Rim Road sections "on the hill" above the school as well as by students from modest homes in the flatland below. It was a relatively successful mingling of rich, poor, and middle-class. Then Coronado High School was built in northwest El Paso, and school authorities gave parents the choice of sending their children to Coronado or El Paso High. The Anglo rush toward a lily-white school began and thus El Paso High – finally cut off from the Rim Road and Kern Place areas through obvious gerrymandering – has had its enrollment drop by approximately 1,000 students.)

If school administrators genuinely want to educate students for the lives they will be leading in the seventies and eighties – rather than just keeping them quiet and off the streets – they must provide courses and teachers that are meaningful to both the highly motivated academic students and the indifferent, withdrawn couldn't-care-lessers. They must also determine which teachers do the incredibly difficult job of plunging into their subjects and making them exciting, challenging, alive – and which teachers merely show up for work, "keep order" with a deadening fervor, and then go home again.

And the principals: they should be energetic, widely read men who are conversant with the issues of the times and the problems which face students in their schools. They should be men who are constantly mingling with their students – staying in touch, hearing what they have to say in this era of intense social concern and audacious questioning of the status quo – rather than presiding over their desks in their offices. They should be shirt-sleeves-rolled-up administrators of the seventies, moving among students the way Mayor Lindsay moves through the people of New York. They should be courteous, open-minded, contemporary men whom the students feel are on their side – which, of course, they will be if they are successful principals.

...The pictures on the wall at Austin High will continue to look out from a simpler time. Whether it was also a better, more just, more democratic – more American – time is still to be decided. If we truly wish to educate everyone and not just an elite – and if we find ways to turn that wish into a reality – then the glory that was yesterday will pale beside the glory of today.

*"Requiem for a WASP School" received the 1970 Stanley Walker Award for journalism from The Texas Institute of Letters.*

# The Making of a Legend
## (1973)

### Amado

One summer day in 1968 I was walking around downtown
El Paso and happened to stop in at Zamora's Newsstand on Paisano. As
I glanced at the magazine rack I noticed a tabloid I had not seen
before – a little newspaper-journal called *The Mexican-American*. What
caught my eye was the anti-Vietnam war editorial – something unusual
for El Paso in 1968 – and a group of unsigned short sketches about
hobos. The sketches were authentic-sounding little chunks of realistic
reporting. I liked them.

I came back to Zamora's several times that summer, picking up
other dime copies of *The Mexican-American*. One issue had a front-page
article about a boy named Manuel whom the writer, a Cleveland newsman, had known in childhood. (Although the piece – a reprint – was a
well-written human interest story about a Mexican-American, it
seemed to lack a specific connection with the El Paso scene. A connection existed – but it was one I would not understand until four years
later.) There were also more hobo sketches – again unsigned.

Out of curiosity I sent a letter of inquiry to the P.O. box listed for
*The Mexican-American*, asking in a general way about the journal and,
specifically, who was doing the hobo pieces. I thought the writer
might be a good contributor to line up for *The Texas Observer*. I waited,
but never received a reply.

Months passed. Then one day while reading an *Arizona Quarterly*
in the UTEP library I came across "Night Train to Fort Worth," a hobo
story similar in tone to the sketches in *The Mexican-American*. The
author was given as Amado Muro.

More months passed: the war was dragging on, the Chicano
movement of the Southwest was gaining impetus, and I was coming
across, in both new and back issues of the *Arizona Quarterly* and *New*

*Mexico Quarterly,* more bum-and-drifter sketches by this interesting fellow Amado Muro.

In the spring of 1971 I finally heard someone mention his name.
Several Chicano and Anglo students were talking in the Union building at UTEP and one Chicano young man was making the point that
Amado Muro not only wrote with "class" but was definitely "a writer of
the people." The students agreed that he was an important voice of the
movement – a genuine new talent – and they expressed an interest in
meeting him. No one, however, seemed to know where he lived or
anything about his personal life.

During the summer I bought an anthology called *The Chicano:
From Caricature to Self-Portrait* and encountered my first Amado Muro tale
that was not about boxcar transients or down-and-outers. It was
"Cecilia Rosas," a well-told story about a fourteen-year-old boy,
Amado, who worked in La Feria Department Store in El Paso and who
was in love with a beautiful saleslady, Cecilia Rosas. After reading the
story I turned to the introduction of the book and found – at last – a
bit of information about Amado Muro: he was identified as "a young
Mexican-American" who "works for a railroad in El Paso and writes in
his spare time."

It seemed logical: a Mexican-American who writes a lot about
Phoenix, Bakersfield, San Antonio skid-row types must have a railroad
job. And being a railroad man would naturally put him out of town,
out of contact, much of the time.

Except that when I checked with the railroad offices in El Paso
no one had heard of an employee named Amado Muro....

Something, indeed, seemed curious about this man who was
increasingly being praised by those interested in writing and in the
Chicano movement but who did not really seem to exist. Thus I was
still unable to be of any help when Molly Ivins, co-editor of *The Texas
Observer,* asked me in July: "Who *is* Amado Muro? Doesn't anyone
know?" The *Observer* had run a number of his sketches and Molly had
become a great fan of his work. She reasoned that since I lived in

El Paso I surely ought to have come across such a talented writer by that time.

In August I finally made a breakthrough in "the Amado Muro story," as I had begun to think of it – and got more than I bargained for.

At a teachers' meeting I asked Dr. Phillip Ortego, then head of the Chicano Affairs Program at UTEP – and whose story, "The Coming of Zamora," had been included in *The Chicano* – what he knew about Amado Muro. His answer was a stunning double-burst: First, Amado Muro was dead. He had died of a heart attack in El Paso the previous year – October 3, 1973 – at the age of 56. Secondly, Amado Muro was not a promising Chicano writer; he was a blond-haired, Anglo-American newsman named Chester Seltzer who had used a variation of his wife's maiden name, Amada Muro, as his pseudonym. Dr. Ortego – who indicated he had just recently found out this information – said he understood that Amada Muro Seltzer still lived in El Paso.

A few days later I picked up an August 31 copy of *The New York Review of Books* – a journal I did not buy regularly – and read a long special supplement called "The Chicanos" by a Harvard historian, John Womack, Jr. In it he reviewed fifteen recently published Chicano books and had this to say about Amado Muro: "The funniest, brightest, most moving, accomplished, and prolific 'Mexican-American' writer used to be Amado Muro, a veritable Isaac Babel of the Southwest.... But Muro was really an Anglo, Charles [sic] Seltzer, and is now dead." In a footnote he gave Dr. Ortego as his source of information.

I couldn't get this remarkable turn of events out of my mind – the rising Chicano writer who suddenly turns out to be a middle-aged, deceased Anglo reporter. "Amado Muro" seemed to be the stuff out of which myths were made. Therefore one afternoon in September, when I happened to be talking to a former student of mine, Diana Weir, I told her in detail the whole Amado Muro story – stressing the role that coincidence had played up to then.

A week later, on a Saturday night, I got a telephone call from Diana: While doing voter registration work on Prospect Street that morning, she said, a woman had called out to her, asking her to please stop next door before leaving the area. She wanted to be sure that her two sons were registered. "I went over and we started talking.... It was Mrs. Amada Muro Seltzer," Diana said.

## Chester

The following Saturday I drove over to Sunset Heights, a quiet, hillside neighborhood near UTEP, and walked up the steps of an aging, but well-kept, two-story house. In the living room I sat down with Mrs. Seltzer, a neat, composed woman in her fifties, and her two sons – Charles, twenty-one, and Robert, eighteen, both UTEP students. Mrs. Seltzer spoke easily, calmly, respectfully about her husband, as did the sons about their father, and before long an outline of Chester Seltzer began to emerge from our conversation: As a young man he had left Ohio, where he had grown up, and after working for a while as a sports reporter in Florida had come to the Southwest to live. Apparently he was bowled over by things Southwestern, Mexican, Spanish: the people, the Spanish language and culture, the look and feel of the land. He had met Amada Muro in El Paso, married her within six months, begun to travel here and there working on newspapers in Texas, California, New Mexico, and Louisiana. He wrote stories as well as news articles, and he seemed to have a strong need to keep his journalist-identity and his author-identity separate. He not only adopted the "Amado Muro" pen name but as his two sons grew up he asked that they keep the name within the family.

I was listening to the talk there in the living room – thinking, well, all right, I guess he was just an exceptionally modest or shy man. Still, there was bound to be something else – the *real* reason....

Then, toward the end of our conversation, the name *Seltzer* once again hung in the air. Mrs. Seltzer was making another reference to Chester's father – who, she said, had been "the famous editor" in Cleveland.

And a final ball bearing, one that I had almost been expecting, rolled into place: Chester-Seltzer-Amado-Muro was not just a guy from nowhere or anyplace but was the son of Louis B. Seltzer, famed editor of the *Cleveland Press*. The elder Seltzer was for many years editor-in-chief of all the Scripps-Howard papers in Ohio. He was a political king-maker whose clout reached onto the national political scene. For years no mayor of Cleveland, no governor of Ohio was ever elected without Seltzer's endorsement. He hobnobbed with kings and presidents and was known as "Mr. Cleveland."

I left – after requesting permission to come again for further talks – and as I walked toward my car I suddenly found myself seeing the whole Amado Muro story as a 1940s movie: the restless young man from Ohio refusing to stay home and work his way up in Dad's Business, cutting out in order to make his own life in his own way, coming west on the train to the border country, taking as his wife a young woman from Chihuahua City, Chihuahua, publishing under a pseudonym so as not to trade on Dad's name, riding the rails from time to time for personal reasons – reasons that the viewer would learn toward the end. (Pan here to close-up of Dan Dailey-Seltzer, battered suitcase in hand, stepping off the Southern Pacific and sniffing the dry, clean desert air, then idling down San Francisco Street toward the cluster of transients standing in front of the Rescue Mission....)

I did return to the Seltzer home – several times – and the Amado Muro mask began to fade as the Chester Seltzer features continued to take definite shape:

Chester graduated from Cleveland's University School High School in 1935 and after a trip to Mexico with a friend entered the University of Virginia. He played guard on the freshman football team and was considered a promising athlete. (An anecdote about the

University of Virginia years: Chester was majoring in journalism instead of English – which was considered more prestigious – and as a consequence some of his fellow students tended to look down their noses at him. One day, to shake up the stiff-necks, he matter-of-factly ordered mashed potatoes with scrambled eggs on top while he was going through the university cafeteria line. There were incredulous stares at first, then a giggle or two, finally a good-humored, appreciative response to Chester's put-on.)

He transferred from the University of Virginia to Kenyon College, where he continued to play football and where he also studied creative writing under John Crowe Ransom, who wrote as a critique of Chester's first autobiographical sketch: "It is a strange combination of genius and illiteracy." Chester was on the advisory committee of *HIKA*, the undergraduate literary magazine – Robert Lowell was an associate editor of the magazine. (Charles Seltzer said that his father often spoke of Randall Jarrell, who was also at Kenyon and who roomed at Ransom's house in Gambier.)

Chester's first job after college was working as a sports reporter for the *Miami Herald* – covering regattas, swimming meets, and up-and-coming boxers like the Yucatan Kid.

In 1942, when Chester was twenty-seven and working on the *San Antonio Express*, he refused to enter the military service on the grounds of being a conscientious objector. (Incident: One night government investigators came to his apartment in San Antonio and began to quiz him, telling him he knew, didn't he, that being a conscientious objector was about the same thing as being a Communist. Where did he get his weird ideas? Seltzer said that although his conscience was his own, he did believe in the teachings of Leo Tolstoy. The government man thereupon took out his note pad and asked: "Where can we get a hold of this Tolstoy?")

As a result of his not complying with the Selective Service Act, Chester served three years in various federal prisons. He worked as a hospital attendant in Chicago and in a labor camp in Colorado.

(Charles said that in one prison in Pennsylvania his father met Dave Dellinger — also serving a sentence as a conscientious objector — who made a great impression on him. Charles feels that his father's experiences in prison marked him deeply and that his father never fully recovered from them.)

In 1946 Chester began working in El Paso. According to Chester Chope, retired former managing editor of the *El Paso Herald-Post*, Louis Seltzer arranged with the then editor of the *Herald-Post*, E. M. Pooley, for Chester's job. Mr. Chope remembers Chester as a "quiet, self-effacing young man who never raised his voice and had a pleasant smile." He remembers Chester most of all, however, because of the following occurrence: Mr. Chope was sitting one morning in the slot at the copy desk; Chester was sitting on the other side. Suddenly Chester rose from his seat and said: "I have to go to Albuquerque." He left the office and Mr. Chope never saw him again.

(Mr. Chope says that he read the works of Chester's grandfather with great pleasure — his grandfather, it turns out, being Charles Alden Seltzer, the author of over two hundred magazine articles and forty-nine Zane Grey-type books about the West such as *Valley of the Stars, Treasure Ranch, Two-Gun Man*.)

During the years after his marriage Chester — sometimes with his wife and sons, other times by himself — worked on newspapers in Bakersfield, Las Cruces, San Diego, Dallas, New Orleans, St. Louis, Galveston and Prescott, Arizona. In 1965, while in Bakersfield, he wrote hard-hitting editorials against the John Birch Society, American involvement in Vietnam, the Ku Klux Klan, the exploitation of farm workers.

He worked for a while on a pea farm near Bakersfield to get first-hand information about the conditions stoop laborers faced each day and later wrote in an editorial entitled "These Men Are Americans, Too": "U.S. Sen. George Murphy...wants to exploit chaotic conditions in Mexico and bring *braceros* back. Senator Murphy apparently isn't interested in what George Santayana once termed one of the most important raw materials of industry: Man.... It's just about time Murphy gave something more than the back of his hand to the American field hand. It's just about time he went out at four o'clock in the morning and saw the men some growers call 'bums' and 'derelicts' shiver on street corners waiting for day haulers to carry them out to the fields. It's just about time he started digging to find out a little about the other side of the story."

Chester was fired from the *San Diego Union* because of his antiwar sentiments.

El Paso, however, was his home base, and he worked at four different times for the *Herald-Post* – writing about street cleaners, ninety-year-old peanut vendors, invalid domino parlor operators, blind yodelers. Virginia Turner, present city editor of the *Herald-Post*, remembers Chester this way:

"Chester honestly suffered for the poor people of the world – and on one occasion literally gave the shirt off his back to a hobo. He had to go home and get another shirt to wear before he could come to work.... He was a gentle person; he never bragged, was never cocky. And he suffered a lot from insomnia. Lots of times he came to work worn out – simply from walking the streets at night, unable to sleep."

In checking through Chester's memorabilia I found out that early in his career he published stories under his own name – stories that were mainly about blacks and which reflected, perhaps, his experiences as a newsman in Florida and Louisiana. Chester took a pen name, Mrs. Seltzer said, only after he married and became deeply interested in the Mexican culture of the Southwest.

By the mid-1950s Chester was already experimenting with his role as "Amado Muro" – and in marking false trails concerning his identity he was perhaps having a little fun as well as adhering to his own artistic principles. (Items: A note on contributors in the 1961 *New Mexico Quarterly* informed readers that "Amado Muro's delightful stories about life in his native Mexico have appeared in *Americas Magazine*." A 1955 letter of acceptance from the associate editor of *Americas* commented: "...you say you graduated from high school in 1944 and have worked on the ice docks ever since. Is writing your hobby?")

I found that critical recognition of his stories in Martha Foley's annual *Best American Short Stories* ranged from 1944 – "A Peddler's Notebook," by Chester Seltzer, in the *Southwest Review*, cited as "Distinctive" – to 1970 and 1972: "Maria Tepache" and "Blue," by Amado Muro, in the *Arizona Quarterly*, also listed as "Distinctive."

During one visit I asked Charles about the hobo sketches: Did his father really take off and live the hobo life?

"Oh, yes," he said, "and sometimes got thrown in jail for it. He told me once about being picked up on a vagrancy charge in Big Spring. He stayed in jail until the police checked him out with Washington."

"Chester was a very compassionate man," Amada Seltzer added. "In Bakersfield and in El Paso he was always buying groceries for the hobos that would turn up at our door."

How about Chester's method of writing the sketches? I remarked that it was almost as if he had used a tape recorder to get down some of the hobos' talk.

"No," Charles said, "he just had a very good memory. And he really listened to people.... You know, in a way he was against the written word. He was for letting the people speak, not the writer; he felt the writer should be subservient to the people he wrote about.... It's ironic that he valued the oral tradition more than he did writing."

"My father admired the writers that did their work in the 1930s," Charles continued. "He was not in sympathy with writers who published after 1945 – after World War II. He rejected the philosophy of existentialism and was against the death-of-God in literature. That's why he celebrated Dostoevski and Tolstoy – all the Russian, nineteenth-century novelists. He thought they were the best.... When I was in high school he would give Robert and me lists of books and authors he felt we should read: Flaubert, Gorky, Chekhov, Sienkiewicz, Dreiser, Dos Passos."

Besides not wanting to trade on Louis Seltzer's name, I wondered, was there any other reason why Chester Seltzer should become Amado Muro?

"My father always pointed to the example of Steinbeck and Hemingway," Charles said, "as writers who finally yielded to commercialism – who got caught by their fame and lost their feel for people." Charles added that his father also admired the works of B. Traven, who had remained anonymous. (Another ironic twist to the Amado Muro story: that B. Traven, a legendary man of letters in Mexico whose real name was Traven Torsvan Croves, was admired by a man who may become more legendary in the Southwest than B. Traven himself.)

I asked Charles about *The Mexican-American*: After my first visit to the Seltzers I had gone home and pulled out the copies I had kept of *The Mexican-American* and found the issue with the article entitled "A Boy Named Manuel." I looked at the author's name and one more little riddle was solved: the writer, of course, was Louis B. Seltzer, editor, *Cleveland Press*.

"Yes," Charles said, "my father published *The Mexican-American* and ran his sketches in it, but it was a short-lived affair – only two years. He had an office in the Banner Building, and I used to run all over town trying to collect from people who owed us for advertising. But they just wouldn't pay their bills.... I thought we ought to distribute the paper around the college area but my father said no. For one thing, he felt that it ought to be sold near the South Side, where the people he was writing for could buy it easily; another reason he always gave was that if he sold it at the college some professor would get interested and want to find out more about it and come around and – you know, learn who my father was. He didn't want that."

We talked a bit about Chester Seltzer's last days. Charles said that during the year before he died his father was working on more short stories. "He was freelancing then," Charles said. "He worked on the stories in the morning, then he would sometimes go over to Juárez to take steam baths and walk around. He believed in keeping his body in shape – he did not drink; he was a vegetarian.... And oh, yes, there's an unfinished novel in a box down in the basement that I'm going to take a look at. My father put it away and never talked about it."

Had his father ever suffered any heart attacks before the one that killed him, I asked.

"Not that we know of," Charles said.

And it was in South El Paso that he died?

"Yes, he had stopped in at a newsstand to buy a paper and talk. He had the attack right there and died before the ambulance could get him to the hospital."

At a newsstand?

"Yes. Zamora's...Zamora's Newsstand on Paisano. My father used to go there often."

*"The Making of a Legend" received the 1973 Stanley Walker Award for journalism from The Texas Institute of Letters.*

# The World on Its Own Terms:
# A Brief for Miller, Simenon, and Steinbeck
## (1968)

There are three world-famous and popular writers who are ignored by the makers of literary fashion in the United States today. Scratch any professional critic and you will find very little blood shed for these unsung three: Miller, Simenon, and Steinbeck. Therefore, in the accounts that follow, I would like to go to bat in their behalf – in hopes that even such brief attention might start to fill the vacuum of neglect.

## Henry Miller

For almost ten years I was part of a conspiracy against Henry
Miller – an unplanned conspiracy, of course, but an effective one nev-
ertheless. You see, in the ignorance of my twenties I went along with
the people who were supposed to know about modern American literature, the critics who made up the Lists. There have always been lists:
the list of the Big Ones – Hemingway, Faulkner, Wolfe, Dos Passos,
Fitzgerald; the list of Stout Fellows – James Gould Cozzens, James T.
Farrell, Theodore Dreiser; the Most Recent List – Mailer, Malamud,
Updike, Bellow; the Intellectuals' List, headed by Nabokov; the Sick
List, headed by Burroughs. But despite the variety and frequency of
the lists, there was never one which included Henry Miller.

Who was he, anyway, I wondered: that strange-looking man in
the golf cap? Was he being rightfully ignored, kept in his place in the
Outhouse of Literature?... I knew that every time I went into a big-city
newsstand I would see his paperback trilogy, *The Rosy Crucifixion*, down
among the sex books and girlie magazines. I knew that the two *Tropic*
titles had been banned at various times and places in the United
States. But for a number of years that was just about all he meant to
me: the Four-Letter-Word Man of Big Sur; Mr. Pornography himself....

Then my period of innocence and mis-enlightenment came to an
end, and I entered Phase Two: the pursuit and reading of all the books
of Henry Miller. This period began about two years ago when I came
across the correspondence of Miller and Lawrence Durrell. I marveled
at both men's prose and decided it was high time I saw for myself what
was going on with this Miller fellow. So I began making my way cautiously through *Tropic of Cancer, Black Spring, The Air-Conditioned Nightmare,
Sunday after the War*. I knew I had come upon an honest-to-God writing
man, but I did not have the feeling that he was pure gold, that I could
ever make a good enough case for all his works. There was much
excellent writing, but jammed up against it was very routine stuff –
sometimes whole blocks of pages that were downright boring. So I

kept on, still in doubt: *The Cosmological Eye, Quiet Days in Clichy, Max and the White Phagocytes*.

And then *Plexus*. Reading it, I knew that my case – that is, his case – was made; *Plexus* alone would be enough. It was the mildest book in the world as far as sex was concerned – and certainly a better book about New York than Wolfe's *The Web and the Rock*.... I had the same sense of bewilderment and pleasure that I felt after accidentally stumbling onto *Steppenwolf* by Hermann Hesse, and I found myself asking the same questions: Where had this book been hiding? Why had no one said anything about it?

I simply could not figure it out. *Plexus* should have been enough of an achievement to establish Miller in the literary world for keeps, yet it remained unknown. And ironically, it wasn't even an under-the-counter sex book: A Baptist deacon could glean all the four-letter words from its 682 pages and still not have enough to cover the bottom of a spinster's thimble.

I have wondered about the professional critics and their attitude toward Miller. Since many critics have only a single point they want to make about a writer, a specific thesis to prove – "Latent Auto-Eroticism in the Brer Rabbit Tales of Joel Chandler Harris"; "Ernest Hemingway as Neo-Neanderthal" – they tend to pass over whatever does not fit conveniently into the limited framework of their analysis. They ignore the body of the writer in order to carve out their scholarly pound of flesh. And because Miller could not be categorized as an essayist or novelist or short-story writer or seminal thinker, it is as though the critics decided to take such nose-thumbing at form as a personal affront.

Another reason why Miller has apparently turned off many critics is that he often represents himself in his works as a character they simply cannot approve of. The "Henry Miller" they read about in *Tropic of Cancer* and *Sexus* is offensive to them, and thus, both consciously and unconsciously perhaps, they are tempted to down-rate Henry Miller the writer. They end up as moralists rather than literary critics.

It is true that Miller, as he chooses to portray himself in some of his writings, appears uninvolved in social causes and uninterested in "progress." Indeed, he seems utterly selfish. Yet it is hard to say what another man's duty is. If Miller has considered it his duty to think, to act, to react as that unique personality that he is, as well as to search out the depths of this huge strangeness we call life ("We live and move and have our being in utter, absolute mystery," he once wrote), I believe he has performed these self-imposed duties with a fidelity that is rather staggering to consider.

There is also an undeniable charm about Miller. Once I am in his pages I seem to relax a little; I feel less down at the heels; I smile. For he does not say, Woe is Me, Woe is Man. He does not say that living is a Totally Serious Business. In this guilt-ridden world – "Shall I, or shall I not, be my brother's constant keeper" – Miller audaciously says: I'm going to amuse myself by doing what I jolly well want to do. I'm not going to put aside the childish things of childhood. And you want to know why? Because they are not childish. To have a sense of personal, physical freedom; to dream, to think, to play – why, that is man's *birthright*.

In other words, he has been interested in himself – which ought to be pretty good news to us, since most people today are trying desperately to escape themselves. Yet critics find this self-interest of Miller's reprehensible. To be happy in the presence of so much world-unhappiness – that is considered an intellectual crime. (Indeed, Camus is respected by the intelligentsia *because* he anguished over the condition of man in an apparently indifferent world; Miller and Steinbeck are not respected now because both men seem to accept too much of the world on its own terms.)

You can find almost any kind of writing in Miller: straightforward prose; surrealistic flights; dull "talk" pieces; vomit-and-cockroach stuff. And even when he is at his worst – off on one of his long windy jags – you know that in just another moment or two he is going to

shake off the nonsense and slap down something remarkably – stun-
ningly – right.

Perhaps this is what one needs to have in order to appreciate
Miller – a certain tolerance and endurance, a willingness to go the full
distance with the man. And isn't that generally the attitude a serious
reader takes when he approaches those writers who tumble out their
words instead of squeezing them: a polite ignoring of what is less than
the best, an embracing of that which is good? But who is polite to the
bad in Miller, and who has really embraced the good? (Case in point:
Miller and Wolfe. Wolfe will remain a Great American Author because
fate was kind enough to bring him not only an immense talent and a
hunger for experience but also Maxwell Perkins. In contrast, Miller will
probably stay a minor figure – basically unread in his own country –
because no editor-friend was around to help shape and cut and mold
his huge outpourings.)

Yet no matter who does or does not read his own works, Miller
remains an enthusiastic reader of the works of others. I am never quite
so eager to read a book as when Miller recommends it. Let him talk of
Knut Hamsen, Anais Nin, Elie Faure, Blaise Cendrars – wondrously
new names to me – and immediately they become necessary to me and
life. I rush out to the library and search hopefully through the stacks
(finding, if I am lucky, *Hunger* by Knut Hamsen, part of Anais Nin's
*Diary*), and then I walk out slowly, ready to spend the rest of the day
listening to the voice of this compelling new friend.

Thus with his facile use of the language, his deep interest in people, his wide-ranging mind, his tolerance of the world as it actually
exists, Henry Miller is an important writer to know. He is, quite simply, an education – a torch that you pick up and become illumined by.

### Georges Simenon

When the taste of daily living goes flat and my thoughts turn
gray, I go to Simenon, the amazing healer. With over two hundred
books in print he is the well that never goes dry, and I have come to

depend on him the way you rely on insurance, or gravity, or a staunch friend.

It is hard to separate the awe you feel at his fantastic productivity from the admiration you have for the man himself – this tireless genius who seems to care so intensely about life.... You finish *The Bottom of the Bottle*, or *The Brothers Rico*, or *The Man Who Watched the Trains Go By* – or perhaps a *Maigret* – and you sigh with wonder and affection. You say to yourself, He has done it again: he has once more isolated himself in a room somewhere for the necessary twelve or fourteen days and produced another little masterpiece. He has briefly, intimately held life in his hands the way a man holds a burning match – to illumine a bit of the surrounding dark – and now he has snuffed it out. Yet the job of creation is never done so he will always be starting over, in another room, with no less urgency than before....

I have not known of Simenon very long – perhaps five years – and I don't recall the exact circumstances of my discovery. I think I began with *Inspector Maigret and the Burglar's Wife*, a light, casually turning story set in a Paris suburb. But with that first, low-keyed little book I fell in love with Simenon's bare style, the rigorous simplicity with which he constructed a scene, his skillful development of atmosphere and exact use of detail.

In the months that followed I began to haunt secondhand bookstores, plowing through tables and shelves full of worn paperbacks in hopes of coming across a Simenon. (Curiously, that is the way you soon begin to think of them: not so much as specific novels but, because of the sheer number of them, as "simenons" – as varied but basically similar re-creations of one man's method and view.) The title, the subject, the setting of the paperback never really mattered. I knew that once I got inside the cover Simenon would be in charge and therefore I could settle back – ready to be fascinated, even hypnotized, by the immense reality he would bring to the page.

Reality – that is perhaps the key word one must use in attempting to explain the art of Simenon. For despite his being a supreme storyteller, it is not the plot of his novels that you mainly care about. You are lured back to his pages again and again because of the terrific sense of life he establishes in each work. A ranch in Arizona, a bistro in Paris, an oil port in Russia – it does not matter where the scene is laid or who the characters are; Simenon knows them so completely and describes them so tellingly it is as though God Himself has decided to become a writer and is now creating in words what He had once created in spirit.

After finishing one of Simenon's psychological studies you wonder how he can feel so much, so variously – can understand what being alive means to so many different people. How can he possibly know, in such depth, the emotions of has-been actors, prostitutes, alcoholics, aging farm women, tycoons, clerks? He continually knocks you over with his perceptiveness, his grasp of human situations, and you are soon ready to believe that he knows more about human beings than any other man alive – that he is able to see through human personality to its very core.

Yet much of Simenon's appeal is not to the mind but to the senses. He always puts a man *in a place* – and that place is created with such loving and expert skill that the reader would sometimes be content with just about any resolution of plot as long as he could remain there a while longer: near a village in one of the French provinces, say, watching the red slugs trace their furrows in the ground, and the small barges moving along the canal beneath tall trees, and the leaf in the nearby hedge finally tilting over and spilling the single drop of water it had been collecting out of the day's thin mist.... For even though Simenon pares his novels down to the bone – ten chapters or less – they are never dry or brittle. To Simenon, the right detail is everything. He is the consummate painter, touching every corner of his novel-world with just the right color to make it glow with life.

Whereas Simenon's more serious books are like high-tension wires – thin lines of steel stretched from an ordinary moment in a character's life to an extraordinary but inevitable consequence – his

Maigret novels are more like strolls through a pleasant-looking yet always threatening countryside. Unlike Graham Greene's "entertainments," Simenon's detective fiction leaves you strangely refreshed. Perhaps it is simply because you become so familiar with the habits and routines of Chief-Inspector Maigret that you regard each of his cases as a chance to pay a visit to an old friend.... Maigret, in his office at Quai des Orfèvres, sending Sergeant Lucas out for four more pints of beer while they continue to interrogate a stubborn suspect around the clock; Maigret lighting his pipe and gazing moodily at a woman shaking carpets above a courtyard, still waiting for the first twinges of understanding that will make all the pieces of a troublesome case fit together; Maigret ordering a calvados in a cafe and then staring at a pair of bricklayers in white smocks, trying to divine which of the two is actually a bricklayer and which is a murderer. These are the quite commonplace moments which the Maigret enthusiast comes to enjoy, for they reflect the very human, very unspectacular behavior of a reasonable and trustworthy man as he deals with the world. Maigret always wears well, as a good friend should.

There have been complaints about the limited scope of Simenon's novels: Why doesn't he ever write a *War and Peace* or a *Crime and Punishment*? Can he ever hope to capture life in just 150 pages?

I believe that Simenon wants to capture life as much as any artist that ever lived. But he knows that all meaningful responses to life must be passionate, and that if his books are to remain meaningful he must continue to write them in his own passionate way: isolating himself in his room for two weeks or less, plunging so completely into a book that he exhausts not only the potentialities of the main character but his own physical resources as well.

...Simenon's books, then, are arrow flights: They leap forward without pretense or prelude, they hum with the distinctive tone of their carefully tailored feathers, they follow unerringly their predetermined arc over specially chosen ground – and come to rest in the

heart of a target that only the Master Archer of Lièges could have
selected or even identified.

## John Steinbeck

In 1962 the third American writer in thirteen years and the sixth
during this century was awarded the Nobel prize for literature. Yet had
John Steinbeck belched loudly at a cocktail party he could not have
been treated with any greater disdain by those who deal with
American letters.

Today, six years later, critics continue to turn their backs on
Steinbeck and I continue to wonder why.

Why was he shoved under the carpet so easily by critics after the
Depression – and why did he suddenly come back to do such an
embarrassing and inappropriate thing as win the Nobel prize? Why
should *Time* magazine, in reporting the news of Steinbeck's honor
(under "Sweden," perhaps to avoid sullying its "Books" section), call
forth its ace hatchet man to chop Steinbeck not only down to *Time*-
size but to no-size – that is, the size that Granville Hicks, Edmund
Wilson, and others wanted to have him? Why did *Saturday Review* –
which in recent years has run special memorial issues on Hemingway,
Faulkner, and Robert Frost – not even bother to mention the prize
news at all?

In an age which has come to equate prose complexity with High
Seriousness, has Steinbeck been crossed off simply because he seems
too readable – and thus, apparently, lacking in weight? Or is it that he
has failed to create around himself a myth and a legend – that is, has
existed solely in the words he has written and not as a literary personality? Is it that he has just gone ahead, writing, and has refused to put
forth that *solemn image* which critics like their literary giants to have?
Also, has he failed to pronounce the world a sorry mess and thus, lacking existential despair, is he considered hopelessly old-fashioned? And
perhaps worst of all, is it that he has periodically pursued *humor* – when
we all know that a writer who lays a light hand on the throttle may be

a fine fellow and all that but hardly a profound and dedicated novelist (for who would expect chuckles out of Thomas Mann)?

Or is it simply that, much like Miller, he has never adopted an easily identifiable tag – has been too varied in his writings and has never kept rewriting the same book over and over, as Wolfe did, or using the same technique, like Hemingway, or describing the same social class, like Fitzgerald? Would the critics be happier if he had become a kind of smooth-writing Dos Passos, or a Marquand of the lower classes? Would that have given his work a nice *wholeness* – so prized by those dealing in professional exegesis and literary pigeonholing?

Had Steinbeck been farsighted enough to die in the early 1940s – as a war correspondent in North Africa, perhaps – critics would thereafter have found it easier to let him ascend a couple of steps toward the Parthenon of American letters. He would have been judged solely on his best work – that sustained creativity during the thirties which only Faulkner, among writers in the United States, excelled.

Yet look at the curious critical astigmatism regarding Steinbeck since he has, indeed, lived on. It is all right, say the critics, that Faulkner wrote his finest books in the thirties and then tapered off in the following twenty years – we will judge him by his best. It is all right, too, that Hemingway did his main work – excepting, perhaps, *The Old Man and The Sea* and *A Moveable Feast* – in the twenties and thirties and never fully regained his stride. But for Steinbeck to have done the most outstanding things of his career in the thirties and forties and then do less memorable work later, this somehow makes him solely a Depression Writer – forever the author of *The Grapes of Wrath* in the college literature books, and nothing more.

Literary fashions, if inevitable, nevertheless do little more than reveal that they serve no lasting purpose: What is good may or may not be what is currently fashionable. The Steinbeck-Faulkner seesaw provides a good example of the vagrancy of literary taste. During his most creative years in the thirties Faulkner was given a rather negative reading by many critics not only because of his demanding prose but also because he was not engaged in any kind of social protest: he was creating Ikkemotubbes and Major De Spains instead of Studs Lonigans and Ma Joadses. Then, with the printing of Malcolm Cowley's *Portable* in 1946 the main body of critics suddenly began to "discover" and "re-evaluate" Faulkner – and went on to re-evaluate him right to the top of the literary heap. (Who can say? Without Mr. Cowley's timely *Portable* perhaps the Faulkner boom would have been delayed for a number of years – and Faulkner might have missed the Nobel prize.)

In contrast, with each new work he published in the thirties Steinbeck progressed steadily in the eyes of most critics – until with the publication of *The Grapes of Wrath* in 1939 he lacked only a muscle or two of standing shoulder-to-shoulder with Hemingway. Yet in the up-and-down world of Critic's Choice, as Faulkner's stock rose Steinbeck's began to fall – with neither of the men's books changing a period or a colon (which merely serves to reinforce a feeling of mine: that some critics never read what is actually written before them on the page; they are always too busy reading *for* something – Freudian symbols, *leitmotifs* – since their whole professional existence depends on finding something to *do* with an author's work. Critics today thus like Joyce, Kafka, and Faulkner because of the rich tangled world these authors left behind to play with. But Steinbeck, in not offering a jungle to explore, leaves many critics with pith helmet in hand and no place to go).

Ironically, it seems that *The Grapes of Wrath*, Steinbeck's most wide-ly acclaimed book, ultimately caused his downfall among the critics. For he did not immediately set about to top it with something even grander, more sweeping; he came out instead with *The Moon Is Down* and *Cannery Row* – and the critics never quite forgave him. Like reli-gious devotees, they had been ready to bow a little in his direction – as they had been bowing so long toward Hemingway – if only he would prove, with another blockbuster, that he deserved a piece of the literary godhead. Yet when the succeeding books came out and none was the desired colossus, the critics seemed to shrink back in righteous dismay. They would not have cared, particularly, if the books had been artistic failures or near-failures – *Midcenturys* instead of *U.S.A.s* – as long as they were sociological epics. They wanted Steinbeck to grind out realistic sincerities à la Farrell and Dos Passos so they could file him away as Good and Solid – and safely predictable.

With me, the subject of Steinbeck is not just one for literary footballing; it is deeply personal. For I go to him, and to Faulkner, more often than to any other two American writers – to Faulkner for his immense plungings in, his uncompromising commitments to the depths of things, his utter power; to Steinbeck for companionship and serenity, for a sense of light and life, for affirmation of my own vision and feelings, and – perhaps more than anything else – for his word artistry. Because that is what the man is, at his best: as fully conscious a prose craftsman and technician as Hemingway.

He uses words with a beautiful rightness and clarity yet does not, as Hemingway was prone to do, set up a self-conscious interline chant of Look At My Words, These Words That Are So Lovely And Fine And True. Steinbeck's words do not seem as if they had been put into place by a surgeon wearing a mask and rubber gloves and then a spotlight labeled Art had been focused just above to illumine them properly. Instead, Steinbeck seems to sit back and write about things with a kind of clear-eyed sanity, letting it appear to the reader that the people and places and words just logically got together there on the page out of a natural affinity for one another. It is a deceptively simple style – yet one as artistically sophisticated as Colette's and equally hard to duplicate.

In order to prove my contention – that not only has Steinbeck been unjustly downgraded and neglected by the critics but that he rightly deserved the Nobel Prize (even though he received it twenty years late and after publication of an unimpressive book) – I would have to give excerpts from some of his best works: passages of earthy power from *In Dubious Battle*; passages of simple narrative excellence from *The Long Valley*, *The Red Pony*, and *The Pastures of Heaven* (a most amazingly neglected book); humorous passages from *Cannery Row* (which is artful, beautiful, and generally misread).

Yet such quoting, of course, could not begin to give a true picture of the beauties and terrors of life which Steinbeck has written about. The only possible way for one to do justice to his work is to say, Read him; don't read about him. Read again, or for the first time, the man who wrote *To a God Unknown*, *Of Mice and Men*, *The Pearl*, *Tortilla Flat*.

There are some of his books which I cannot recommend – among them *East of Eden*, *Sweet Thursday*, *The Winter of Our Discontent*. They seriously lack the essential Steinbeck flavor and reflect the fact that after World War II, after the death in 1949 of his friend Ed Rickets (Doc in *Cannery Row*), after his move from California to New York, the quality of his books began to suffer. Something happened to all the good words. Perhaps he lost contact with people and places he really cared about and could not get started again. *Travels with Charley*, though not front-line work, does indicate that his language is back in gear, so perhaps he is not to be counted out even yet.

But if Steinbeck's best work is behind him, it is all right with me. He has put down plenty already – quite enough to last. I plan to go on rereading his books the rest of my days because whatever he wrote about, he wrote as a man whose sentences are connective tissues which subtly tie the bloodstream of his books to the bloodstream of your own experience and which thus manage to transmit that rarest of rare gifts: a literature as believable as life.

# Livestock Show
## (1978)

They come in pickups and Blazers, campers and Mobile Chalets – mainly from Texas and New Mexico but from Oklahoma, Iowa, and Indiana too. Plump sixth-graders in pigtails, beanpole freshmen in

T-shirt and jeans, ag teachers, parents, county agents, hangers-on –
they have gathered the clippers and combs and brushes and water
buckets, have slapped and poked and prodded their hundreds of
calves, pigs, sheep, and horses into trucks and trailers, have driven the
interstate and farm-to-market roads and are finally arriving for the
week-long bash: the 49th Annual Southwestern International Livestock
Show and Rodeo. They enter the dusty grounds of the El Paso
Coliseum, unload their stock into the assigned stalls, buy their bales of
hay, start wandering the aisles of the big livestock barns and inserting
their first lip-full of Copenhagen snuff.

The 4-H and FFA-club exhibitors, following in the bootsteps of
their country-and-western fathers, waste no time in getting ready to
show and hopefully to sell animals that for the past year they have fed,
exercised, pampered, and in some cases loved. They put their radios
against the wash-rack wall – tuning in a Willie Nelson song or the
theme from *Rocky* – and begin scrubbing down their Hereford steer or
combing out the wool of their Southdown lamb.

The nerve center of the livestock show, the judging barn, has
bleachers on each side of the sawdust-filled arena and a concession
stand at one end. A visitor can sit in the stands in the late afternoon –
overhead heaters taking out the February chill, the smell of sawdust
pleasantly in the air – and drink his coffee and watch the people and
listen, if he wishes, to their endless talk.

It does not matter if the women are from Fort Stockton or
Abilene, Vernon or Tularosa; they are country-rural and speak as if
they were reared in the same extended family, had picked up from the
same momma-and-daddy the telltale, flattened umlauts: they want
*Caokes* to drink; they talk about their *faolks* back *baome*.

One watches the sideburned men in hats and puffy, stitched jackets, and wonders about them. When swarms of neighborhood children
come after school to the Coliseum – to look at the animals and play in
the sawdust of the judging arena – the men seem curiously tolerant
toward their swirling feet and heads and arms. As the men move

through the aisles they do not seem to see the paper cup-footballs thrown through the air, do not actually hear the shouts and whistles of the children rolling around in the sawdust. When the men cross the arena itself they look neither right nor left; it is as if they are wading among invisible porpoises sporting in a sawdust sea. (It is the women who become upset at the gliding cups, the hail of sawdust in the air: they come out of the livestock offices to shoo the boys, to clap hands and scatter them – like elementary school teachers disciplining a class.)

The men, one decides, are not being tolerant or patient; it is just that they are not easily deflected from what lies within their field of vision. Thus they are not actually aware of the cups, the flailing arms; they see, as always – in the air before them – breeding heifers and vaccinations and range cubes and the faces of other men who see these essentials too. They appear tolerant only because they are indifferent. Such men are not basically concerned with others – the problems of others, the presence of others: with nuclear disarmament and sexism and racial tensions and civil liberties and all the rest of the city-man's world. They are single-minded men concerned with their own – with their grain crop, their mortgage, their tractor. They respond more to the feed prices in Marfa and Hobbs than to Moral Responsibility and the Human Condition.

...It is curious. After World War II most men in the United States generally gave up on the idea of wearing hats. But not country men. They still wear hats – western hats – or else wear, as a substitute, strangely enough, caps. They doggedly keep their heads covered, indoors and out.

You sit in the bleachers and ponder this phenomenon: Rural men keep their hats on when they dance, when they sit together at cafe tables, when they drive their pickups and cars to town, when they tend to business in stores – perhaps even when they sleep or couple conjugally in the night. Why? Is it Freudian, this hat fixation – a subconscious act of sexual aggression? Does the point of the hat or the bill of the cap reinforce the penile protrusion of their boots? Is it a matter of basic identification: We can tell who you are, we can trust you, we can know that you are for us instead of against us, if you wear a hat? Or is it simply that traditions – all traditions – last longer among country-living people: Men of the West wore hats in times past and by god they still wear them now, if they are still men. By definition, a man is a person in a hat....

It seems that almost any kind of head covering will make do: a hunter's furry, red-checkered cap; even a colored knit cap. Give a livestock-tending man the choice of going bareheaded or wearing a stew pan, and he will wear the pan.

Hats come in endless varieties: Brim rolled neatly in front, dipped down smartly in back; brim curved deeply down in back, also curved deeply down in front – as if the wearer had on a hat-banana; some hats with crowns level on top, others with crowns rising like the prow of a Viking ship; some resembling Halloween hats: extravagantly wide, flat brims, hanging down front and back like awnings; some scarcely bigger than the wearer's head – dinky Stetsons almost comically small; some with such a luxuriously deep dip in front they could be used as grain scoops; gunfighter hats; some square-crowned, some round-crowned, some creased; blacks, browns, pearl-grays, showman white; some almost fluffy felt-and-feathers – as though half a dozen bedroom slippers had been compressed and then shaped into a hat.

And the caps. Apparently every commercial firm serving rural America now makes a cap. Sober, gray-haired grandfatherly types, acned young CB-and-longneck boosters, plump-cheeked eleven-year-olds – they walk the aisles in caps advertising fertilizers, feed stores, John Deere, Coors, insecticides, Phillips 66. A cap – formerly just the practical headgear of baseball players and auto mechanics – is now combination billboard and status symbol.

Like the separate points of two huge, incompatible wedges – one Anglo-Saxon/Teutonic, stretching south from Montana to the Texas border; the other Hispanic, reaching north from South America to the same Rio Grande – the blue-eyed, sandy-haired livestock raisers and the dark-eyed Mexican-Americans of South El Paso meet on the Coliseum grounds but do not blend. They are oil and water.

The brown-skinned boys in long hair and tennis shoes come to the livestock show after school to play in the sawdust (it fascinates them: they run, fall, throw handfuls at each other, laugh, run some more, jump, slide; it is an exotic element, like snow, and they cannot get enough of it – how it feels on the skin, how it feels underfoot, how it clings to their clothes and hair), to look at the animals and chase each other endlessly through the barns and aisles and bleacher stands. They come to have a brief diversion from daily life, to jeer among themselves at the gait of these alien Anglos who walk around so solemnly in their boots and hats and take their fancily groomed animals so seriously – washing and combing and blow-drying sheep as if they were human babies; charging around on horses as if they were on TV.

These kids from the Paisano Street projects: they do not arrive at the Coliseum gates in sleek Oldsmobiles to show fat Angus steers. They are here because the livestock show – this temporary island of Country-Western just a good tobacco spit from Juárez – is located in their neighborhood. These are Juans and Ramons and Miguels whose culture does not embrace raising Appaloosa horses and driving Mobile Chalets.

Although one in a hundred FFA exhibitors may be a Mexican-American from Clint or Pecos, it is difficult, nevertheless, to imagine a Jesus Attaguile from Littlefield winning grand champion crossbred steer; a Maria Mendoza from Big Spring – in black riding cap and shiny, stovepipe Princess Margaret riding boots – receiving a first-place trophy in the English Pleasure horsemanship class.... One watches the eyes, registers the body language of the livestock people from Sweetwater, Seminole, Lampasas – men and women to whom a Rodriguez has generally meant a laborer willing to work for $75 a month and board, a *wet*, a *meskin* – and as they pass the swarms of kids, as they buy a Coors or a hot dog from the brown-armed women in the concession stand, there is a mask that automatically drops into place: Hear No Mexican; Speak to, Touch, Think About No Mexican.

And once, as if on cue – as if a malevolent Anglo deity were orchestrating events at the Coliseum for the Good Old Boys – a work crew of five hard-faced, tattooed Mexican-Americans in their late teens and early twenties pass by the bleachers carrying shovels, pushing wheelbarrows of trash and manure, their shoulder-length black hair held in place by Cochise-style bandanna headbands. They do not smile. They do not look as if they are interested in junior barrel racing. The livestock men, smoking and drinking beer from cups – and accustomed to seeing brown-skins in such menial, caretaking roles – do not give them a glance as they pass.

Yet it is, after all, the animals themselves – over 2,000 of them – that are the focus of the show. They are constantly being bathed in Ivory liquid, exercised, weighed, brushed, watered, fed.... Certain sheep, sheared and washed and blocked, are rubberoid sculptures, their neatly trimmed assholes resembling, from a distance, dark little valentines. Other somber Suffolk blackface sheep – their dark eyes showing through the holes of their protective body cloths, their black nose and mouth covered by a square wire cup – look like clusters of benign Darth Vaders. Still other sheep, with their blank, guileless, eyebrowless gaze, give pleasant shocks of recognition, for among them one can spot familiar faces: Lewis Stone – Mickey Rooney's father in the Andy Hardy movies; Ike Eisenhower; several aging female relatives; a mild-mannered rancher from Fredericksburg with badly fitting false teeth. (In contrast, there are no calves that look like anything except calves: they are true beasts, large and healthy but lacking souls.)

Pigs. In the swine barn, in its dusty and dim afternoon light, a storybook image materializes before your eyes: a young man in a yellow Cat-hat strolls by with a trio of sows, the pigs moving along in an almost comradely fashion toward their stall, the young man walking amiably behind, guide pole in hand, whistling: a medieval Swineherd

Going to Market.

Nearby a boy in jeans and boots, about ten, a Confederate cap on his head, swings on a post above the stalls. "Last year my pig was Wilbur," he says, "and he was just as *gentle*." Where is he now, he is asked. "Well, I done eat part of him."

Down the aisle a freckle-faced boy in a blue cap and horn-rimmed glasses – Jimmy, it says on the back of his belt – is lying in the straw of a pen, carefully brushing his huge white barrow. But he is not just brushing his back; he is almost lolling about on him. He brushes a while, stops, takes the pig's ear in his hand, begins to flop it about gently, experimentally – drawn into considering the weight of it, the texture of the skin, the way the ear feels in his hand: this familiar yet foreign pig's ear, so touchable yet so strange. He pats the pig, slaps him and makes him grunt, tickles the pig's crooked gash of a mouth with a piece of straw – continues to mess around fondly with this pet of his, this huge and indolent pink-fleshed buddy.

Suddenly, in a pen of four, then in a pen of three, finally in a whole pig-neighborhood of the barn, there begins a Walpurgis Night of hysterical, high-pitched, almost metallic pig squeals – as though a dozen street cars were coming to a halt – with a *Boris Goudunov*-basso profundo counterpoint added by other hogs. Something is in the air, some threat or need or excruciating delight, and the pigs join in a swelling, sustained swine chorus.

Each day the exhibitors take their animals into the arena where a judge, godly in hat and tie and boots, moves carefully about, saying nothing, his gaze continuous, penetrating; stooping here to feel the flesh on an animal's back, there to feel its hindquarters or brisket; straightening up, moving about some more, the contestants watching him intently, their eyes riveted to his face, waiting for his nod or hand gesture that means they are to move to first or fifth or eighteenth place.

Each day spectators sit in the stands and watch a girl in tight jeans and a white T-shirt that says "Flick My Bic" lope around and around the arena, followed – like a well-trained dog – by a trim-bod-ied, blackfaced sheep, obviously a pet of long standing. The girl, somewhat boyish, runs tirelessly in her rocking, side-to-side gait, and the lamb – neurotically dependent now on the neat-jeaned buttocks in front of it – dutifully goes lap after lap, black ears rhythmically flop-ping.

Each day townspeople wander through the barns, fathers wearing soft-shiny leather jackets and checkered dress pants from Union Fashion. They are squeaky-clean, Bank Americard middle-class, as con-spicuously out of their element as the kids from the Paisano projects. They stroll by, hands in pockets, tolerant, detached, Saturday casual, viewing horses in stalls as they would giraffes in the zoo.

Finally, after the last lamb has been judged and the last ribbon draped across a Duroc hog, the winners line up behind the auction barn; the prospective buyers from the gas and electric companies, the banks, the service clubs, the shopping centers, the automobile dealers get out small calculators and take their seats among the spectators in the auction room; and the stock show draws to a close. Amid cheer-leader clapping by mothers and friends from Alpine and Fabens and Las Cruces, the exhibitors, one by one, lead their animals into the ring and the auctioneer begins his tongue-twisting chant, "Sayyyy, I-have-one-fifty-one-fifty-one-fifty-one-fifty...." The auction assistants roam about in front with rolled-up programs in their hands, seeking out the bidders in the stands, pointing toward them, waiting, catching an affir-mative nod, signaling with a sharp "Yaa-ooohhhh!" to the auctioneer, moving on. When the bidding stops, the exhibitor leads Madge or Curly or Whimpy – this lovingly packed body with its prize-winning conformation – out of the ring to the back lots where packing house trailers are waiting to load it and carry it off to slaughter.

The show is over. Dust hangs in the air as trailers and pickups pull out through the main gate – past the same county sheriff cars that have been parked there all week. Pigeons return to the sheep pens and begin their bobbing-necked pecking in the spilled grain. Sparrows fly in through the barn windows and talk wildly to one another in the rafters: the empty stalls, the aisles, the sun rays are theirs again. Broken styrofoam cups lie in the scattered straw. And in the doorway of the judging arena the five maintenance crew Indians, in their faded jeans and red headbands, lean on rakes and hoes and stare out at the deserted grounds. Two of them are smiling.

# A Trip South
## (1976)

I will have to go into training if I want to develop the proper Graham Greene spirit – if I ever decide to board a steamer for Montevideo and live for six months in a cockroach-and-wash-basin hovel. You see, one night several years ago in Mobile, Alabama, I discovered I was middle-class to the core.

...The house: it stood on a corner in the fading light. A three-story Gothic monster. Built and painted at the turn of the century perhaps and then stripped down to cottony fiber by seventy-five years of coastal weathers. Room and board, the barely distinguishable sign said out front. Well, I thought, this might be interesting, and I knocked on the door.

It was opened finally by a small, corpulent man in house slippers and rimless glasses (surely Truman Capote's twin, alive and well on Mobile Bay). Yes? he said, in a high, flat voice. I told him I would like to see a room. He said he was just a boarder but to come on in. Mrs. De Ridder would be with me in a minute.

I followed him down a dark hallway. Then he opened a door and we were in it: the living room. Or better: The Morgue. The Cave. Fagin's Place. Ward Seven. A stage set designed by some young playwright-of-the-absurd who decided to take Tennessee Williams, Ken Kesey, Dickens, and Flannery O'Connor and scramble them together in order to come up with...Mrs. De Ridder's Boarders.

They were seated, seven or eight of them, in a circle around the gloomy, high-ceiling room looking toward the oldest television set in the Western world. It flickered its vague images as they sat there, watching, unmoving. Blank faces, blasted faces. Crooked bodies sunk in chairs. Toothless mouths and rolling eyes and twisted hands.

Mrs. De Ridder was apparently busy with a woman who was sick – or insane perhaps – in an adjoining room. I got a glimpse of the woman's thrashing white head above the bed covers as Mrs. De Ridder's hand passed a ring of keys out the door.

"The rent is ten dollars a week," the small, corpulent man said as he led me upstairs. The yellow light bulb hanging in the hallway had burned out so we moved along slowly in the dark. Trying several keys before he found one that worked, the man finally opened the tall, scarred door. We entered. The man stood patiently, serenely – as if ready to say, "And this is the master bedroom" – while I looked around, still holding my two suitcases. Torn shades hung from the windows. Knife messages were carved into the walls. There was a faint smell of mice.... I looked at the bed and imagined lying there in the dark, waiting for the bedbugs to come out. It was eight o'clock and I was hungry and at that particular moment I did not feel the least bit like Graham Greene.

I thanked the man and told him I would like to take another look at the room when it was daylight. We locked the room and left. I walked six blocks to a Travelodge and lay on the clean-smelling bed and watched color TV and for thirty minutes or so felt like a million dollars.

But I'm getting ahead of myself. My trip actually began on a March afternoon in Kerrville, Texas, in a light mist: one week on a Greyhound bus. One week to enter part of the Deep South and see what I could learn by just keeping my eyes open and wandering around.

As I settled back in my seat and watched cars going by on the San Antonio highway, it seemed that just sitting higher off the ground, in a bus, offered a traveler new angles of vision, new possibilities.... There would suddenly appear the white overpowering burst of a pear tree blooming by a fence, a rain-glistening horse, head down in a field. Trees stood in groves, somber as committees; the tin roof of a barn was visible through surrounding oaks, with streaks of rust making for a casual rural elegance. (And on one barren stretch of dirt sat that blunt, oblong obscenity, a trailer house – the Flem Snopes of all human living quarters.)

In the Houston terminal, at one o'clock in the morning, the sandy-eyed, dry-mouthed, downcast mood of the all-night traveler began to settle over me as I watched toothless men in dirty, wrinkled pants standing near the bus station door, looking out vaguely into the night. I was already identifying with the transient's life: feeling how it was to be uprooted, for whatever reason, and to be moving about from place to place – not elegantly, easily, comfortably, by jet or air-conditioned family car but by the cheapest way possible: by bus or hitchhiking or trudging down a road: guys out of work, just standing around, waiting; guys moving from one Skid Row to another; young mothers with a couple of kids asleep in their laps.... Outside the terminal more run-down-at-the-heel men stood around, more men without teeth: they moved toward each other, vaguely joined for a moment – for a cigarette, a quarter, some bit of information – then walked on down the sidewalk to stand some more, looking at the dark streets as if the streets themselves – since they were so familiar, so intimately a part of the men's lives – could somehow give them help.

We crossed Lake Pontchartrain in a 9:30 drizzle. My first glimpse of New Orleans was a continuous line of trucks and cars, their headlights on – as if everyone in town were part of a dreamlike funeral procession left over from Mardi Gras. Then, on the left, a gigantic cemetery greeted us.

I rented a room at the YMCA and in semidarkness lay dead-tired against the thin little wafer of my YMCA pillow. I listened to the echoing voices of the black cleaning women in the halls as the New Orleans rain kept pouring down. I tried to sleep but couldn't, and lay there remembering another narrow room at another Y: in New York, twenty years before, when it was also raining and I would look out of the window my first day there and see the gray solid slabs of buildings and say reassuringly to myself: Well, this is New York.

At noon I had breakfast at the nearby Hummingbird Cafe: two eggs, grits, toast, thick bacon for $1.10. A twenty-four-hour cafe underneath a small walk-up hotel – a gathering spot for Skid Row, waterfront types – the Hummingbird was a pleasant, warm place to be in while the streets grew grayer in the rain.

A balding young Captain Kidd, his hair shoulder-length in back, an earring in his left ear, methodically washed dishes behind the counter and sucked a tooth. The red-haired waitress, with catfish-white skin, had veins running like blue rivers at the back of her fleshy legs. During a lull the waitress lit a cigarette and stood beside Captain Kidd, who had stopped working too. The cook, in long sideburns and apron, also turned around. The three of them stood there for a moment, motionless, gazing blankly, privately, across the cafe toward the wet sidewalk – looking like a strange trio of performers paused in a silent movie. Gazing straight ahead and barely moving her lips – the cigarette still in her mouth – the waitress said to no one in particular, "God, am I tired. I could stay drunk for a month."

On Bourbon Street that afternoon, in a bar, a waitress was reminiscing to several customers as she watched the rain. "It's all gone to hell in the past five years," she said. "Everybody used to hang together – the street people, you know. I worked as a stripper before I got fat, and I walked out of there every night with $150-200. But no more. Nobody's spending – it's the dope. It used to be just grass and pills, but now it's all hard stuff.... And the pimps: you see, they'll play up to a guy that looks like a good prospect; then when they figure he's ready they'll line him up with a girl and roll him.... People are afraid to go to the Quarter. It just ain't like it used to be."

...Nighttime in New Orleans. I ate a Whopper Burger while a Cajun without teeth swept the floor of the cafe and talked to a friend about something or other. He was incomprehensible. It was like listening to the double-talk of Professor Irwin Cory of the old radio days.

On my way back to the YMCA I stopped in at the Paddock Bar for a beer. A balding young man broke the stillness of the bar as he suddenly punched in the side of his empty Jax can. It was as if he were trying to shatter the universe with the single abrupt motion. The night – another night in the Paddock Bar, a night just like all the other previous nights in the same bar, with the same half-light, same dim heads of patrons, same pictures of horses and jockeys in their silks – had been too much for him. With a single motion of his thumbs he tried to destroy it.

I went up to my bare room at the Y and listened to Jim Croce on a transistor radio while I sipped cheap whiskey out of a paper cup.

The next morning, in the New Orleans bus terminal, a boyish young security guard leaned against a chair, cap pushed back, toothpick at the side of his mouth: he was talking to two faded-blue-jean girls. He seemed genuinely interested in where they were going and where they had been – even envious of their foot-loose life: "Been down in Mexico, huh?" He tried to keep the conversation spread equally between the short-haired pretty girl and her plain-Jane companion, but his face just kept on drifting back automatically toward the pretty one. He smiled, shifted the toothpick to the other side of his mouth, reached down to touch the girls' backpacks on the pretext of feeling the texture, shifted his position against the chair, recrossed his legs – all the while soaking up their presence: two girls in blue jeans and bandannas and sandals, loose on the world, doing what he would like to do but never would.

..."What are you, some kind of troublemaker?" the Houston-to-Birmingham driver asked a young man who rushed up at the last minute and wanted to check his bags. "This is union shop. I don't load no bags and he" – the driver jerked his thumb toward the baggage man at the side – "don't drive my bus." The young man persisted, politely enough, saying that he was told inside the terminal that the bus was already loading and he would have to check his bags outside. The driver refused further talk, but as the young man struggled to get on the bus with his bags the driver begrudgingly held out his hand to assist. The young man wordlessly refused the offer to help and bumped his way onto the bus and into his seat. Immediately the driver came charging down the aisle after him: "That's what I knew you were – a troublemaker.... See this?" He held up the blue sleeve of his driver's jacket that had a red spot on it. "That's blood. A man was killed on my bus last night.... *Troublemakers.*" The young man sat in his seat, stunned, as the driver went back to take more tickets.

(Blacks sit at the front of the bus now; young counter-culture college students seem to purposefully, flauntingly, dress in old, patched, ragged clothes; foreign students with AmeriPass tickets speak halting, difficult-to-understand English. In reaction bus drivers seem to be hardening up, pulling back from easy-going courtesies – despite the metal plate at the front of the bus which still says, "Your driver is_____. Safe Efficient Courteous." They give their set little speech over the intercom about smoking and intoxicants as they pull away from the terminal, then they take off their cap and drive on silently down the road. They seem to feel they have nothing in common with their passengers any more. They could just as easily be transporting sacks of feed or window sashes.)

The sun finally came out on the North Shore of New Orleans, just before Slidell, and shone on the East of Eden Lounge, on bayou shacks and small prefabricated houses. In Slidell there were pines and oaks and brilliant red azaleas; shadowed yards ran along shadowed streets.... I found myself thinking: These are Southerners now, walking in Southern sunshine, under Southern trees. How does it feel to have lived here in this place under this moody sky?

We passed through Picayune, Mississippi, where the bus station was located in a small grocery store. (A few miles on down the road a green interstate sign solemnly informed us we were approaching North Picayune.) In Hattiesburg I enjoyed the good sight of porches still going casually around the front and side of Southern homes.

I looked out intently at the landscape as I rode along, but with my inner eye I kept expecting to see Scout Finch of *To Kill a Mockingbird* cross into Boo Radley's side yard, or Carson McCuller's Frankie standing with her nose pressed against a screen door, or a young Willie Morris gazing up at the bus — or Faulkner's Lena Grove and Horace Benbow and Jason Compson and Eula Varner moving along the sidewalks and crossing the town squares. Southern writers had already powerfully shaped this land for me, and the South meant nothing more than the words that I had read about it. The pine trees and the houses and the flowers struggled for verisimilitude against the almost overwhelming reality of the books I had read, movies I had seen. I wanted to see with my own eyes, feel with my own body what it was like here, but there had been too many news reports, too many stereotypes — too much Faulkner and slavery and Civil War for me to see the South simply, of a piece, as I might see Denver, Colorado. I wanted to look deeper — for essence — but all I was seeing, as a visitor passing through, was just more pines, more sweet gums. The interstate highway kept going ruler-straight through the countryside of central Mississippi, away from the towns and farms and people I wanted to see. I could just as easily have been going through Oregon.

In the late afternoon we crossed into Alabama and its gentle hills. After the few small Southern towns and the isolated stretches in between, the University of Alabama in Tuscaloosa came as a shock — as an unreality. Our bus, with its load of half-asleep, head-wobbling passengers, was suddenly rolling right past fraternity-and-sorority row, past timeless, tree-shaded brownstone collegiateness. It was like turning a familiar corner on your way home from work and finding that a movie set of "The Halls of Ivy" had been built on what had always been a vacant lot.

The next day I sat in a park by the Jefferson County Court House in Birmingham. It was a cool morning with subdued city sounds in the background. Old men were reading newspapers. Secretaries on their lunch hour nibbled the remains of their sandwiches while thumbing through magazines. Pigeons coasted above the grass; electric drills whined from a construction project on a side street. I felt as if I were back in Austin, Texas, in 1954. There was that same sense of fifties promise in the air, the sense of a leisured future waiting, beckoning.

In the afternoon I walked through the downtown streets of Birmingham – past the Protective Life Building where, at 3:00, the chimes slowly rang out "Dixie"; past a black billiard parlor where, in the window, men's mismatched shoes were strung horizontally along a piece of string beneath a sign, "Shoes for Sale"; past two men sitting on a bench, one of whom was engrossed in telling the other the following joke: "Seems there was these ten niggers in a Cadillac that went around a curve too fast one night and crashed through a farmer's fence. The Cadillac hit a tree, scattering niggers everywhere. The next day the farmer calls out the Highway Patrol and tells them what he's done. He said, 'I took my bulldozer and buried 'em right where they all died.' The Highway Patrol says, 'Buried 'em? Why, how did you know they was all dead?' 'Well,' the farmer says, 'I know eight of 'em was. Two of 'em *said* they wasn't, but you know how niggers lie.'"

At six o'clock I was visiting an old air force friend at his home among the tall pines in suburban Homewood. Boys in the neighborhood were shooting baskets at the side of their red-brick homes, fathers stood in wide, unfenced yards with drinks in their hands, blond-haired daughters rushed up front walks with tennis rackets and tennis sweaters, leaving young male companions waiting in sports cars.

After supper I took a leisurely walk around the edge of the nearby country club and then circled back past other quiet, wooded homes. I stopped a moment at a street corner. It was a lovely, easy dusk – the smell of burning leaves was in the air along with a lingering clean dampness from a brief afternoon rain. Small fast cars took the hilly curves now and then. A neighborhood patrol car cruised slowly by. (I had asked my friend's wife at supper: Is this suburb restricted? Yes, she said: no blacks, no Jews.)

Then I noticed him: a middle-aged man in a T-shirt and sneakers ambling about the yard. He had a large stomach and walked like a man who had just finished a satisfying meal.... Standing on the street corner in Homewood, Alabama, I tried to put myself in the man's place – tried to see the man as he saw himself: Expensive homes all about him. A golf course just down the hill. The Alabama-Auburn basketball game on television the following day.... Here was a man who had it made: a restricted neighborhood; a sports event to look forward to; a beautiful place among the pines. For him day was nicely done, and he walked peacefully on the smooth, pine-needle-soft lawn of his life.

Sunday, and it was time to move on. At the Birmingham station I caught the noon bus to Mobile. Riding next to me was a laboring man with a strong body smell and super-thick glasses. Even though a chunk of chewing tobacco swelled his right jaw, he smiled easily, showing small, brown-stained teeth. He was reluctantly going back to Mobile to work in the city parks department. "It's regular young New York," he said. "I don't like it, I can tell you that. I'm a country man, you might say." As he drowsed in his seat I noticed that he had a brown plastic artificial leg showing above his white cotton sock.

We passed through Selma – coincidentally on the tenth anniversary of "Bloody Sunday," 1965. I bought *The Selma Times-Journal*, a progressive-looking paper, and read about the commemorative march, led by Mrs. Coretta King. This time the marchers crossed Edmund Pettus bridge – on the way to Montgomery – without any problems, the paper said. Instead of bloodying heads, the police directed traffic to make the marching easier. The newspaper gave front and back page

coverage to the march, and there were more non-sports page photographs of blacks than I had seen in any other Southern newspaper.

A stunning, part-Indian young black woman got off at
Thomasville. With her hair sleeked back across her head into a tight
bun at her neck, the prominent Indian nose, the dark elegantly oval
face, the quick flash of strong perfect teeth, the almost palpable intelligence, she stood next to the outside trash receptacle – waiting for her
ride – like a totally self-possessed figure of royalty. (Again, not being
able to see the South with just my own eyes, I immediately thought of
Faulkner's Indian stories – of Issetibbeha and Doom and Herman
Basket.)

Looking out of the bus, mile after mile, I wondered what it was
like to live in the South among tall trees – trees that were always
above you, around you, making a daily backdrop to your life. It was as
though the trees, the constant sense and presence of them, had created
a vital extra dimension in Southern people's lives – as if all human acts,
black and white, had been hidden within them. It was as if the trees
were not mere phenomena, like sunsets or snows or deserts, but
instead were undrawn curtains for the drama of Southern history....
They did not just form a horizon to Southern lives: they got closer
than that, were more intimate. They were, indeed, witnesses – almost
like eunuchs in the courts of pashas: privy to events but not
threatening.

...The trees, the trees, in small country towns and sprawling
cities: inevitably, I felt, they were symbols. They were, perhaps, the
blacks still too silent in the presence of whites. Perhaps – if the South
were truly ever to "rise again" – it would be as trees suddenly losing
their immobility and beginning to walk – armies of silently advancing
pines, making their way across the red clay fields, moving with relentless intensity: not as an act of redemption or vengeance or justice but
with the elemental force of an ice age or a prairie fire: trees: not bringing destruction or chaos but, anticlimactically, simply moving silently
away.

What would the South look like, feel like, be like after all the trees went away – the landscape denuded, the houses starkly one-next-to-another and lacking the touch of grace that pines can give even the flimsiest shack, the undeniable charm they lend to a suburban home.

Yes, indeed, I wondered, what would happen to the South if its trees deserted it, leaving the land bare and the people naked to one another (like Adam and Eve who, suddenly, became ashamed?).... To remove the context of trees; to remove that which had provided elegance and beauty; to let the unredeemed flat earth remain, with the people on it, black and white, looking at one another, shack to Tudor home, face to face, experience to experience. To no longer have trees that soften the harshness and camouflage the grimness ( – shacks as studies in cosmetized poverty). To let the trees march away, to let the Southland see itself finally in terms of people only and the quality of their lives; to strip off the mask of beauty and let the stark light of no-trees come flooding in.

The country man with the plastic leg got off the bus at Prichard, a little town north of Mobile. I watched him limp away down a street of azaleas toward whatever rooming house or relatives' home he lived in during the week. He didn't want to be here this quiet Sunday afternoon; he wanted to be back on the farm in West Blocton with the wife and kids, spitting his tobacco juice into an empty coffee can on his front porch.

In Mobile I read the faded notice on the door of the YMCA – "Closed in 1972" – then walked with my two suitcases past Greek waterfront bars, looking for a rooms-for-rent sign in a gray, dreary town.

No one was in sight in Bienville Square – downtown Mobile – after dark; not a car was moving. It was like a scene from a science fiction movie in which the entire population of a city has been annihilated by Martian death rays.

At midnight I had a cup of coffee next to a wiry, white-haired man in a leather cap. A self-possessed, calmly speaking man, he was traveling with the Royal Lipizzan Stallions show. He said he had been laying off for most of the winter, letting his son do a little horseshoe-ing to bring in grocery money. They had been staying near Newport News in Virginia in "the best little town in the world." He said the people up there care about one another: "you get sick and the next door neighbor lady brings over a bowl of chicken soup...*fusses* over you, you know."

Four black queens got on the bus the next morning. Betty Ann was their leader. He wore a black sequined tam, sandals, three rings on his little finger, long fingernails painted yellow. He carried a small wooden traveling case with his name painted on it in orange, and a portable TV. Christy Star, wearing a black tam, sat across the aisle from him. He was smooth skinned – apparently beardless – and had plucked eyebrows. They made crooning, unending talk and gave each other frequent hand touchings across the aisle.

Also boarding the bus was a young couple – both red-haired, fleshy, pale-skinned and freckled – who never once saw a pond or a pine during the ride to New Orleans but just moved with the blind rhythm of the tides from tranquil hand holding to bone-jarring embrace. She would lick his ear, in and out, like a cow cleaning her newborn calf; he would slide his fingers through her hair, twisting, clawing. They would rest and doze, then gradually begin to work each other over again. In between rounds their lips looked like orange-red blossoms that had fallen from their hair.

In the midst of his fellow travelers, trying to ignore them, was a slim elderly man who looked like Thomas Mann on a sabbatical. He sat in his overshoes, wearing a gray, small-brim fedora and horn-rimmed glasses, and read stock quotations from the *Wall Street Journal*. Periodically he cleared his throat and gave the paper brisk little shakes – dignified protests, perhaps, against the unseemly worldliness of his traveling companions.

The sudden stretch of beach at Biloxi was welcomed and dramatic. It even caused Betty Ann and Christy Star to stop talking for a moment — their intense private world finally eclipsed by the overpowering presence of natural grandeur.

And there was this too along the Mississippi Gulf coast: just a small white farm house sitting off by the side of the road, with an azalea bush in the front yard: a quite ordinary house, yes, but illumined by that single, blazing ornamentation.... Homes with their modest Eternal Flame, their own holy Burning Bush.... Azaleas: rouge on the face of the South.

The afternoon was bright as we came into New Orleans. After checking back into the YMCA I walked up Canal Street toward Woolworth's and the source of the loudspeaker music on the sidewalk: "Oh, Savior, tell my mother I'll be there...." The singer, a neat handkerchief around her head, was smiling pleasantly to curious passersby while she sang her gospel songs. Her companion, a man in a green lightweight sport coat and green slacks — looking vaguely like a small-town grocer — was praying a long prayer over a man in a muddy brown suit whose face was covered with welts and cuts and dried blood. It seemed that the man had been beaten up while he was drunk and had been robbed of all his money. He stood abjectly beside the Woolworth front glass with his head bowed and his hands folded. His wife had broken down in the midst of the prayer and was moaning and crying with the release of having found Jesus.

When the prayer ended the man in green stepped back and turned away from the couple. He began to straighten his clothes and make his move toward rejoining the singer at the microphone. But when the beaten-up man formed words of gratitude through his puffed-up mouth, the prayer man became ill at ease. His business was bringing another lost sheep to the fold, not having this smelly, hang-dog-faced man in the dirty wrinkled brown suit hold his hand like a souvenir.

He tried, somewhat gently, to remove his hand, but the beaten-up man just hung on, pumping it thankfully. They continued to stand in their awkward frozen handshake while the wife hugged her black purse to her breast, crying in her deliverance, and the singer kept artfully whipping her microphone cord out of the way of people going by and sending her cheerfully mournful songs up and down Canal Street.

On the Mississippi levee at dusk people sat on the gray boulders, looking out to the river and soaking in its quiet, muddy hugeness. Across the street in Jackson Square, in a tree, a mockingbird was almost loony with its private ecstasies.... Three long-hairs were meeting by a bench. "Did you score?" ...As darkness fell I strolled along with other tourists and had French doughnuts and chicory coffee in a sidewalk cafe.

The French Quarter that night – to me – was not Al Hirt, not the blasting Dixieland combos, not the serene Preservation Hall old black musicians – none of these. It was, instead, a young, long-haired transient who stood for a while on the sidewalk next to "Your Father's Mustache" saloon, beside three plastic trash cans. He was wearing a frayed Mexican vest and brown flare pants; sweat was popping out all over his face; his stringy black hair was swinging around, partially covering his face and eyes. He was playing a mouth harp and a strange hand instrument, and he was raising goosebumps all over my back and arms with his frantic, driving music.

With his left arm and hand flailing away, his foot tapping, his hair swinging, he poured himself into "Cherokee Trail," "Truckin' with the Blues," "Melody and Rhythm," while the nine o'clock tourist crowd stopped, watched, and drifted on down Bourbon Street.

After listening a while I went over to talk to him. He was Raymond Simmons, he said, from Wisconsin, and he had just made it in from Florida that morning. He called his hand instrument a symbal-lows – a finger cymbal mounted on a strip of wood plus two little bars of aluminum that he hit together in a tap-dancing, castanet fashion.

He flicked his hair back from his eyes and added, in his soft-spoken voice, that he was half-Indian.

I thanked him, wished him luck, and moved away. He began playing again – playing with passion – his body in a constant pumping sway, the beat infectious. People continued to stop, stare, move on toward the gay bars and strippers with forty-four-inch breasts. (One man in an expensive suit and a toothpick in his mouth glanced briefly at Raymond Simmons from Wisconsin, shook his head, and remarked to his companion: "Takes all kinds, doesn't it.")

Two policemen finally came walking slowly up the sidewalk and told the young man to shut it down and move it on. Sweat still dripping, he said yessir politely and began putting his instruments into their case (...he will pick up and go, say yessir to other policemen in other cities; he will sleep on his dirty blue jacket in other doorways and he will stand against other buildings in Baton Rouge and Houston and Albuquerque, shaking his arm, sucking and blowing on his harmonicas, creating his beautifully frenzied, haunting, one-man-show for himself and the gods).

On my last morning in New Orleans I stopped at a park on Camp Street and watched as, one by one, they came out of an old, three-story frame house: bearded young men in cut-offs and tennis shoes; bright-eyed, bra-less young women in jeans and polo shirts. They began to jog around the park, to run unending laps – never seeming to tire, just getting redder in the face and gaining continual second wind.... Afterwards I spoke briefly to a girl named Susan as she walked down the sidewalk. "We're keeping our circulatory systems in shape for Jesus," she said, panting a little but smiling. "We came down at Mardi Gras and we've been busy ever since – saving souls for the Lord." Still smiling, she told me to have a good day as she turned in at Shiloh House. On the steps, reading the Bible with almost painful attentiveness, was a shaggy-haired fellow with a skull and crossbones tattooed in red and blue on his arm. (Across the street, on the steps of a house with broken windows, a couple of dudes and their old ladies balefully watched the Jesus Runners while passing around their early morning joints.)

Before leaving New Orleans I thought I ought to take at least one ride on the St. Charles Street trolley. So I had a farewell cup of coffee in the Hummingbird Cafe, paused for a moment at the corner of St. Charles and Camp to have a last look at Skid Row before catching the trolley at Lee Circle – and couldn't budge for an hour or more. The men: they were sprawled out across the sidewalk, up and down the street; they sat huddled, hunched, fallen in doorways; they stood around in staggering bunches trying to get together enough nickels for another bottle of Hurricane wine. They would never pull out, none of them – that's what overwhelmed me. There was not a single day of dignity, of grace, left for any of them. They were all doomed to sit in one alley or another, one city or another, until they froze to death or died of malnutrition or staggered out, intentionally, in front of a warehouse delivery truck.

The trolley carried tourists and townspeople along a stretch of Showcase South – past magnolia-shaded yards and elegant-looking old homes. To get off the trolley, to walk through Audubon Park across the street from Loyola University, was like waking up after a bad dream. There was an incredible sense of freedom and the goodness of living. Kids played baseball surrounded by idyllic, lush, Audubon greenery. Students, in twos and threes, studied crosslegged by a pond beneath huge oaks. Leaves were picked up by random breezes and scattered gently across the ground. There was warmth and light and bicyclers and kites and the smell of spring oak blooms. It was all so much the way life ought to be lived by everyone everywhere that I almost couldn't stand it: the sheer physical contenting joy of humans being in the right place in the right way.

The irreconcilable opposites: that's what I felt, finally, about the South as I checked out of the YMCA and walked to the bus station. Which was perhaps only to say: that's what I felt about life. The sane, pleasant, leisurely pace at one end of St. Charles Street versus the sound of crashing wine bottles at the other. Failed, fallen, lonely men versus the self-assured, well-dressed patrons of the Old Absinthe House in the French Quarter. The lobby of the Fairmont Hotel versus the collapsing porches of black families on the outskirts of Meridian, Mississippi.

I also had a bone to pick with tourists who seemed to keep reality at arm's length by having convenient words to describe it so that they would not have to experience it. To experience would be to *become*, imaginatively, empathetically, that which they were observing – to see with the same eye that looks out from the center of the experience. Thus tourists had found parts of a city "fascinating" and bums, drifters, derelicts (again, easy words which describe a man but which were one remove from being the man himself) to be "disgusting" or "pitiful." The tourists I listened to seemed to be taking in experiences like a child gobbling down jelly beans: they remained unaffected, unchanged because after their experiencing they did not have the urge to *act*. And to act, to do something in response to that which you have experienced, seemed to me the only verification that you had, indeed, experienced.

It was almost over now. Just a final, flat, monotonous stretch of Louisiana, and then Texas and home.... Tall, straight, leafless trees growing in the swamps like fleets of ruined sailing ships run aground.... Grim-looking beer joints, abandoned filling stations, mobile home graveyards, coastal drabness.... Unable to tell if those were low clouds boiling around or scattered plumes of industrial wastes.

And the last, lingering vision of my trip? We were in the San Antonio bus station, one o'clock at night. The rain which had started in Beaumont had stopped but the air was biting cold. A man in an overcoat and an old hunting cap was crouching outside the bus station door – immobile, like an Indian on a rock. I glanced at him when I went out to the news rack to buy a paper: a small neat man, clean-shaven. He had probably been run out of the terminal but had no place to go.

As the bus pulled out for Kerrville I looked back: the man was still there, collar up, facing the street, crouched there for the night.

# VIII

# JOURNALS

# 1954–1961

# Central Texas

I don't think I am *interested* in God as such; it's just that, having a mind, I feel logically compelled to find Him. It's like being involved in reading a fine book: a tremendous desire arises in you to know who wrote it and to stare into his face; but all the while, despite the looking, it is the work that he did you are attracted to. The creator can never match his creation, if the creation is any good.

There is only one way in which I can ever be at peace with myself – to be convinced that I have within me a steady source of significant things to say about life and have the ability to write them down so that others will value them. If I were Jesus Christ and Abe Lincoln rolled into one, I would nevertheless carry within me a sense of failure if I did not write because to create memorable things out of my head is the only challenge I accept. I must be able to look at the world, perceive truths about it, and write them down – or fail.

I sit in my car on Sunday afternoon beside a plowed field, writing a little about isolated sights and sounds: the beauty of a tree shadow; the sound of a dog barking as a group of children run unseen through distant trees; the smell of grass and flowers and fresh dirt that a breeze brings to you; the steady heavy-sweet smell of acres of mesquites in bloom; a few bobbing-necked doves eating hurriedly, suspiciously along the railroad track; a bird – far out in the mesquites and hidden – that makes a quick, incessant sound that is useless to describe unless you have heard it once on a hot, quiet afternoon in South Texas.

And with the air smelling the way it does, and with the dark plowed field stretched out in the low sun the way it is, and with unseen running dogs and children, and gradually shadowing grass, and a light continual breeze, and night coming out of nowhere like a slow ground mist – you feel you must put something down. It won't be much, but you feel you must pay homage to the day.

Cypress Creek Road: I drive along, seeing the country stretch out into the morning and I become limp with the sense of greenery and peace and sun and air. The simple magnificence of trees, of bird-sounds, of grasses – it washes over me, possesses me, makes me joyful and clean.

I look at the narrow road left over, undisturbed, from the thirties, with grass growing into it from the roadside; at the Spanish oaks and pecan trees taking all the shining ten o'clock light into their leaves; at weeds along the creek and prickly poppies in the field, at cattails and gourd vines and clumps of horehound and cedar posts and windmills and a farmhouse partly hidden in a distant joining of the hills. These things I see clearly, and yet I do not understand what feelings I can express about them. It is as though I want to say, without knowing why, that...*nature never lacks*, it never fails to satisfy, it is the only paradise which I am always ready to enter.

I love the ranch – the ranch house itself, primarily, and its yards, but also the lots and fields, the pastures that go to the horizons with trees and varied risings of land, the seasons that come and go and the animals and birds that remain. The ranch means my grandparents who have lived there for over half a century. It means good morning breezes, and wasps crawling into the mouths of front-yard hydrants, and windmills turning, and boards weathering. It means the smell of homemade pillow cases and the feel of cool kitchen linoleum against your bare feet on late summer nights.

The ranch is a near-completeness, a near-perfection; it allows for human living at an unneurotic pace. It is what the body of a woman is to a man, a church is to one devout. It is uncomplicated peace.

I wait for this August day to present itself to me: for the trees and houses to break their afternoon silence. You see, a town, a neighborhood, a street has a quiet life of its own that goes unnoticed – separate from the lives of people. But everyone is too busy to notice. Mothers, delivery men, carpenters, boys walking to town – they do not see the life of the day because it is too familiar. It is right there before them and is therefore invisible.... Cars turn corners, cats cross yards, rocks sit whitely in a two o'clock glare, but they are expected, they are routine. They are ordinary sights of a day and thus no one ever sees them.

The context: that is what I am talking about. The total mood of a day or place, not just what happens to *people*.... The context is always taken for granted unless something happens within it – a car wreck, a sudden rainstorm. Then the day is changed by News. A man gets up from his chair on a porch, or stops his truck, or goes to the yard fence to watch, or gets on the telephone to call. People become momentarily concerned; they are aware of the day because it is no longer the day they had taken for granted.

Without obvious little dramas to distract them, people do not look at two o'clock very deeply – at the *way* an afternoon is, the *way* a street is. They travel many miles to Carlsbad Caverns, or to Yellowstone Park, but they will not look out from their own living room windows to see *this* moment of *this* day: the way the sounds of a neighborhood are when the summer wind is moving about and there are whirring insects and birds and drifting afternoon voices and sun glintings on carpet grass. Or just the simple sitting of buildings and plants on this earth, where we are; the deep wonder of any single moment.

...One window in the side of any house is a mystery – one tree trunk, one door slamming, one glimpse of sky.

I am stuck here in the middle of eternity and I don't know what to do about it.

Sundown on the Pedernales: It is summer, and you are standing in that casual stretch of time in late afternoon when the sun is going down and the river air is so strongly peaceful that you can almost hear the greenness of the weeds along the bank. You are fishing, and from time to time you look out to where your cork is riding the surface of the water, comfortably. You do not mind too much if the cork doesn't move, for it is the atmosphere of the river that counts – the long ending of the summer day, the gnats milling in the sun-washed light, the deep presence of trees.

During the early afternoon hours you wandered along the river, fishing in the sun. You stood on big whitened rocks, watching your line drift toward the shadowed ledges and the perch that waited below. You cast out from the shade of willow trees, and from the end of logs. You stood long moments not fishing at all. And whenever you wanted to you could look up and see the red-dirt road that curved up from the river toward the Hoenig house and you could hear the sound of Mr. Hoenig on his tractor – the small German man in his small straw hat, in khakis, riding tirelessly back and forth across his sunlit field, the dust following behind like an obedient German cloud.

And now, finally, the day has come to this huge resting moment. The sun is behind the trees on the opposite bank and frogs are beginning to experiment with familiar night sounds. On the ridge behind you cows are moving out of the hay fields and into the light-and-shadow of a wide pecan grove. Tails swinging, they move with easy slowness toward the shallow crossing of the river and the barns at the top of the slope.

You look again at the cork. You smell the richness of the weeds. You watch the small circles spread as fish come to the top of the water. And as you stand there beside the long sweep of the darkening river you are without motive or malice, desire or specific need. You are content to have a fishing pole in your hand and to feel the gigantic earth-peacefulness around you. There is no other place you want to be. You are in the heart of a moment, next to trees, smiling.

I seemed to want an altar to lay my body on.

As a sophomore in college I began standing at the corner of Sixth and Congress on Sunday mornings, not understanding why, just knowing that watching people pass by on the street was the one deeply important thing I had to do. College was nothing; the faces on the street were everything.

Without loneliness in its deepest form I would have never been driven to write a single line. Count the words, multiply by hours, and arrive at the length and depth of isolation.

My writing is a puzzled striving toward the most intimate thing I know.

If you're a writer, you will write. If you are not, you won't. It's as simple and complex as that. You may fret and worry and self-doubt yourself all over the place, may try and abort, may start over again and despair and give up, eyeing the words jaundicedly, then creep back once more. It's the nature of the game. But if you're a writer, good or bad, you won't ever give up trying to write and won't stop thinking about writing. It will possess you – *it* being some vast, partly unseen and unknown feeling about life. It always seems so huge and just-around-the-corner that you feel inadequate for the job; you believe that you don't think big enough or clearly enough.

But if you are a writer, you will keep on trying despite yourself, despite everything that is reasonable and safe and evident. It will cause many afternoons and nights of inner fury and self-contempt and missteps. But somewhere along the way the cement of desire will begin to mix with the elusive vapors of experience, and you will begin making something solid. You will sense – suddenly and joyfully – that you can do it, that you can and must write.

There is a pasture in my life – a little stretch of flatland beneath a
hill, with oak trees and many leaves – that I carry within me as a private place. It is where I would go, I think, after a time of great despair.
I would park my car and walk from the road into the woods and I
would come to that spot which would not have changed since the
time I had been there last. The dirt would still be richly dark under the
trees, there would be leaves and grass, and if I looked I would be able
to see goats grazing in the distance and maybe a few cows. I would
touch the rough wood of the oaks, I would walk through the grass
slowly, and I would know that I was home: I would know that the
place contained an essence which was both deeply me and something
deeply beyond me: something I could not identify but which I could
respect, be awed by, and love.

Poetry is what you see when you take one step to the side of a
familiar path and look at ordinary things with suddenly extraordinary
eyes.

I like sheep. I'm one of their few champions. But just *look* at them
sometime – maybe when it's the heat of the day and they are bedded
down underneath a big live oak, all bright-eyed and waiting for the
sun to go down. They are like a massed meeting of retired simpletons,
gathered to hear a speech by Ike Eisenhower.

The time was the thirties and the town was Center Point, where
the Harlesses lived in the dark rooms of their unpainted frame house.

When we went to visit them we turned off the San Antonio highway and went down the slope to the Guadalupe River crossing – I
would listen to the tires change their hum as we drove over the low-
water bridge – and then we climbed to the opposite side and were in
Center Point. It was Sunday and the streets were quiet – although
Center Point was so small and bypassed and full of shade trees and old
people that the town always seemed like Sunday to me, no matter

when we went. We drove slowly past small wooden houses and small yards full of flowers, and when we got to the Harless place we parked by the fence in the shade of a chinaberry tree. We looked once toward the house, then got out and walked toward the front-yard gate.

(Yet there was more to it than that, for the ordinary slamming of our car door, in the silence of Sunday noon, sounded like a thunder-clap before a storm. It was as if the trees and grass of the yard, the vine-tangled porch, the old couple poised like museum dummies inside the museum-like house – it was as if they had been waiting all morning long for that one sudden sound, had been dozing within Center Point timelessness until the shutting of the car door abruptly announced: *Sunday visitors; time to come alive.*)

Mother, Daddy, and I would go inside the Harless house and there they were, the two of them: a very old, very small, white-haired woman, her hair parted in the middle and pulled behind her neck in a bun: a barely-able-to-move old woman, coming toward us like a slow-motion swimmer through the deep-sea shadows of the living room; and a very old man, in his nineties, with black moles on his forehead and cheeks, tall and bald-headed except for a fringe of very white, very fine hair above his ears: a bony old man dressed in black, almost invisible to us except for the shining whiteness of his hair.

Mother would take Mrs. Harless by the arm and guide her care-fully back to the screened-in side porch. They would sit at an oil cloth-covered table in the center of the porch and shell the rest of Mrs. Harless' garden peas while they talked. Daddy and Mr. Harless would continue to stand there in the living room – Mr. Harless look-ing as if he were not aware that he was standing at all, as if he had for-gotten where his body was after he had risen from his chair to greet us.

Finally Daddy would suggest that it might be cooler if they sat on the front porch. Mr. Harless would open his mouth and his jaws would begin to quiver a little and he would manage to say it: *yes:* the word strange and distant and hollow and fragile, sounding as if

someone were talking through a very long rusty pipe. Then with
Daddy holding the door open, Mr. Harless would shuffle out onto the
porch. They would sit there on the smooth wooden bench, looking
toward the deep greenery of the yard through the deeper greenery of
the vines.

For a while I would look at the walking canes hanging by the
fireplace on pegs, at the old photographs in their oval, glassed-in
frames. But I did not want to stay inside the house; there was too much
darkness, too much that was old and faded. A dim hallway went down
the center of the house, with a bucket of well water on a stand silhouetted by the back yard light at the other end. I would get a drink from
the dipper and then wander outside to stand under the chinaberries.

The Harless house was the only one I had ever visited that rested
on small posts, that was completely open underneath. I would sit on a
stump and watch the huge gray-and-white dominecker chickens walking around underneath the house — half naked from molting, fluffing
themselves in the gloomy dust.

We — I — keep asking: is there a purpose for Man, for Me? Well, is
there a purpose for spiders? I see none beyond the simple purpose of
their continuing to act like spiders. Their purpose is to *be spiders*.

Are we different, any more than cats are different, from spiders,
as far as a purpose goes? Spiders and cats go on being what they are,
for whatever it is worth to them. But we humans, with reflective intelli-
gences: we are not content with *being*. We question where we are going
and why we came. Cats don't. They do what cats have always done,
and so do spiders. They roam through weeds or hang from threads,
and are content.

What could possibly be man's purpose? He assumes — through
viewing his heritage and noticing his present supremacy on earth —
that he has some special place, some special end and significance:
some *purpose* that, though inscrutable to him, is one not assigned to
cats and spiders. Yet if we suppose that a cat's "purpose" is simply to be

fully that unique creature he is – a fur licker and a graceful mover –
then we might suppose that a man's purpose is likewise to be himself in
all *his* uniqueness: to be the one special being that can wonder, imagine, strive, hope, and search – especially into the farthest limits of all
things of which he can conceive.

However, there is something wrong here. A cat's purpose brings
him contentment. He seldom wants to do things other than cat-things;
he thus carries the mantle of catliness rather lightly. Similarly, the spider seems to go right along with its destiny: it does not sit on a log
and mope, refusing to spin. It does not rage against having a tail end
full of silk. The burden of being a spider is not more than what a spider can rightly bear. But a human: he seems to find a certain *weight* in
being that which he is, and would many times alter the structure of life
because it does not make for one vital condition: his happiness.

The cat, now, is neither happy nor unhappy; he simply *is* and
thrives on being that way. He cannot conceive of a different life for
himself. Yet if a human is the only living creature that can evaluate his
own state and perhaps find it wanting, does this intellectual capacity
alone imply the presence of some special *purpose*, some essential *godli-
ness*? Is a man more like God than a cat is simply because he alone can
feel unhappy and unfulfilled and therefore strives out of this discomfort to be more like something else (that "something else" being God)?

Setting aside the possibility of "becoming more like God," can we
say that there is more *of* God in a man than in a spider? Is man more
*like* God than a spider is? Some have said – mainly those expansive old
pantheists – that God *is in all things;* He *is* all things. Well, now, if God
is not some special unit, some separate force, but instead the total of *all*
things – spiders, cats, men – what is a man striving after with his "special purpose"? He cannot be *more Godly* since he, along with the rest of
living things, is already part of God.

Is he, perhaps, to strive to be more fully himself, more *man*-ly? Is
this his responsibility, just as a cat's "responsibility" might be to act
more *cat*-ly ( – ignoring the fact that man's striving involves a sense of

constant unfulfillment, as opposed to the cat's sense of constant contentment). Or will we simply have to say, after all, that there was no
special creation of man, and therefore no special function? Will we be
obliged to recognize that the range of all living things is like the range
of the spectrum: just as there are bright colors and somber colors and
many intermediate shades, so are there many living forms on a huge
evolutionary scale, ranging from primitive to advanced, each with a special nature but none with a special calling, none more Godly or divine
or favored in the universe than any other?

Why the continuous beginnings of life? Why do eons pass like
colored slides in a projector, and history seem no more than a spilled
pile of typewriter ribbon on which words were written. Why keep
having these individual exercises in Lifemanship; why always the infinite perfection of *one more*. Why one more piece of throbbing conscience, one more set of eyes. Why one more of her, the little girl in
the drive-in laundry: why another starched blue dress and black patent
leather shoes and white socks neatly turned down one turn. Why
another unsuspecting, unknowing, innocent face. (Instead of smiling at
her, I should have yelled: It's too late now; you're already in for it.
You're alive now and you've got to go ahead. But that starched dress
and that candy bar you're setting so much store by now – they won't
be of much use to you. Try them for a while, but you'll see.)
Why the continual lighting of fires, why the brief glows and
quivers of flame that reach up and attain one concentrated point and
for a moment seem to beg for just one worthy object to consume, or at
least scorch; why the gradual disappointed sagging down of the flames
upon themselves, why the gradual growing into yellowness and sput-
tering and a final dying out, why another small patch of white ashes
on an already ash-covered ground.

There are places in the hill country – river places – that stay in
my mind like love affairs, and on hot city days I think of them: I

remember the delights of river rocks and river air; I remember river-bendings and river spaciousness.

There is a stretch of the Llano, up above Harper, where the rock bed of the old river is wide and flat; where water moves down the center in a bare shallow stream, dropping here and there into pleasant little pools; where bluffs rise on either side to remind you of the way the river used to be in the giant, silent times of eons past.

The place is called Cedar Springs, and during the summer ranch families go there in the late afternoon to spread checkered tablecloths near the spring and eat supper as the sun goes down.

You can still go there, in the heat of the day, and wade barefooted in the narrow rock-bottomed stream. You stand there, minnows waiting near your toes, and you look up and down the wide river bed. You see its wet places and weeds, the easy sweep southward as it curves out of sight, the sky and the light and the trees on the bank. You stand bareheaded on the rock floor of the Llano, in July, in the sun, with willows nearby, and a spring, and shade. You stand very still, feeling the presence of this river place – its silence and heat, its beauty, its earth-godliness – and you feel like a saint.

I wanted to *love* God, as I had loved or tried to love everything else. But I couldn't work it that way. It seemed that to be in the proper swing of things you had to back up, cool off, straighten your tie, brush the sweaty hair out of your feverish eyes, and *be nice* to God, be respectful and courteous, since the relationship between creator and subject is to be considered a decorous and rather impersonal one, what with his being *God* and all. The less you were preoccupied with God – the less you were *truly concerned* – why, the more pure of heart you were and the better your mental health. "You're trying to *understand* God!" one lady said, with insight, meaning: YOU BETTER STOP THAT RIGHT QUICK: YOU BETTER GO BACK TO HOEING IN YOUR OWN GARDEN AND CONFINE YOURSELF TO MAKING PLEASANT COMMENTS NOW AND THEN ABOUT HOW THE

LILIES DON'T TOIL OR HAVE CONCERN FOR THEIR RAI-
MENT (AND ABOVE ALL THEY DON'T ASK QUESTIONS:
THAT'S THEIR MAIN FORTE).

To try to *know* was the sin, the blockage, the alienation. It was all
primarily a matter of human impertinence, an absence of the prostrat-
ing spirit, a matter of "pride." To be nicely and comfortably normal,
one should want to take his God like bedtime Ovaltine: lukewarm.

I think I have been, without knowing it, trying to give life to
things which have no voices. It is as though I want my words to set
free the things which, without a voice, would have no meaning. It is as
if I am saying to myself: There is a beauty locked in many places; people will not find it unless you lend them your eyes and let them see.

# 1962–1966

# El Paso

Sometimes I think I am too pleased by life, too satisfied by its
daily simplicities. Say I am out walking on the edge of town some
sunny morning – I find that all I would ever care to express about life
is right there before me: the mountains lying in the distance in the
early morning smoky-haze; the fields spread around me, plowed and
ready for planting; the sound of tractors running and cars moving
along the highway. If I wrote, I would just want to lift that whole satisfying piece of earth and sky and air and place it down on paper. So
most of the time I have to ask myself: why write? You've already got
what you want – *there it is*, right before you. Why not go ahead and
enjoy it? Why not continue to be delighted in it and stop feeling
guilty because you are unable to capture it on paper with the same skill
that God used to create it?

Much of the time I follow this advice – I walk about finding pleasure and contentment just in perceiving my surroundings. Perhaps I see
an old punctured oil can in a ditch. Fine, I say to myself. It exists, I
exist, the two of us are here together; we have a relationship, and I am
pleased by it. We are two things in life side by side – what more can
you want? Or perhaps I see two women talking in a small roadside
dry-cleaning shop. Again, fine; lovely. At such a moment I prefer seeing them – and listening to them talk – to reading Shakespeare. Or I
see a sign on another building: "Ed's Welding." Also fine. I prefer looking at those black, irregular letters to seeing a play. Or, to be perfectly
accurate, I had *just as soon* see the sign "Ed's Welding" as read
Shakespeare or see a play. Because to me there is no hierarchy of
things in life. Everything that exists is a phenomenon; everything has
its own wonder. *Life* is a wonder – how, then, can anything in life not
help but share part of that wonder, that mystery? To be sure, it is perhaps a matter of seeing it – like picture puzzles in childhood: a cow,
for example, is camouflaged by its surroundings and you keep looking
and looking and finally shrug and say, There's no cow there; and then
someone points to a certain area of the picture and sure enough, staring out at you is a cow.

Most people don't find the cows in life – the everyday, ordinary
phenomena. And those who do become a little paralyzed from the
awesomeness of such simple delights. For if you have the right eyes,
*everything* intrigues and captivates. Everything is of value simply
because it *is* – it exists in the magic of its own incomprehensible being.
Bums, babies, trees, filling stations, grass – all exist, and thus all are
worthy of your interest, reflection, and bewilderment.

Just living: that's more than enough, any time. Living, and thinking hard as you do the living; and remembering the past, when you
lived there too; and trying to put the two together – yet always finding the past hazy and strange and vaguely unreal, as if it had happened
to someone very close to you but not you; and coming to feel that you

are always living a bunch of separate, barely connected lives, with only childhood and boyhood approaching anything definite and real and lasting; and always wondering if that's the way it is with everyone, or just you.

Art results when the passion of living becomes too much to bear. If there is no passion, or if it can be tolerated, there is no art.

It is a wonder that all human beings do not become insane as a matter of course.

First child: It is a cool summer morning and Deborah, the baby, sits in a slanting infant seat beside a pleasantly shining mahogany door.

Outside the house little is stirring – a few casual branches of a salt cedar by the porch, a leaf or two of the young mulberries along the street.

From where I sit I can see her in the front doorway and can hear her small noises. They are very much like the sounds of the morning – melodious, periodic, peaceful. I listen first to the back-yard doves, a few neighborhood cars, a lone plane passing over the mountains; then from the living room I hear the baby shaping her broad, breathy, sighing sounds.

Occasionally there is a cool trace of air that makes its way through the open doors and windows of the house – touching the white cabinets of the kitchen, the lamps and chairs of the living room. The baby feels the air, too, and is pleased. Her small, beautifully molded legs rise together like a pair of delicate sea flowers drifting above the ocean floor; her toes move in a slow curling and stretch. As the light in the doorway shines through the edges of the toes, it pinks each one with inner halos.

After a while I go to the baby and take her from the seat and feel her small intense baby heat against my body. I stand in the doorway, the whole beautiful weight and length of her familiar flesh there in my arms, and I am empty of words.

What I am can only be found in my childhood. That is the wood of my life; everything else is simply paint.

Romance is music, the smell of Bermuda grass, a girl, all the vague yearnings of youth. Romance is when you have not learned how to defend yourself.

Since no one else wants the job, I will be the poet laureate of these city things:

Red bricks placed diagonally around front-yard flower beds.

Small printed cards stuck behind fly-specked windows, announcing, without too much vigor: Apartment For Rent.

Locusts singing in tall hot elm trees at two in the afternoon.

Pipes jutting through the walls of downtown laundries, spurting steam into the tall grass of vacant lots.

Empty wine bottles lying in recessed doorways of padlocked clothing stores.

Old homes sitting naked in a block of rubble, waiting for the freeway to come on through.

Bay windows in red-brick old homes, gazing out like eyes that have gradually gone blind from the harsh glare of the twentieth century.

Eras pass, and whole blocks of cities are left to winos, thugs, indigents, and poets.

You finally arrive at a fact you simply can't deny: that the world is incomprehensible. God, order, truth — such finalities may exist, but they cannot be dealt with by any of the human resources. Accepting this, what kind of daily stance do you take in order to live on? Do you

simply ally yourself with recognizably human causes and ends, saying,
This is all I can do or know; the rest of it – the lurings of the spirit –
will have to remain beyond us and our immediate concerns. Or
indeed, do you keep on, doggedly, in a willful denial of all that seems
sensible and reasonable, always pursuing the invisible hand that apparently set you and your kind into this terrible and beautiful human
motion.

The world as it exists is that perfect spike upon which minds can
burst themselves like so many fragile balloons.

It is twelve o'clock at night and I must put the sick cat in the
garage. With her purring contentedly against my side I step out into
the cool October air. Fellini, the big pet lamb – the long-tailed, badly
spoiled child – immediately comes across the back yard in his saunter-
ing yet quick-footed gait. He knows it is improbable that I am going
to feed him again but then there is always a chance. He sniffs at my
legs and shoes as I open the side door of the garage and put the cat
inside. The cat likes it there, and so does Fellini. That is where his feed
is kept. He sticks his nose through the partly opened door. "Get back,
Fellini," I say, and he retreats a pace. I close the door and then hunker
down to pass a few midnight words with him. I ask him how things are
going, if life is treating him well, and he sticks his head close to my leg
and breathes contentedly against it. After a bit I rise and move on to
the small ligustrum tree by the back door where Mrs. Garvin, the bantam hen, is roosting. As I address her and smooth a couple of fingers
along her back, she responds with little singing, sighing croons from
her throat. I bid her goodnight, go inside the house and lock the door.
Through the kitchen window I see Fellini lingering near the steps,
looking in wistfully. Finally he decides that I will not be coming out
any more for a while and begins to move along, head down, back into
the darkness of the yard.

I breathe easiest when I am fully on the land. I look out to the day unnervously. I am friends with air, with grass, with country sounds. The heat of the sun delights me, and the cool of shady places.... I listen and touch and see and life seems very real.

All acts seem right in the country: a tractor plowing in a field; a gate closing; a woman hanging washing on a line; a window facing toward the afternoon; ants crawling.

There is time for sitting down and time for walking about; there is no need to hurry. I move to the tempo of dogs barking, flowers growing, cows eating in a pasture.

Everyone is a cripple (I was thirty-two years old before I learned *that* little truth).

It is in hearing old songs again and feeling the goosebumps rise throughout your body that you suddenly realize how much, for you, *the past was never completed.* A hundred familiar doors are still ajar inside you, and to hear the songs is to look again down yawning passageways of the past, to feel once more the cold drafts coming off broken dreams and love affairs.

It is always with a sense of unfinished business, then, that you write, trying to do at last what you could never do before: give to things a final shape that pleases you.

Sometimes, with luck, you actually can: by calling forth imagination, and using the special power over past events that time alone ultimately gives a person, you can say the magic words that will cause one of the doors to swing shut on its painful memory. At other times, however, despite the same careful attempt at mastery, the words fail and the door remains open as though rusted into place by permanent tears – as if allowing its room of old defeats to go on echoing for a lifetime its nostalgic melodies.

Death, pain, and despair are like patient pendulums that swing across human life in monstrous silent arcs. Whenever they happen to pass near us – and miss – we compliment ourselves for being invulnerable. Convinced that the forces of darkness have forever fled the light, we continue to putter about smugly in the little gardens of our delusion – never seeing the shadow that is sweeping in close to clip us from behind.

Well-to-do women: In black Cadillacs and white gloves, their red-ringed Saturday morning smiles flashing behind cool, air-conditioned window panes, they sit securely as their sleek cars roll through gently curving streets lined with tall green trees and stately houses. Scrubbed and powdered and perfumed, their hands manicured and their legs sleekly sheathed within fine-mesh hose, they are El Paso's composed and elegant matrons. They taste the leisured life of Saturday morning like hummingbirds sipping bright red wine.

The more I live, the more it seems that the concept of sin was introduced by men in a desperate effort to preserve their sanity and their idea of God: for man seemingly has a great capacity for feeling his own guilt but could not long tolerate the idea that *God* is guilty.

What a writer does is mark off a piece of land or group of people and stay right there working until he makes the land or the people his: the country becomes Faulkner Country, the people Steinbeck People. A man and his material become so much one that they cannot be separated. And it's not just art; it's chemistry: hydrogen finds oxygen – marvelously, with beauty, for keeps.

Of course someone else can always try to take over ownership of that very same land or people or way of life, but it will probably not do him much good. He can never get a clear title. Someone may make another canoe trip down the Brazos River in November, say, but what he writes about it is apt to be pale stuff, or derivative. For John

Graves has already made that particular trip, and felt it, and did the writing about it, and there is little way that further writing and feeling can bite more deeply into that same material.

This is what classic means: that the job was done, and need not be done again.

I would like to write paragraphs that kicked hell out of a reader – that pulled the rug out from under his feet and put him back in the emotionally vulnerable, off-balanced position he was in before he smugly began to think he had learned so much and began to forget about mystery and beauty and terror and awe.

The mystique of the Other Sex – that strange and constant awareness of femaleness which makes a man willing to serve – so to speak – another master. A woman's foot, half-raised, slipping into sheathing nylon hose; the sudden faint aroma of face powder; the white skin of belly and thigh suggesting an inner body richness....

Men in their thirties and forties, with their new hostilities. They are getting pudgy in the middle, they drink to excess, they have become a little too dissatisfied with their jobs and wives. So – their bodies sagging, their lives increasingly humdrum – they look around irritably for someone to blame.

Preserve the heritage; preserve what was good. Reach back; find a way to keep the best.... Too many days pass, and gradually the things that once stood as little pinnacles of glory above the flatlands crumble and are buried. Before long we do not even remember what was worthy of saving.

This is the ache: a sense of responsibility for what was important, what was greater than you; a feeling that good things must be preserved; a feeling that although we don't know where we are going, we must know where we have been.

I think every adult is close to tears – the tears he would shed if he ever paused long enough to confront, genuinely, the memory of himself as a child. They would not be tears of emotional release – of suddenly felt love or guilt or anger or self-pity. They would be, instead, tears of wrenching sadness, of profound loss. For as the adult confronted moments of the past – as he experienced once again the intensity of forgotten childhood moods and people and days – he would be overwhelmed by the mystery of human living, by the wonders of time and memory and change that could allow him to look, in his mind's eye, at the dim outline of his past self and still be that self in the present.... What was it like to be me then, the adult would ask; or, *Was* I really me, that long ago, in that shadowy place? And in asking he would perhaps understand a little more about the process of life and death: about how the child he once was had died and yet had lived on.

...So it is: We lived so intimately there in the past, and then we left it, and forgot it, as though indeed, we had never lived there at all; yet it remains, that strange and distant childhood, within us always – shaping our wishes, our fears, the very outline of our days.

If there is, indeed, a God, and if indeed He made everything and everyone there is, has been, and ever will be: *What in the world does He want?* What can we do to repay Him – or make Him stop?

# 1967–1971

# El Paso

I started back toward the center of town, taking my time, looking at chinaberry trees, sleeping dogs, buses lumbering through the narrow streets. But mainly I found myself looking at faces, the faces of the poor: the constantly, extravagantly, unending poor of the back streets of Juárez.

My feet hurt but I kept on walking. By the time I came to the market district I was drunk on old cars and old clothes, on worn-down bodies and faces – drunk on the wine of poverty. I stopped beneath the roof of a melon stand, among the people, saying to myself, dazed: The human spectacle is too intense; I cannot bear it.

When routines of work are done and I am driving slowly home, I think again that one unforgettable thought which has been waiting for me all during the day: the thought of death that slams through me like the quick surge of an electric current and makes me almost recoil physically against the back of the car seat. I continue to gaze ahead through the windshield, looking for all the world like any other home-bound, five o'clock driver, yet I am sunk into depression, paralyzed by the awareness that all my daily concerns add up to nothing. I turn familiar corners, getting closer to home, and all I can think of is: All in vain, All in vain....

You know, I accept the unfathomable mysteries of space, the tragic cast of all human experience, the ultimate question mark of life – but let me also say this: One night I went into the bedroom of my five-year-old daughter and laid my face close to hers as she slept; I listened to her, breathing and sighing in that semidark room; I looked at the lovely, satisfying curve of her neck and cheek; I all but tasted the sweet-flavored childish essence that seemed to emanate from her body. And so satisfying was she to look at, and touch, and consider – such a *gift* she was, deep within her covers, with her soft, glowing skin and good-smelling hair – that I could not help but say to the nothingness as I left her room: Good-God-a-mighty....

Beauty and the beast: People feel better when they see cripples with redeeming features: the paraplegic with a good sense of humor;

the cerebral palsied child with a high intelligence; the deaf, one-armed boy with great athletic skill.

And of course a blind street singer should always have a beautiful voice.

But Eugenio, who is blind and enormously fat, has a rasping, tuneless, ugly voice. Each afternoon during the summer he sits on Sixteenth of September Street in Juárez, across from Our Lady of Guadalupe cathedral, and makes loud cheerless noises. He sits on a stool with his legs spread apart and sings his songs and it is as though a very dull needle, placed on a warped and worn-out record, is creating sound through a loudspeaker with loose connections. Eugenio, sweating even in the shade, bawls out his songs toward the invisible cathedral and the invisible people moving by – his mouth wide open, showing his rotting teeth; his eyes wobbling about in their wrinkled sockets.

And standing next to him each afternoon is a very pretty little girl. She comes out of a dress shop two doors down the sidewalk and takes up her waiting position there beside him. It is as if Eugenio is a handsome operatic tenor and she is his modest lady-in-waiting. She listens patiently, attentively, her large dark eyes never seeming to blink as she gazes out toward the hot afternoon. Eugenio bellows, strikes clumsy chords on his old guitar, rolls his clotted, marble eyes. The child stands quietly beside him, listening closely to his anguished cries.

Words cheapen experience. We assume that since we make use of a word which describes or stands for a thing, then we are actually coming to grips with the thing itself. In having available such words as *miracle, holy, awesome, profound*, we believe that the mouthing of them somehow makes us participate in some act other than mere speech. Thus we never really try to enter deeply into experiences which words stand for. We dismiss miracles from our minds simply by calling them that: miracles.

To see...is astonishing; to think...is fantastic. Yet even to use such words – *astonishing, fantastic* – is to stop trying to grasp the essential nature of seeing and thinking. Words, in becoming such easy substitutes for the thing-in-itself, have gradually robbed life of its (glory) and (awe) and (power).... Name it, and it dies for us.... Yet apparently the urge of civilized man is to do exactly that: to name, to categorize: to attempt to master life through a continual verbalization of things in it: to reduce its mystery by giving mystery various labels.

To name does not explain, and long after we have said, "I am," we still do not know what we have said.

We must remember that there was, indeed, a ninth century and that it was fully a hundred years long: that people lived, day by day, in 836, in 837, in 838, and looked forward perhaps to 839 in hopes that it might bring a change of fortune.... A man in 838 would finish his midday meal, belch, scratch a scab on his arm, and wonder about those things which men wondered about in 838. He was a man like any man anytime: caught up in daily routines, unsure of tomorrow, surrounded by the mysteries of living.

...We accept so much intellectually. Why, yes, of course, we say, men lived in the ninth century – but we fail to be humbled or amazed at such a fact because we do not really feel the words as we say them. We do not react to knowledge imaginatively. And yet it is only through imaginative perception that we ever change mere facts into understandings.

I am teaching at 3:15, standing before a class of failures. I have been talking quite a lot – hard, with genuine bursts of passion – and have been able to get the class to talking some too. They are a discouraged and discouraging lot, for the most part, yet just for this brief span of time it seems that the artificial structures of the room have fallen away and we are simply gathered together to talk things over:

students and a teacher linked only by circumstance yet for a few
moments genuinely exposed to one another.

As I stand before them, very tired, ready for the school day to
end, a curious thing happens. A sudden emotion surges through me,
and I find that I am saying to myself, "Why, I love these people."

It has happened before: being around the weak-eyed, the down-
and-out, and suddenly – because I had come to know a little about the
hidden shapes of their lives – feeling a great respect for them and then
a sense of love.

...I look out at those in English IIM, just as the bell rings, and all I
can see is their humanness: they hurt, they are vulnerable and unsure,
they have had a rough go of things. But for a while their defenses have
been down, and for the better part of an hour they have been sitting
here as rather pleasant folks, really; rather ordinary human flesh.

Experience, of course, is simply chaos presented in a straight line.

Mae, remembered: At 11:30 and 5:00 each day except Sunday I
could back off from my college despairs and forget them for a while in
table-waiting routines at the boarding house. I could slice lemons and
fix pitchers of tea and carry out bowls of rice and carrots and peas to
the tables and then, when the doors opened, I could stand at the back
of the dining room in my white apron and look out across the heads of
future engineers and drama majors and fraternity boys and be rather
content.

Thirty minutes before the evening meal I would take my apron
off the hook behind the hall door and, whistling, begin to lay out
plates in the dining room. Mae would be limping around in the
kitchen – checking rolls in the oven, washing pans, wiping sweat,
sweet-Jesusing at all the work that still needed to be done before five-
thirty. After I would pour up the ketchup and get out the jelly and butter and set the silverware and napkins beside the plates, I would come
back to the kitchen doorway and, leaning against it, pretend to drum

my foot. Mae – usually washing a pot at the sink, her arms deep in
suds – would turn and slide a look towards me. Then she would stop
washing and let her big-lipped grin make its way out of the sweat and
meaty blackness of her face: "Shi-it, Leroy," she would say, her words
exploding a little, her head dropping forward. She stayed that way a
moment, shaking her head from side to side before throwing back her
head in a long, throat-throbbing laugh. It was the laugh of an always
fat, always tired colored woman ( – still Colored, then in the fifties,
not Black): a fat colored woman looking over at a skinny white col-
lege-kid in tennis shoes and thinking that he meant no harm of course
but that he didn't know his ass from a water pitcher when it came to
understanding how an East Austin cook felt in a white woman's
kitchen in the late afternoon of an ordinary work day.

But for both of us I think it was a pleasant communication and
release: that head-shake, that look, that laugh, in that quiet, 5:20
house.

I have backed away from intelligence and have come to embrace
a kind of divine idiocy. Human intelligence, I mean. Intelligence that
prides itself on mastery of facts. Intelligence-test intelligence.
Computer intelligence.

I identify with weeds and sun and ground. I give up thinking.

I am content to sit beside the chicken house and blend into the
morning: to be as a post is, as grass is.

I look out at the radiant earth and I want to ask: Who is in charge
of this production?... Why, that is a beautifully placed clump of
Johnson grass over there; and that mountain range is elegant.

I am in this June day, on this plot of ground, the way my foot is
in my shoe. I inhabit myself comfortably. I am friends with myself,
with the water from the yard hydrant, with the passing hours.

I saw the pleasing profile of a girl; I saw the shape of her face,
turned sideways.

She was in class, listening to a record I was playing, and she was turned a bit in her desk, looking toward the windows. She was a straight-D student, limp, disinterested; brown hair parted in the middle and stringy; no make-up; child of divorced parents.

Yet as I looked at her, turned in her desk, she was suddenly someone special. There was in her profile the outline of a human personality – no, more than that: the outline of all human personality. Suddenly, listening to George Harrison's "My Sweet Lord," she became a quietly pretty girl, a thoughtful girl, she was Potential and Sensitivity and Feeling and the History of the Race. She was not just another face-among-faces; she was everything we have been living throughout history for; she was the end product of several billion years of evolution. In that split moment when she turned in her chair and gazed toward the window she was more than herself: she became immortalized, my own sixth-period Mona Lisa.

Always, in the summertime, when I am released from the routines of teaching and have time on my hands, when I sink into myself again – always when I turn myself over to the rhythms of nature and the universe, I think of death. I focus deeply on non-human purposes and things. Like a piece of wood gradually dislodged from shore by the slow working of the tide, I am floated outward.... I drift among the weeds, the breezes, the gradual turning of morning into noon into evening into night. I become a piece of paper blowing across a cotton field, a flower wobbling along a fence, a bird passing.

A writer is a cripple who uses words as sutures to bind together the fractures of his life.

# IX

# WITNESS

# On the Coast

When I was a boy my family occasionally went on summer trips
to the coast. We were not vacation-taking people – those were the
1930s and 40s, Depression-and-war days – but my aunt and uncle
lived in Sinton, near Corpus Christi, and every few years my parents
and I would go visit them. We loaded our Chevrolet and headed out of
the cedar hills of Kerrville into the farms and fields and grasslands
below San Antonio. As my father drove through Floresville, Karnes
City, Beeville, he talked about the hay crops and watermelon stands,
but I kept watching the high buildup of clouds ahead of us, trying to
detect in them the first signs of bright, coastal glare.

We would stop in Sinton to spend the night, and in the late afternoon I would walk around in front of my Uncle Mitch's house, getting
the feel again of new territory – looking at the white, crushed-shell
streets, the oleander bushes in people's yards, an occasional palm tree
jutting above a roof. There was a heaviness in the air and the dramatic
smell of oil wells.

The next day we would pack my uncle and aunt's car with fishing
gear, tents, food, pots and pans, ice chests, and drive toward Port
Aransas, forty miles away. As I looked out the window it seemed that
the coast was already a gigantic, invisible presence hovering over the
land. Buildings and telephone poles had lost their sharp edges: they
shimmered in the air. Everything was distant, on the horizon. It was as
though we were already surrounded by water – as if the buildings
across the heat-and-haze of the cotton fields were not farm silos and
industrial plants but ships far out in the gulf.

When we got to Aransas Pass we were still not quite to the coast
– at least I wasn't. There were faded houses on the blazing-hot streets,
rusted cars, shrimp boats in the harbor, but the exotic sign of the coast
I had been waiting for was still missing: the smell of it. That unmistakable moment came as we drove onto the causeway leading to Port
Aransas. I would be looking at the pelicans standing in the blue bays,

at fishermen casting from their small, anchored boats, and it would come through the window: the first breath of pure salt air, the incredibly rich and sensuous gulf breeze that was different from any other air I had ever known. The coast was no longer a memory, a destination, a jagged line on a Texaco map; it was there in the wind on my face.

We crossed to Port Aransas on the ferry – I would stand outside the car, feeling the salt spray, watching the porpoises leap out of the channel water, hearing the horns of pleasure boats in the docks – and then we would drive through town and out to the beach.

The beach. Each time I saw it I could not believe it, could not take it all in: the water, the sky, the sand, such huge, calm expanses blending together, so endlessly blue-and-white: everything bigger-than-life – as if the universe itself had been born right there in dazzling June light – yet totally serene, with the surf rolling steadily in to shore and sailboats fixed on the horizon like white triangles in a painting.

I would change into my bathing suit and walk along the edge of the water as the seagulls wheeled and called above me. I dug my bare toes in the sand, making holes, and watched the watery, jelly-like sand quiver until mysteriously the holes were filled again. I waded into the gulf – ankle-deep at first, with seaweed and broken shells flowing between my legs toward the shore: then deeper, with the water green and foam-filled around my thighs; finally deep enough to swim, the waves swelling, cresting, curling rhythmically over my head, pulling me sideways and under. I would let myself be carried along, luxuriating in the idea and the presence of water: *I was in the ocean.* It was ocean water in my mouth, salty and warm; it was the ocean floor beneath me. I floated and wallowed and smiled.

I swam some more, I walked along the shore and found sand dollars and hermit crabs and jellyfish, but mainly I fished. I would change into my long-sleeved shirt – buttoning it at the neck against the sun – and put on my baseball cap and with my father and uncle I would walk

out on the pier and we would spend the afternoon and part of the
night fishing.

I never tired of holding a pole, of watching my cork. I would peel
a shrimp, bait my hook, angle the line over the railing between the
lines of others fishing around me, and wait. I waited with no thought
in mind. I was simply an extension of my cane pole. I was content.
Sometimes I would feel a muscular tug as the cork went under and I
yanked up hard. Usually a scavenger cat – no good to eat – would be
flopping on the line. I would pull the catfish onto the pier and then,
holding its mouth with my uncle's pliers, remove the hook. Sometimes
when I wasn't careful enough the catfish managed to jab me with the
toxic fin on its back and my uncle would come over, laughing, and
give me a wad of moist chewing tobacco. I would hold it on the jab
for a while to take away the sting.

The hours passed, the sun beat down, and all of us on the pier
fished as if hypnotized – bony old men in yachting caps and worn tennis shoes; red-headed fat women in bonnets; big, brown, bare-stom-
ached hairy men; men with crab nets and live-bait buckets and chunks
of meat to catch tarpon. We were a quiet community focused on the
single business of catching fish – with everyone seeming to wish the
other well. We always admired a man's impressive string of redfish or
gaff-top cats as he walked by. We would gather around to stare at the
strangeness of another man's stingray or porcupine fish. We listened to
the surf rods whine. We watched boys using perch hooks keep pulling
up from among the pilings small-mouthed, beautifully striped angel
fish. And occasionally someone would call out, "Hammerhead!" and we
would all look over the railing, trying to see the shark in the gray-
green water below.

At sundown – I would finally notice it, the huge fan of rays slanting across the western half of the sky – my father and Uncle Mitch
and I would go back to the tent we had set up next to the car. My
mother and my aunt would have supper ready, and we ate fried

chicken and potato salad out of paper plates as the surf rolled in and
the breeze blew as if it were going on to China.

After supper my uncle would ask, "Well, now, did you finally get
enough of fishing for one day?" and I would say no. The others
laughed because – as my mother told me later – with my sun-flushed
face and sweat-matted hair, I looked as though I had had enough of
everything for that day.

But my uncle lumbered around, getting the poles and gear boxes
ready, and we went back to the pier again to fish under the lights until
midnight.

The next day would be more of the same: fishing – on the pier,
down the beach at the granite-rock jetties, back across the channel in
the bays. My uncle would let me use his rod and reel and I would
wade out into a bay up to my knees, casting out. I would stand there,
the salt breeze blowing, the pelicans flapping around near the causeway, oleanders blooming pink and white in the sun. I would feel something hit my line and I would reel in furiously and there it was, finally,
an elegant, glistening, foot-long speckled trout.

In the late afternoon it would be time to go. We would load up
the car and cross on the ferry and start back to Sinton. The adults
talked; I didn't. I sat in the back seat, the hot wind blowing in on my
sunburned face and arms and neck. I was sweaty, my clothes had sand
in them, my eyes burned, my hands smelled of shrimp and fish and
tobacco juice. I was so tired I felt as if I had almost disappeared: somehow the Me that had come down to the coast from Kerrville had been
used up. I would look at the gas flares of oil wells burning near
Ingleside, at the huge sunflowers along the highway. Then, with the
wind like the open door of an oven on my face, I would sleep.

# An Early Summer Morning

I was drinking coffee in the living room at six-thirty in the morning. No one was moving in the house. I looked outside to the small back yard. The dog lay curled against the living room wall. Shadows stretched here and there. On the patio two chairs were still turned slightly inward toward the charcoal grill, left that way from the hamburger cookout the night before.

It was just another early summer morning, quiet and subdued, but it was the kind of moment people would like to keep, if they could: to put away in the bank and then use again when needed. It was like a clear essence of life at its most human-sized: a distillation of tranquility.

I got a second cup of coffee, and as I returned to the sofa a thought came to me:  On the day of a funeral or the breakup of a marriage, this is exactly how a morning would be: outrageously, gloriously normal. No one would be paying any attention to it, of course. People would be walking about aimlessly in rooms – faces grim, lives shattered – yet the cool breeze would be easing indoors through the half-open screen, shadows would be splashed beneath the trees, the grapevine would be looped across the back rock wall and the morning glory vine with its flaring white petals would still be climbing up the metal post. A white-winged dove would be calling from a hidden perch.

...The universe knows no grief. During human tragedies the sun keeps on shining, the roses still bloom.

# In Gruene

In the mid-1800s when Cotton was beginning to be King in the rich farming lands of Central Texas, Henry Gruene's family settled along the Guadalupe River northeast of New Braunfels. By the late 1800s Henry was doing quite well. He had twenty to thirty families sharecropping on the Gruene family acres. He built a mercantile store and a cotton gin that was run by water from the nearby river. He built a lumber yard, dance hall and beer garden, and donated land for the town school. He built a Victorian home complete with gazebo, wrap-around porch, and second-floor galleries. In 1904 he put up a new mercantile store which also housed his bank and the post office. By the time he died in 1920 Gruene, the man, and Gruene, the town, had seen prosperous times.

But during the 1920s the boll weevil appeared, devastating cotton crops in the area. The Depression followed, farmers went broke and moved away, and Gruene became virtually a ghost town for the next fifty years. Then in the 1970s a new type of entrepreneur appeared, saw possibilities in the handful of buildings that had survived the century, and invested in a new cash crop: tourists.

...When I lived in San Antonio during the 1980s I would decide on a late Saturday afternoon in spring that it was time again: time to get in the car, drive east on I-35 toward Austin, exit onto the farm-to-market road just past New Braunfels, head in the direction of Canyon Lake, and then at a convenience store turn onto the narrow, winding road that leads into Gruene.

On one of these mild afternoons I arrived at five o'clock. The Gruene water tower was just ahead; the sun was below the level of the trees. As I pulled off the road and parked next to the small winery set back among the oaks, I felt as if I were being rewarded for something I must have done right. Just to be in Gruene for a little while – to get out of the car, to walk down the roadside in the cooling air – was enough to loosen a person up, to get the kinks out of mind-and-body.

Gruene is essentially one main street with a dozen-plus businesses and a scattering of small, old-fashioned wooden residences. It is tourist-y, but low-key: not overly commercialized. It is like a stage set where people wander around and are both the actors and the audience

– or like someone's nicely kept up rural compound where friends drop
by to eat, buy a few knickknacks, and in general participate in weekend and summertime rites of leisure. Its "downtown" is two blocks
away from the countryside and a few hundred yards from the
Guadalupe River low-water crossing.

I got there before the main thrust of the tourist crowd arrived. I
eased through the screen door of Gruene Hall – said to be the oldest
dance hall still operating in Texas – and after buying a long-neck Pearl
sat at one of the tables in the front barroom. Joe Ely and his band
wouldn't start playing in the main hall until nine, which was fine with
me: I had heard enough country western, country rock-and-roll to last
me several lifetimes. I was content just to sit there at my table with its
red-checkered cloth and listen to the college-age bartender swap small
talk with the guy in black motorcycle boots and black motorcycle cap.
The room was pleasantly high ceilinged, airy, full of light; the wooden
floor creaked as the bartender moved about. Through the window I
could see the side beer garden with its cedars and picnic tables. The
small red-and-yellow lights strung among the trees would be turned on
at dark.

When I left the hall, tourists were already in full force: couples,
families, dates: in walking shorts, open-necked shirts, stylish casuals,
fashionable footwear. I sat on a low rock wall and watched them
strolling by in the elegant gloaming. They flowed down the street,
poking about in antique shops, the general store, the handicraft and
gift places. (Tourists: recognizable anywhere by their slowed-to-a-
crawl, almost deferential gait. Cooperative, genial – like eternally
retired golfers on a celestial putting green – they exhibited the relaxed,
middle-class bonhomie that wells up almost automatically in people
with nicely filled wallets and secure bank accounts.)

Some were already in line outside the Gristmill Restaurant – the
boiler house of Henry Gruene's old cotton gin. Others had put their
names on the restaurant waiting list and had congregated on the grassy

reception area – listening to the blue-jeaned young guitarist as he entertained them with his easy-on-the-ears folk ballads.

In the last light of dusk I wandered down to the Gruene Mansion Inn, the refurbished Henry Gruene home. It was an undeniably fetching house-and-grounds, and once again I thought: One of these days I'm going to call these people up and make a reservation.... Imagine: spending the night in this old place: padding down the narrow hallways, letting turn-of-the-century ghosts beckon to me from claw-footed bathtubs and dumbwaiters.

I had tarried outside the white picket fence a good while before I saw her: the woman sitting in the yard swing. She was the bare outline of a figure – how old she was, I couldn't tell. She was in deep shadow, sitting there, just barely rocking in the swing: alone, in Gruene, Texas, at the end of a long spring day: a woman – I fantasized – who came each year at this time to sit and savor a special poignancy, a loss, a deep sadness in her life.... I imagined that one day John Fowles, happening by, would see her – just her silhouette, her aloneness, her enigmatic shadow in the swing beneath the trees – and out of such a brief glimpse fashion a companion novel to *The French Lieutenant's Woman*.

I continued on the road toward New Braunfels a way, turned around, went again along the main street, bought a hamburger at the barbecue-specialty cafe, and decided to walk down the dark slope to the Guadalupe River crossing. During the summertime it would be alive with tubing enthusiasts and rafters. Now, beneath the tall cypresses, it was alive with moonlight and the sound of its own rushing river voice. It was a strange place: the unrelenting, timeless water, flowing on in darkness, unmindful of human presence, human need: as strange as the universe is, as life is. I got my fill of it – meaning, I stood for a long while beside the river the way a blind man would stand before a painting, trying to penetrate its mystery.

Finally I yielded, shrugged, turned away. I saw the lights up above on the hill and walked toward them with a quickened step: Good old Gruene.

# The Fig Tree

For adults every paradise is a paradise lost or a paradise to regain:
it is never in the here and now. Only as children can we know a timeless little world complete and perfect in itself. Only as children do we
move freely, thoughtlessly among sensory delights in a sun-bathed,
unchanging corner of the earth.

I knew a paradise once: my grandparents' ranch. I can still see the
house and yards, the back lots, the windmill, the rock tank, the pecan
trees, the corn and oat fields, the sheep grazing in the front clearing
and the goats trailing out to the back trap, and of course – as in any
paradise – the garden.

I can see Gram in her apron and canvas shoes opening the old
wooden gate to the garden. The rusted gate spring gives its drawn-out
complaint and then the gate collapses and shuts behind her. It is a
clear June morning and the sunshine is bright on the squash, the corn
stalks, the strands of the smooth wire fence, the fig tree in the corner.
My grandmother begins gathering string beans for dinner while the
sheep bleat to each other in the front clearing and pairs of wild
canaries flash across the garden and into the front yard. I can see the
part in Gram's braided gray hair as she bends down, straightens up,
puts the beans into her gathered apron.

I can see Grandpa in his frayed work pants and crumpled, sweat-
stained Stetson. It is now late afternoon – after his nap, after coffee
with Gram at the dining room table, after fixing a broken saddle girth
in the harness shed – and he has shifted the pipe from the windmill so
that water flows down the next row of potatoes. He stands beside the
garden fence in the shade of the woodlot pecan trees, eating a fig,
watching the water spread down the row and looking out to the cattle
grazing in the front pasture.

The fig tree: it is strangely memorable to me now. I have never
really liked figs and as a child never paid much attention to the fig tree
itself growing in an ungainly sprawl by the gate. It was hardly

classifiable as a tree – had none of the appeal, the beauty and majesty
of the ranch house oaks and elms and pecans – but I knew it belonged
in the garden simply because my grandparents wanted it there:
because they and others of their generation, of their same rural traditions, liked figs the same way they liked buttermilk and clabber and
stringy, cooked okra.

Each year – after the summer and fall growing seasons had ended
and the beans and peas and corn and onions had disappeared – the fig
tree was still in its corner. It had lost its broad, rough leaves but it
remained intact – had once again outlasted the richer produce of the
earth around it.

My grandparents are dead, the ranch and garden have gone to
ruin and decay, yet whenever I notice a fig tree in someone's yard it
reminds me of my childhood paradise: it is symbolic of days long past,
things out-dated but once simple, satisfying, enduring.

# Vacant Lot

As I stood at the wire fence and the three o'clock sun played
across the brown landscape of Central Texas, I entered, once again, the
sunlit now and its strange depths.

I had parked my car on a side street in Comfort and walked over
to a vacant lot green with rain-soaked winter grass. I stood beside the
fence, listening to the stillness. Everything in the lot and on the streets
beside it – the weathered garage, the tool shed, the cistern – was
sharply defined: luminous beyond description, beyond words.

I had been here before, of course – not this place, but this
moment. I had seen this sun, pale in a winter sky; smelled the cedar,
the river, the hill country air; listened to the silence that was just
another voice for some greater reality. It was as though I had been
born to stand beside fences: It was my primal moment, my opportunity
– my privilege – to experience the secret nature of things.

So I stood and listened. The lot was like a stage where quiet dramas were unfolded. Each blade of grass, each slant of sun was part of the drama, and it seemed that if I could remain still enough – long enough – I could see past the familiar outlines of rocks and posts and boards into the heart of creation itself.

I waited – trying to see as the afternoon saw.... Those long-stretching shadows: why, they were not shadows at all; they were prodigal sons of the land who had finally returned at midday and were now lying passively beneath the pecan trees. At nightfall, at a signal, they would blend together and re-enter their rightful home, the earth.

And those rusted barrels, those scattered piles of leaves: they –

But a car cruised by, and another, their radios blaring. Then a jogger worked her fierce way down the street, looking neither right nor left, locked into her determined stride and the hidden rhythms of her Walkman.

The silence returned, and I thought of the Bible: "Be still and know that I am God." Yes: that was the kind of stillness I was trying to hear at the fence: the unattainable silence that allows, finally, a burning bush to speak, a mountain to move: the silence that a human keeps straining to hear.

I got into my car and left Comfort. As I joined the lines of cars on I-10, the intimacy of the vacant lot disappeared. Trees along the roadside seemed blank, withdrawn – like family servants decorously resuming their unnoticed – their traditional – poses. I drove along the interstate with my speeding humankind: enclosed, insulated, focused on our human concerns. We looked straight ahead, paying no mind to the Otherness that lay around us.

# Seeing, Knowing, Remembering

My past is an October seashore. I go there periodically to pick among the debris left by personal shipwrecks and storms, to walk in the pale sunlight of my recollections.

Stooping, considering, I recently sorted among random memories and stopped at this one:

I was in the fifth grade. One afternoon after school I turned the corner of the elementary building, going home, and there he was, Charles Tamplin, thrashing on the ground with fluids coming out of his nose and mouth. I didn't know what to do except stare. I knew he was Charles Tamplin and that he was several years older than I was and that he lived in the corner house across from the Red and White grocery store, but I did not know he was having an epileptic seizure. I just stood there, holding my Hardy Boys library book and looking down at his dark eyebrows and slick dark hair that he always combed straight back across his head. His eyes were closed and he quivered as he breathed.

I remember that it was late in the afternoon and the sun was low in the oak trees. I had stayed with Mrs. Rose to work on a geography project, and the big shadow of the elementary building had already reached past the trash incinerator. Charles was lying out in the sunny part of the playground, but I didn't know if his eyes were closed because of the sun or because of what was happening to him. I could smell the smoke from the incinerator and I could hear radios playing in the houses across from the school.

It still seemed like a normal day except that Charles Tamplin was there on the ground. I looked at him a while longer and then I walked in a wide semicircle around him and went on home. I never told anyone about it.

When I was in high school I would see Charles sitting in the swing on his front porch. I knew about him by then – about his epilepsy, that he didn't go to school any more. I would be walking along the sidewalk past the Red and White and Charles would be there in the porch shadows—not swinging, just sitting Indian-like, looking ahead, with his smooth black hair still combed straight back. I guess I passed him a dozen times or more.

I began to wonder, years later, about the curious burden of responsibility borne by the one who accidentally sees rather than by the one who is seen: by the one who knows instead of the one who does not know: by the rifleman in war who finds the unsuspecting figure of his enemy within his gunsight yet decides not to shoot – lets his enemy walk on across the jungle road and then remembers him, his human vulnerability, for the rest of his life.

I used to wonder what Charles Tamplin would have thought if he knew I had seen him curled up that afternoon on the ground with pieces of caliche rock stuck to his chin.

...Abraham "knew" Sarah, the Bible says. Always, to *know* is an intimate act.

# Arrivederci, Winn's

I am a reluctant consumer and thus have no warm feeling for picking among bargains; I have no real interest in shopping. But I confess to a sentimental liking for Winn's Stores, and it pains me that they seem to be losing out. The Targets and Sam's and Wal-Marts – megamonsters of retail – have tolled the death knell for smallish five-and-dimes and are sending them to join Mom and Pop groceries in the business boneyard.

I miss the simple charms of the neighborhood Winn's where I used to take my nine-year-old son on a leisurely Saturday morning: where the two of us could ease back to the model airplane counter and stand for long, satisfying moments while he sorted through a dozen or so tempting little boxes before deciding on a Messerschmitt or a P-38: where we could afterwards meander on to the back of the store and look at the canaries and love birds in their cages and finally select three exotic-looking tropical fish which we carried with us in sloshing plastic bags.

Wandering around Texas in the summertime and feeling a bit out of sync with myself and with life, I have gone into a Winn's on the main street of Llano or Kerrville or Pleasanton, and as I moved through the aisles looking for a pocket comb or a birthday card it has been good – reassuring, somehow, like dropping in to visit a relative – to touch base with the store's homely merchandise: the plastic kites, assorted children's socks, party favors, Mr. Bubbles refillable bubble blowers, soaps and brooms, yarn and fly swatters and jelly jars and Indian Chief writing tablets. Nothing is fancy in Winn's – nothing for swingers or the *haute couture*. Shoppers just poke about, looking for simple items to satisfy simple needs. And sometimes, with only half a dozen customers idling around at a time, the store can have a comfortable feeling to it – almost like that of a small-town church.

Such moods, such days are about to fade away; the trend is set. We have entered an age in which corporations put up their Colossi of Commerce on sprawling acres of cement, and into these somber depots of unending supply come shoppers who seem ready to buy by the gross, the van-load. The day is coming when all such stores will be merged into one gigantic chain – Corp, Inc. – and all of us will take our government-issued plastic purchasing card, board a monorail, and do our decade's worth of shopping in Unimall, U.S.A.

# Canals

If I could give them as gifts, I would give canals.

If I were a painter, I would paint them. If I were a moralist and wanted to improve society, I would get on a soapbox and tout their virtues.

As it is, I simply walk them – frequently, gladly. Give me a choice between MTV and the Montoya Canal, I'll take the canal any time.

I need canals, and I go to them the way other people go to church. They heal, offer sanctuary, help lead my thoughts forward under a canopy of green.

Farmers irrigate from them, of course, and occasional joggers use their pathways, but for the most part they remain invisible to urban El Paso – these thin brown veins of the Rio Grande that run past alfalfa and cotton fields, past Upper and Lower Valley yards from Old Mesilla to San Elizario.

Last week I took my constitutional along a canal. As always, it was a private symphony of sight and sound, of honeysuckle along fences and roosters crowing in the distance. Tree shadows – casual, alluring – moved across the ground: suggestive of river banks and Sundays in other good places. As always, there were favorite things to see: old sheds with slanting tin roofs (streaks of rust looking as if they had been added with an Impressionist's skillful brush); woodpiles and long adobe walls; whole communities of doodlebugs in sandy dirt as soft as talcum powder; rows of red cannas looking like stringy-necked turkeys poking their heads over tops of cages; horses, heads down, tails switching, grazing slowly across the long shaded lots as if they were moving across Time itself; cottonwoods filled with grackles wheezing out their metallic calls; pink oleanders – hints of the far-off seacoast South – rising above the rock walls of subdivision homes.

(The trees themselves: great weeping willows, flowing downward in fragile streamers, making their elegant tents; unglamorous but serviceable elms, fanning upward and outward with a commendable grace; a random sycamore with its rather grand, broad-fingered leaves; and the globe willows: a bit dumpy, but nice: looking vaguely like Jazz Age flappers with bobbed green hair.)

At a break in the trees I stopped to look out at El Paso mountain-and-sky stretching behind cotton fields still yellow-topped with blooms – giving a sense of absolute space joined with local, neighborly containment; then I reached down and picked up a handful of dirt. I held it, judging that it was a pleasant and worthwhile experience to be in contact with dirt again. (A homely personal verity: *Dirt is good.*) While I was there, hunkered down, two brown goats came up close to the fence to see if I might have anything interesting for them in my hand. They walked as if they were trying out for drum majorettes: with short, precise, almost prancing steps, tails held high, heads cocked somewhat demurely to one side. I pulled up a clump of Johnson grass from the bank and offered it to them, but they were a bit too prim and proper to try it.

Of course, not everyone is charmed by the world of canals....

I remember one midday last spring when I was idling along a West Side waterway. Across the canal, to the south, the stylish homes in Stonehenge Estates sat in the shade of luxuriant front-yard trees. The houses had ivied archways; hunks of bronzed rock were artfully placed in desert gardens; spacious back yards were bordered by Spanish-style, cream-colored walls. From time to time sleek gray Audis and Cadillacs purred along Meadowlark Drive and out of sight.

I was on the north side of the canal, following a sandy path that went through dry grasses and salt cedars. It was April, and the hot earth smells made the path a rich sensory corridor. Such a canal in France — or so I liked to imagine — would have been typical Colette Country: a Burgundy coast setting for sensual awakenings, bared bodies, eager young love. Here, in spring, near the Rio Grande, it was simply a place of bees and butterflies, of doves calling placidly to one another among the trees.

The brown canal water was moving rapidly, and ripples glinted in the sun. As I came around a bend, two ducks rose in alarm from their resting places along the bank and flew down the canal toward the west. A nutria, unperturbed, kept on nibbling among the reeds.

To take a break from the sun, I stopped for a while and stood within the branches of a salt cedar — within the low, constant humming of bees. As they explored the sweet-smelling tips of the cedars, it was as if they were carrying from limb to limb the steady sound of life itself: unobtrusive, timeless. I listened, pleased by their noontime music.

Then it began. A high-decibel car stereo started blaring forth songs – if that is the correct term – by Iron Maiden, and for the next ten minutes it was Confrontation: the electric wailing of "Seventh Son of the Seventh Son" and "Bring Your Daughter To the Slaughter" versus the seductive droning of the bees among the blooms.

I left my salt cedar resting place and walked on until I saw the car parked along Meadowlark. It was a spanking new Corvette and the driver – a young man in reflective sun glasses – sat low in the seat. With his stereo cranked up full volume he did not take note of me as I passed by. We inhabited different universes.

Like Woody Allen and Duke Ellington – other unswerving urbanites – the Iron Maiden young man will probably never find time – or reason – to scoop up a handful of dirt and pronounce it good. So be it.

Sometimes I believe that the most rewarding activity for me is just to walk along, putting one foot in front of the other, feeling the earth – the sun at my back, water at my side, a breeze in my face. Just that: mobile, independent, a survivor of things past, unaware of things future: a human, "lost in the stars," moving along in the ageless human way beneath the trees.

# Mercedes Man

Excellence and perfection are curious attributes. They distance those who seek after them from the sadly imperfect masses....

One Sunday morning as I entered a Furr's supermarket in El Paso a sinewy, sandy-haired man in his early forties strode past me in his white golf shirt and shorts. He had muscular calves and wore a beeper at his hip. As he pulled loose a shopping cart and detoured around a

large, rather shapeless woman who was quarreling with her two whin-
ing boys, I tried to sort out my reactions to the man.

His physical appearance, his movements, his air: they were the
embodiment of a familiar type. They conveyed the haughtiness, the
sense of aloofness from the crowd that is radiated by a person who
Excels and Achieves. He was someone who was confident, secure,
*better*: indeed, how could he ever manage to feel humble displaying, as
he did, those sculpted calves molded to such perfection at a Gold's
Gym?

He was, I decided, a Mercedes Man forced to endure, periodically, the ineptitude, the lack of competence and efficiency – the sheer
awkward messiness – of a Used Car, Bargain Basement world. (I could
visualize his quick contemptuousness, his explosive anger during morning freeway traffic as he came upon an old truck with Juárez license
plates chugging along in front of him up a West Side incline – loaded
with collapsed cardboard boxes, with blue-black smoke pouring out of
its exhaust.)

I lost sight of the man, did my few minutes' worth of shopping,
stopped a moment to browse at the magazine rack, then heard a com-
motion. In the detergent aisle the shapeless woman was jerking hard
on the arm of one of her boys. Apparently he and his brother had
been chasing each other and he had knocked over a display pyramid
of Tide boxes. A white splash of granules was scattered across the floor
from several broken boxes. The woman was yelling, the boy was trying not to cry, his brother stood to one side, smirking.

The Mercedes Man came by with his well-stocked cart. Glancing
at the woman, the boys, the scattered boxes, the white trail down the
aisle, he gave a brief, almost imperceptible headshake of annoyance
and disgust; then, calf muscles flexing, he rolled on toward the check-
out counter – cataloguing, I assumed – yet another example of the
graceless souls who manage to make such a mess of their bodies and
their lives.

# A Day in the Country

Driving past fields of the Mesilla Valley one summer noon, I stopped, got out, and stared. I could not help myself. I stood on the roadside in the midday sun, trying to take it all in: the green of the cotton fields, the mountains, the land, the sun.

The sun: it burned with clarity and distinctiveness – it burned with beauty – into every leaf, every dirt clod, every stick and weed and blossom. Each surface shone in the brilliance of the light; each shade and shadow was rich with the absence of light.

I walked into a field until I reached a line of pecan trees growing beside an *acequia*. It was a pleasant oasis, and as I stood beneath the trees the countryside seemed to grow quieter. A killdeer called, and then called again. Yellow and white butterflies jiggled and danced through the nearby patches of alfalfa. There was the random coursing of flies and from time to time the faint thunder of jets far overhead.

It was all familiar, all satisfying. The heat waves shimmered in the distance; the breezes moved like friendly visitors through the leaves.

Beyond the trees, in the great peaceful glare of the summer sky, I could see trucks and cars on the high ridge of the interstate, moving with their strangely unreal lack of speed and lack of sound. They had lost size and significance; they were no longer central to the basic reality of the day, which was heat and sun and land and sky – and pecan trees: As they stood there, limbs bending down toward the earth, their knotholes resembling leathery old eyes, they were like peaceful tree-elephants who had lowered their trunks into the coolness of the *acequias*.

I walked back to my car and drove about for the rest of the afternoon. I drank coffee, I drank Cokes, I read for a while beside a barn. Then, at almost sundown, I stopped again on another country road. The seven o'clock sun was now a bright flare across acres of plowed earth and acres of pecan trees. I looked again at the unbroken symmetry of row beside row, plant beside plant, green beside green, tree beside tree.

...The sun was sinking, the dogs were barking in the distance, the doves were calling back and forth, the sand hills lay sprawled across the horizon in the west, the ducks were rising and circling and settling toward unseen canals, the summer air was moving with an idly caressing carelessness across the twilight earth.

It was just the end of another summer day – a day in the countryside. Incredibly, that's all it was: just desert farmland of the Rio Grande turning inward upon itself, toward night. Yet in those quiet shining rows – rhythmic as ocean waves, intense as a Van Gogh painting – the silent, ceaseless furnace of creation burned and roared.

# Wilfred Gaither

In elementary school we all knew he was "different" but we didn't know exactly how or why. He was small and soft and plump, like a Humpty Dumpty, with his dark hair oiled and combed carefully across his head. He made all S's on his report card, and when he went to the blackboard he wrote in big, round, looping letters. He smiled a lot. He did not join in most of the games we played, but we did not expect him to.

I remember once, however, in the fifth grade when Mrs. Rose made Wilfred take part in the class baseball game during recess. When it was his turn to bat, he stood at the plate, every hair in place across the top of his remarkably large head, squinting into the bright morning sun but nevertheless smiling that almost tolerant smile of his and holding the bat in a way that nobody else held a bat – sort of letting it hang down over his shoulder the way a person might carry something in a sack.

He stood there as Joe Lopez pitched to him with less than his usual speed. The first two pitches were perfect strikes but Wilfred

stood looking out at Joe and let them go by. He just smiled, as if –
now that I think back on it – the whole business of people throwing
balls and hitting at balls and running around bases was complete nonsense and he was merely indulging us all on that spring morning.

Everybody was yelling, "Swing, Wilfred, *swing!*" so on the third
pitch he obliged us somewhat and brought the bat down across the
general area of the plate. He missed the ball, or, rather, the ball was
already resting in the catcher's glove when Wilfred swung. Whoever
was umpire called "Strike three!" and Wilfred handed the bat politely
to the next batter – holding it straight out from his body in a way that
none of us ever handed somebody a bat – and walked in his curious
little precise way over to where a group of girls stood watching the
game from the shade of an oak tree. Even while some of the cruder
guys jeered at him and called out his name in high, mocking tones, he
never stopped smiling – not a big smile, just something private and
constant.

I guess that even in elementary school Wilfred had developed his
own survival skills: his smile was his wall, his shield. He could never
have defended himself in a fight – he knew that – but he also knew
that he would probably never need to defend himself. He was
untouchable. He was not like others. He was, in some private way,
supremely himself and that gave him strength. And he smiled in the
confidence of that knowledge.

# Church Words

I remember sitting in a back row of the Methodist church in
Kerrville. I was seventeen. The preacher was going on again about
Jesus, the Trinity, the Holy Ghost – all the familiar, singsong words I
had listened to for years. But I had a problem – actually two problems.

One was that I didn't believe in sin – the whole long-faced, buga-
boo concept of it. *Sin* just didn't jibe with what I knew of trees, of

camping out along the Guadalupe River, of my grandparents' ranch, of the hill country.... *Sin?* Where? To me it was an unreal, holy-Joe scareword that I heard each Sunday and forgot about during the rest of the week.

Also, I couldn't work up any enthusiasm for "Jesus" – the idea of Him. He was strictly a secondary figure, vaguely out of focus – a picture on a Sunday school wall and nothing more.... "Son of God"? That just didn't seem right: a God wouldn't need to have "sons." Or "daughters," for that matter. As a high school senior I didn't have the concept of anthropomorphism down pat, but nonetheless my gut feeling was that the whole business of Mary and Joseph and the Virgin Birth was a hocus-pocus cooked up in order to soften the hard mysteries of life and make them more palatable to churchgoers.

Now God: that was a different matter. God – the word, the idea – was serious stuff. I definitely felt the need to find out all I could about *God*. I was drawn – like an arrow to its mark – to the puzzle of First Causes, the world and its meaning, its origin.... Thus *Creator* had a strong ring to it, as did words like *Cosmos* and *Infinity*. Those were great, grand words – challenging words – as I sat in the back row of the First Methodist Church. They belonged rightfully to the awesomeness of the universe. Jesus? He seemed too earth-bound, human-sized, parochial, of lesser import. He belonged to preachers and Holy Rollers, not the stars.

# I Am Mourning Robert Ingersoll Today

It is a summer morning and the sun is shining. Lawns are being mowed and mail delivered. Clerks in white aprons stamp prices on cans of tuna fish in the aisles of grocery stores. Mothers drive their children to swimming pools. Workmen work and dogs lie in the shade. I walk about the house, subdued. I am thinking of Robert Ingersoll, 1833-1899, who has just died.

I knew nothing about him until recently – nothing other than his being, vaguely, a line or two in a history book. Then suddenly, last month, there he was: Royal Bob, as Garfield called him, the Great Agnostic, a man no longer a nobody but, instead, the storm center of religious controversy for a quarter of a century, a man admired by Clarence Darrow and Walt Whitman and detested by ministers. Lawyer, orator, family man, skeptic – he was, as I began to read what he wrote and what others wrote about him, an immensely compelling man.

He loved his wife, he loved his family, he loved good food, he loved music, he loved Shakespeare and Robert Burns. He could come before a hostile audience – listeners gathered grimly, prepared to hate him as the Anti-christ – and before he was through speaking his wit, his word-artistry, his contagious good humor would have the crowd applauding. Praising a speech by Ingersoll, Mark Twain said, "It was the supremest combination of English words that was ever put together since the world began."

It was a life I came upon – a full, important human life. Ingersoll, colonel at Shiloh, 1862; Ingersoll, man with a photographic memory; Ingersoll, free-thinker and hater of humbug. Then, in his sixties, a stroke and death. A man whose life I had become immersed in was there on a bier in white linen – his funeral one without prayers or sermon, his wife in mourning, flowers piled high.

...And I close the biography and leave him there – just words now, no flesh. Just the record of another dead man who was once alive. Ingersoll just a part of history again, perhaps to be discovered by some other reader.

I look out to the street and cannot see death anywhere – Ingersoll's, my own, anyone's. I see young girls in white tights hopping into a church building to take ballet lessons. I see grass growing. I see boys on bicycles in baseball caps.

I mourn Robert Ingersoll – which is to say that I mourn me, everyone, our deaths. We all enjoy it so much, this life, this air, girls in white tights and boys on bicycles, and it is so very good and seems to last so very long, but doesn't, and the end comes, and then it is history. It is always out there, in the sunlight somewhere, our mortality, but we can never see it. We live in our skins between the cracks of eternity, convinced we will never die.

But: Ingersoll is dead, his chapter ended. I think of him, and me, and I walk about the house, subdued.

# The Last Moment

I never knew Delpha Starcke well, but I knew about her all my life. She and her husband Archie were contemporaries of my aunt and uncle – friends on nearby ranches for almost fifty years. My aunt was attractive in a severe, dark-eyed way, but Delpha was indisputably classy: a beautiful, poised woman who always knew that she "turned heads" in any gathering. Archie Starcke and my uncle were both good ranchers, but Archie seemed to be a bit more concerned with social status: he was the first one to buy a new car, to remodel his ranch house.  My uncle was strong featured and muscular; Archie was a little less so. Both families had well behaved and ambitious children although when they grew up none of them carried on the ranching traditions of the parents.

When Archie died of cancer in his early seventies, Delpha leased out the pastures and continued living on the ranch – continuing, also, to look like a stunning, barely aging Gloria Swanson. I would nod to her sometimes in town in a department store or see her profile in the window of her Oldsmobile as she turned off the highway and drove up the lane toward her ranch. She stayed on the go and – so my aunt told me – kept up her shopping trips to Houston and Dallas.

Then two years ago she had a stroke. One side of her face was paralyzed for a while and she had trouble speaking clearly. She gradually recovered, even began driving into town again to shop.

Apparently, as far as friends could tell, she was in good spirits.

One morning this past spring my brother called me: Delpha Starcke shot herself, he said. Suicide.

As I say, I really did not know the woman – would just hear about her occasionally when I went back to visit relatives in the hill country – but I couldn't get her death out of my mind.

I went to see my aunt and uncle last summer, and as they sat at the supper table – my aunt staring ahead, going over and over the little that she knew, that anyone knew – I tried to imagine what those last moments of Delpha Starcke's life were like.

My aunt said it was Susan, the daughter, who had found her: "You see, Susan went shopping with Delpha just that morning. Susan said they looked all over town for the face cream Delpha liked.... She said her mother was even talking about going on a trip this summer, maybe down to New Orleans."

My uncle, in his undershirt, sat at the table wheezing with his emphysema, looking ahead at the blank white door of the refrigerator, thinking his thoughts about the woman he had danced with for fifty years at community dances.

"...So when Susan still couldn't get her mother on the phone that afternoon, well, she decided she'd better drive on out. And of course she found her that way in the bedroom.... The bedroom door was locked and she had to break it in." My aunt kept circling it, again and again: "No one knows, of course, why she would do a thing like that, what was on her mind. Susan said she didn't seem at all depressed in town."

Indeed, no one will ever know, but the maybe's are plain enough. Maybe Delpha Starcke simply could not face the idea of getting crippled and feeble and dependent like all the old people she saw when she had visited her father in the Kerrville nursing home (old people: when casual acquaintances of Delpha read her age in the obituary column they were shocked: she would have been eighty her next birthday yet looked twenty years younger). Maybe she told herself, "I don't want to live if I have another stroke" and maybe that night she began to feel the first telltale signs – a numbness in her arms and legs – and while she still had mind and will power enough to act she opened the drawer by her bed and took out the loaded revolver.

There are probably other maybe's, but none of them counts. It's only that last moment that matters to me: it's trying to imagine what it was like to be Delpha Starcke in her house in the country as she locked the bedroom door (one more maybe: maybe she thought if she locked it her daughter would not be able to open it by herself, would have to leave and come back with help, would thus have someone with her to cushion the shock). Then she got the plastic bag from the kitchen and sat on the pink counterpane and put the bag over her head and after sticking the gun in her mouth pulled the trigger with her slim, liver-spotted, cream-moistened hand.

# Along the River

I want to spend, once again, a day along a river. I want to take cold fried chicken and potato salad and pork-and-beans and buns and an ice chest with drinks and go in midmorning to a river place in Central Texas. I want to get an old quilt from the trunk of the car and spread it beneath a sycamore tree and stay there near the river for the rest of the day.

I want to lie on the quilt, reading, and then put a marker in the book and close my eyes and hear, once more, the leaves of the sycamores and oaks and willows moving in the breeze and the sound of water running somewhere over rocks. I want to walk along the river through weeds and clumps of grass. I want to stand in the deep river shade, feeling the sense of the river, its large open silence, the all-enveloping heat of the summer afternoon.

I want to take an old coffee can that is half-filled with moist dirt and fishing worms and bait my hook and edge out onto a mounded rock along the bank and, sitting beneath the overhang of trees, fish throughout the rest of the afternoon. I want to watch the ripples begin to circle and then spread away from my cork as small unseen perch nibble at my bait, but mainly I just want to continue being where I am. I want to sit and lose track of time – letting four and five and six o'clock blend into the flow of the river and the muted, random call of birds. I want to become the reflection of the trees on the water, and the idle swarming of gnats in the shafts of the setting sun, and the periodic surfacing of turtles.

And then, after the sun goes down and the river settles into its deep twilight mood, I want to walk back to my car – slowly, deliberately, as if each step is giving something back to the riverbank, as if the river and the gathering night can know, somehow, that I am offering a thanks.

# The Living Room

One summer morning I was walking through a neighborhood in an older part of El Paso. Delivery trucks rumbled around corners and the shrill sound of locusts filled the air. As I passed a modest frame house sitting in its small square of yard, I happened to glance toward the porch and the front door, then at the dim rectangle of living room that lay behind the screen.

I stopped, moved back a pace or two, looked again – feeling compelled to gaze more deeply. I was caught, you see, by the hidden *something* suggested by that screen door and the almost invisible living room framed within it: some emotionally charged scene, perhaps, from my childhood, some truth, some irritation or even anger. I knew I should not stand there too long, staring so obviously and openly, but nevertheless I wanted to penetrate, to become that door: to feel what it was like to face outward to the street day after day from that particular house: passive, restrained, waiting – always waiting – for some routine happening to mark the passing of the hours: a phone to ring, a breeze to blow, a cat to cross the yard, a letter to be placed by the postman's hand into the porch mailbox.

Standing in the street under the hot July sun, I tried to understand what the door – but more precisely, the shadowy living room – seemed to suggest or symbolize.... I did not need to go inside the house; I could visualize well enough the sofa frayed at the arms, the curtains drawn shut over the windows, the small radio on its black-varnish end table, the floor lamp, the collection of knickknacks, the arrangement of artificial flowers.

It seemed as if the living room was the stage for the depressing drama-less dramas of human life: the dreary everydayness that seeps in once the children have grown up and moved away, once puttering about replaces the eight-to-five work routine, once laughter and competence have begun to fade, once health and vigor give way to illness and physical debilities. It is as though the very objects in such a room begin to set themselves more closely together, the way wagons in the West were drawn in a protective circle against the threat of a common enemy.

...The living room: a safe haven with only one tempo: the slow moving about of people among familiar things within safe walls.

...The living room: a place where the photographs on the bureau seem more animated than the people who are still breathing.

...Then someone appears: from the harsh glare of the almost forgotten outer world – the vague world beyond the four plastic ducks in the yellowed yard, beyond the sidewalk, beyond the familiar whir of locusts in the neighborhood trees – someone steps upon the porch at 10:15 in the morning and knocks on the door. In response, a woman – a wife, a housekeeper, a widow – appears from the unseen kitchen, wiping her hands on an apron, and crosses the living room to stand at the door. Or perhaps an old man in undershirt and slippers struggles to rise from his arm chair, shuffles past the unlit lamp, peers toward the figure outlined within the screen: perhaps not fully believing that the figure really exists since the nature of reality has gradually changed over the years and is now something that appears more believable over the radio, on the TV set.

I walked on down the block, trying to sort out my conflicting emotions.... What was so bothersome to me about that gloomy human cave? Maybe it was not just where the old got older; it was also where people backed away from life, narrowed their scope and expectations: felt they had sucked out all life's juices and were then content to exist on mere dried pulp.... I had unpleasant memories of childhood visits to such stifling, hermetic places that were more like museums than homes: where towels were hung with an intimidating exactness from bathroom racks, where visiting children were smiled at but not for very long, where order was so orderly it gave off an odor. It was where discontented people had somehow become proud of their discontents and thus were self-pitying and boring. It was not just their bodies' infirmities, or a husband's death, or reduced income that set the mood of these airless cells; it was that they had drifted into a daily drabness, into pettiness and resignation.

(...I am eight or nine, I walk up concrete steps with my mother, she pushes a bell; I hear it ringing faintly within the two-story, brick building. We stand next to a palm tree in the morning heat of San Antonio. No one comes. After a while she rings again. We wait, and finally the door opens and Aunt Bessie in her long housecoat is standing there – her hair still a bit brownish but mostly grayed on top, parted in the middle, pulled back in a bun. We follow her down a hallway, past closed doors, to her set of rooms. Aunt Bessie and my mother sit close together in stuffed chairs and talk – Aunt Bessie bent forward a little, her voice low and resonant and constant, as if she were finally revealing terrible secrets. I sit in another chair and look around at the dark wood paneling, the heavy drapes, the low line of dancing blue flames in the gas heater. I know there was once an Uncle Henry who is dead, and that the various somber faces within their oval frames, hung about the room, are photographs of distant relatives, but most of

all – though I say nothing, just wait, look ahead at my shoes, at the rug
– I know that I want out of there.)

Getting into my car, I think: *"Living* room? No, the dying room."
That was the "something" I had tried to identify as I stared at the
house: my own mortality trapped inside. Anyone who stayed for long
within the confines of such a room was simply inviting death to join
him. But I would not be lured inside. The boy in me from long ago
was insisting: Not me.... I would rather crawl up Kilimanjaro on my
hands and knees – freezing to death along the way.

# Weekend in Silver

Let's say it has been a long week and you are a bit more restless
than usual – the daily work routines seem to be more deadening, the
responsibilities of your life less satisfying – so you do it: on Friday
afternoon you toss a few weekend essentials into your car and head out
from El Paso to Silver City, New Mexico.

It's always good to start a little trip after work on Friday. You slide
into the I-10 traffic, feeling kind of smug about cutting loose from
your customary weekly rhythms. You've made an extra thermos of
coffee and you sip from the plastic cup on the seat beside you – the
travel thermos, the travel cup. You put a travel tape into the cassette
player, and the pulsing sounds of Woody Herman's "Wild Root" fill the
car as the green interstate signs begin to glide by: Canutillo, Vinton,
Anthony, Mesquite.

As you turn truly west at Las Cruces it's nice to see the Deming
sign along the highway. The trip is for real now: you have broken free
from the "gravity" of El Paso. Deming is a traveler's town, a highway
map town, a town to pass through when you're on the road to distant
places.... You look out your window to the mountain ranges pale and
hazy in the distance: Cookes Peak to the north, Florida Peak to the

south. Already they offer the satisfying lure of things-on-the-horizon, things unknown.

You take Highway 180 north out of Deming. The sun is low; you have gone through the tapes of Stan Kenton, Artie Shaw, Peggy Lee; the coffee is still a worthy companion. You slow down, trying to decide: Should you swing off the main road and check out the City of Rocks — that strange cluster of rusty-orange, hill-sized boulders dumped in the middle of nowhere as if they had fallen from Mars?... You decide against it, keep on climbing toward Hurley and the sprawling, open-pit copper mine. In Bayard you park, get out, stretch your legs on a walk through the darkening side streets. Nice little upland, hillside community, Bayard. (Too bad the drug-store has closed for the day; it is one of your favorite stopping places: a small-town drugstore left over from the 1940s: wooden floors, narrow aisles, chock-full of every possible item from copper plates to packets of *yerba buena*; with a long-time clerk named Irene or Wilma at the front cash register buffing her nails and a smiling man in spectacles, a Gene or Lewis, visible in his small, arched pharmacist's window at the back.)

In Silver City — just "Silver" to the locals — you get a room at the Drifter Motel and drive on downtown. You order a Chimichanga at the long-tunneled Mexican-food restaurant that was probably a dry goods store at the turn of the century. Once again you are the only customer, and once again you wonder how the restaurant manages to stay in business. It's as if the owners keep it open as a service to family and friends rather than to make a profit.... You eat; the middle-aged waitress gazes into some private reverie; the grandmotherly gray head of the cook is barely visible above the back partition. No one talks or moves; no dishes rattle. It's like dining out in a private club: dim light, high ceiling, unobtrusive movements and sounds. You feel this is a fitting way to end a Friday.

On Saturday morning you gas up and head out toward Glenwood and Mogollon. It's desert and ranch country you begin driving through: the far western edge of New Mexico. In Glenwood you

pause at the sign, "Catwalk," and consider the length of time it takes
not only to walk out to the Catwalk bridge but to dally along the
creek.... Next time you'll do it; next time you will spend the entire
afternoon just poking along the trail among cottonwoods and aspens.

At Alma you take the road to Mogollon. It goes across open,
serene highlands for a while, then begins the winding climb and pre-
cipitous descent with its hairpin turns. You glance across the valley
toward the site of the old Fanny mine, then finally you are down: in
Mogollon, once the pearl of the mining region and now a ghost town
preserved in pine-scented historical amber. A dozen or so people move
about: some are tourists, some are residents. You walk past restored
miner shacks and adobes as breezes flow through the canyon.

Back in Glenwood you treat yourself to a steak in an oak-paneled
little cafe. It has red-and-white tablecloths, sensationally cold bottles
of Coors, and an adjoining room where blue-jeaned men in western
hats leisurely shoot games of pool in shafts of Saturday afternoon sunlight. You sit at your table – tired, relaxed, content: thinking that you
had just as soon not move again for perhaps the next month or so.

On Saturday night Silver City has a tradition – a local spin-off
from the more widespread teenage ritual of driving mindlessly around
a neighborhood Dairy Queen. In Silver, teenagers and college students
and whoever else wants to join in the procession drive almost bumper
to bumper down the main street and keep on driving in a slow, continuous ebb and flow until – who knows, maybe midnight: you've never
stayed to observe the spectacle from beginning to end....You watch
from your parked car and at ten o'clock it's rather a sight to see: one
line of trucks and cars meeting the other line that is returning from the
turn-around spot: everyone driving calmly, almost sedately in their
methodical, young folks' parade past the dark store fronts.

On Sunday morning you drive to Pinos Altos, another historic
mining community a few miles north of Silver. Pinos Altos: High
Pines: each time you go you want to rent a cabin, pitch a tent – whatever – and spend a summer there. You walk and walk; you feel you

could keep on walking down one of the dirt roads, past another of the apple orchards, on up through the pines, and never come back....

You check out of the Drifter at noon and begin the return trip home: along the upper route past Hanover and San Lorenzo (a heart-breaking little river town drowsing in the sun); through the Mimbres Mountains and the Black Range of the Gila forest.... You have the thermos at your side and sweeping vistas out your window, and, my-oh-my, the land is still strong stuff.... Great looping ascents through the mountain passes and long, snaking declines above occasional streams bring you at one point to an observation site where you get out and look down on the world: the horizon-to-horizon desert world sprawled from Alamogordo to Las Cruces; a godly, sobering view.... At Kingston you stand in its quiet Sunday isolation, trying to imagine – to feel – how it was in the boomtown days of the 1880s when 10,000 gold miners camped there among the junipers.

Finally you're just about through with soaking up mountain byways and ready to call it quits. You take one brief look-about in Hillsboro (mighty interesting little town...you need to spend a few days there some time) and then, like a rider letting the reins go slack and allowing his horse to set the pace, you aim your car toward Caballo Lake and I-25 South. You still have a couple of hours to go on the interstate so you put a Duke Ellington tape in the cassette and let the remaining good times roll.

# Angie

Angie was probably the most popular girl in my high school class. She was easy-going, low-keyed; she was everybody's buddy.

Angie wasn't pretty but she didn't need to be. She had a round-faced, regular-featured pleasantness and by our sophomore year she was comfortably, womanly fleshed. She had brown eyes, shoulder-length dark brown hair, a smooth healthy-looking skin, and full lips.

(Her lower lip was especially large and ripe – almost motherly, like a red-glossed breast.)

In our junior year she went steady for six months or so with Junior Mayfield – a handsome-enough, good-natured guy who played first-string right end and always snorted a little when he laughed. They broke up, and Angie dated just about anybody who asked her out. It was the 1940s, the smooching era, and Angie had the reputation of being a good smoocher. That meant that after a movie at the Arcadia and a hamburger and a shake at the Dairy King and then just driving around town for a while Angie's date would pull off Cypress Creek Lane onto the edge of the golf course and park under the live oaks and settle in for an hour or so against Angie's face. Angie didn't mind who her date was, within reason. She would slide across the front seat and yield up her fleshy flesh – lips, arms, breasts – to trumpet player, college guy, ordinary Joe, whoever.

At school dances after the Friday night football games you would stand around in the intimate almost-darkness of the gym – you and the other stags – and watch familiar couples lock together on the dance floor. Then you would wind your way through the bodies and tap Tunstell or Fred or Billy Ray on the shoulder. Angie would already be releasing him and turning now toward you, smiling, her dress damp with sweat, her hand automatically reaching up to clasp your neck: whoever you happened to be among the numerous, interchangeable Friday night bodies. And after a brief, obligatory arching backwards so she could give you the full measure of her smile, her teeth, her direct and friendly Good Ole Girl gaze, she would place her sweaty hair and face against your shoulder and the two of you would snuggle your way around the gym for the rest of "Moonlight Serenade."

It was years later – at our twenty-year class reunion – that I heard the rest, the last of Angie: how she had gone on to college but had dropped out after her freshman year; had moved to Canada; then had killed herself at age twenty-two with an overdose of barbituates in a suicide pact with her lesbian lover.

# Loneliness

It is early summer, the windows are open, and at ten o'clock in the morning the bird has started to call. I stop reading and listen. It is the sound – the voice – of my childhood calling again in the trees.

I have heard it, off and on, for a lifetime, but I still do not know its proper name. My mother called it a raincrow – the hill country term she had learned while growing up on the ranch – but I doubt that it is actually a crow or that it has anything to do with rain. Nevertheless, its sound never fails to haunt me. It is my own personal Raven.

On Gilmer Street in Kerrville a border of trees lay around our house and yard, and it was like a safe perimeter around life itself. As I played beneath the huge oaks during those endless childhood days the raincrow would call in its sustained, hypnotic, unobtrusive way: just two hurried notes, the first rising, the second falling, over and over, throughout the sunny small-town mornings. Delivery trucks would lumber down our unpaved street, the postman's car would stop just before noon at the mailbox on the corner, dogs barked, certain doors and gates opened and slammed; then, afterward, all grew quiet again in the yards and neighborhood and the raincrow – hidden, as all oracles are – would continue to hint at things I did not understand but would always remember.

For over fifty years I have listened to the raincrow, but only recently was I able to understand it: "Loneliness" – it is saying – "loneliness is constant; loneliness is everywhere." In the midst of life – in the midst of security, family, trees and yards – the bird of loneliness has been calling out to those who can hear.

I listen to it now outside my window. Its monotonous message is clear, unchanged.

# Desert Place in December

It is not a rare day; it is, in fact, a typical one, this sun-warmed, early-December afternoon on the outskirts of El Paso. The sky has all the blue it can hold, the sun is as bright as a person would want it to be in late fall, and the air has just enough of a cold bite to make it jacket weather – although you can move about comfortably in short sleeves. The sun warms even as the air chills. The air is so clear and clean that everything in the landscape – houses, trees, mountains – is sharp-edged to the eye.

People are out in their back yards, but they seem to move a fraction more deliberately, more patiently than on other days, as if they are listening or waiting, as if attentive to the remarkable *something* in the day but not quite sure what the nature of that remarkableness is: as if they have suddenly found themselves in a play and are uncertain of their role. They understand that the day is a kind of gift, a blessing – but, well, weather is merely weather, after all, and they do not want to seem excessively conscious of it.

The grasses in the yards and along the roadside have finally turned yellow; the salt cedars are faded to rusty-reds; tree limbs loom up brown and bare. Nonetheless, as a person walks across his yard the leaves crumpling beneath his feet make a crisp, satisfying music. An insect in a pyracantha bush begins its long whirring sound that, in a wolf, would be a howl but in the insect is simply its own sustained hymn to the universe. Birds move about almost invisibly in hedges and trees – noiseless, secret, busy.

...Mid-afternoon becomes a deepened, private time. Children stand along a canal, throwing rocks into the water and watching the ripples spread. They wait, filled with a sense of inwardness and wonder. They throw again, watching the water, listening – without knowing it – to themselves and the afternoon.... As people rake leaves, as they take walks, shadows fall not only across their lives but into them – vague and suggestive of unknown depths.

The earth lies still, sunning itself.

Goats snort in their pens, then fold down upon their front legs to ruminate on the goat world in front of them.

A horse breaks into a run across its enclosure, stops, shakes its head, stares, gallops back.

Eight peacocks sit on a fence, the blue of their necks still iridescent within the deep shade of a globe willow.

Two brown bantam hens lie side by side, feathers fluffed and overlapping onto each other, eyes closed, drowsing in their little hollow of barnyard dust.

A boy and his dog race together across a field: a story in motion.

And because it has to be there, because the day would not be complete without it, a lone Piper Cub moves along in the distance, droning its patient, knowing commentary to the horizon.

# Hildegarde's Dream

Everyone has a lost girl, beautiful in memory, fixed like a hidden valley in the plains of youth. Mine is Hildegarde Kimmel of Cologne, Germany – lovely to look upon, painful to remember. When we met she was caught up in a dream of love that did not allow entry of mere mortals.

White-gloved, white-hatted, adroit Hildegarde: at twenty-three she was half-woman, half-child, moving through her well-ordered world of wealth, culture, and travel. Hildegarde: translator at the U.N., speaking in her low, quiet voice, ripping r-r-r's off her throat like someone gargling. Hildegarde: of the pointed meditative shoe on the hot New York sidewalk – walking slowly, gracefully, partly because of her aristocratic bearing, partly because of her very pretty but long and narrow and restrictive brown skirt. Finger-snapping, jazz-loving, Americanized Hildegarde: giving her quick shudders and shakes to express the simple joys.

In 1955 she was like a smooth-sailing swan on her calm international lake: womanly serene, but girlishly watching for the sudden, electric, emotional storm that she assumed was bound to come her way – upsetting her deft, independent sailing and sweeping her thrillingly into some hidden port of love. She had no doubt it was there somewhere on the horizon – that romantic and deliciously consuming storm. She wanted it to descend like a thundercloud from heaven and unleash itself upon her – scattering her senses and tearing her heart loose from its moorings and throwing her headlong and panting into its bright lightning and roaring waves. And after the first terrible sweet thunder had rolled over her body she wanted to open her eyes and find Him there. Without words, this prince of Heart-storms, this golden-maned Neptune would lift her with his marvelously restrained passion and carry her off to his sheltered lagoon. There she would live forever – her old poise gone, her independence gladly surrendered. She would mend his sandals, tend his fire, bear his sturdy young.

Ah, Hildegarde: her god did not descend from the clouds, but she did manage to get along well enough with a reasonable substitute, a young blond heir to the Krupp munitions fortune. On the day she left New York I went to see her off on the Liberté. Smiling, she sat on the edge of the narrow berth, holding her drink and making conversation with the small group of friends and relatives who had come to wish her a pleasant trip back to Germany. She sat with her smooth, firm legs crossed, the bottom of her skirt slanted artfully across her kneecap. Every now and then she reached up with the little finger of her drink hand and removed a fleck of lipstick from the corner of her mouth and smudged it away into her palm. Red-lipped, clear-eyed, oval-faced, self-possessed, she gazed into my camera with a cool readiness to be immortalized.

# Salvation

During the summer after I graduated from college I was working as a camp counselor in Central Texas. It was my Sunday afternoon off duty and I had driven down the road to a pleasant little cafe in Hunt. I went to the screened-in back porch that perched above the greenery of the Guadalupe River and I drank iced tea and read in *The Sound and the Fury* for an hour or so. It was mid-July and the four o'clock heat hung like a curtain across the land.

I closed the novel and walked down to the river. Sycamores and cypresses stood along the bank, and the river ran over a shallow, sandy bottom. Small perch, curious and detached, waited about in the shade of the trees as if painted there in the water. I sat against a big cypress and smelled the moss and the clean river freshness and heard coming from downstream the sound of the water as it moved across a layer of rocks. It seemed to be the sound that the afternoon itself would make if it could be heard moving slowly toward night.

I walked a while along the bank, and in an open space I reached down and broke off a piece of sage. I crushed it, rubbed it in my palm, then inhaled it: that familiar, fragrant smell warmed by the sun. I stood with the sage in my hand and suddenly it was not just that specific smell I was experiencing: I was smelling all of the summer afternoons of my childhood at my grandparents' ranch: the hot clearing in front of the ranch house, the cries of killdeer at the water trough, the flash of black-and-white wild canaries above the clumps of oaks, the casual clanging of a goat's bell as he rubbed himself against a shed.

As I walked back up to my car to return to camp, I understood something: that no matter how often despair or loneliness would be having its way with me, I could always head out to the rivers, to the fields, to the countryside. There were sounds and smells of the country in my past, in my bones, and I could rely on them the way others relied on incense in a church. Nature would be my private place of refuge, my salvation.

# Sunday Nights

For many people – sitting in the air-conditioned sanctuaries of their living rooms, tranquilized by a television screen – Sunday can be a peaceful, manageable day.

Not for me. I have been fighting it for years. When I was in college the sense of gradually increasing despair began at Sunday noon, grew through the long, empty afternoon until, at times, I thought I would not survive another six o'clock on Sunday night. I would stand on the darkening Austin streets and feel life draining out of the week like my own blood seeping through my shoes. *Desolate* is just a word, but when I was twenty-two, that word, on Sunday night, was me. And although I wandered past other students down the main drag of the university campus I might as well have been alone on Alpha Centauri.

Sunday still affects me – like a malaria that never quite leaves the body. I have learned to take my personal doses of quinine for it – mainly, trips to the countryside – and I seldom get the old painful sweats, but nevertheless Sunday-at-six is always lurking nearby – a vague but formidable ghost of city-times past.

Even now, let me be on downtown streets at Sunday dusk with all the stores closed and slow Sunday cars cruising about; let me catch a whiff of stale beer and refrigerated air coming from the doorway of a down-at-the-heels bar; let pigeons be sidling along near a fallen drunk, scavenging crumbs from between his legs on the sidewalk; let shadows start filling the broken windows of warehouses; let the first neon signs of upstairs rooming houses start to blink; let entropy drift into the vacant streets like sewer gas seeping up from cracks in the earth – and I am once again twenty-two: vulnerable, uncertain, adrift in an unfathomable universe.

# Redemption

The little house was at the end of a long side street in Reserve, New Mexico – the humblest kind of residence, more of a shed than a house. It had once been yellow but the paint had faded. It had a sloping tin roof. A porch of sorts extended over a brief yard of bare packed earth. Rags poked out of an old sofa that sagged beside the front door. Several cars and trucks – apparently no longer fit for the street – were angled about in the side yard.

The little house seemed willing enough to say – to anyone who cared to notice – that it made no effort toward middle-class pretensions.

Yet as I drove past – several times: turning around at the vacant lot at the end of the street and then looking again at the house as I drove back by – I knew I would like to be sitting there on hot New Mexico afternoons. I wanted to be in that wooden chair beneath the front porch overhang, looking out at the day and the mountains because in front of the house stood its redemption: a row of four, slim, impossibly green and shimmering cottonwoods towering sixty feet high.

The house – well, it was what it was, yes. But those trees – their leaves moving and glistening and shimmering like thousands of little green waves in a sea of air – made the yard as peaceful and contenting as a Roman villa. The cottonwoods, like a phalanx of imperial guards, not only shaded the house, protected it, but by their very elegance they canceled out the meanness of the abandoned cars, the dilapidated sofa, the flaking yellow paint. The trees, rising up – soaring – elevated all within their domain.

# The Smile

North of Las Vegas, New Mexico, on the way to Taos, a road turns west to Sapello Creek and the foothills of the Sangre de Cristo mountains. It is a world of narrow valleys and brief hillside fields, little communities of adobe houses, barns, mobile homes. Horses idle along beside ponds, their tails switching rhythmically: princes of their highland kingdom. At 6,000 feet the clouds gather, the breezes increase, the leaves of the aspens shimmer and shine. Death and commerce are elsewhere; only the sky and the evergreens and the blue jays are real.

At the end of day one afternoon – with the mountains rising on all sides, a clean dampness in the air – a blond-haired woman came toward me around a curve in the road, riding bareback on a dappled gray horse. The woman was smiling, and what a smile it was. It was not social or perfunctory; it was more like a rose blooming. It said all kinds of things.

It said: "I may look slightly ridiculous to you, sitting as I am on this old horse, my bare legs and knees and feet angled down, and looking as I know I look: like a socialite, a woman of means, of style. But even though I have worn expensive jewelry and eaten at the best of restaurants and at this very moment could be lounging with friends beside our California condo pool – yes, of course I have money – I had rather be here, in ragged and faded cut-offs, riding bareback on this dirt road along Sapello Creek at sundown – with miles of mountains around me – than anywhere else on earth."

That's what the woman said with her smile as she passed slowly by. And on that dirt road at that time of day – with the smell of pines in the air and the lingering hint of mountain rain – I believed her.

# Couple in the Park

I was wandering through downtown San Antonio one afternoon and decided to see what Jazz in the Park was all about. It was an easy-going Sunday in September and the people in Travis Park were milling around near the outdoor stage – eating sandwiches, drinking beer, listening to the music. Local bands had been playing since noon and Dave Brubeck was scheduled for eight o'clock.

I got a Coors in a paper cup and watched a pair of Frisbee throwers charm a group of kids. Then, as the Herbie Mann Quartet began setting up on stage, I noticed them: the couple on the blanket.

The woman, in her late thirties, was pretty and fair-skinned – with the kind of soft flesh that bruises easily.  She had a neatly lip-sticked mouth, carefully made-up eyes, and I could almost smell the powder and moisturizer. An expensive red-and-white striped dress smoothly outlined the hourglass curves of her body.

She was lying back on her elbows beside her husband – obviously trying to be a good sport on the blanket-island beneath the tall pecan trees. But she just couldn't keep from yawning – graceful little partings of her lips half-covered by pats of red-nailed fingers. From time to time she would lean close to her husband, trying to make comments that he could hear above the music. Occasionally she would slowly, lovingly rub her nose against the hair of his arm. Sometimes she even remembered to move her feet a little with the beat of the music – politely, mechanically.

Her husband – he with the tan walking shorts, the meaty legs crossed at the knee; he with the freckled arms and reddish, clipped beard: did he ever turn in his wife's direction to smile a bit or nod at one of her comments? Did he ever break his sphinx-like stare into the legs of the spectators standing in front of them? You can bet your sweet *fajita* he did not. He remained there, thrust back on his arms – angled away from his wife for an hour or more. He offered her his pro-

file, his crossed legs, his impenetrable isolation. Toothpick in mouth –
in beard – he faced outward like Napoleon gazing across Elba.

So there she was: pretty and affectionate and ignored in her pep-
permint-stripe dress: an upper-middle-class matron linked on a Sunday
afternoon outing to her reclining statue of a husband. What to do?
How to pass the time?...She twitched her cupid-bow lips in more sup-
pressed yawns. She crossed and recrossed her sweetly calved, moistur-
ized legs. She looked about at the crowd with slightly widened eyes.

I watched her husband and wondered: Oboist with the San
Antonio symphony? computer programmer? psychologist? clothing
store heir? I could not tell and did not really care to know. I just wanted to reach up and break off a tree limb and rap him a couple of times
across his freckles to get his attention. I wanted to yell at him through
Herbie Mann's wildly driving solo: You jackass, that's no way to run a
marriage!

But I knew it would do no good. I've been around such marriages
before. She would immediately grab his arm and hold him tight while
trying to kick at my shins with her glossy-red toes. And even then he
would not respond – would not bother to look at either of us: would
just keep on staring ahead, toothpick intact, while his wife carefully,
solicitously, began to brush the pecan leaves off his beard.

# Four O'clock, 1937

Mrs. Colbath was in her back yard across the street, hanging
laundry on the clothesline; the mailman had turned the corner and was
headed down the hill; I was on a branch of my favorite front-yard tree.
It was four o'clock on a spring afternoon in 1937. I was six years old.

I liked it there and never bothered to wonder why. The tree was
simply good: I was up there in the limbs and leaves, above the grass,
the walk, the fish pond, the fences, the dusty streets. The tree was like
another home.

My tree limb was private and sort of hidden, yet it was where I could see things too. It was a lookout on the neighborhood. I could see Mrs. Colbath's yellow hair and the way her cigarette dangled as she moved along putting clothespins on socks and shirts. I could see the Albe house where Mr. Albe sat in his front porch swing and leaned forward in his undershirt to spit into the yard. I could hear organ music from the radios in all the houses: "Lorenzo Jones" was over and the announcer was starting "Young Widder Brown." Sparrows raced each other across lilac bushes and through the trees.

My mother was down the street at Miss Bertie Barrett's, taking her some flowers from the side yard because Miss Bertie had broken her hip.

Hugo Maese walked by in the middle of the street, jerking his head up, over and over, and talking to himself in a loud way. I knew Hugo wouldn't see me there in the tree. Hugo never looked anywhere but straight ahead. He lived with all the Maese children in the unpainted little house down by the creek. My father had said that Hugo was "not right" and people shouldn't tease him. Hugo was big and didn't go to school any more and was usually barefoot and wore faded overalls.

I sat holding on to the smooth oak limb and started to think about Mr. McCaleb. For as long as I could remember Mr. McCaleb had come across the street and talked to me through the back wire fence. He showed me little smooth black elephants and pieces of ivory that came from parts of the world that Mr. McCaleb had gone to when he was in the army. He had white hair and wore a hat and sat on his porch like Mr. Albe, but he never spat in the yard and he was always reading in his newspaper and once he had shown me where he didn't have a finger on his left hand. He had lost it in the war.

I was eating breakfast that morning when my mother told me that Mr. McCaleb had died. My father had already gone to work at the feed store and it was just my mother there in the kitchen. She said Mr. McCaleb was a good man but it was his time to go. I finished eating

my Post Toasties in the cereal bowl and didn't say anything as my
mother looked at me from where she was washing dishes at the sink.

I got down from the tree. The mockingbird was still singing on
top of the telephone pole at the corner of the yard and the radios were
still playing in the windows along the street. I went into the house.
My mother was still down the street at Miss Bertie Barrett's. I picked
up a Tinker Toy windmill I had made that morning and then I put it
back down on the lamp table and went to the back screen porch and I
stood looking out toward the White Leghorn hens that walked around
in the shade of the garage. I thought about Mr. McCaleb, who was
dead. Mr. McCaleb was seventy years old, my mother had said.

I looked out the window and the longer I stood there the more I
began to think: "Mr. McCaleb was alive and now he's dead. Mr.
McCaleb lived until he was seventy years old. He was a person and I
am a person too. When I am seventy...." And I began to count upward
by fives: "5-10-15-20-25-30-35-40...."

It was strange. When I reached "70" it was as if I were suddenly in
a box that had begun to close down on me, a box that I had not
known I was in before: a box that was going to squeeze the Me out of
me and there was nothing I or anyone could ever do about it. There
was no way out. I was trapped; I was doomed to die like Mr. McCaleb.

I had nowhere to turn. I began to scream.

Mrs. Colbath had finished hanging her clothes and was taking
her washtub toward the back steps when she heard me from across the
street. She did not know what was wrong, but she dropped the tub
and came running.

# Sunset Heights after Dark

In the late 1950s, when I moved to El Paso, I walked in Sunset
Heights, just west of downtown, and tried to get a feel for this city at
the edge of Texas — so far from home, so close to Mexico.

At nightfall I walked along Porfirio Diaz Street. The porch lights were on and lamps shone within living rooms behind thin curtains. It was romantic to me — nothing less: the faint smell of October-night dust, the cool air, the chinaberry tree on the corner, the sounds of children's voices — their Spanish words, their laughter — as they played on the dimly lit porches. The moon had risen in the east, a train was rumbling at the station below the hill, and as I stood on Porfirio Diaz it was as if I were in Paris, in Madrid, in some fabled city of the earth.

I look back, and I think of how crickets and shadows and children and barking dogs set the tone of that time of my life, my twenties, more than philosophies and ambitions. As I walked at night I was constantly pleased by the sides of the half-darkened buildings and small front yards — as if they held, somehow, important answers to my as yet unformulated questions. I was looking — constantly — but I had no idea what I was looking for.

So I kept walking — roaming through the streets of Sunset Heights, past the red-brick homes that for decades had been facing west toward the desert, south toward Juárez and Mexico. It was as if they were still faintly flushed from the dramas of the past, and now, though solemn and decorous in the early-night darkness, their burnt-red bricks carried within them the fever of memory, the warm crimson trace of history.

Prospect, Upson, Mundy: they were strange streets to me, but as I walked them those first October nights I knew I wanted to know them, wanted to stare past their lighted porches and learn of their hidden lives.


# Father and Son

They came one late afternoon into Favello's Spaghetti House in Albuquerque and took their seats at a table next to mine. The father — balding, in his late thirties — wore a white T-shirt with designer logo,

blue jogging shorts, and running shoes with no socks. He was a slender, spare man apparently "into" jogging. His son, about eleven, wore a
T-shirt, brown walking shorts, and Adidas. With his fleshy arms and
wide thighs he seemed more into snacks and MTV.

A waitress took their order for spaghetti and meatballs. Pepsi for
the son; just water for abstemious Dad.

After the waitress left they sat there. The father, who was facing
the window, looked past his son toward the street. The son looked
vaguely in the direction of the salt shaker.

If I read the situation correctly, the scenario was something like
this: Divorced father and son were on their weekly night out. Son still
lived with Mom and was basically satisfied with the arrangement.
Whatever Dad had lost in his marriage he was attempting to regain in
clean living – something like that.

They did not have anything special to talk about. Occasionally
the father turned, asked a negligible question about sports or school;
the son gave a half-shrug/half-no answer; the father turned back and
continued looking out the window. He jiggled his right leg – not wildly but constantly, enough to make his well-developed calf muscle
bounce.

He was a good man, I felt: this restrained and none-too-buoyant
father with the bare spot that was creeping across the center of his
skull. I assumed he watched his cholesterol in the same way he
watched the stock market. At almost-forty he could seek fulfillment in
health and handball if not in meaningful dialogue with his son.

The waitress brought the spaghetti and meatballs. She asked the
man if he needed anything else. In the split-second that she stood
there, waiting for a reply, I waited too – hoping that the man would
reach for his fork, pause, consider things, and then, looking up at the
waitress, say, "Yes.... Help."

But he just shook his head no. The waitress said "Enjoy" and
turned away. Father and son ate in silence.

# Unseen, Unheard, Unnoticed

For several years I have tried to come to grips with the notion that the hunting cabin doesn't exist when I am not there to experience it. To me the cabin is not "alive" unless I am there to give it life – to wrest it out of its off-the-road, in-the-woods isolation and silence.

Related in some way to this curious and illogical attitude is my inclination – or compulsion – to "appreciate" the accomplishments of others: to prevent them from existing unseen, unheard, unnoticed. For example, let's say that I am in San Antonio and have gone to hear Noboko, the talented Japanese pianist who plays at Arthur's Restaurant bar. Let's say she is giving another of her knockout performances. Let's also say that the other patrons – businessmen, mainly – really don't care about Noboko and her music. They just want to drink and talk and laugh and carry on. They are paying no real attention to Noboko – are not impressed by the brilliance of her playing – and do not clap in appreciation when she finishes a number. They just continue laughing and talking as if she had not played at all, as if she had not "existed" during her moment of artistry.

But I always make it a point to applaud – to let her know that at nine o'clock at Arthur's she has been heard, she is valued.

What I am saying is that all my adult life I have responded strongly, empathetically to the accomplishments – and needs – of others. I have automatically tried to put myself in their place.

Not only that, I have had a strong sense of responsibility to do something when I experienced a good thing – Noboko's piano playing, the family cabin. I feel a need to celebrate it, to keep it from "dying" unheralded, unrecorded. I feel obligated to rescue a person or moment or place from the indifference of others or the uncaring flow of time.

I suppose loneliness enters in here, somehow. If Noboko's performance goes unnoted – or if the hunting cabin remains unspoken of, ignored – then to me it seems too "lonely" and I must take it upon myself to see that it gets its proper recognition and its isolation is broken.

Perhaps this is all a mirror-situation: perhaps I, as observer, am actually the only one in need. Perhaps Noboko is one tough cookie who is never affected by a lack of applause for her work. Perhaps it is a matter of my reading into a situation the dynamics of my own emotional state. Perhaps I have a loneliness which I constantly project onto situations around me. Perhaps I am simply an over-active tuning fork responding to vibrations that I alone pick up, that I alone care about.

I think this need, this awareness, this sense of responsibility is rooted in a single event I remember from my childhood. I was three or four years old, and my mother took me with her one morning to see a neighbor girl, Dorothy Burnet, perform in a play at the school auditorium. I was seated there in the semi-dark next to Mrs. Burnet and my mother, watching the eighth graders move about on the lighted stage. At one point Dorothy forgot her lines. She stood there – it seemed forever – and the play could not go on. Everyone on stage and in the audience was waiting for Dorothy to continue, but she was frozen.

I couldn't stand it. I couldn't face Dorothy's embarrassment. In order to get away from it, I crawled under my seat.

It was the first empathetic act of my life – at least, the first that I can remember. During that long moment when no one could move I was in Dorothy's shoes. It was as if I, not Dorothy, were there on stage. It was as if all eyes were focused on me: watching, in silence, my humiliation.

# In the West Pasture

In the heat of a summer afternoon, while my grandparents took their naps, I walked into the pastures. I opened the back yard gate and went through the wood lot past the windmill, past the garden and the pens and the shearing barn and the dipping vat, and walked toward the first big live oaks in the west pasture.

Beneath the trees sheep lay in small clusters, their stomachs moving in and out, steadily – as if connected to the rhythms of the afternoon, to the almost tangible pulse of the heat and the sky. As I stood within the trees, next to the sheep and their rising and falling stomachs, I felt I belonged there with them – among the leaves and limbs of the oaks, the filtered sunlight, the hot smell of wood and needlegrass.

I walked on across the pastures until I reached an open rise of ground. I could see across other people's land, to the neighbors who had come to the hill country before the turn of the century at the same time my grandparents had settled there. I looked at the sun shining on the trees of the Russells, the Harlesses, the Perils – old people living on their own stretches of grass and ground. I thought of them in their homes now – taking naps in the mid-afternoon, lying on their beds in small cool ranch-house rooms.

At the windmill in the far side of the west pasture I got a drink of well water from the pipe that went into the low rock tank, and then I sat for a while in the windmill quiet – within the scattering of shin oak brush. It was as if I were in a place that went on and on to never-ending horizons: as if the ranch land – pastures, the oaks and the sheep, the birds, the deer in their hideaways – was not only the way the world was but was meant to be: all of it under the hot, cleansing sky of summer, all quietly being itself, and me peaceably in it.

# Sarah Ann Vance

We were standing around in front of the First Methodist Church that Sunday morning in May, getting ready to go down to the basement for Sunday school. It was our usual bunch, five or six of us who were sophomores in high school. On Wednesday nights we came to the church for scout meetings. On Sundays we came to Sunday school and usually stayed for church. All of us were in the high school band.

That morning we had begun to gather, as usual, by the stairs leading to the basement, and as each new arrival sauntered down the sidewalk, the others who were already there sort of turned a little and waited.

"Did you hear about Sarah Ann Vance?"

No, the newcomer had not heard.

The others of us waited, looking at the newcomer's face, as one of us told it: "She was killed last night at that low-water bridge this side of Bandera. She and Harold Spaeth and Juanita Crenshaw and Marvin Tomlinson were coming back from a dance at the Broken Spoke and hit a bridge post. Marvin Tomlinson was driving."

The newcomer stood there, not saying anything, looking at the others and the others looking back at him.

Sarah Ann Vance.... We couldn't take it all in, the sudden enormity of what had appeared out of nowhere on that sunny morning in May with car doors slamming along the street in front of the church and someone practicing on a piano inside the fellowship hall.

Sarah Ann Vance. She was the drum major of our band and the daughter of the school secretary. She was valedictorian of the senior class and she was going to give the valedictorian's speech at graduation in just two weeks.

It was unreal. We stood there, our faces blank as we tried to find expressions appropriate for what had happened. We had not known anyone at school who had died before. We had heard of several kids who moved away and something had happened to them somewhere. But this was different...Sarah Ann Vance.... She was small, almost like a doll, with doll features. She had an oval face and dimples in her cheeks and in her chin. She had big Cupid-bow lips and the dark red lipstick she wore made them look like real rose buds. She was the editor of the school yearbook and she helped her mother in the office. If we passed by the office window on the way to our lockers after school we could sometimes see them in there among the desks, and when Sarah Ann and her mother smiled and laughed they looked like sisters.

Marvin Tomlinson was a senior too and everybody always said that he drove too fast.

We stood there. Mr. Thurman, our Sunday school teacher, came up from the basement. He looked at his watch, then looked at us. He said it was time for us to come on down. He did not even seem changed that morning. It was as if everything was still the same to him – as if our Sunday school and church could go ahead and start on time because Sarah Ann Vance didn't go there. She was Presbyterian.

We began to file down the stairs but we didn't want to. It was as if we needed to stay outside a while longer. Because we knew Sarah Ann Vance even if Mr. Thurman didn't. Because she was our drum major and she had a kind of low, throaty chuckle when she laughed, almost like a woman's – which was strange in someone so small. We could see her in our minds – smiling with those big dimples – and she had been killed during the night at a low-water crossing while we had all been asleep. Her head went through the windshield, they said.

And what would Marvin Tomlinson do now?

We went on down into the basement, but we had wanted to stand around a little longer and maybe tell somebody else who came late what had happened. We would tell him and then we would watch his face.


# On Doniphan Drive


At just past dark I turned right off Mesa Street at the Crossroads – leaving Chili's and Pizza Hut and Carrows and Sam's and all the relentless suburban traffic and neon glare – and I was on old familiar Doniphan, my street of simple charms in El Paso.

The wattage dimmed, the road surface became a more sober and shiny black, a line of trees outlined the horizon to the west. I turned in at the Riviera Restaurant and sat for a while, letting the Upper Valley darkness settle in. The Doniphan traffic hummed past, then faded. There was an agreeable spring-night silence.

I started to get out of my car and go inside the restaurant but found that I was looking at the small, white-walled house on the east side of the parking lot. Out front a young man was leaning into the open trunk of his car. A light bulb shone dimly above the doorway of the house. A radio played inside. A white curtain was pulled shut behind a front room window. Through the partly open doorway I could see a young woman placing a baby in a high chair.

A house, a family, a bare bulb burning in the night: it was nothing unique, of course. The scene was not freighted with drama or tragedy or any kind of special beauty. It was just a familiar time and place after dark on Doniphan Drive: a pause at the end of day and a modest place of human habitation. It was one of a thousand such moments a person sees out of the corner of his eye, yet somehow this simple domestic scene seemed to be a kind of summing up for me: a philosophic statement.

...All my life I have tried to find in such ordinary – "meaningless" – moments a clue, a key, an answer. We searchers for the Ultimate keep looking around us for that magic occasion when all the flow and randomness of life will finally become clear: when, at some turn of a street, in some common event, the yin and yang of the universe will join right before our eyes. It's as if all of us grim seekers after truth think that one day we will find it: that all the potentialities, all the infinite variables of human experience will, at a moment of perfect clarity, coalesce into a meaningful whole. We will, at last, be able to see into the elusive but luminous core of reality and *voila*, the synthesis will occur: we will see all things in their simple-yet-profound essence the way we see an apple in a tree, a shadow on the grass, a face.

# The Bar Sevilla

For several years during the 1960s doctors of philosophy, flamenco enthusiasts, *novilleros*, college girls, casual drop-ins, and tourists congregated at the Bar Sevilla in downtown El Paso. They felt it was their kind of place.

In 1959, before it became a popular hangout, I enjoyed going there in the late afternoon. I could sit at a corner table and look at the bullfight posters and think my thoughts. Pepito, the owner, moved around smoothly in the dimness behind the bar. He was a jockey-sized man from Spain who wore a white apron and a red fez and made idle, teeth-clicking noises with his mouth like little castanets. Occasionally a customer would call out, "Pepito, a song!" and he would turn, flash a professional smile, and come out from behind the bar. He would assume his pose – almost soldierly erect, hands clasped behind his back – and when he sang it was as if an amplifying device had been placed in his throat. His voice exploded into the small room: megasounds from a micro-body. When he finished he said *"Arrivederci, ciao, sank-you-very-much!"* to the applause, bowed, again gave his fine, shining smile, wheeled around on his neat little pointed black shoes, and went behind the bar to resume his graceful pacing.

Sometimes the late-afternoon shadows deepened into night as I sat reading in my corner. Other loners, couples, groups would have filled up the tables. Across the room a young man with a goatee hiding his badly receding chin would be speaking loudly and pedantically about orgasms – as though he were simply discussing motor repairs or the gold standard. The immensely plain young woman at his side tapped her cigarette and nodded sagely. At another table a world-traveled and life-weary history teacher sat before his pitcher of beer. His bald head as smooth as an onion, he squinted into his cigarette smoke and read the *New York Times*.

One night a drunken young newspaper reporter – a firebrand of sorts – attempted to offer various pronouncements about religion and world affairs but could never make himself heard above the noise. Half-smiling, searching for any faces that might be turned his way, he stood in a kind of crouch at his table and tried to rise above the drone of voices and bursts of laughter as well as the sound of "Granada" that kept playing on the jukebox. No one paid him any mind. He would sink back into his chair, still half-smiling, half-talking, and take another deep drink from his beer glass.

When the Bar Sevilla finally became "in" – when business was so good that Pepito had the back wall knocked out and added an extra room – it was no longer a place I could ease into after work for a Budweiser and a bit of quiet time with *The Brothers Karamazov*. Teenagers had joined the tourists in checking out the Action on weekends, and the regulars had taken to pouring wine from wineskins onto each other's faces. It was just another loud, crowded place filled with drunks.

# At the Kerrville Mall, 1984

At five-thirty I was through with work for the day and drove across the bridge to River Hills Mall at the edge of town. I pulled into the parking lot – acres of it shining in the pale November sun – and began walking toward the entrance. I walked slowly. I lived alone in those days and found that I no longer enjoyed a number of things – visiting relatives; hearing certain painfully evocative songs; smiling – but what I especially did not enjoy was coming to the mall.

(Most people, of course, like malls. They find it a pleasure to stroll past the doorways of shops; they like to select and possess. They buy in order to spruce up their lives. But I go to a mall the way I enter a cemetery or an apartment complex on a gray Sunday afternoon: it is unrelieved isolation, numbing loneliness. To me, malls pall.)

In River Hills familiar signs announced the drearily predictable stores: Radio Shack, Waldenbooks, J.C. Penney, Hallmark Cards. I passed them by, wandered into the bright glare of a Walgreens. I picked up a magazine, leafed through an article I did not want to read (another profile of Bruce Springsteen, another feature on Cher), replaced the magazine on the rack. I walked through the aisles and in passing glanced at the labels of household products – Carpet Fresh, Downy, Grecian Formula – that I never used.

At the checkout counter I reached for a package of Spearmint, then changed my mind and walked on out the door: At a low point in the day I refused to buy meaning for my life, to purchase a cheap sense of self. I refused to say, "Hey, guess what: I'm alive! And how do I know for sure? Because I have just *bought* something!" I refused to place a quarter in front of a Walgreen cashier in order to buy twenty-five cents of human worth.

(...Spearmint, Porsche – the cost does not matter: the result is the same. Consumers keep asking the world fundamental questions – Am I lost and alone? Do I really count in the scheme of things?  Can I perform some meaningful act to prove my existence?  – and the world keeps giving an answer: "*Of course* you're all right: you have just *bought* something. Money buys identity in addition to everything else.")

I walked on through the mall, resigned to the fact that consuming was a religious rite and I was a lapsed believer.

At Kmart I bought my three pairs of Fruit of the Loom shorts and drove on home.

# The Earth at Noon

One day last summer – about noontime, with the June sun blazing down – I wandered along the river near Canutillo. No longer a fabled stream to write poems about – humbled, tamed by New Mexico dams – the Rio Grande still offered a satisfying river-timelessness as it moved steadily south. Pink-tipped cedars grew along its banks, and killdeer had made tracks in the mud of recent rains.

As I stood beneath the heat-filled sky, the shallow saucer of the old flood plain provided a curious sense of primordial dinosaur-days: Lone black birds were slowly flapping their way across country like pterodactyls, and small cloud puffs above the Franklins were like vapors rising from unseen volcanos — or smoke-signal messages from the mountain gods. To the west huge cloud formations were massing along the horizon as if above an unseen sea. And to the north, over the Organs, still other clouds were thrusting upward in silent explosions: building their enormous cataracts and chasms out of the sun-brilliant whites and grays. Their cloud-shadows lay draped across the shoulders of the Organ peaks and were folded deeply into canyons.

Everywhere I looked there was the balance of field and mountain and sky: long stretches of green alfalfa blended into the sands, making a pleasing horizontal sweep; cottonwoods and willows thrust up here and there — offering, vertically, their satisfying geometric counterpoints.

And above it all — above this grand expanse of the earth at noon — loomed the encompassing desert-dome of blue.

# Air Force Blues

It was peacetime, 1955, and as a second lieutenant I wandered around Randolph Air Force Base in San Antonio trying to keep from doing something wrong. I wore stiff, starched, awkward khakis, a visored hat, black tie, blunt-toed black shoes. For two years I was obligated, during duty hours, to suspend the essential Me. Encased in my khaki prison, I looked like, and felt like, a goon.

After work I walked about in the big, nearly bare sitting room of the Bachelor Officers Quarters, my footsteps echoing as I paced the smooth wooden floor. I stared at the brown woods of the walls and chairs, the white plaster, and tried to think of what to do with myself. I was clearly not meant to be a military man.

Outside, on the cool second-floor walkway, Major Witherspoon would pass by, laughing, with a nurse. He was friendly, dark-haired, youthful looking – remarkably young, I thought, to have a gold leaf on his open khaki collar. He seemed to be all that I wasn't: a confident bachelor officer accustomed to traveling here and there, dating secretaries and nurses and laughing his hearty, young-major's laugh. He was friendly with other young officers in rooms nearby and played cards with them late at night in his slippers and maroon robe. He did not bolt the base each afternoon as I did and head down the farm-to-market road toward San Antonio – to the lure of the streets and the night – but instead walked casually back from his accounting office to his quarters, enjoying the look of the Spanish-style buildings and the quiet, enclosed quadrangle of grass and roses.

I suppose it was the BOQ refrigerator that gave me, for a while, a passing sense of worldliness. It was my first personal refrigerator, so to speak, and on Saturdays, with a box of soda and a wet rag, I cleaned its insides. Afterwards I went to the PX and bought lunch meat and cheese and put them on the bright metal racks of the gleaming ColdSpot. For a while I felt almost smug: there I was, a college graduate, a lieutenant, carrying out my lone, independent little duties like all the other solitaries of the world. And I could snack whenever I wanted to. I didn't have to go out every night and order the same hamburger-and-coffee at a cafe. I could be casual and sedentary.... Why, I might end up buying a television set to look at while I ate – who could tell? I might even buy a pipe. Then if friends knocked on my door, I would look the way a young officer ought to look in his quarters after his day of duty – sitting there in his room smoking his pipe and reading *Saturday Review*.

But I never even came close to pulling it off. True, I did have the refrigerator. But the lunch meat curled up at the edges and the limes shrunk into rocks and the half-cartons of milk grew sour because, as it turned out, I seldom fixed myself a meal in the room more than once a week – and never again thought of smoking a pipe. Something had happened. During those unprepossessing, goon-like days in khaki I had made an important discovery: the world could be written about. Not a vague Shangri-La "literary" world but the one right outside Randolph Air Force Base: the world of personal experience.

So each night I was on those dark San Antonio streets, looking, walking, listening: afire with the stunning new idea that my life could read like a book and – incredibly – I could do the writing.


# Back Roads


Narrow roads wind through the Texas hill country – past winter fields and pastures, past little places that are still on the map but just barely: Cain City, Sisterdale, Waring, Welfare. These are the back roads going by settlements left over from the Old Order: from the pioneer times when German immigrants saw the shoulder-high grasslands among the Central Texas hills and decided to settle along Grape Creek and the Pedernales, built their stone houses as they kept an eye out for the nearby Comanches, and established the farms and ranches that their descendants would continue to work for the next eighty to a hundred years.

But times changed. Some of the old-time ranchers and farmers have finally sold off, moved away – given up the heritage of their forebears – and now millionaires from Houston and Dallas and Minneapolis as well as two-paycheck families (sending their kids to school in nearby Boerne and Fredericksburg; seeking the rural good life) live along the narrow roads among the elegant oaks.

New money, old way of life.... Small holdings with weathered barns and trailer houses sit next to large, well-kept spreads. An old rock-wall fence built in the 1880s still borders a bottomland oat patch; across the road an impressive new limestone-wall entrance announces the acres of an oil-tycoon-turned-cattle-baron.

Once in December I drove up and over the cedar-covered hills:
into valleys where sheep were scattered like miniature chess pieces
across huge fields of lush, green, winter grass; by the mailboxes of the
Rausches, the Doebblers, the Kothmanns and the lovely Germanic
geometry of their neat fields and orchards.

I eased down toward a low-water bridge (Madonnas and Michael
Jacksons come and go, but the Guadalupe River, beneath its border of
cypress trees, flows on forever) and I was in Waring, a riverside cluster
of toy-like buildings. The schoolhouse – white, with green-trimmed
windows and a slanting tin roof – had been long closed except for
occasional community gatherings. A flock of guineas paraded along
the school grounds; a trio of white turkey gobblers strutted and
chuffed across a quiet yard.

I drove through and out of town – past the gas station-store, several turn-of-the-century, embossed-tin houses, the abandoned yellow-
walled depot sitting on its grassy railroad right-of-way – and I stopped
on the side of the road. I got out and listened to the great afternoon
stillness. It was silence I heard, but it could easily have been called
Time or History. A breeze came from the south; a hawk circled low
overhead. An armadillo came rattling through dry Spanish oak leaves,
then waddled along the fenceline to snuffle in dried cow manure.

We were both content.

# Deborah's Shoes

It was January 1965, and cold, and in the mornings I stood
around in the front room watching for the mailman, hoping he would
stop. But he always went on by and I had to go another day without
letters from El Paso – letters that would have brought me both news
and warmth.

After the mailman turned in at the next house, I continued to
stare past the porch – a *wooden* one now, not stone, for this was indeed

Fort Worth – and into that small, dispirited square that was to be my yard for the coming year. It had a mimosa tree, a patch of Bermuda grass, nothing else.

I had no job. We had moved too suddenly, with no chance to oil the wheels of change. After a week of filling out applications only Judy, my wife, was able to find work. She began substituting in the public schools while I stayed home and kept Deborah and looked out the window – waiting for mail that did not come.

Sometimes, instead of gazing out the window, I would watch "Mr. Peppermint." He was on morning television and Deborah, who was three, thought that his striped jacket was nice. So we would watch him together. Out of our general despair, I even let her suck her thumb. If I hadn't been trying to set a good example, I think I probably would have sucked mine, too.

After the second week Deborah began to cry out in her sleep. I first assumed that the North Texas rainstorms and lightning were scaring her – there had been no such lightning in El Paso the previous three years, and very little rain – but I began to wonder if the crying wasn't really her reaction to the change of houses. She had been wrenched out of pleasant winter days in the sun and brought to a house with shadowed, high-ceilinged rooms and boards in the floor that creaked. It was a gloomy house she lived in now, in a neighborhood without friends, in a town without sun.

During those January days in the Grim Place – as I began to call Fort Worth – Deborah and I would sometimes walk over to the zoo that was nearby. We crossed the wide greenery of the adjoining park and then moved slowly along in front of the cages. Small baboons clutched each other in desperate embraces, flamingos regarded us serenely from ponds, zebras stood there in their long pens, not doing much of anything except looking exactly like zebras.

When Judy came home in the afternoon, I was free to get into the car and drive slowly down red cobblestone streets – that

is, I was free for awhile to explore a town I did not think I could
ever like.

It was midnight, and from my chair I listened to the refrigerator
whirring, the mantel clock clicking along. Mrs. Garven, the bantam
hen, snuffled in her sleep as she sat perched on an orange crate on the
back porch. Tom, our lean and elegant cat, purred soundly in the big
arm chair near the bedroom door.

I gazed about the sleeping house: Judy, another child growing
inside her, lay partly out of sight in bed – the thrust of her hip beneath
the sheet like a small mountain range looming from a white and placid
sea. I turned and noticed Deborah's new shoes sitting in the middle of
the floor. They were shiny red ones, fresh that day from the shoe store
shelves. Proud of them, she had put them that way before going to
bed: side by side, the toes perfectly together.

I got up from my chair and stood over them wanting to see
exactly what a three-year-old's pair of shoes looked like when the
house was still. I told myself they were merely laces and soles and rub-
ber-heels – just ordinary footwear put together somewhere by
machines and now sitting routinely on the living room floor.

But I got down on my knees to look closer and they were something beyond mere shoes. Already they had the definite – the *personal* –
shape of my daughter's narrow foot: I detected it easily in the flat curve
of the arch and the corrective wedges on the heels and the crusts of
front-yard mud – they were now part of the life of the shoes themselves, part of that half-day's worth of living they had spent in covering small, unique, human feet.

And it seemed all right, in that midnight hour, to be jobless in
Fort Worth for a while. The three of us, soon to be four, were bound
together in a way that pleased me. We were okay; we could make it.
We had the look and the feel – the substance – of a family, and it even
showed in Deborah's shoes.

# Glenwood

There is a country tune that Eddie Arnold used to sing in his mild, shoes-off-in-the-living-room tenor: "Make the World Go Away." I did that this summer when I went once again to Glenwood: I made the day-to-day, city-streets world go away. Yet the world of western New Mexico was never more with me. I just can't get enough of that place.

I took I-10 out of El Paso to Las Cruces and Deming, slanted up U.S. 180, and at Silver City I was there – in the foothills of the Gila forest and the Black Range – but I drove the farther few miles north to check out Pinos Altos, as I usually do. With the windows open I breathed in the gorgeous smell of the distant rain, the cedars and pines, the greasewood, the roadside weeds and flowers.

At dusk thunder started rolling around, the sky clouded over, there was an upland chill: the summer afternoon had turned autumn. As I walked down a bare, sandy road I could hear children at a trailer house giggling in their games while all around us the mountains were as quiet and ageless as China. A wild plum tree was so sharply defined in the air it looked stereoscopic. I wondered how it would look out-lined in snow: in wintertime, when the reality of Pinos Altos would be mountain isolation, mountain cold.

The next morning I drove west out of Silver City, climbing up and over the Continental Divide. Sunflowers and yellow-tipped mullein stalks lined the highway; yucca plants and white poppies were scattered across the pastures. As I eased past Mobile Haven and Wild Canyon Estates, the quarter horses grazed on the hillsides, and the rounded crests of the land rose and fell like swells of an ocean. The sweep of the hills, dotted with cedars, made a pointillist painting.

It was familiar territory: the turnoff to Tyrone, where open-pit copper mining had hollowed out another gigantic scoop of earth; the long flatland of Mangas Creek (named after Mangas Colorados, the Chiricahua Apache chief who had raided Mexican settlements and mining camps in the area); the constant, dune-like, gingerbread-colored mounds and ridges; the long, hot, waterless draws where cattle stood among the scattered mesquites; the Gila River, running fast and shallow as it wound its way into Arizona; then the valley of the San Francisco River, almost Day-Glo green: a sheltered oasis; and finally Glenwood resting beneath its own arbor of cottonwoods along Whitewater Creek.

The Whitewater Motel is a single line of fifteen units on a rise above the creek. Each room is simple, clean, cabin-style, more like a back bedroom in someone's rural home than a sterile motel room. The front door is made of bolted planks of rough-cut pine; the back door opens onto a long narrow porch that runs the length of the motel. The back yard, a grassy rectangle with well-tended shrubs and flowers in stone planters, is anchored at each end by enormous sycamores.

I registered, parked in front of #12, and after unloading a few things from the car went outside to the back porch to put my feet up on the railing and read a while. I opened my book – but once again the hummingbirds did not let me get very far.

Hummingbirds: From their perches in the sycamores they flashed to the back porch feeder above my head in a constant ebb and flow, a dozen or more of them in a hovering swarm. They hung in the air in their pulsing cluster: tireless, aggressive, jockeying back and forth for their minuscule territorial air-space; inserting their needle beaks, sipping the sweet sugar water, then whirring away to sit a moment in the trees as sedate little bird-curiosities.

At four o'clock the clouds in the west darkened, the wind came, the temperature dropped, and it was smiling time on the porch: a time of lovely coolness, with the limbs of the trees along Whitewater Creek swaying in their graceful, slow-motion frenzies.

I stopped watching the hummingbird sideshow, read for a while, then walked across the bridge past the realtor's, the scattering of modest roadside houses, the Blue Front Bar and Cafe, the Lariat Motel, and bought a Coke at the Glenwood Trading Post. Roses grew across the driveway near the two Chevron pumps, and the white-haired proprietress sat inside the store in her chair – ready, if someone wanted to buy something, to get up and go behind the counter to the cash register but otherwise quite satisfied to keep on sitting there, staring out.

It was late Saturday afternoon, a casual time almost anywhere, but in Glenwood it was as though I had wandered into a time warp – as if the curving highway in front of me did not lead on to Alma, Luna, and Alpine, Arizona, but to Oz. A couple of the locals sat on a low platform in front of the Coke machine, drinking Dr. Peppers and talking about horse trailers. They would watch a car go past, checking out the license plate. Much of the time they stared past their Dr. Pepper cans, not saying anything, just sort of studying the shape of their boots.

Standing there, I had the feeling that the rest of America – really, the rest of the world – did not exist. Presidential politics, Third World upheavals, famines and riots: They were as unreal as the rainbow that had arced for a moment to the east over the Mogollon Mountains and then disappeared. I felt that I had wandered into a novel, a play – maybe *Our Town* – and if I stayed still long enough all of us there at the Trading Post would just gradually fade into the timelessness of the pages.

At suppertime I crossed the road to the Blue Front – the other daily gathering spot for tourists and locals. When I went inside I slowed my pace a bit to match the tinkling, honky-tonk rhythm of "Crazy," Patsy Cline's song, that was playing on the jukebox. A couple of Ol' Boys in hats were hunkered over their beers at the bar; several Young Ol' Boys in baseball caps and tank tops slouched their way around the pool table. In a shadowed booth a little girl was asleep, face down, her bare feet hanging out over the edge of the seat.

In the cafe section I ordered my chicken-fried steak and had a look around. Seated next to me a couple of the regulars – coffee-drinkers, mainly – were tapping their Marlboros and exchanging weather reports. One of them – an every-other-week bather, apparently – sat in his soiled khaki shirt, soiled khaki pants, soiled brown fisherman's floppy cloth hat, and rubber boots. He looked up as a third regular pulled out a chair from the table.

"Where'd *you* come from?"

"Bad pennies always show up," the newcomer said.

"Well, sit down and tell us another of your windies."

They talked and nursed their coffee along – occasionally laughing themselves into cigarette coughs ("...you could take one of them rubber snakes, y'know, and shake it at ol' Buddy when he was wakin' up and he'd be runnin' clean over that mountain before he'd stop.... Scaredest fella I ever seen about *snakes*").

The next morning I headed out of Glenwood: just driving, just looking at creeks where horses stood under cottonwoods at noon, shifting lazily about, their tails flowing in the shade like hair in water: just thinking how a person experiencing such moments – the horses, the shimmering trees in New Mexico sun – could be ruined forever for another kind of place, another kind of life.

# Among the Rabbits

My marriage of many years was falling apart and I did not know what to do about it. I felt that I had to get out, get away, think. I finally decided to ask for a leave of absence from my job, take a trip – by bus – to Alabama and stay a while with a friend of mine and his family. From that perspective, miles away, maybe I could decide what to do.

But my *children*: Deborah was fourteen, Byron was eight, and I had not been away from them for more than twenty-four hours – two days at the most – since they were born. How could I get on a bus and leave them – even for a few weeks, a month? And what would I say? Deborah knew that things were not right between her father and mother – she and I had talked a good bit and she was going to be okay – but Byron: he was as innocent of domestic troubles as an Upper Valley breeze. How did I go about telling him – this little boy that I loved, that I had carried around the living room each night on my shoulders? How could I bear to say to him, "Byron, goodbye for a while; I'm going on a trip; I don't know when I'll be back," and just disappear?

The morning I left was in January, and Byron was outside feeding Sniffles, his dog, before school. I said, "When you get through, let's go to the rabbit pen. I need to show you something."

I thought it would be easier there, somehow: away from the house, in a place where he did his chores.

We walked across the back yard – past his rope swing hanging from the big elm tree ( – I had pushed him there a thousand times, his bare feet arching up toward the low branches), past his bicycle leaning against the garage door ( – and I had walked beside him around and around the church parking lot across the street, steadying him, giving him more and more freedom, then had watched his first solo ride that ended in the rectory hedge), and went into the little feed room where we kept the rabbits and hay and sacks of grain. The three gray rabbits moved slightly behind the mesh wire of their enclosure but kept on chewing their alfalfa.

I looked at Byron in his faded corduroys, blue tennis shoes, Dallas Cowboys jacket, and the lump grew in my throat, but I had to go ahead. I told him that I was going away for a while. I told him that he knew how to take care of the animals but I just wanted to double check. I put my arm around him and told him to change the water regularly for the ducks. I told him to give hay to the sheep and grain to the bantams and quail. I told him – a number of things, but I am not sure he heard them all or that I actually said them all because the pressure in my throat and the tears welling in my eyes made it impossible to speak.

I held him close to me so that he could not look up into my face, and I wondered if he were waiting for some next thing I was going to tell him: that these sudden and unnecessary instructions about the chores were for that day only, for that single afternoon when he would come back from school and do the chores by himself. The next day, I would surely tell him, I was going to be home.

...Someday I will be a very old man and I will have accumulated all the experiences a long life can offer, but even then I will be able to smell the mashes in their sacks and hear the quiet in that cold little room: feel the long, goodbye silence of that winter morning with just the rabbits and Byron and me.


# The Secret Twin

The other day I was in the bathroom brushing my teeth and I looked over at a can of Comet sitting next to the mirror. I simply noticed it, as a person will, then kept on brushing. When I glanced back I didn't look at the can but at the reflection of it in the mirror. And it was one of those little sudden, sharp, dramatic moments: the words on the label were not just reversed; they were fundamentally different – incomprehensible – and it was as if I were staring at words in Arabic.

Such a moment is no big deal, or at least it's not supposed to be. But to me it is another instance of the hidden strangeness all around us, of things not really being what we assume them to be – that is, safely themselves. People go along thinking everything just *is*. But to me the unknown and unseen are right there, right next to the *is*, like an unseen shadow. It's as if everything has a secret twin, as if there is an invisible two-sidedness we never see.

People say: "There's a dog." Or "There's a chair." Or "That's an apple." And it's as if they are *through* when they say it: they've announced the agreed-upon territory and everybody is supposed to nod and agree about the dog and the chair and the apple because they are so familiar and real that there couldn't possibly be any mystery about them.

There *is* a mystery to them, but nobody seems to recognize it because we are so used to dividing everything into separate categories – into being and non-being, familiarity and strangeness, mystery and the commonplace. But just because we assign names to things doesn't mean we understand them. An apple is still a phenomenon long after we have called it an apple.

For thousands of years a rock was incontestably a rock. Humans saw it, hefted it, threw it, *knew* it. Then the twentieth-century physicists came along and said that such an oh-so-solid object was made of atoms, which happen to be mainly space. And now, at the end of the century, the physicists are telling us that the particles inside the atoms are really not at all what they first thought they were. They are not bits of matter; they are things that *move*. They're waves – like light. They are matter-in-motion, not just matter.

We spend lifetimes never quite understanding that the real is always a fraction away from being *un*real – or rather, that the real is real in a way that is radically different from how we are used to seeing it: real in a way we can never actually know.

...Last month I got a new prescription for my glasses. The ophthalmologist had dilated my eyes so after I left his office and went out to my car I waited a while since the sun was particularly bright even in the late afternoon. Finally, after dark, I eased into traffic and started to drive home.

The lights! My God, they were incredible. Every pair of headlights, every star in the sky: they were startling exaggerations of how they usually are. Light rays were shooting forth great Fourth of July skyrocket beams. And why? Because my pupils were still dilated. I was seeing things abnormally, but that "abnormality" had just been waiting for me. The beauty of those distorted lights had always been there if I could have seen them with wide-open pupils.

Then this: Yesterday I was driving to work on the interstate and I looked over at a woman driver in the lane next to me. She was a nice-enough looking woman – bright red lipstick, some eye shadow, wavy brown hair – and she was in that early-morning interstate trance, staring ahead at the cars in front of us.

I don't know why but I got to thinking: How would it be if human eyes were so constructed that we could see right through flesh to the skeleton within? What if we went about our business that way – every day, all of us, by the millions – seeing each other as the skeletons we are instead of as the fleshly packaging that covers us?

We were side by side on I-10, going our sedate fifty-five-miles-an-hour in the 7:45 traffic, and there I was trying to visualize the driver next to me as a woman with a white skull and bare, grinning teeth – no lips, no lipstick: a woman gripping the steering wheel with her bony fingers and staring into traffic with her eyeless eyes.

We *are* skeletons who meet and talk and smile with other skeletons. All we have to do to see our secret skeleton twin is sit in a doctor's office and look at ourselves up on the wall inside that lighted panel: at our X-ray: at that sudden bunch of whitish-gray cavities and sockets.

Every day we are just as much what we don't see as what we do see. The reality we think we see is never the reality that is.

# The Quiet of New Mexico

After I went north out of Deming and turned right on the road toward the City of Rocks, I could see the long green smudge of trees in the Mimbres Valley. The hills in the area – low and rounded and bare – were hardly picturesque. But I kept going east, just beyond the Faywood community, and then parked along the side of the road. I crossed over the wire fence and walked through the greasewood and came to where the Mimbres wound its way. It was an intimate little river, creek-like really, but it was nicely framed by arching trees and I sat beside it for a while and felt that I had come to the proper place. I considered how pleasant a cabin would look in the filtered afternoon sun and shadows, and how, if I lived there, the world would seem to make sense.

I saluted this little spot among the cottonwoods, marked it down for a longer visit another time, walked back to my car and drove on down through the narrow strip of valley that was serene, archetypal, like Steinbeck's *The Pastures of Heaven*: the brief fields, the horses and corrals, the occasional cluster of frame buildings, the cottonwoods, the ever-present sense of the mountain-fed Mimbres coming from a place of winter snows.

I pulled off the road again at San Lorenzo and walked in the quiet of New Mexico. I stopped along the deserted main street and listened to the deep, continuous lack of sound. (It would not be an easy silence for those who need the background distractions of an urban hum.) I moved a step or two and heard the small, explosive rub of gravel beneath my shoes. I listened to the doves in the distant, riverside trees: sighing their benedictions to the ever-abiding land.

I stood looking past back-yard windmills to a rock wall crossing a rise of ground. I had no real need for drama to end my day, but if I had I knew that the wall – radiant with itself in the last glowing of the sun: holding, somehow, all the silence of the afternoon – was drama enough.

# Supertramp

Originally, it had been my daughter's album during her teenage years, and from time to time I had heard it in her room: back in the 1970s before the divorce, before the breakup of the family, before I had left El Paso and started driving Central Texas highways by myself again, before I finally bought a portable cassette player and began to accumulate the cassette car-library of a lone traveler.

As I say, at first Supertramp was just another of the strange '60s names for me: a British-sounding group with shrilling voices, wild keyboards, soaring tenor saxes performing to a driving, hypnotic beat. Perhaps in San Antonio I bought my own Supertramp cassette in a half-hearted attempt to capture something of my daughter's room. Perhaps I just wanted to revisit a stable time and place as my life kept on unraveling.

Sometimes when I could not handle my middle-age misery I would take it out of town. After work I would head north out of San Antonio, put Supertramp in the cassette player, and crank it up to high as I drove toward creek banks and crossroad stores. It was my road-to-the-hills-in-slanted-sunlight therapy. Somehow the sounds of the tape bonded my misery – took it from me and gave it voice. Supertramp became my misery's twin, and the two of us, wailing – the band loudly, me silently but vibrating in every nerve – went through the late afternoon cedars-and-oaks like a hatchback ambulance on a mission of mercy.

...I think I want that tape played at my funeral whenever it comes. I want no sermon, no eulogies, no quavering hymns. I just want assembled family and friends to be seated in a small hill country church and a sensible spokesman to make the necessary funeral remarks. Then I want whoever I have entrusted with the task to put the last cut, Side 2 of my Supertramp tape into a player, and I want the sound of it – full volume – to fill that little church building for a startling, soaring two and a half minutes. I say "startling" not only because it won't be traditional funeral music but also because it will seem so outrageously inappropriate – so unlike the Dead-and-dearly-Departed that the assembled have come to mourn.

But the tune – if I can call it that – will not be played in order to shock or upset. It will simply be my final statement, a kind of aural epitaph that says: Hey, No One Ever Really Knows Another.

Which is true, and that sometimes serious, sometimes clownish merry-go-round of a tape – that keening, melodic cascade full of whistles and bells – was actually me. Along with the predictable and recognizable me was – always – the anarchic, curious, desperate, ecstatic, privately wild other.

Indeed, if I could manage to speak from my coffin into the somber silence that would follow "Child of Vision" I would say: "Don't you see: we are born – all of us – into a mighty mystery, and for a while, just like you, I was part of it. There has never been a proper description of this mystery, nor a proper representative sound. I don't think that the music of the spheres is church music; I believe its sound is the sound of galaxies expanding and cells multiplying, of the surf crashing and winds moving through pines and caves.... For some, maybe, it is the music of Beethoven and Mozart and Bach. But for me Supertramp will do just fine."